grand slam

A Novel

Samantha Brenner

kedziepress
INTERNATIONAL

Kedzie Press International
37 Rosebank Grove
London E17 6RD England

Suite 8042
2647 N. Western Avenue
Chicago, Illinois 60647 USA

Visit us on the World Wide Web at:
www.kedziepress.com

Disclaimer: This book is a work of satirical fiction. The characters, conversations, and events in the novel are the product of the author's imagination, and no resemblance to any actual conduct or real-life person, or to actual events, is intended. For the sake of verisimilitude, certain public figures are briefly referred to or make appearances in the novel, but their descriptions, actions, and words are wholly fictitious and are not to be intended to be understood as descriptions of real or actual events, or to reflect in any way upon the actual conduct or character of these public figures.

Grand Slam is published by Kedzie Press U.S.A under license from Sigel Press U.K.

Visit our website at: www.kedziepress.com.

Cover design and Interior design by Harp Mando
Author photo by Hillary Olsen

Library of Congress Control Number: 2006935133

ISBN-10: 1-934087-42-4 and

ISBN-13: 978-1-934087-42-8

Typeset in 10 pt Columbus MT

Printed in the United States of America by United Graphics
10 9 8 7 6 5 4 3 2 1

Printed and bound in Great Britain by Henry Ling Limited, at the Dorset Press, Dorchester, DT1 1HD

The publisher's policy is to use paper manufactured from sustainable forests.

For Hillary

Thank you for showing me that love does mean something.

Acknowledgements

A warm thank you to my friends of the court— Caroline Vis, Conchita Martinez, Dana Davis and Patricia Tarabini— whose valued friendship has always been inspiring, uplifting and treasured.

Special thanks to my early readers— Leanna Creel, Beth Friel and Michelle Archer—for their time, input and invaluable encouragement.

Special thanks also to Megen Macdonald for taking flight with me and to Amy Mallon for clipping my wings and for always being devoted friends.

Many, many thanks to Hillary Olsen for enthusiastically and tirelessly reading various drafts of this book, for her incredible patience and for her undeniably generous and steadfast love and support.

Abiding appreciation to Dannielle Thomas for always believing in this book.

Particular thanks to Andrea Killian, a very special friend, without whom this book would never have happened. It truly is all her fault.

Thanks to Tyla Berchtold, Michele Alexander, Joan Kochan, Thomas Sigel, Andrew Hogbin, Jim Downs, Anthony Tabasso and Neal Tabachnick.

An extra-special thank you to my dad for the constant deliveries from John & Pete's—they were sometimes a source of great inspiration and other times a fantastic break from sitting in front of my computer.

Lastly, I owe a debt of gratitude to my mother for her immeasurable and unwavering love and support since the day I was born, but especially in the years since I have begun this journey. Thank you for not having a nervous breakdown when I quit practicing law. I'm no longer a Philadelphia lawyer, but I am a published author.

From moot court to centre court

Let me tell you what it's like to walk onto the grass at Wimbledon.

Rested and refreshed from first class, I emerged from Heathrow's customs area and politely greeted the chauffeur awaiting my arrival. Even without the sign he displayed, I couldn't have missed the snappy gentleman. He wore the classic garb of Wimbledon— a green and purple polo shirt and khaki britches with pleats so perfectly ironed I marveled at his ability (or daring) to walk in them at all. As nonchalantly as possible, I glanced around to catch glimpses from the wandering eyes of curious bystanders until the baggage carrousel began to turn and spit out bags. My priority-tagged baggage was among the first to tumble down and into my driver's waiting hands.

I followed him outside and hopped into the big black sedan that reminded me of something out of a romantic, soldier-falls-in-love-with-grieving-dying-widow-nurse-WWII flick. Everything in England just smacks of history. I was like a little kid in a candy store the entire drive from the airport to the small, but world-famous village of Wimbledon. Granted, it was a challenge to adjust to driving on the "other" side of the road and I lost track of how many times I shouted, much to the surprise (or dismay) of my driver. "Jesus, these bloody Brits drive like crazy people!" Clearly, not used to some ballsy, raucous, loud-mouthed, slightly crass American in his backseat, after each of my little explosions he'd simply respond, "Yes, Miss." As if decorum might prevent any further outbursts. Yeah, right.

Finally, we peeled off the A3 and my heart started quivering with anticipation. As the driver slowed reverentially, we arrived at The All England Lawn Tennis Club, home to Wimbledon, the most prestigious and famous Grand Slam tennis tournament in the world. The grounds were manicured within an inch of their lives and adorned with a tasteful plethora of purple, yellow and white flowers. As we approached the club entrance, photographers and fans waved and yelled, hoping to snap a shot or catch a glimpse inside the car before it disappeared behind the gates that separate "us" from "them."

Almost simultaneously, the car came to a halt. The driver opened the backdoor before I had a chance to open it myself. Other official tournament cars lined the driveway entrance and all began to empty. I could hear cameras clicking behind me and fans shouting for autographs. I threw one bag over my shoulder and wheeled the other one behind me, stopping briefly at the security checkpoint before being granted entrance to the club.

I was tingling with excitement. It was, afterall, my very first time at Wimbledon. This is the only Grand Slam tournament steeped in history and majesty, quite literally— grass courts, white clothes, kings and queens, strawberries and cream! Wimbledon is *the* crown jewel of tennis.

My skin was covered with goose bumps. Of course, I wasn't sure if it was because I could smell the freshly-cut grass or because Andre Agassi was two feet in front of me. Almost immediately, the lobby was flooded with names and faces recognizable to just about anyone in the world. Jennifer Capriati was standing so close behind me that I could feel her breath on the back of my neck. By now I had become accustomed to seeing these famous faces in person but, somehow, being in the presence of tennis greats at Wimbledon was just a little more special— just a little bit surreal. I still chuckle to myself when I see John McEnroe, tennis' consummate "bad boy." In fact, I'm chuckling now because he just walked past me with Martina Navratilova, who gave me a wink and a wave. I'm important but not important enough to break her stride with "Johnny Mac," so I waved back and borrowed one of McEnroe's famous lines, "You cannot be serious!" They both glanced back with cockeyed smiles... McEnroe as if to say, "Hey that's my line!" and Martina with a look of, "Why you quoting him? I'm the Queen of this court!"

I finally made my way into the credentials office and waited patiently in line behind Maria Sharapova, one of a handful of Russian tennis phenomena who had broken into the Top 10 of the Women's Tennis Tour. Despite her early-round loss at Eastbourne (the women's grass court opener to Wimbledon), Maria greeted me cheerily with her usual lovely and gracious demeanor. At last, it was my turn. I smiled for what would certainly be another dreadful credentials badge photo and, within minutes, I was handed a badge granting me access to almost anywhere on the grounds. Thankful the photo actually showed my pupils and not just the whites of my eyes, I threw the badge around my neck and flipped my cell phone open to read an incoming text message. *Glad you made it safely. Meet me outside the locker room.* My lips curved into a grin.

As I walked toward the locker room, I was overcome with a euphoric feeling. It was Wimbledon and I was walking in the footsteps of champions! I tried not to think about where I was or the glitterati that surrounded me, but I couldn't help it. I was basking in my own private glory with every step I took and every jingle of the metal clasp attaching the badge around my neck. No one could burst my bubble. Well, no one except for the escorts who "politely" shoved me out of the way to make room for Lindsay Davenport to pass. *Lindsay Davenport. Whatever. I mean, I know she's won Wimbledon. Okay, and like every other major tournament, but you don't have to push! A simple 'Excuse me' would have worked just fine!* This witty banter I was having inside my head was cut short when my good friend, Saskia Van Voorst, emerged from the locker room, flanked by her own attendant. Saskia is one of my very close friends on the Tour and is a veteran doubles player whose career spanned fifteen years. If you're picturing some withered eighty-year-old because of my use of the word "veteran," let me clarify. She's only thirty-three, but in tennis terms, this is considered old— even ancient. Saskia had decided that this would be her final Wimbledon before her retirement later in the year.

"Christ, it's about time. I thought you'd never get here!" she squealed, as I threw my arms around her and we greeted each other in the traditional Dutch manner— three alternate kisses. Within seconds, my bags were tucked inside the locker room and we were following the furor created by the Lindsay & Co. entourage.

I then found myself walking in the area restricted to players, their guests, coaches and officials. Awe-inspiring would be an understatement! At the end of the hall, Saskia and I climbed a final flight of stairs and a pair of very proper-looking tournament officials opened the set of doors before us. An explosion of light and bright blue brilliance filled the hallway and I wondered if this was like the tunnel one hears about ascending to heaven, because I was fairly certain I heard the undeniable strains of angels and harps— along with the loud beating of my heart. I was about to step onto the grass at Wimbledon.

Before I even touched the grass, I could smell it…an intoxicating combination of honey and straw. And every time I inhaled, it smelled even sweeter. Mesmerized, I followed Saskia toward Court 18. The bright sun made her customary all-white ensemble even more brilliant and I squinted as we walked through the gate opening onto the court. Finally, I stepped onto the soft, springy bed of grass; barely damp, but still glistening from the morning's watering. The Saturday before the tournament starts is the only day players are allowed to practice on the courts at The All England Lawn Tennis Club, which are otherwise reserved for match-play during the fortnight. Though most of the players had already arrived, the grounds still looked pristine, as if not a single blade of grass was out of place. The mossy bed of green was outlined by the thick, freshly-laid white chalk that defined the court. Wooden posts stretched the dark black net with its stark white tape top the width of the court and the bronze crank on the side of the post near the umpire's chair shined brightly in the sun. The net sank ever so slightly in the middle of the court.

The glorious Centre Court stood just across the way. My feet rooted themselves in the grass and my eyes widened even further as I stared, transfixed, at the perimeter of the incredible stadium. Its beauty was breathtaking— almost paralyzing. Television truly cannot do its elegance justice. Similar to the club entrance, the outside walls of Centre Court were adorned with purple and yellow flowers. As I was relishing the majesty of it all, I heard the familiar "*crack*" and "*whoosh*" sound of a brand-new can of tennis balls opening. I turned to find Saskia standing at the net, opening the first of two cans of Slazenger balls, the official ball of Wimbledon. I was standing a few feet from her and the distinctively pungent smell of fuzzy rubber and plastic quickly enveloped me. Saskia had a wide grin on her face. One by one, she crammed three bright yellow tennis balls into her shorts pocket and gripped another three in her left hand before grabbing her racket. Still smiling, she pointed the head of the racket toward me and said, "Take those flip-flops off, grab one of my rackets and get your ass on the baseline before someone comes and kicks you off the court for being dressed like an idiot!"

I pursed my lips into a half-smile, half-smirk, rolled my eyes and said, "Ha, ha, ha. Very funny." I had no intention of doing what she so politely demanded and wasn't convinced that she was serious anyway. Looking down at my tattered gray-and-black Perfetto sweatpants and flip-flopped (albeit nicely manicured) feet, I thought, *she's right. I don't have the right clothes on and I do look an idiot.*

As if *this* would be the *only* reason I'd get booted out on my ass— not the fact that the last time I was even remotely *ranked* as a player was when I was seventeen years old and even then, it might have been considered something around number 109,385 in world standings.

Oh, I'm sorry— did I give you the wrong impression? You thought I was competing at Wimbledon?! Are you nuts? No. I'm just...

* * *

... Stephanie Alexander, a "nice" Jewish girl from Tulsa, Oklahoma, and this is the story of the nine most insane months of my short life.

O-k-l-a-h-o-m-a. Now, doesn't *that* just conjure images of TV evangelists, rodeos, pork rinds and cowboys and Indians?

And it was as absurd as it sounds. I am living proof that we— Jews in Oklahoma— do, in fact, exist. Or, perhaps, did so incognito because, in second grade, my parents transferred my sister and me to a Catholic private school. I have an older sister, but that's likely all you'll hear about her (a word is coming to mind that I could use to describe her, but it's not normally used outside of a kennel). My parents put their faith in Sister Mary Margaret of Monte Cassino because they felt her tutelage would practically ensure my acceptance at an Ivy League university. Thus, I became the token Jewess amongst the Gentiles.

My reputation as being the anti-Christ preceded me when I entered the classroom at Monte Cassino for the first time. Much to my fellow eight-year-olds' surprise, I didn't have horns or a tail (characteristics that, apparently, most kids in Tulsa thought were standard of Jews). And, every Friday, I was the only kid left sitting in the chapel pews while everyone else lined up to receive the Eucharist. In all my years of Catholic school, I never did get to taste that little wafer. Hell, I may have just earned my horns for referring to it as a "wafer." Bless me, Father, for I have sinned. Now can Polly try the frickin' cracker?!

Growing up, I was always the "good kid"— obedient and reverential, driven by the all-pervasive fear of disappointing my parents. I was no Goody Two-Shoes, but I was the furthest thing from a curious child whose sense of adventure trumped any potential parental punishments awaiting rule transgressors. While I dutifully played tennis after school and on the weekends with the private coach my parents had hired, I lived vicariously through the rebellious kids whose extracurricular activities included things like toilet papering homes and tipping cows (some people consider sneaking up on a cow while it's sleeping and tipping it over onto its side a recreational activity which, according to my mother, was something only "hillbillies" did).

I'm not sure if I was a rule-follower because I felt it was my moral obligation to do as my parents said or because I was deathly afraid of getting caught for doing something I shouldn't have. I was in constant search of my parents' approval. For the most part, I successfully maintained the label that my mother gave me upon birth. I was "Mommy's good little girl." She'll be the first to tell anyone that from the day I was born I have brought her "nothing but joy and happiness." Yeah, right. No one's *that* perfect! I can name at least five instances where my actions weren't exactly pleasing to her. Similarly, my dad considered me his "perfect angel." I might still have the halo somewhere.

As a twelve-year-old, I thought Tulsa was the most boring place on earth, but my parents would prove me wrong when they moved us to Florida. Longboat Key, with its white-sand beaches and gray-haired population, turned out to be an even more challenging playground for a pre-teen girl. But, contrary to my opinion, the goal was actually not to bore me to death. As with everything my parents did, there was a master plan. If you ask them, they'll probably say the move was inspired the summer before, when I was eleven. We had a vacation home on Longboat Key, which was a thirty-minute drive from the world-famous Nick Bollettieri Tennis Academy in Bradenton, Florida (now, Bradenton truly *is* the most boring place on earth!). My parents will also tell you that Nick "recruited" me to come and play tennis at his academy. If, by recruited, they mean Nick wanted their sizeable tuition check in his back pocket in exchange for my joining his merry little elite group of students, then, I suppose, this assessment is accurate. We've all experienced it— the fabulous parental prerogative: revisionist history. The truth is, I was only a somewhat talented tennis player, with a nice topspin backhand but I was by no means a prodigy.

My parents had a vision for me which included national tennis, collegiate tennis and maybe even professional tennis— ideally in that order. God bless them, they believed in me and thought there was *nothing* I couldn't accomplish. They truly and honestly thought I had a shot at being one of the best. From the first conversation with Nick, they saw junior championships, NCAA titles and Grand Slam victories.

My summer session at the Bollettieri Academy turned into a five-year stay. My mother took early retirement from her career as CEO of a fiber optics company in Tulsa and moved across the country in pursuit of *our* dreams. I played hours and hours of tennis everyday and she got her real estate license and sold house after house. Meanwhile, my dad held down the fort back at the ranch in Tulsa as the last remaining senior partner in his family's third-generation law firm and commuted back and forth to Florida on the weekends. Longboat Key and Bradenton became my new home, tennis became my life and instantly my formative years were changed.

Although my total immersion in tennis at such an early age did not produce a champion, it did instill in me a love of the game which is still alive today. From the first time I ever held my Prince Junior tennis racket in my hand at the tender age of five, I loved tennis, but I never had that insatiable tennis fire in my belly. While I was at the Bollettieri Academy, however, a different kind of passion ignited inside me.

As if being a teenager isn't hard enough, I compounded my teenage turbulence by coming to terms with my sexuality. For my "sweet sixteen," my parents gave me a brand-new BMW convertible. I know, so *Beverly Hills, 90210*. But the little twist is, I drove right into my first gay relationship. In search of nectar from an entirely different fruit, suddenly I found myself in a distinctly dissimilar world from the one where Brenda, Dylan, Brandon and the Peach Pit gang lived. In what could have foreshadowed my future demise, my first girlfriend, Chelsea, was also my tennis doubles partner. She played the backhand side and I played the forehand, and together we volleyed our way into each other's hearts.

At seventeen, Chelsea and I were barely able to admit our attraction toward each other, let alone deal with the terrifying prospect of our "secret" being exposed to anyone else. We didn't even know if we really were gay. We only knew that we loved each other deeply— and that we *really* loved kissing each other. After all, how could I be gay? I had seen gay women on television and I looked nothing like them. Sure, I was a tomboy, but I didn't have a mullet atop my head and I certainly couldn't be mistaken for a man. The closest I came to fitting the lesbian stereotype was that I owned every Ralph Lauren Oxford Polo shirt and preferred wearing one with jeans any day of the week versus the more *feminine* option of a skirt. Other than that, I looked like a total girl. I had a long, preppy, brown bob. I owned pearls. Hell, I even liked wearing them. I knew how to gracefully stride in heels, though I can't say I often chose walking on the stilt-like soles to the more comfortable option of dragging my feet in broken-in loafers.

Before Chelsea, I had boyfriends, like all of my other friends. Without question, my boyfriend was the cutest boy in the class. So there was no way I was gay! I just had a really close friendship with my best friend! I was a debutante, for God's sake! I had a traditional "Coming Out Ball" (if that isn't a double entendre, I don't know what is!) and was presented to society in a fluffy, pristine, white wedding dress like a seventeen-year-old bride-to-be.

After one year of living in blissful denial, I finally entertained admitting to myself that my connection to women transcended the boundaries of what most people would consider friendship. But, remember, it was still "early" by some standards, 1992, and it was Longboat Key. And it was still Florida— and that's *still* the South. Florida was and remains a distinctly "Red State," home to Katherine Harris, Jeb Bush, and the hanging chad. Luckily, both of my parents are as open-minded as they come, but their liberalism is somewhat more limited when it comes to their daughter. So, I adopted a "Don't Ask, Don't Tell" policy. Eventually, I would implement this policy in other areas of my life.

Chelsea and I stayed together until the geographical challenge of going to colleges on opposite sides of the United States pulled us apart. She was my first girlfriend and, despite my broken heart upon our demise, I knew in that broken heart that I was gay. (Chelsea went on to date her college doubles partner. What is it about lesbians and doubles?)

With no girlfriend to distract me, I spent even more time on the tennis court. Chelsea and I had gone to the Bollettieri Academy during the Monica Selles/Andre Agassi/Jim Courier era. The forty-hour tennis week propelled Monica, Andre and Jim to professional greatness and Chelsea to celebrated collegiate success. On the other hand, my training at the Academy catapulted me onto an operating table with a "career-ending" back injury.

During my second collegiate match of the spring season at Harvard I whaled (tennis jargon for "I hit the shit out of the ball") on a topspin backhand. I won the point but fell to the baseline writhing in pain. My coach carried me off the court, and that was the end of my tennis career, as well as my parents' dreams of tennis greatness. The orthopedists informed me that due to years of overuse and strenuous high-impact training, a vertebra in my lower back had snapped. It was traumatic, but eventually I bounced back, albeit with a foot-long scar at the bottom of my spine as a reminder of all my years of hard work.

I spent the summer after my freshman year at home in Florida in a removable plastic body cast (imagine how comfortable that was in the Florida summer heat and humidity!), recuperating from my back surgery. It may as well have been plaster, given the lack of mobility it left me with. For weeks, I filled my days by watching tennis— the French Open and then Wimbledon. It was consoling that I wasn't the only one bidding adieu to my tennis career that summer. I was in good company. Two months after I swung my racket for the last time, Martina Navratilova— one of the top three players in the history of the game— made her final appearance in a singles championship at the tournament with which her name as winner had become synonymous. Seeking her tenth Wimbledon singles title and her last crowning victory before retiring, Martina squared off against Conchita Martinez. Unable physically to cheer, I watched the riveting three-set match as the skillful

Spaniard deposed the Queen of the Wimbledon Centre Court.

During the lull after the grass court season, just when I thought the ennui of being bedridden would make me absolutely crazy, I became addicted to reruns of *L.A. Law* on Lifetime. From the first episode, I was hooked. I was immediately drawn to the glamour of the character, Grace Van Owen, played by Susan Dey. She had it all— the money, the power, the fame. I wanted to *be* Grace Van Owen.

Pleased with my new obsession, my mother handed me an intricately wrapped book (judging from the silver Barnes & Noble sticker holding the ribbon in place) and insisted that I read the card before opening my present. It read: FOR THE FUTURE STEPHANIE ALEXANDER, ESQ WITH OUR UNWAVERING LOVE AND SUPPORT. LOVE, MOM AND DAD. Without the slightest clue as to what the card meant, I ripped open the wrapping paper to find a Princeton Review LSAT book. It was larger than any textbook I'd ever held. Not exactly what I'd call light summer reading! Before I had a chance to enquire as to the meaning of the card and present, or even thank her, my mom proudly announced, "I think it's wonderful that you want to be a lawyer! You're going to be even better than Grace Van Owen! I've already called and enrolled you in the Princeton Review class." She then propped the card on my bedside table, close enough for me to read but far enough away so that my brace-restrained arms could not tip it over. I stared at that card for the rest of the summer. *Oh, great. More 'goals.' Look where our last goals got me!* My scar hadn't even healed, and already I had another monkey on my back.

My parents took my fascination with *L.A. Law* seriously and translated it to mean that I wanted to be a lawyer, which at the time I suppose I did. They quickly repositioned me from the "star tennis player" track to the "star corporate lawyer" track. Who says parents can't adapt? But, to them, it made perfect sense. My dad, the successful attorney, would gladly lend a hand and outline all the courses I needed to study in order to achieve "our" goal of getting me into law school (Boston University, because Harvard liked my GPA, but not my LSAT score) and ultimately passing not one, but two bars. Dutifully, I followed the course they charted, because really, what else was I going to do? I was thankful I hadn't become addicted to reruns of *E.R.* that summer. The sight of blood makes me faint.

Suddenly, I was twenty-six, living in Boston, and I had it all— two diplomas hanging on the wall of my office, one of which was from an Ivy League university (one out of two's not bad!). I had mahogany furniture, a secretary, and a view of downtown Boston. With "ESQ" after my name, I spoke on speakerphone to handle "matters" which all had severe consequences and repercussions. I wrote letters by way of Dictaphone and sputtered phrases like "heretofore" and "notwith-standing the aforementioned," all while remaining "very truly yours." I wore designer clothing, drove a luxury car, ordered martinis with imported vodka and owned a gorgeous condominium in Beacon Hill with not one, but two doormen.

Sure, on the surface, I *was* Grace Van Owen and yet, I was absolutely, unequivocally and hopelessly miserable. I was making piles of money, but I am living proof that money can't buy happiness. The novelty of the corporate legal world wore off very quickly. I became disenchanted with my profession and loathed pretty much everything about it— the politics, the hours and the work. But, what I found most hateful was how corporate lawyers treated other people, especially their junior associates like me. I was no longer amused by the "ghost deadlines" given by surly senior partners. You know the ones— it's five minutes until five o'clock on a Friday afternoon and somehow a crotchety partner gets wind of a Happy Hour gathering organized by a handful of junior associates. He walks into your office with a shit-eating grin on his face, only to dump an outrageously tedious emergency research project in your lap with a deadline of 8 a.m. Monday morning and then strolls out of your office without apologizing for ruining your weekend, muttering, "This is for one of our biggest clients, so please be thorough," just to dig the knife further in. And of course, after spending your *entire* weekend doing research and preparing a brief, you hand it to the senior partner who blithely says, "Oh, I no longer need that. The client left a message on Friday evening. The matter has been resolved." After about the third of these fun weekends, I was done.

Before I jumped ship, I considered the two years of hard work I had already given to the firm, not to mention the combined seven years of study in college and law school. Then there was that last, minor detail that I had to consider— the parents. After all of *their* hard work and positioning to get me to this very prestigious place, how could I

11

abandon our dream? According to them, "anyone in their right mind would give their eyeteeth to be a lawyer" and have the opportunities that I had. Their words constantly reverberated in my mind (although, to this day, I still don't know what "eyeteeth" are), and I questioned how I could so flippantly disregard such a great thing. But this "great thing" that anyone else would have killed for had come to represent traps to me.

Traps. I was trapped.

Still seeking approval, I didn't want to ruin my life or shatter my parents' dreams— the dreams that had required studying constantly, graduating *cum laude*, foregoing a graduation trip to Europe for a prestigious internship, graduating *cum laude* again and immediately going to work for one of the biggest corporate law firms in Boston. I swallowed my bitterness toward my career and adopted the same "Don't Ask, Don't Tell" policy I mentioned earlier. As long as my parents didn't ask, I didn't tell them I was miserable.

But, no matter how hard I tried as the months dragged on, I could not recapture the enthusiasm with which I had entered the legal profession. My disenchantment with law became diabolical. The scenes in *Nine to Five* where Jane Fonda, Lily Tomlin and Dolly Parton fantasized about getting even with the boss who tortured them on a daily basis paled in comparison to my fantasies, which were of a slightly darker bent.

I knew it was time to quit. *Res ipsa loquitur* (a legal tenet from the Latin meaning "the thing speaks for itself"). See, Mom, I am using my law degree!

Abandoning my post as an attorney was the first major decision I ever made by myself (not counting decisions like, "I'll have nuts on my banana split but no whipped cream"). It was a Friday evening after a grueling eighty-hour workweek. Walking home from the office, something snapped inside me. I knew that my days as a practicing attorney were numbered. In fact, there would only be ten more of them because come Monday I intended to give my two weeks' notice. I was so nervous that I went home and literally wrote out word by word what I was going to tell my dad. It seemed ridiculous to me that I was twenty-six years old and was still afraid to confront my parents with what I wanted to do or didn't want to do. The fact that I should have been old enough to stand on my own two feet didn't change the reality that the mere thought of it was making me nauseous. As I stepped into the elevator, dreading being closer to making the call, I wondered if I was ever going to be old enough to make my own decisions without not just seeking but *needing* the approval of my parents.

If only I had a plan! But I didn't. All I knew was that I had to quit my job, and I needed to do it fast before I was persuaded not to. I knew there would be a burning question on everyone's mind— even my own. "Okay, but, if you're giving up law, what *are* you going to do?"

I didn't have an answer. And I knew I couldn't shrug it off and say, "I don't know. Maybe I'll go to Disneyland! I hear that's the happiest place on Earth." Yeah, witty sarcasm was probably not the right tactic to take on this one.

I stared at the various drafts of my handwritten speech for what felt like an eternity and finally bit the bullet. I picked up the phone and called my dad first to deliver the news because I thought he would take it harder than my mom and I wanted to get the worst of it over sooner. Turned out, it was my mom who was actually more devastated. Well, I suppose both of them would qualify as devastated, but I really couldn't blame them. Everything they did, they did in hopes of securing happiness for me. If I were them, I might have gone through the roof. But parents can surprise you in good ways too, and I have to hand it to mine. They only dwelled on their shock for a few days before they both kicked in and started helping me plan the next phase of my life.

At precisely the same time that I resolved to quit my job and go in search of the something different that would interest me, I confirmed that my girlfriend of four years, Paige, was also in search of something different…or rather, *someone* different.

* * *

One of the only perks given to me by my law firm was tickets to the US Open. The year before I quit, by some fortuitous twist, the head of my department offered me the use of his tickets. Formerly a collegiate volleyball legend, Paige remained a sports enthusiast and jumped at any opportunity to watch a live sporting event. Despite having to share box seats with the partner I despised most, I excitedly snatched the complimentary pair of tickets, and Paige and I rode the train from Boston to

New York.

A quick glance at the daily program left a huge grin on my face. Conchita Martinez was scheduled to play her third-round match, and I had courtside box tickets in the Arthur Ashe Stadium. Seven years after watching from my bed as she claimed the greatest victory a tennis player can hope for, I sat just inches from Conchita and cheered her to victory— this time flailing my arms wildly and even jumping to my feet after especially exciting points.

Unbeknownst to me, our seats were directly next to the players' box, and the person sitting to my left was none other than Pascuala Toribio, commonly known throughout the tennis world as Ribi (pronounced with a Latin flair and a roll of the R— R-r-ree-bee). In addition to being Conchita's coach, Ribi was also a top doubles player on the Tour. Despite my fervent desire to lean over and tell her that she was sitting next to one of Conchita's biggest fans, I let my enthusiastic cheering speak for itself, occasionally catching a smile of encouragement from Ribi. Once Conchita had claimed victory, Paige and I pushed out of the stadium next to Ribi and the masses of other patrons. As we moved shoulder to shoulder, Ribi spilled the Diet Coke she was sipping— and not on herself. The front of my new white US Open T-shirt was now distinctly brown. (I know it's cheesy, but purchasing and actually wearing my brand-new overprized and overpriced guilty pleasure took first priority upon entering through the gates.)

"Very sorry," Ribi said, in an extremely thick Spanish accent. "Please, come with me. I fix it."

Before I could exonerate her and tell her not to concern herself over my stained souvenir, Ribi grabbed my wrist and insisted that we follow her. She led Paige and me through the crowd, stopping near a guard posted in front of a wrought-iron gate. She asked us to wait for her and flashed her badge before disappearing through an entrance marked: PLAYERS AND COACHES ONLY. Within minutes, she reappeared with a brand-new T-shirt, which I, of course attempted to politely decline while blotting my shirt and trying to convince her that the stain was not that bad. Not only did Ribi demand that I accept the replacement gift, but after chatting with us for over an hour she also insisted that Paige and I join her for dinner later that night.

When Paige and I walked into the small Italian restaurant in

Midtown Manhattan, I had no idea that we were joining Ribi *and* Conchita (Conchi to her friends). I suddenly found myself sitting across from Conchita Martinez. Even before she beat Martina at Wimbledon, Conchi had been one of my favorite players of all time— a true champion of tennis whose classic backcourt game overpowers her opponents with long rallies, incredible spin and delicate finesse.

Finding myself only slightly more articulate than the two Spaniards at the table, who spoke very broken English, I desperately tried to regain my composure, certain that baby babble would not impress the tennis goddess across from me. Blessedly, Erin, Conchi's fitness trainer who travels full-time with her, joined us. An American with full use of the English language, Erin gently coerced me out of silence and my ability to carry on an intelligent adult conversation returned before I had completely embarrassed myself. Countless bottles of wine later, we all stumbled out of the restaurant barely able to grasp our newfound friendships.

Thanks to that spilled Diet Coke, my friendship with Conchi, Ribi and Erin developed and I would find myself grateful to be their guests at numerous tournaments around the world. Exactly one-and-a-half years later it was Ribi who insisted that I come to Europe immediately when she heard I had quit my job and that Paige had quit me.

Fed up with my life and not knowing in which direction to go, I accepted Ribi's invitation and, just days after I turned my professional life upside down and Paige did the same to my personal life, I boarded a plane for Hamburg. Since I was a guest of a "main draw" player (as opposed to a "qualifier" whose ranking is not high enough to grant automatic entry into tournaments and must play preliminary matches to qualify for the main draw), I enjoyed the same perks that Ribi did— a beautiful hotel room paid for by the tournament, as well as a car service and driver.

Initially, I felt somewhat out of place as I traveled amongst tennis icons and champions, similar to how I felt being the only Jew in an entire school filled with black habits, white collars and wooden crosses. But by the second tournament, in Berlin, I had a new handful of friends (including Saskia) and I'd begun to get the hang of life on the Tour. And, instantly, I knew I could get used to it— a new city every week, top-notch hotels, drivers, restaurant owners catering to our every whim and gift bags. Oh, the freebies! One quickly falls in love with the word "swag!" It's hard not to. Tournament sponsors throw things at the players like iPods, designer watches, cell phones, digital cameras, concert tickets, clothes— you name it and they get it for free! And, they get so much of it that often, they just hand it right over to their friends like me. There's one tournament that even hands out Porsches to the top players— just for entering! Pity, I never got one of those.

I was no stranger to five-star hotels and the finer things in life, but my newfound relaxed lifestyle was distinctly foreign. With no hours to bill, no parents or senior partners to answer to and no ghost deadlines to obsess over, my only obligation was simply to have fun. Gallivanting in foreign cities, staying in beautiful hotels, dining in posh restaurants, and watching icons play tennis was not exactly an onus, and my maiden voyage on the Tour sped by.

For two months, I'd been having the time of my life, traveling through Europe with the Tour. I suppose I was making up for lost time since the last time I had taken two months off from anything was the summer I had back surgery. But tournament-hopping was not reality and my vacation had to end. Structure had to return. I'm not really sure why I felt this sense of "responsibility"— perhaps it's that kernel of Midwest work ethic left over from Tulsa! More likely, though, it's an inherited quality from my mother.

I arrived back in Boston refreshed but still uncertain what my future would hold. My dad suggested real estate as my new career choice, adding that my legal training would be of the utmost value to negotiating transactions. I didn't think it was a bad idea and decided to follow in my mother's footsteps— which were huge footsteps to fill since she is *the* real estate diva in Florida. On a whim, I sold my condo in Beacon Hill and replaced it with one in West Hollywood, moving across the country to Los Angeles to become a real estate agent. My mother cringed at the thought of my title changing from Stephanie Alexander, Attorney at Law to Stephanie Alexander, Realtor. But, true to form, she quickly kicked into gear and handed me a six-page list I'd need to strictly follow in order to achieve the same great success that she had. And then she surprised me with a box of new business cards that read: STEPHANIE ALEXANDER, ESQ/REALTOR. Instantly, *we* had new dreams of grandeur.

* * *

So there we have it— a little Jewish girl's journey from Tulsa to Longboat Key to Boston, to a regular guest on the Womens Tennis Tour to Los Angeles. Once a tennis player and now a tennis fan. Once a lawyer and now not a lawyer (or a practicing one, anyway). Once coupled and now single. And, that brings us back to where we left off— my debut at Wimbledon, where I went to visit my friend Saskia for two weeks as she bid adieu to this most glorious Grand Slam tournament.

2

Going home with a trophy without winning the tournament

Standing barefoot on a tennis court at Wimbledon with hot cheeks, trying to maintain my composure, I was speechless. Saskia wasn't kidding. And she was right. How many people can say that they have played tennis at Wimbledon? And when else in my life will I ever be able to do this again? But, shit, how embarrassing! A princess I am not, but, seriously, I was in my tattered gray-and-black Perfetto sweatpants. And, I hadn't hit a tennis ball in years! As these inane thoughts bulleted through my mind, I didn't have time to put together a persuasive argument because suddenly one, two and then three balls raced by me. As I ducked and darted to avoid being hit, Saskia, now empty-handed, was walking backward on the other side of the net. She made her point without saying a word. I met her gaze and said, "Okay! I'm going! But don't tell me what to do!"

As Saskia had so delicately instructed, I grabbed one of her rackets and took my place on the baseline, hoping she'd be the only witness to my Wimbledon performance. Fortunately, I didn't make a *complete* ass of myself. Granted, more balls went out rather than in and at times, our hitting session looked more like batting practice than a refined tennis rally— at least on my part. But I was truly having the time of my life and eventually I calmed down enough to somehow pull a passing topspin backhand out of nowhere and rip it down the line past Saskia. As I jubilantly pumped my fist in celebration, I imagined that the shot had just won me *my* first Wimbledon title in front of all of my thousands of adoring fans. The award ceremony playing out in my head was cut short and the deafening shouts and claps from the stadium were silenced by a simple "Nice shot!" from an unfamiliar face approaching the court.

I glanced at the stranger nearing, attempting to discover her identity as well as the country from which her accent originated. Having only two words to analyze, I guessed that the new arrival was British. The face became recognizable once it was closer to me, and I realized I had guessed incorrectly. There, just outside the court, was *another* of the greatest players in the history of women's tennis. I didn't have time to pinch myself, but I knew that, unlike the fantasy of holding the champion's trophy, this time I wasn't dreaming. Little Stephie from Tulsa, Oklahoma, had just received praise from Sydney Foster! Her career statistics raced through my memory and the smirk immediately disappeared from my face. Seconds before, I was aglow with joy and self-adoration, and before I could unclench my fist, the muscles on my face froze, preventing me from holding a smile. I have never been able to relish compliments, and even if I had wanted to gracefully accept the accolade handed to me by a celebrated champion of tennis, I was incapable of doing anything but will myself not to pass out. As if being stunned into a zombie-like state wasn't sufficiently torturous, I felt as if, one by one, goose bumps were popping out on my skin to remind me of how embarrassed I was.

Although I didn't know it at the time, the ruination of my life was about to walk onto the court and life as I knew it was about to change. I was about to embark on the craziest nine months of my life. In this period you can produce a baby, but what was born out of these nine months was far from any new life I'd like to consider; not tenderness, infancy and innocence, but an insane and unbelievably tumultuous love triangle.

Saskia formally introduced me to Sydney as her "lawyer-friend from Boston who recently quit her job." She didn't have to preface her introduction of Sydney, her friend who'd won virtually every tennis tournament there was to win. Sydney Foster held the distinction of being New Zealand's most famous female tennis player, as well as one of the most successful players on the Tour in recent years. Despite my numerous appearances at various tournaments, Sydney and I had never met. I knew her through her reputation and I'd surely seen her play.

Not only was she a champion of the game, but she was a woman off whom I couldn't take my eyes. Her features were precise— defined cheekbones, dark brown hair, and sharp green eyes. Her wet hair was pulled back into a tight ponytail and a red baseball hat shaded her sunburned, button-shaped nose. I gulped as she tightened the laces on her shoes and confidently swaggered onto the court to hit with Saskia. Not many things make me speechless, but I found myself searching for words— for something witty and impressive to say. But, as I walked past her and retired my racket against the net post, I could utter nothing. Not one word came to me. I sat on the grass in silence with my back against the fence and watched as Sydney and Saskia began to rally.

I couldn't help but think about how thrilled my dad was going to be that I'd met Sydney Foster. He followed all sports and was familiar with every athlete. And he was a huge fan of women's tennis. He once hoped that my sister and I would go to college together and bring home an NCAA doubles championship. I knew in the juniors when she served a ball into the back of my head that he was dreaming. The only trophy that my sister and I would bring off the court would be a broken racket inspired by flaring tempers. We gave new meaning to sibling rivalry.

Thankfully, I regained some control over the muscles in my face, otherwise my mouth would have flung open when Sydney took off her white shirt and continued to play scantily clad in only a white sports bra and white shorts— the Brandi Chastain look of tennis. Her face was only moderately attractive, but I was mesmerized by her body. I tried not to stare but could not help myself. She had toned and developed muscles that were humbling. If I had a type, Sydney was definitely it— a brown-haired, olive-skinned, green-eyed, chiseled athlete.

Once their practice was over, Sydney interrupted the call she'd just answered on her cell phone and reminded Saskia, "Don't forget, mate— party at my flat tonight in honor of this glorious event. I'll text you the address. Oh, and bring your attorney." She smiled and turned her attention back to her phone.

I guess Saskia could see me swooning because she immediately pounced on my silence as we exited the court. "Okay, Stephie, what the hell is going on with you?"

Covering, I said, "Nothing. I just can't believe I'm here." More silence. "Sydney seems really nice, and God, what a body that one has on her." I fanned myself as I got ready to throw out my line on my fishing expedition about Sydney.

"Yeah, she does have a nice body…if you like muscles."

"Is she single?" *Bloop!* The fishing line just splashed loudly into the water.

Saskia firmly placed her hand on my shoulder and responded, "Oh no, Stephie! Stop right there! Sydney's a good friend, but she's not for you. Trust me. She's *not* for you!"

My line had just hit a snag. Shit. I trusted Saskia, so she must have had good reasons for not wanting me to be interested in Sydney. But the damage was already done. My interest was piqued and I'm not sure *anything* Saskia could have said— if she'd talked until the end of time— would have dissuaded me.

* * *

I met Sydney wearing torn up sweatpants and a tank top; probably not my best look. I was determined to up my ante considerably the next time she saw me. I wanted to look cute and thin. I had a problem because I wasn't feeling very svelte. As I squeezed into my "skinny jeans," which snuggly (but not absurdly) hugged my size 8, 5' 8" frame, I cursed the chocolate cake I'd eaten for dessert the night before. Inhaling laboriously, I buttoned my Sevens, which were an investment with a promised ass-minimizing return. I turned to the side to check myself out in the mirror and was thankful that the denim curved in just the right places. My favorite red Elie Tahari shirt (unbuttoned just enough to show my healthy cleavage) and a pair of simple DKNY leather sandals completed my ensemble. Red is my color— it brings out my complexion, dark brown hair and hazel eyes.

I plucked a stray gray hair from just above my forehead and ran my fingers through my "I just fell out of bed with sexy 'Rachel' hair." Refusing to admit to Saskia that I was trying to impress anyone, I subtly applied lotions and beauty potions and topped everything off with a few sprays of Gucci Envy.

During the drive over from our hotel, I digested the backstory on

Sydney that I had carefully and nonchalantly extricated from Saskia during the day. She was twenty-nine years old and originally from Auckland. Like many professional tennis players, tennis became Sydney's life before she entered her teenage years. At fifteen, she began playing on the Tour. Once her talent was identified by the New Zealand Tennis Federation, they provided a tutor who traveled with her to tournaments in lieu of her having to attend her last two years of high school. Although singles was her forte, she enjoyed great success in doubles as well. She and her former partner, Casey Matthews, had built an impressive doubles empire together that had recently crumbled.

Until the previous fall, Casey and Sydney had been girlfriends (not exactly in the sorority way) and doubles partners for three years. Their relationship, as well as their partnership, ended due to irreconcilable differences on and off the court. The rumor was that Casey fell out of love with Sydney when she could no longer deny her love for her best friend, Trish. How unique. Imagine that! A young lesbian falling in love with her best friend. It turns out, the best friend, Trish, is straight— very straight. Casey dumped her girlfriend and doubles partner for her straight best friend.

Sydney, the more talented tennis player of the two, suffered a broken heart and a shattered ego which severely impacted her tennis. Since their breakup, Sydney's singles ranking plummeted from Number 1 in the world to her current ranking of Number 42. Her doubles ranking fell as well— from Number 5 to 26. Accustomed to receiving byes first round, Sydney now counted herself lucky not to be eliminated in the opening round. To make matters worse, the upheaval of the breakup had virtually no negative impact on Casey's tennis career. In fact, at Number 59 in the world, her singles ranking was steadily climbing, and she immediately partnered with another of tennis' greats on the doubles court. Together, Casey and her new partner captured the World Number 1 ranking— a ranking that had eluded her and Sydney— within a few short months of her split from Sydney.

As I processed my newly acquired information, it occurred to me that Sydney and I had quite a bit in common. I was finished licking my wounds of rejection from Paige, but I was still hurt. I'd had a few quick flings just after I arrived in LA but hadn't dated anyone seriously since I left Boston. I only had myself to thank for turning my professional life upside down in Boston, but I'm pretty proud of the way I bounced back and settled into my new career as a realtor in Los Angeles. I was building a client base and had a partner of my own. Unfortunately, that partnership wasn't long-lived. My ex-partner and I had different ideas on how to run a business (specifically, he didn't agree with pages three and four of my mom's how-to-be-successful-in-real-estate list) and just before I left for Europe, we ended our partnership. So you see, Sydney and I were in similar positions with one small difference. I was on vacation, thousands of miles away from anything resembling my life and the "real world," while Sydney had to go to the courts everyday and face the one person who had single-handedly made her entire life personally and professionally miserable.

It was time for us both to move on. And we did. With each other.

Loud music was playing and Sydney was busy arranging bottles of wine on the counter when we arrived. My eyes flashed immediately from the impressive selection of Burgundy and Bordeaux wines to our hostess. Her skimpy white denim Hollister Co. skirt hung low on her hips. A simple black tank top accompanied her miniskirt and her feet were bare. Her toenails were painted a vibrant red and she wore a silver toe ring on her left, second toe. As she waved us toward her, her sterling silver Tiffany & Co. oval tag bracelet clanked ferociously against another silver bangle. After greeting us with quick kisses on the cheeks, she announced to Saskia, "Mate, there's a pack of smokes with your name on it on the terrace. Just give me a second to pour us some wine, and out we'll go." She smiled widely, exposing two rows of slightly crooked teeth.

I counted ten bottles of red wine, four bottles of white, and predicted a night of blistering intoxication. Even after traveling to countless tournaments with my friends on the Tour, I was still amazed how these world-class athletes could perform with such finesse on the tennis court after a night of (over-) indulgence. Some of them smoke, most of them drink and hardly any of them count calories. Everything they do—whether executing the most perfect one-handed backhand down the line, or single-handedly polishing off a bottle of Château Margaux—they do with the same intensity.

Sydney joined Saskia and me on the terrace and handed us full glasses of deliciously aromatic red wine. Saskia toasted, "Proost!" and we all lifted our glasses.

Sydney winked at me, and I flashed my most alluring smile before averting my gaze for fear that Saskia would catch me gawking at her friend. I traded one breathtaking view for another. Sydney's flat was stunning. Her home for the next two weeks was newly renovated and had an expansive terrace overlooking the Wimbledon practice courts. It was huge by anyone's standards, but especially by European standards. Her jaw-dropping pied-à-terre was the epitome of excessive, which I would only later come to learn was synonymous with Sydney Foster.

Main draw players are given a per diem at the Grand Slams to offset their daily expenses. At Wimbledon, the per diem is generous, but it's safe to say that it didn't put a huge dent into what this place must have cost Sydney for two weeks. I'm guessing her flat came with a $10,000 price tag.

After giving our livers the daunting task of processing more than just one glass too many of red wine, Sydney and I separated from the rest of the party. Kicking shut the bedroom door behind us, I landed on top of her on the bed. It wasn't as dramatic as those sex scenes in the movies where lovers with limbs and tongues intertwined slide everything off a china-filled table in one smooth motion in order to make room for their bodies, but it was close. Her silky shoulder-length brown hair fanned out across the crisp white 1,000 thread count Egyptian cotton sheets. Our lips met and we began kissing with urgency. I tasted tannins on her tongue and smelled fragrant musk on her skin. Immediately, our hands wandered underneath our disheveled clothing. The awkwardness of our position— me on top of her propped up on one elbow slightly so that I had a free hand— lent itself to hasty disrobing. I'm pretty sure I lost one, if not two buttons on my shirt as Sydney ripped it open. I would have returned the favor, had she not been wearing a simple cotton tank top, which I immediately pulled over the top of her head and tossed onto the floor. She fumbled with the hook on my bra for a few seconds before she gave up and just slid it over my head. Shimmying, I impatiently backed my bare arms out of it and threw it down. I had the luxury of not having to maneuver around her bra since she wasn't wearing one— her martini glass-sized breasts were so perky that unlike me, she did not need a bra to help push them up.

Our sizzling attraction and sexual craving for each other intensified and seemed animalistic. Forget tenderness and passion; I saw her toned, tight body and had to have it. My physical attraction to her was magnetic— the mere anticipation of touching her muscles sent me into a euphoric state. We slid to the end of the bed and I rolled off her so we could stand and free ourselves of the rest of our clothing constraints. We barely broke our kiss as she unbuttoned my jeans and I unzipped her skirt, as if it were a race against time to get our clothing off and explore each other's bodies. Once naked, our lips parted long enough for me to push her back onto the now wrinkled sheets. She crawled back toward the inviting pillows on her elbows and I followed on my hands and knees. My bare body absorbed her warmth as I straddled her at the waist. Inhaling deeply, I stared in amazement at her perfectly sculpted physique.

Her arms were extended above her head as if she had just done the "Nestea Plunge." I leaned forward and with one hand gently ran my fingers up her arm from the inside of her elbow, tracing the outline of her rock-hard bicep. When the tip of my index finger reached her shoulder, I lifted my hand to my mouth and wetted my finger. I lowered my hand and with that same finger circled her nipple as it became even more erect. My other hand cupped her breast and I squeezed firmly with excitement and desire. Looking down at her body, I felt short of breath. As I pinched her nipple, her body tightened beneath mine and her breathing increased. I counted eight perfectly defined abdominal muscles popping out of her stomach. *Eight!* I felt like I was going to explode!

As I lowered my body onto hers, our kissing grew more intense and our bodies began to move rhythmically with each other, causing blissful friction. I started to sweat, and within minutes we were both glistening. Her hand slid down my damp back leaving a cool trail behind it as the air brushed against my skin. I pushed my body down hers until my mouth found her breasts. Shifting to the side slightly, my tongue flicked one hard nipple back and forth as my fingers squeezed the other one— gently at first and gradually firmer. Slowly, she widened her long, smooth, sinewy legs. One leg was now bent, and her knee rested nearly even with her chest. I caressed the inside of her bent leg, starting with her ankle. My fingers traced the lump in her calf muscle to the crevice beneath her knee and continued up her inner thigh. Her breaths increased and, as I eased one finger inside her, she let out a moan of pleasure. When I felt her warmth and wetness on my finger, a surge traveled down my body, resting between my legs. Slowly but then faster and faster, I slid two fingers in and out of her. "Is this okay?" I whispered.

She answered with a sexy sigh of pleasure and opened her legs wider. "It's more than okay," she purred.

Her muscles contracted around my fingers as I plunged deeper inside her. I watched her body move, writhing with pleasure. As she gasped, she gripped my arm and squeezed every time I thrust my fingers into her. Her moans got louder and louder with every exhale. I closed my eyes and fantasized about tasting her. I wanted to slide my body down hers until my tongue found the warmth that my fingers were feeling. As my fantasy became more and more erotic, my hand pumped faster until I heard a climax in her voice. Without warning, her hips lifted from the bed and her body began to shake. I exhaled a sigh of satisfaction with her and felt as if I had almost reached orgasm myself. She hadn't even touched me and I felt tingly from excitement. I opened my eyes and could see her chest moving up and down rapidly from her breathing. Her heart was literally pounding beneath her skin. I collapsed onto my back and tried to catch my breath. It took her a few minutes to move, and then she rolled onto her side facing me and threw her arm across my still sweaty chest.

Panting between words she said, "I cannot tell you how incredible that felt, love. That's the first orgasm I've had in months." She gazed at me with her limpid, sexual eyes.

Her accent was every bit as delicious as her body and I told her as much. "Please don't stop talking. That accent is one potent aphrodisiac!" I whispered softly.

"I've never been told that before, but I'll gladly accept the compliment and the request. Hey, if you're from Oklahoma, why is it that a southern drawl doesn't come out of your gorgeous mouth?" Her thumb traced the outline of my lips as she awaited my response.

After kissing the tip of her thumb, I answered, "Because my mother refused to let me talk with a southern accent. As a child, I was taught that there was nothing refined or intelligent about employing such words as 'ya'll' or 'ma'am'." Technically, Oklahoma is the Midwest, not the South, but it may as well have been in my mother's eyes. And in her humble opinion there is nothing elegant or prestigious about anything south of the Mason-Dixon Line. Most of all, talking with a drawl wasn't charming or endearing. It was, according to my mother, just plain ignorant.

Inching toward me, Sydney seductively whispered, "That's classic, but I'm not fussed one way or the other about your accent so long as I don't hear it right now. Kiss me!" The warmth of her breath in my ear made me flinch, and her hand started to move slowly down the side of my body. Just as she reached below my naval where my skin was stark white under my bikini line, my body began to tremble. I closed my eyes again and replayed in my mind her moans, her orgasm and the warm silky feeling on my fingers. Savoring that image, a bang startled me. My eyes darted open, and I looked toward the direction of the noise. It was coming from the door. Saskia, Conchi and Ribi were on the verge of falling over into the room as they peeked through the door. Sydney and I covered our naked bodies and were then blanketed with laughter. As much as I wanted to continue touching Sydney's body and feel her inside me, the three stooges had just shattered the moment. But nothing, and I mean *nothing,* could kill the images of us frantically ripping off our clothes in order to satisfy our carnal desires.

Saskia and I had been among the first to arrive at Sydney's kick-off soirée, and I may have been the last to leave. It was that night that my romance with Sydney began.

From that initial evening, Sydney and I were inseparable for the rest of the Wimbledon fortnight. There's an old joke: "What does a lesbian take with her on her second date?" Answer: "A U-Haul." I wish I could say that joke was not tailor-made for me but, when it came to Sydney, I'd certainly have to plead guilty. I only spent one night in the hotel room that Saskia had graciously offered to share with me. The rest of my nights were spent at Sydney's apartment. We were captivated by each other— I was in awe of her accomplishments as a player on the court and she admired that I was a bar-appointed member of the court. And, we couldn't get enough of each other in the bedroom.

* * *

I met the infamous heartbreaker, Casey Matthews, a few days after meeting Sydney. I distinctly remember the first time I ever laid eyes on her. I was sitting with Erin in the players' lounge ogling over Sydney. Barely able to contain my excitement over my infatuation with her, I didn't notice Casey until Erin leaned over and whispered, "That's Casey."

Casey who?

Scratching underneath my favorite Boston Bruins baseball hat, I looked at Erin with confusion and stared at the stranger across the room for a few seconds until I focused enough to finally realize that I was looking at Casey Matthews, Sydney's ex-girlfriend. And then the scrutiny of the "ex" began. Immediately, I noticed she was physically very different from Sydney. She had streaky platinum blonde hair peppered with black roots. A dark blue bandanna held her jaw-length hair out of her face. I'd been told that Casey was one-half Puerto Rican, which explained her golden-bronze skin. The sun had not merely kissed her gently but had stolen the freshness of her youth and aged her well beyond her twenty-six years. She was several inches taller than Sydney, and thin, but not particularly lean or noticeably muscular. I tried not to stare at her right ear as I silently counted six earrings. My eyes bounced from her silver studded ear to the small dolphin tattooed on her bare left shoulder. Streaky blonde hair, piercings and tattoos aren't exactly commonplace among tennis players so I was somewhat mesmerized. Upon first glance, I would have guessed she was a member of an alternative punk rock band, not a professional player of the refined game of tennis. But, it was her face I found myself most drawn to. In fact, I immediately joked to myself, *H-E-L-L-O, Pinocchio!* I wondered if her beak of a nose had its own zip code. There was a tiny pin-sized hole on the top of her left nostril that had obviously once housed a piercing. Why she'd want to draw attention to that monstrosity was beyond me! As I cattily analyzed Casey, I tried, mostly in vain, to stop myself.

Over the past several days, Sydney had regaled me with more details about Casey and their relationship than I cared to hear about. Despite her new obsession with me, Sydney was clearly still fixated on Casey and the demise of their relationship. It seemed like she could not finish a sentence without saying "Casey." Apparently Sydney the tennis champion was not well versed in the rules of the dating game— Rule Number 1: you don't mention ex-girlfriends (let alone dwell on them) when you're in a fledgling relationship. Sydney's constant banter about Casey made me a little nervous, but I was comforted by what I saw when I gave her ex the once-over. I was no longer threatened by this person with whom Sydney still had somewhat of a lingering obsession. By my estimation, aesthetically, Casey was in a different league, and that league was definitely beneath me.

I leaned over to Erin and spitefully said, "She's not very cute." Erin tried to disguise her laughter as Casey approached.

Erin and Casey exchanged pleasantries before Erin introduced me as her "friend, Stephanie, from Boston."

Casey had no idea who I was or what *connection* I had assumed with Sydney and enthusiastically greeted me as a fellow Bostonian. "You're from Boston? I've lived there my whole life. I love that city! Where do you live?" She spoke without even the slightest trace of a Boston accent.

Suddenly, I was nervous and became extremely and unnaturally verbose. I launched into a bio of my life, "Actually, I live in LA now, but when I was in Boston I lived in Beacon Hill and worked downtown. It's a great city. The restaurants are the best! I definitely miss it, but I love LA." I stopped myself when I realized that I was speaking a million miles a minute, my sentences colliding into one another. I had not taken a single breath since opening my mouth to speak.

Excited by my enthusiasm about her hometown, Casey smiled and crinkly lines formed around the corners of her eyes. "I know…Boston's the best! It's definitely my favorite place in the world! I could never leave there again and be happy!"

Just then, a short, rail-thin Asian woman, wearing tons of makeup came out of the bathroom a few feet from us. The stranger walking toward us in tight jeans and three-inch heels looked out of place among the athletes and their friends donned in sportswear. She resembled someone who walks the streets at night offering her services to gentlemen— not a tennis fan. She looked like the kind of girl in high school whose name and phone number were written on the Boy's Room wall with "call for a good time" underneath. In fact, she actually did remind me of one such girl I went to high school with, Peggy

Kossoff. Peggy fancied herself a home-grown beauty queen (and dressed the part!), but I didn't think it was a coincidence that her name was only one vowel away from "Piggy." She was one of those girls who thought her senior prom picture should be a shot of her seductively positioned on top of her parents' baby grand piano, with her date on the bench nearby. She even topped off the ensemble with a tiara. As I stared at the girl before me, I just knew that she had both worn a tiara and posed for an equally cheesy picture at her senior prom.

Casey introduced her friend Trish Avalon from Boston to Erin and me.

Trish Avalon. That sounded like some sort of bad porn name. What is it with these girls whose names could so easily be changed by substituting one vowel for another? First it was Piggy and now Trash. Did I say "Trash?" Surely I meant Trish?

As soon as we exchanged pleasantries, Trish shrieked, "Like, omigod! Andy Roddick, like, just walked by. He's, like, sooo hot!" Her high-pitched, valley-girl voice was piercing. I repeated her sentences in my mind to confirm that she had, in fact, used the word "like" in each of them. Before I could decide if her enthusiasm for Andy Roddick was facetious or genuine, Trish adjusted her push-up bra, nearly spilling out her disproportionately large breasts (clearly the result of a foray into the world of plastic surgery) over the lacey cups. Desperately trying to catch a glimpse of Andy, she skirted by us mumbling, "He's freshly single— he and Mandy Moore *just* broke up!" For a second, I actually thought she was going to run after him into the men's locker room and ask him to autograph her Victoria's Secret undergarment.

Just then, Sydney strolled around the corner, fresh from practice. Clearly unprepared to join the conversation, she continued past us with a look of shock and horror on her face. I probably would have done the same thing. There I was, the girl she was now sleeping with, chummily talking with the girl she used to sleep with. I watched her continue past Trish who was now busy craning her neck as Roger Federer emerged from the locker room.

Erin was barely finished raving to Casey about a new Indian restaurant in the village when Casey spotted Sydney. Her demeanor changed immediately. As soon as Erin finished her sentence, Casey pleasantly excused herself to leave for practice and dragged her gawking friend away from her post just outside the men's locker room. I wished Casey luck in the tournament, as I would any other friend of mine. *She seems really nice. She's not cute, but she's nice. She doesn't seem like the nightmare that Sydney made her out to be, but what do I know?*

When Casey and Trish were out of earshot, I turned to Erin and mumbled, "Well, that was awkward. I take it she has no idea I'm sleeping with her ex-girlfriend."

Erin laughed and said, "Totally awkward. And you do realize who Trish is, don't you?"

I looked at her blankly. I didn't have a clue who Trish from Boston was aside from some girl who must have purchased one of everything at her favorite makeup store and decided to apply every product at the same time. I wondered if she knew that her makeup mirror needed to have a daytime setting. "No. I have no idea who she is. Andy Roddick's Number 1 fan?" I offered sarcastically.

"That's the 'best friend'— the one that Casey's been in love with forever. The one she left Sydney for— well, not 'for' exactly, but definitely because of."

I didn't believe her and was waiting for her to tell me she was just kidding. My gaydar is finely tuned and it certainly wasn't sounding at the sight of Trish, who was very obviously salivating over the male players. I stopped trying to convince myself that Erin was telling me the truth and said, "Nice try. I don't believe for *one second* that girl is gay!" To me, Trish was as straight as the bangs that crossed her forehead (which looked like they'd been cut using a ruler!). I replayed her heavily-made-up face in my mind, but it was her "fuck-me heels" that really solidified my categorization of her as heterosexual— very heterosexual.

Erin shrugged her shoulders and smirked, "Whether she's gay or not, she's who Casey's in love with. The three of them used to be friends, and now not so much."

She really wasn't kidding. Trashy Trish was the woman who had broken up Sydney and Casey. I shook my head disbelievingly. "You're not kidding, are you?"

"Nope," Erin answered wryly.

"Those two look like complete opposites. I would never, in a million years, guess that they were together. C'mon! They *can't* be together!"

"No one really knows if they are or aren't. Trish always flirts with men— you saw that just now. The other day she was drooling over Rafael Nadal. So, if they *are* together, they don't admit it and they must have some sort of arrangement. As far as we know, Trish is still *just* Casey's best friend. Whatever's going on between them, they certainly seem obsessed with each other."

I thought back to a conversation I had with Sydney in which she had described Trish as "straight as a pool cue." According to Sydney, Trish knows Casey's in love with her but has made it very clear she could never be in a gay relationship. She told me that Casey and Trish became close friends years ago when Casey's hitting partner was Trish's then-boyfriend. That relationship is long over, but Trish clung to Casey, who apparently misread Trish's intentions and has been steadfastly trying to persuade Trish to fall in love with her ever since. Sydney claimed that Trish is in love with Casey's tennis celebrity status— like she gets part of her identity because her best friend is a famous tennis player, but that is as far as her love for Casey goes. My eyes were almost glazed over. Turning to Erin I said, "I don't know either of them, but from what Sydney says, they're *both* obsessed with something they can't have."

"Yeah, that's what I've heard too, but you gotta figure Casey hangs on for a reason and it doesn't look like Trish tries to discourage Casey's obsession with her. I see her all the time at the tournaments— the glamorous ones, anyway. She deals blackjack at some casino outside of Boston, and they give her all the time off she wants so she can travel." Erin smiled as she snickered an insinuation, "Apparently, the gambling men rush to her table in droves. Judging by her looks, I'd bet lots of them get lucky." Her innuendo was followed by a smirk and a wink. "Anyway, either she's a tennis groupie or there's something more to their friendship than they're admitting because my best friends don't follow me around the world to tennis tournaments."

Something didn't make sense to me. I still didn't know if Casey and Trish were romantically involved. Sydney insinuated that they had an affair that couldn't exactly be considered platonic, but now that I had set eyes on Casey's "straight crush," I was just certain that a sexual relationship was impossible!

In response to my furrowed brow, Erin said, "I can't imagine those two in bed together, either. I'd love to be a fly on the wall of that hotel room! Do you think she takes those heels off?" It was Erin's turn to adjust her eyebrows— one was raised while the other remained level, but both were accompanied by an uneasy frown. "Who knows what's really going on between them? The only thing we know for sure is that there were a bunch of rather inappropriate e-mails and countless phone calls between those two at the end of Casey and Sydney's relationship."

I cringed, knowing exactly what Erin was referring to. Just before their split, Sydney had broken into Casey's e-mail account by guessing Casey's password. She read every e-mail she could find that was to or from Casey to Trish and unabashedly bragged about it.

Clearly, Erin had heard as much from Sydney herself. "I guess it was a little bittersweet after she started reading how Casey was head-over-heels in love with Trish. Kinda creepy, if you ask me," Erin admitted.

I agreed. It was and still *is* creepy! What I didn't get into with Erin— because, frankly, I had found it so utterly appalling, even in the throes of a relationship meltdown— was that, just to be certain, Sydney had gone to the extreme of cracking Casey's cell phone account code, giving her access to all of her soon-to-be ex-girlfriend's incoming and outgoing calls as well as the itemized, monthly bill via the Internet. She'd scrutinized Casey's call logs for further proof that she was in touch with Trish morning, noon and night. What I then heard from Erin was how Sydney had created this huge drama and told everyone how Casey didn't just have feelings for Trish but that she was having a torrid affair with her. Only in the twisted world of lesbian romances would you enjoy being seen by your friends and peers as a victim of betrayal by your girlfriend and her straight best friend. I mean, really, what's juicier than that? Apparently, everyone on the Tour was talking about it.

Suddenly, I realized I'd drifted off into my own little mind spin, but Erin was still relating more of the blow-by-blow: "No one knew what she was going to do next. She even followed Trish and Casey around— in a stalking way."

Erin was making me nervous. I didn't like what I was hearing. Sydney's behavior sounded disturbing and destructive. I was starting to feel as if I were infatuated with someone who could have authored a book entitled: *How To Stalk Your Ex-Girlfriend And Make Yourself Look*

Absolutely Insane.

No shit, Sherlock! Here I was, falling head over heels for Sydney. Could a bigger, louder warning bell not have just started ringing over my head?

Obviously, Erin could read the shock on my face and attempted to assuage my concern. "Oh, don't worry about it. It's over and done with. She got that craziness out of her system and she and Casey are working on re-building a friendship. They're taking baby steps, but they are making progress. In fact, Sydney told me that even she and Trish are becoming friends again."

"Okay, just to make sure we're on the same page and that there's no confusion, let me reiterate succinctly." I took a deep breath and blurted my summary, "Casey left Sydney for Trish, who is not gay but is totally obsessed with Casey. Trish welcomed the attention but rejected the attraction. There were major fireworks, some minor stalking, and now the three of them are on their way back to being best friends again?"

"Exactly. You got it," Erin laughed.

Fucking women! They really are crazy!

But I quickly convinced myself, in a self-delusional happy way, typical of all young love-struck girls with flushed cheeks, that there had to be a good reason for Sydney's past behavior. My romance with Sydney had just begun. The Sydney whom I had woken up with that morning was not the type of person who would violate *my* privacy and break into *my* e-mail account.

Yeah, no warning bell ringing in my ears. Can you spell r-a-t-i-o-n-a-l-i-z-a-t-i-o-n? Don't we all do crazy things when our hearts are involved? After all, we're only human.

I had heard enough and wanted to stop thinking about all of the off-court craziness I was learning about Sydney. I chalked it up to a "temporary lapse in judgment" on her part and put it out of my mind. You had to kind of feel bad for Sydney, though. Whether she deserved it or not, she had been through the wringer because of Casey. Last year was the greatest year of Sydney's career and her most successful Wimbledon ever. She was the Number 5 singles seed and had overcome the odds to capture the Wimbledon trophy by ousting the Number 1 seed in a straight-set victory. In addition to her singles championship, she and Casey won a hotly contested victory in the doubles draw, handing them their second Wimbledon title. This year, because Sydney's rankings had dropped, she wasn't even seeded in singles, and she didn't bother entering either the doubles or the mixed doubles draws.

Now ranked 42, Sydney drew the Number 1 seed, Lindsay Davenport, in the first round. Talk about luck of the draw— or lack thereof! The match was played on Wimbledon's famous Centre Court. Thousands of clapping fans rose to their feet as the players walked onto the grass. I flashed an uncontrollably shiny smile when Sydney stepped onto the court with her bright red Wilson tennis bag draped over her stark white Addidas ensemble. She graciously waved to the on-lookers and immediately spotted me in the players' box. I watched the match courtside in an awe-inspiring stadium full of people as Sydney gallantly fought to the death. It was a nail-biter of a three-set match and although Lindsay struggled with Sydney's left-handed kick-serve in the final set, Sydney didn't come out on the winning end. Damn! I knew I should have hip-checked Lindsay in the hallway that first day when her entourage pushed me out of their way. Sydney Foster, who had once proudly held the Wimbledon trophy above her head on Centre Court, had been eliminated from the tournament before the end of the first week. It was a devastatingly early loss for Sydney, but she kept her chin up and found a positive twist on the situation— me.

I nervously waited for Sydney outside the women's locker room— the one reserved for the past Wimbledon singles champions. Having known her less than a week, I wasn't sure how to comfort her. When she finally walked through the doors, I solemnly said, "Bad luck." This was Tour vernacular. I'd heard my friends say it to one another after a loss, and not knowing what else to say, I extended the borrowed phrase to Sydney.

She smiled. "No worries, love. You win some, you lose some," she said blandly. "Lately, it seems I'm losing more than I win, though."

I grinned silently.

"I've just hung up the phone with my agent. We both agreed that I need to take a little time off and regroup, so I told him to book me on a flight at the end of next week. I don't suppose you'd care to join me for a week's holiday in this fantastic flat I've already paid for and don't see the point of not using? I promise you it'll be a fortnight to remember."

Normally, players leave the tournament with haste once they've lost. Completely taken aback by Sydney's departure from the norm, I accepted her invitation with rushed eagerness, thinking, *now this is an opportunity I'd give my eyeteeth for!* Just when I thought my vacation couldn't get any more spectacular, I had been handed the unexpected gift of seven uninterrupted days with the object of my affection.

Donning a permanent smile for the first time in months, Sydney was thrilled and proud to parade me around as her new paramour. Although she did not conceal her sexuality on the Tour, she didn't exactly broadcast it to the world. On the other hand, my fingers couldn't type salacious e-mails fast enough to my friends around the globe. My enthusiasm in front of the computer screen attracted Sydney's curious eyes, which occasionally caught a glimpse of the screen as I typed my flattering daily e-mails describing my excitement and involvement with "the great Sydney Foster."

Night after night, we enjoyed each other in the secluded splendor of Sydney's flat. And, during the days, we'd sit courtside and watch our friends play, occasionally taking refuge in London during the rain delays for which Wimbledon is famous. I actually got lost in Harrods—twice. Who can blame me though? I was busy thinking about how fantastic my life suddenly was, despite the upheaval of the past year. I couldn't be expected to remember if I'd last seen Sydney near the Burberry display or the Paul Smith offerings, much less how to find my way back to either of them. My little vacation to the most glorious Grand Slam had turned out to be much more than a vacation. It was finally my turn to wake up happy.

Eventually, my time at Wimbledon had come to an end. The same driver who'd picked me up from Heathrow a couple of weeks earlier now delivered Sydney and me back to the international terminal. The one thing that I have to admit was a little disappointing— but also should have been a little telling— his britches. Remember his crisp, pleated pants? Well, on the way out they were wrinkled; only slightly, but still. I should have realized Wimbledon was much like the rest of the world— we can put on a great show, but after the show's over, everyone stops trying so hard. But, what the hell? He probably kept his britches on a lot longer than I did!

After signing several autographs, Sydney and I ducked inside the first class lounge to savor our last moments together before boarding separate planes; hers to her home in Miami, and mine to my home in Los Angeles. We quickly downed one last traditional English breakfast together— bangers, eggs, baked beans and tea— and then an awkward silence consumed us. We both knew that our sexy affair at Wimbledon was more than just that. But we hadn't broached the subject of "us" and hadn't made firm plans to see each other again. I was gripped with anxiety, wondering when I'd see Sydney next— indeed hoping that there would, in fact, be a next time very soon.

"Love, I need to go to the toilet. You do, too, don't you?" Sydney said as she gestured toward the bathroom in an obvious attempt to persuade me to accompany her.

Smiling coyly, I answered, "Uh, yeah, I do," and rose from my seat to join her.

As soon as Sydney locked the bathroom door, she enveloped me with a warm kiss. Her soft tongue frenetically swirled around mine as she embraced me tightly. My body filled with happy adrenaline as we made out like teenagers who sneaked off after school to steal some private kisses.

Please don't let this be our last kiss.

Pulling her lips from mine, I opened my eyes to find a brilliant smile on Sydney's face. "Love," she softly spoke, "I may not have won the tournament, but I'm certainly going home with a trophy."

I felt a jolt of excitement in my stomach as my lips curved into a bright smile. "I had an incredible time. Who knew I'd go on vacation and find— " I stopped myself before I said something neither of us had dared to speak.

"Find such an incredible, funny, smart, beautiful woman?" Sydney joked, finishing my sentence.

And before I could think of a witty retort, she continued, "I do think you're incredible, funny, smart and beautiful. Amazing, in fact. So amazing that I don't think I'll be able to stay away from you very long." She paused briefly and said, "I'm playing a tournament in just over a week in LA. What do you think about me coming in a few days early so I can see you?"

I was so hoping she was going to play in LA!

"I'm pretty sure I'll be around," I said nonchalantly. I didn't want to appear overly eager, but inside I was going absolutely crazy.

"Great. Plan on it, then. It's a date," Sydney announced enthusiastically before giving me one last kiss and unlocking the door.

We gathered our belongings, and I was no longer dreading our good-bye. Sydney threw her large, red Wilson racket bag over her shoulder and I clutched my new Burberry tote. We exited the lounge and walked together toward our gates. Boarding for my flight had already been announced, so Sydney dropped me off at my gate and gave me one last hug.

After handing the attendant my boarding pass, I turned and waved. I got on the plane barely able to grasp the whirlwind of the past two weeks and was completely and hopelessly smitten with Sydney Foster.

3

Calling the score... starting at love

Back in LA, the first phone call I made was to my close friend, Melissa. I was bursting with excitement when she answered. "Oh, my God! Oh my God! Oh. My. God!" I bellowed into the phone. "You have to sit down so I can tell you about the last two weeks of my life! Brace yourself." I paused, purely for dramatic effect, but I could only remain silent for a second. "I met a girl and I'm absolutely crazy about her!"

"Slow down, sugar. First of all, welcome home! Second, who's the new girlie?" Melissa affectionately calls everyone "sugar."

"Her name's Sydney. She plays on the Tour. She's just awesome!"

Oozing with sarcasm in her best you-wanna-piece-a-me Brooklyn accent, she said, "What, they don't have phones in England? Why am I just hearing about this now? It's not like you to keep secrets!"

Melissa is like a sister to me and we talk numerous times a day, everyday. She had not been one of the several recipients of my tell-all e-mails because she is one of the few people I know who refuses to engage in the electronic mail craze (my mother's eighty-year-old aunt being another one). I thought about calling Melissa from Wimbledon, but I was too caught up in the excitement of Sydney to stop and check in. She let me fumble for an excuse before causally handing me exoneration. "Forgiven. This time. Who is she and what's she like?"

We spent the next half hour talking about me. I was pummeled with questions about my new love interest and I gushed on about how funny, thoughtful and humble Sydney was. I took pride in bragging about

Sydney's successes of having won Wimbledon the year before and downplayed her current "slump." I loved telling Melissa that, *for once*, someone else reached for their wallet when the check appeared on the dinner table. Since I always seemed to be the one who spoiled my girlfriends and picked up the tab for everything, this was a welcomed change. Beaming, I described Sydney as "everything I have never had in a girlfriend." As the word "girlfriend" slipped out of my mouth, even I had to admit to myself that the label was somewhat premature. Thankfully, Melissa didn't pounce, so I continued describing how *perfect* Sydney was. Listening to myself ramble, I could predict the response from Melissa and the tone with which she would deliver it. It's the same response that almost any close friend would give to a friend who was swooning overzealously about someone they'd just met.

"Uh-huh…she sounds too good to be true." Delivered with much more sarcasm than I had expected. As Melissa's words reached my eardrums, I really couldn't blame her for trying to inject some reality into the fantasy world that I was presenting to her. Someone needed to look at the situation with clear vision. After all, what are friends for? Thanks a lot, Melissa!

Impervious to her skepticism, I dismissed Melissa's narrow-minded jovial pessimism and continued to flatter Sydney. I have the cunning ability to acknowledge only the things that I wish to and, in so doing, employ selective hearing. I blathered on about Sydney's brilliance on the tennis court, naming specific tournaments that she had won. I boasted to Melissa that I was dating a woman who owned trophies from all of the tournament tier classifications— including all the Grand Slams— some of them more than once. As I was reveling in Sydney's athletic prowess, Melissa interrupted me.

"Stephie, I really appreciate your confidence in my sports knowledge, but you know I'm the furthest thing from a jock. When I watch tennis on TV— because God knows I've never watched it live— I usually pick who I want to win by whose outfit I like better. I have no clue about all of this technical stuff. Here's what I know about tennis— there's a racket, a ball, a net and a scoring system where 'love' means zero. So everything you just said about Grand…what did you call them?…is just a little foreign to me."

I gladly gave Melissa a lesson in Tennis 101 hoping to impress upon her what an incredible athlete Sydney was. I explained that the tournaments on the Tour are either classified as Grand Slams, Tier 1, Tier 2, Tier 3, Tier 4, or Tier 5. The Grand Slams are the biggies— Wimbledon, the US Open, the Australian Open and the French Open. Not only are they the most prestigious and most selective tournaments, they're also the big money makers. They last for two weeks, and the singles champ gets a check for close to a million bucks. The doubles winners generally split $400,000. Not bad for two weeks' work! That's not to say that there is no money to be made at other tournaments. Winning a Tier 1 championship will also dump a nice chunk of change into your bank account. But the Grand Slams are where the "real" money is made.

As Melissa digested her newly acquired tennis circuit information, I threw out the most impressive tidbit. "And, Melissa…" I had to catch my breath. "The body on this one is un-fucking-believable! I mean, outrageous!" I was close to panting, and my jaw was nearly hitting the floor. I didn't mind, in the least, that I sounded like a teenage boy.

"Is she pretty?"

I paused. The question was inevitable. Not only do I always go for the athletes, but I go for the pretty jocks. Paige was definitely both. With Sydney, I got one out of two. I tried to gingerly explain to Melissa I didn't care that Sydney would probably not be nominated for *People* magazine's "Most Beautiful People." And really, I didn't. It was her body I was captivated by, not her face— which wasn't *bad* looking but certainly paled in comparison with her physique. I answered Melissa honestly. "She's no Elle Macpherson, but I don't care. I'm so tired of chasing after beauty queens who have nothing but looks." A tiny part of me even believed myself when I said that.

She snickered, "Ohhh, is my Stephie finally growing up? Sugar, forgive me for asking, but is everyone on the Tour gay?" Melissa herself is not gay.

Melissa certainly wasn't the first person to erroneously jump to this conclusion. I answered her matter-of-factly. "No, Melissa. I know many people consider a female athlete synonymous with being a lesbian, but not all of the players on the Tour are. In fact, far from it! Only small minorities of the women on the Tour are gay and even smaller minorities are openly gay."

I've never noticed a stigma against the gay players and never heard stories about the straight players not wanting to shower in the same locker room or stuff like that. They might not all get along, but that has nothing to do with the fact that some of them are gay. Rather, it's because they often compete against one another. They truly seem to view one another as friends and opponents, not as gay and straight. I've heard of players saying derogatory things like, "I have to play that pain in the ass" or, "I can't believe I drew that bitch with the fucking kick-serve." But never, "Oh crap, I drew the damn lesbo again!"

Satisfied with my answer, Melissa forged on. "This is all *muy interesante,* but more importantly, is she nice and does she treat you well?"

Melissa takes her roles as the sister I never had (since high school) very seriously. Although she will humor me and listen patiently and enthusiastically to my teenage-like excitement, there is really only one detail that she cares about. She will cut through all of the fluff and bullshit to the most important thing, which is how I am treated and appreciated. She breathed a sigh of relief when I happily bragged that Sydney adored me and took any opportunity she could to show me and others how excited she was to have me in her life.

"Good. Athletic *and* smart," she uttered, stifling a laugh. "When do you see her again?"

"She's playing a tournament here next week and she's coming in a couple days early." Melissa paused, and I could hear her draw in a contemplative, deep breath— or maybe she was just taking a drag on her cigarette. No, I was probably right the first time, so I said, "I know what you're thinking! And, yes, we did do the whole 'brunch, lunch, munch' thing."

Bam! Instant relationship.

Melissa hadn't pounced on my use of the word "girlfriend" earlier, but I knew it was only a matter of time until she did. I continued, "I really want to do things differently this time. I told her that we have to take things slowly."

"Oh, I see. And, by 'slowly,' you mean meet, jump into bed, spend two weeks together, label her your girlfriend and now she's coming here? Is that lesbian for 'taking things slowly?' I guess I don't speak Lesbian!"

"Ha. Ha. Ha. Fuck you! I know, I know. But, it's different this time. We're not just two stereotypical lesbians sprinting into a relationship. Seriously. I promise." My delivery even convinced *me*.

"Hey, maybe as a welcome home gift, I'll get you a T-shirt made that says: *AM LESBIAN. HAVE U-HAUL. WILL TRAVEL*."

Now it was my turn to pause. Not that she wasn't right. But, again, when the parade is in full swing, who wants it rained on, no matter how right they might be to do so?

Reacting to my silence, Melissa said, "Sorry, but you kinda asked for that one. You sound excited now, but are you sure you're not going to dive and dash in a few weeks? Isn't that how it went with Karen? And Kristin? And Amanda? It was the same story with all of them— you were crazy about them all at first and then a few weeks later you got so annoyed you couldn't stand to be around them." She exhaled loudly. It was a sigh that could have been construed as disapproving, but I knew better. Once the air was emptied from her lungs, she lovingly said, "I'm not trying to be a pain in the ass. You know I love you and just want you to be happy."

We chatted a few more minutes— Melissa filling me in on what had been happening on *her* side of the pond for the last couple of weeks, while I listened absently. When I hung up, I thought some more about the concern I could hear lacing each of my good friend's supportive volleys.

I knew Melissa was right; Sydney and I were moving too quickly. But, I couldn't bring myself to care. This time it was different. This time I *really* liked the girl I claimed to be crazy about. I refused to think about things too much. When you think too much or too hard about something— whatever it is— it's inevitable that you might have to confront something that you just might not want the answer to. Sydney and I were infatuated with each other, so why not proceed with reckless abandon and just enjoy things? Why slow down and actually get to know each other instead of jumping in head first? Both were intelligent questions.

Sydney and I spent every waking hour on the phone over the next several days before she came to LA. Upon arrival, she would be with me for ten days before going to San Diego for the next tournament. Instead of staying in the tournament hotel as she normally would, she accepted my invitation to stay with me. I ran around like an absolute crazy person readying myself and my condo for my reunion with Sydney. One by one, I ticked off items on my to-do list: manicure/pedicure (do not nervously bite freshly painted fingernails!), flowers (red Gerber daisies— her favorite), wine (Cabernet and no bottle less than $30— that should impress her), new 1,000 thread count Egyptian cotton sheets (just a little reminder of those luxury sheets on which we first tumbled), carwash (dirty cars don't make good impressions), bubble bath (just in case) and scented candles (always sexy).

After seven excruciatingly painful days of separation, finally the day arrived on which I was to pick up Sydney from the airport. I parked my car at LAX twenty minutes early. Pacing the baggage claim area, I nervously awaited Sydney, desperately trying not to ruin my manicure. Suddenly, I felt a tap on my shoulder. I turned to find Sydney smiling widely. Sunglasses covered her eyes and she spoke softly as she embraced me. "What a sight for sore eyes you are, love."

Hoping that my radiance wasn't stupidly obvious, I squeezed her warm body and said, "I can't believe you're here." Truly, I couldn't. I was still astounded that I was dating Sydney Foster. I stood with a perma-grin plastered over my face as Sydney collected her bags from the carrousel.

I directed Sydney toward the garage and stopped in front of my silver BMW 530i.

"Great car. I would have guessed you were more of an SUV girl," she said as she loaded the trunk.

Good thing I had the car washed.

Once inside, I slyly reached into the backseat and handed her a single white tulip. Of course, not wanting to appear too eager, I had labored for hours over whether to bring her a single flower or a bouquet. I opted against the bouquet because although it's a nice gesture, it might also send the wrong message. But then again, I wasn't sure what message I was trying to send. Anyway, after a lengthy conversation with a lovely florist in West Hollywood, I decided on a white tulip— classy, sincere and beautiful, but not scary.

Obviously touched and thrilled with my gesture, Sydney thanked me by leaning over and giving me a passionate kiss on my freshly glossed lips.

I made a mental note to go back to that florist.

I welcomed Sydney into my home, extending her a *mi-casa-es-su-casa* attitude. Immediately, she adapted to my life and my home with chameleon-like ease. She hung her clothes in my closet and even shared my dresser drawers. She freely borrowed my car and filled my pantry with all of her favorites (part of me thought that was a bit odd, but the other part found it endearing). She even gave me a framed picture of her holding the Wimbledon trophy above her head and suggested that my bedside table would be a brilliant home for it. Very quickly, Sydney and I went from courting to committed. Admittedly, at first I worried that she adjusted way too easily to "playing house" with me. But then I dismissed my concerns. After all, I was crazy about her and I'd given her an open-door policy.

Despite knowing that Sydney and I were progressing exceedingly fast, I was enjoying my new girlfriend thoroughly. I did, however, wish she'd wipe her crumbs off my kitchen counter.

After two days of selfishly keeping Sydney all to myself, I introduced her to Melissa and some of my other close friends. She effortlessly engaged them all with her entertaining personality and impressed them with her unconcealed devotion to me. Everyone was fascinated by her and happy for us— and that made me extremely happy.

* * *

On the first day of the Bank of Los Angeles tournament in LA, Sydney and I arrived at the site and went immediately to the credentials office to get our badges. See how easily I now say "our" badges, as though my new role fit perfectly into my back pocket?

Every player is required to wear an identification badge at all times and is allotted two or three extra badges for her coach and guests. I cheerfully smiled as my picture was snapped and, with one quick click of a mouse, a few seconds later my credit card sized badge was affixed to a string and found a home around my neck. I was by no means the only "wife" at the wedding proudly donning a behind-the-scenes pass. The only place where my badge didn't grant me access was the locker room. Don't think I didn't try to peek though!

We entered the club, and already I missed Wimbledon. What a

difference! The walls were stark and the halls not hallowed. I greeted my new friends, the tournament director and the director of communications, as well as my old friends, Conchi, Erin, Ribi and Saskia. Of course, my friends knew that my romance with Sydney had made its way across the pond, but I think our appearance together came as somewhat of a surprise to the uniformed eyes in the players' lounge. They, like my friends, must have thought that our affair would be short-lived. We were now almost one month into it and my friends all had the same raised eyebrow reaction, declaring that my attraction to Sydney was totally "unbelievable." Nay-sayers! I didn't care, though. I couldn't stop talking about my fascination with the physical aspect of our relationship, and although my friends didn't have bets going (at least, to my knowledge), I knew that none of them thought our relationship would last. They all remained true to their original convictions— Sydney and I were not a good match. I was determined to prove them wrong. In retrospect, I really should have listened when they each individually asked me if I were "sick of her yet." I might have saved myself a ton of grief.

Sydney still hadn't found a doubles partner and decided not to play doubles until the US Open one month later. She focused solely on singles, having suffered another dive in the rankings due to her early departure at Wimbledon. Frustrated and disgusted with her current ranking of 48 in the World, she strengthened her resolve and was determined to break back into the Top 10 by the end of the year. But for now, once again she entered a tournament as a non-seeded player. When it was time for her match to start, I followed Sydney, her opponent and their escort out to the stadium court. The stands were only half-full, and the heat was blistering. This venue was more like a concrete jungle than a picturesque and manicured tennis club. Oh, how I longed to see Mr. Crispy Trousers now!

Sydney dominated in the first set, not relinquishing a single game. It was a complete blowout! The second set, however, was not quite so easy. She lost a few games she shouldn't have. I watched the match courtside as Sydney served. The score was 4-3, 30-40. She pulled her opponent wide on the "ad" side with her famous left-handed kick-serve and the rally started. My head flicked from side to side as my eyes chased the ball. I call it the "tennis turn"— imagine a stadium full of people (or in this case half-full) whose heads are turning from left to right, right to left, in unison. Suddenly both players were at the net when Sydney lunged for a backhand volley. She popped it back and it shot past her opponent directly on the other side of the net and landed in the backcourt, on the very outside of the baseline. It was a gorgeous shot. But before Sydney had a chance to celebrate, the linesman called the ball out. I don't know. It looked in to me, but it sure was close. As soon as the word "out" flew past his lips, Sydney went absolutely ballistic. She threw her arms up in surprise and waved her racket over her head angrily. The chair umpire confirmed that the ball was out and refused to overrule the linesman. I wasn't sure how it was possible, but Sydney became even more enraged. It wasn't pretty. She screamed some more, but her tantrum was to no avail. The chair umpire called the game in favor of Sydney's opponent.

In a last-ditch effort to convey her outrage, Sydney took a ball out of her pocket and slammed it with her racket against the back fence. Fed up, the chair umpire announced, "Warning, Ms. Foster. Ball abuse." If I had to guess, I think my face looked like a deer staring into headlights as I flinched unbelievingly at the fit Sydney threw.

I remember the one time that I lost control of my temper on the tennis court during a match. I was eleven or twelve and my dad was watching. I missed an easy volley and I threw my racket from the service line past the baseline. God, it felt good to release that racket with such force! I wound up winning the match, but instead of congratulating me when I walked off the court, I got a talking to like you can't imagine from my dad! That lecture didn't feel nearly as good as watching my racket soar toward the baseline, so I never threw my racket again after that. I had never seen the ball-smashing side of Sydney. Maybe it was just nerves. Or maybe I should have started running in the opposite direction and never looked back.

Thankfully, Sydney regained her composure and she went on to win the next two games which handed her the match. So, all was right with her world— and therefore mine, at least for now.

Two days later, it was my birthday. I was two years away from thirty. Sydney arranged a birthday dinner for me and invited ten of my friends. Unfortunately, she was scheduled to play late in the afternoon so I could not be there to cheer her on. I adored her, but love or no love, I wasn't about to miss my own birthday dinner. Everyone was on their second cocktail when Sydney barged into the restaurant after winning her second-round match. It was a huge victory over the Number 1 seed. Even more reason to celebrate! No one was more shocked and stunned than I when Sydney placed a small, black velvet box on the table. Granted it was unwrapped, but really I would have totally thought that organizing this big, fun dinner was enough of a present. I cautiously opened the box as if something was going to pop out at me when the top was lifted.

Movement of any kind was impossible when I saw what was inside the box. For what felt like hours, Sydney watched me stare, transfixed, into the box. Finally, she broke the awkward spell and put her arm around me and said, "Happy birthday, gorgeous. I love you," and then kissed me on the cheek.

Oh, yeah…we moved on from "I'm crazy about you" to "I love you" almost immediately after she arrived in LA. Yep. No matter what kind of fancy arithmetic you use, it took us less than one month to profess our love for each other.

Melissa was right— she should have gotten me a U-Haul T-shirt after all.

Everyone's eyes grew as big as saucers when they caught a glimpse of my "birthday present"— a white gold ring encased with pave diamonds. I smiled and despite thinking, *you shouldn't have— no, you really shouldn't have*, I uttered a cheerful, "It's beautiful. Thank you." But even as I pushed the sentiment past my lips, I could feel a tightness gripping my throat. Paige and I had been together for four years and neither of us ever came *close* to getting a ring like this. I was completely shocked. Everyone at the table was duly impressed by my shiny new bobble and took turns trying it on.

In hindsight, I don't know whether Sydney genuinely felt the emotion behind giving someone, let alone me, that kind of extravagant, romantic gift— or if she was just really desperate to impress me and my friends and woo us all into submission. She certainly did a great job of it that night. She even earned Melissa's stamp of approval when she very discreetly slipped her platinum credit card to the waiter and picked up the bill for the entire dinner party. I have to admit— no matter how you look at the ring— Sydney handled that part of her plan in a really classy way. No fanfare. No pomp. No attention. Lots of credit!

The next day, I could hardly wait for Sydney to leave for practice so I could call Melissa. (I had decided that using my car as her own *was* a little odd, so I encouraged Sydney to take advantage of tournament transportation.) The second I heard her voice, I shouted, "Okay, we need to talk about the ring. I'm not ready for a ring!"

"Back up. We need to talk about the '*I love you*' part," Melissa insisted.

Calming myself slightly, I said, "Yeah, I meant to tell you that, but I didn't want you to give me shit. The 'I love you' slipped out a few days ago." Before she had a chance to respond, I joked, "We almost made it to the one-month mark. That's a long time to wait to say 'I love you' in the lesbian world because you know we multiply time by six."

But she wasn't about to let me off the hook so easily. "So, how does this work? 'Lesbian years' are like 'dog years?' You multiply by six, so one month is equal to six months? Sugar, I'm not buying it."

"Well, given that most of my dive-and-dash relationships never make it past one month, we should be impressed not only that I can still sit across the dinner table from Sydney after one month, but that I like her enough to tell her I love her."

"You guys are moving pretty quickly, aren't you? Not judging. Just stating the obvious. I thought you were going to do things differently this time and go slowly?"

"Melissa. I know. I wanted to. I've been trying to tell her to slow down. I really like her, though. She's really intense, but she's so good to me. She really loves me."

"And, do you *really* love her?"

Wow. This girl really knows how to bring a conversation to a stop sign.

I fumbled with my words. "Yes…I do…I think I do."

"Well, she certainly seems to love you. I mean, that ring— "

"I *know!* Is it real? It has to be real! She's not the type to buy something fake. But, we've only known each other for a month. Should I be worried that she gave me a diamond ring after only one month?" Did that question really come out of my mouth? Why did I even bother asking?

"Slow down. It's not like she's rushing you to the altar. It doesn't seem like money is a problem for her, so maybe, in her world, this is simply a nice gesture. Just be gracious and keep enjoying each other, but maybe try a little harder to slow things down."

Keep enjoying each other. That's all I heard. Selective listening again. You hear what you want to hear. Enjoying Sydney is exactly what I planned on doing. So, I left my concerns behind and drove to the courts to meet Sydney before her afternoon match. It was the semi-finals and she was playing the Number 3 seed. Sydney disposed of her opponent rather easily. Her performance was riveting. I don't think she missed one return the entire match. Watching her play was like watching poetry in motion. On match point, she hit an incredible two-handed backhand down the line past her opponent to win the match. It was insane! Totally textbook! I think I fell in love with her all over again when that ball came off her strings.

The next day, I was thrilled for Sydney when she won the tournament. Although it was a Tier 2 tournament, it was a great victory for her on several levels. It was her fifty-second singles title. Beyond that, it was her first title without Casey Matthews cheering her on. Sydney was back in the winner's circle and back on track, and I was happy to be right by her side.

After a hearty celebration in LA, I boarded the Sydney Express and headed down to the Southern California Classic in San Diego. Sydney asked me to accompany her to the La Costa Resort, where the tournament was held, and I happily accepted. This was a Tier 1 tournament and most of the top players were there— including Casey, who now knew that Sydney was dating the girl from Boston whom she'd briefly met in the players' lounge at Wimbledon. My interactions with Casey were limited to casual encounters in the lounge, but I found her quite pleasant.

I very quickly became known as Sydney's girlfriend, and lest anyone forgot, she was there to remind them. And, if she wasn't there, all people had to do was look at my badge which read: STEPHANIE ALEXANDER COACH OF SYDNEY FOSTER. Sydney directed the woman in the credentials office to print "COACH OF" and not "GUEST OF" on my badge. I think she thought it was cute and endearing. I'm about as qualified to coach a professional tennis player as Richard Simmons is to coach a professional football team. Okay, maybe I'm slightly more qualified, but not much.

Officially, it was only my second tournament as a tennis wife and I was enjoying myself thoroughly. What's not to enjoy? It was a constant vacation. I put real estate deals together while sitting courtside at a resort having fun in the sun during the day, and went to gourmet dinners at night— and I had a "COACH OF" badge to boot! I didn't quite have "highway patrolman's mentality"— give me a badge, a gun, and a walkie-talkie and I rule the world— but I am the first to admit that I didn't mind wearing my all-access badge around my neck and going places where the rest of the public wasn't allowed. It was fun being warmed by the glow of a spotlight.

Sydney, still unseeded, breezed through her first two rounds before meeting one of her archrivals in the third round. As Sydney walked onto the court, I flashed my badge and pushed my way to the first row of seats next to the court. I settled in as their warm-up began and watched people pushing and shoving to get a view of the court. Ribi joined me courtside to cheer Sydney on (although for political reasons, her cheers were much softer than mine). Almost as nervous as I, she couldn't help but eke out a watered-down *"Vamos!"* or *"Bravo!"* anytime Sydney won a critical point. I don't remember breathing the entire match. It was extremely close, but it seemed just as soon as Sydney would get her game on track, she'd derail. She lost the match and I witnessed Sydney exit a major tournament prematurely for the second time since our romance had begun.

I felt deflated. It's emotionally exhausting sitting on the sidelines and hoping desperately for a successful outcome while knowing that you're completely powerless. I wonder if this is how my parents have felt my entire life? No. Impossible. Since when did they *ever* sit on the sidelines?!

After the match, Sydney rode to the players' lounge in the golf cart with the escort. Ribi and I followed closely behind. As we waited for Sydney to finish talking to the press, Ribi's eyes zeroed in on my left hand. Initially, I put the ring on my right ring finger, but Sydney preferred that I wear it on my left ring finger. I obliged. Ribi's jaw dropped and her eyes widened. I knew what she was looking at.

"What is that?!" she squealed.

I covered the ring with my left thumb and rolled it back and forth, hoping that something would distract Ribi and that she'd forget she ever saw the shiny bobble. She continued to stare so I answered, "A birthday present." I could feel the color draining from my suntanned face.

"Birthday present my ass! *Dios mio!* That's a statement!" Normally, I loved listening to Ribi speak broken English with her Spanish accent, but at that moment I wished she wouldn't say another word.

"Ribi, stop! I'm already anxious over it, so I don't want to talk about it!"

"Your mother— does she know about the ring?"

"Are you out of your mind? Of course she doesn't!" Yeah, right, tell my mother that I have found a new career as a tennis wife? She was still having a hard enough time trying to explain to her friends that I'd given up my law career to become a realtor! Somehow, I doubted that she'd take great joy in having new business cards printed for me that read: STEPHANIE ALEXANDER, ESQ/REALTOR/TENNIS WIFE.

"Stephie, I don't think even *you* can convince your mom that you got that thing from a gum container." I think she meant gumball machine. "When are you guys moving in together?"

"Whoa! I am so not having this conversation right now." I felt short of breath. I looked down at my left hand. The sun caught my ring and I squinted as the bobble almost blinded me. Was I being blind? Maybe this *was* all moving too fast. Shit! There's *that* concept again. Ya think?!

Damn that Ribi! I hate it when she makes me face reality. Melissa too! But, acceleration is the name of the game with these tennis players. They spend all of their time traveling and chasing a ball on a court, so they don't have time to chase love off the court. You either jump on board or let the ship sail away. Apparently, I had leapt on board. Great, and now I was starting to doubt myself. Time to slow things down!

As we drove back to LA later that afternoon, I gripped the steering wheel and tried to think of a way to tell Sydney that I was concerned about how quickly our relationship was moving. I was silent for the first twenty minutes of the drive. Apparently, Sydney knew something was on my mind and asked, "Love, what's wrong? You've hardly said a word since we got in the car."

I could feel the dampness of my armpits and nervously said, "Sydney, I think we need to slow things down between us. I really like you, but things are moving a little too fast for me."

She laughed and cavalierly said, "What are you talking about? We're having fun. These last two weeks have been great."

"These last two weeks *have* been great," I echoed. "But, I'm just not sure I'm ready for all of this...the constant togetherness...the meshing of worlds...the ring." There! I said it! I felt relieved.

Sydney heard what I said but, clearly, was not listening to one word. Okay, I'll admit— that's a bit of the pot calling the kettle black— as I think back to my conversation with Melissa. *We all only hear what we want to hear*— until I heard what Sydney said next.

"Love, relax. We're perfect for each other. You're just freaking out because our relationship is the first healthy relationship you've ever been in. You're not used to being with someone who's so good to you. I think you're just afraid of commitment and that's why you're nervous." Her patronizing voice sent prickles over my body.

Now my silence was inspired by shock and not nerves. Apparently, Sydney was not just a professional tennis player, but she was also well versed in the field of psychiatry— at least in her own mind. I might not have stuck to my guns after first forcing my feelings out of my mouth, but her psychoanalysis angered me. I admit that I've got my issues, but I *hate* being psychoanalyzed. I can only put up with it from my therapist because a) I'm paying her to tell me shit I don't want to hear, and b) I only have to listen to her for fifty minutes— once a week. I wasn't about to put up with it from my girlfriend— completely unsolicited! I tried a different approach, trying not to sound too derisive. "Sydney, your perspective is interesting. Really, it is. But the reality is that we barely know each other and I think we need to slow things down a bit, and get back to our own lives."

She quickly retorted, "Love, I'm going home tomorrow and then we won't see each other for a couple of weeks. How's that for getting back to our own lives? I really think you're making too much out of this."

Again, I echoed, "A couple of weeks?" *What's she talking about now?*

"The US Open. I was going to surprise you, but I might as well tell you. I got you a plane ticket so we can be together in New York during the Open. It will be so much fun! I'm so much happier when you're with me, and when I'm happy, I play better. Please come. You have to come."

Oh, God! More pressure!

As graciously as I could, I sheepishly asked, "You already bought the ticket?"

Please tell me that it isn't already paid for or, if it is, that it's refundable.

Sydney smiled. "Actually, that's only one leg of the ticket I bought for you. I wanted it to be a surprise, but there's no time like the present, I reckon."

Oh God, what have I gotten myself into? Why am I afraid of what she's about to tell me?

"What do you mean, 'only one leg'?" I asked, forcing a smile and suddenly feeling tightness in my throat.

"I know we talked about you coming on Tour with me, and I know you can't go full-time, but I thought you could come to the US Open, then to Europe and then Australia and Japan. Of course, we'd come home in between." She smiled a loving grin and added, "I splurged and put you in first class."

My cheeks felt like they were on fire. I tried to process what Sydney had just told me. *Fuck, I can't even imagine how much that ticket cost her—probably $10,000. No one, besides my parents, has ever spent that kind of money on me! What am I going to do?! And, come 'home' in between? What home is she talking about? 'We' don't have a 'home' to come home to!*

My mission of slowing things down somehow turned into my having to make a decision whether or not to drop everything and travel around the world with Sydney. At that particular moment, I felt like driving into oncoming traffic. I took a deep breath and concentrated so as not to cross the solid yellow line in the road. "Sydney, I don't know what to say."

She reached over and put her calloused hand on my knee. "How about 'Thank you?' No, actually you don't have to thank me. It's my pleasure. It's gonna be great. We're gonna have so much fun. This year has been such shit for me…until I met you. And now you're in my life and I'm finally happy again. I know things are gonna turn around with my tennis now, and it's all because of you! I never want you to leave my side. You're my good-luck charm! I just want to put you in my pocket and take you everywhere I go!"

Oh, God! Oh, God! Oh, God! O-H M-Y G-O-D! This is spinning out of control! So much for taking a step back! Okay, calm down and relax. This is all a bit too much, but we're in love. She's leaving tomorrow. I can regroup from this.

So, of course, I smiled and said, "That's really generous of you, but I don't know if I can commit to all that traveling. I do have a job and I do need to make money."

"Oh c'mon. You're a realtor. You're your own boss and, let's be honest…you don't really *need* to make money. You *have* money. And besides, you won't have to pay for a thing on the road. I'll pay for everything."

I knew I wasn't going to win this argument. When Sydney and I had spoken about it a couple of weeks earlier, I agreed to take some time off from selling real estate and travel with her occasionally. Initially, the idea of traveling around the world with my professional tennis player girlfriend sounded so sexy, romantic and exotic. Who wouldn't like that? But I honestly didn't think she was being serious about having me come with her so quickly. Clearly I had been wrong and clearly I didn't have the presence of mind to deal with this right now. I didn't want to crush Sydney in the process, nor cause a multi-car pile-up on the 405. But there was no question. I was now officially freaking out.

The road sign read: LOS ANGELES 67 MILES. I felt like I was a million miles from home. How did I go from dating this woman to being a tennis wife…essentially over night?

4

Code violation, Ms. Foster: unsportsmanlike behavior

After Sydney left LA, the two weeks that we were apart flew by. I was now relaxed, thanks to the space I'd been given in Sydney's absence, and I was eager to board the plane to New York. After disembarking at JFK, the car service (arranged, surprise, surprise, by Sydney!) whisked me directly to the USTA National Tennis Center in Flushing Meadows, the site of the US Open. I could not wait to see my girlfriend!

The black Lincoln Navigator passed through the security points and dropped me off at the front gates near the players' entrance. As usual, my first stop was the credentials office. Wearing my badge with pride, I glided through the crowd. The grounds were teeming with people and the energy was intoxicating. I could hear the smacking sounds of tennis balls, reactive gasps and cheers from the passionate crowd, enthusiastic applause from the die-hard fans and echoes of scores being announced from the chair umpires. I was camouflaged in the crowd until I flashed my badge to the security guard blocking the door to the players' lounge. Once inside, I quickly found Sydney— or rather, she found me.

She wrapped her arms around me and whispered into my ear, "Love, I have a huge surprise for you!"

Another surprise?

I was afraid her grip around my waist would be the only thing keeping me from collapsing to the ground. I had a feeling her surprise wasn't going to be a commemorative US Open mug. Gently pushing back from her, I looked at Sydney's smiling face. If her grin had been any bigger, it would have formed a perfect circle around the back of her head. My eyes widened, but there was not one tingle of excitement in my body. As she smiled, I was looking at my surprise— staring with my own mouth agape, in fact. I considered for a quick second that my eyes were playing tricks on me. They weren't. I guess, in a way, she *had* given me a commemorative mug. My twenty-nine-year-old girlfriend had gotten braces.

Still smiling wide, Sydney said, "I've never smiled as much as I do when I'm with you. I wanted to fix my crooked smile since I'm using it all the time these days." She pulled me close again and hugged me tighter this time. "Gorgeous, I love you so much. You're responsible for this smile of mine! In twelve short months, I'll have a movie-star smile!"

My mother taught me to give appropriate responses in virtually every scenario imaginable. But, words escaped me at this very moment. What do you say to that? My girlfriend had resorted to cosmetic alterations because of me. Figuring silence was not the response she'd hoped for, I forced a soft laugh and said, "Well, that sure is a different kind of shiny surprise," with as much creativity and enthusiasm as I could muster. To that, Sydney's smile widened again. She gave new meaning to "bright smile." I'm not sure which was gleaming brighter— the three-carat diamond studs in her ears or the freshly laid tracks of silver in her mouth. I needed to sit down.

Before we planted ourselves on a couch just outside the players' restaurant, Sydney gave me a quick tour around the restricted access areas. Talk about a great people watching opportunity! Though not nearly as prim and proper as Wimbledon, the US Open is not lacking in personality. It's the Big Apple of Slams! People were rushing around everywhere. Agents raced by wearing Bluetooth headsets. Coaches dragged boxes containing new shipments of the latest fashions from sponsors. Where the aura at Wimbledon was awe-inspiring and the energy chilling but hushed, you could practically feel the charge in the air at the "Open." It took on a life of its own. Come on, this is New York! The sights and sounds in New York are indescribably unique. New Yorkers are a species of their own, and New York sports enthusiasts...forget about it! They give new meaning to the word "aggressive." They're both loyal and unforgiving. If you have thin skin, the US Open is probably not the tournament for you.

During the first few days of the tournament, New York was blessed with picture-perfect weather. Sydney's title in LA, coupled with her two wins in San Diego, had given her ranking a boost. With a little help from top-ranked players who had pulled out of the US Open due to injuries, Sydney had managed to secure the last seeded position in the singles draw— Number 32. She won her first-round match but had a little more trouble in her second round. The first set was totally one-sided— in Sydney's favor. But the second set was decided by a tiebreak. Sydney was not on her best behavior. Her outburst here was actually worse than the one in LA, but she didn't get a code violation for unsportsmanlike behavior. I guess the Open is still living with the ghost of their resident bad boy, John McEnroe, and the chair umpires are a tad more lenient. But I dare say "Bad Sydney" came dangerously close to receiving a warning several times and I can't say that I was terribly thrilled to be her wife that day, despite her win. Actually, I was embarrassed. I know her intensity level is brimming when she walks onto the court, but her histrionics were really unbecoming. Temper tantrums suited Johnny Mac, but not Sydney. His were amusing, but hers were abrasive and abusive. Okay, his could be abusive, too, but he still managed to get that amusing aspect in there to mitigate the abuse. I wondered if Sydney's parents ever gave her the same kind of talking to about her on-court behavior that I got as a kid? If they did, it didn't make an impact. Doesn't she know that someone is always watching and first impressions can't be undone? It's all fun and games until someone gets a code violation or, worse, a fine!

The brilliant weather was interrupted on the fourth day of the tournament. New York got pummeled with rain for almost one entire week. Play had to be suspended. The US Open is an outdoor event and the courts were transformed into lakes. Not only did Sydney and I not go to the courts everyday as we would have in good weather conditions, but we rarely left our hotel room during the downpour because I wasn't feeling well. I had the misfortune of catching a cold at the end of August. I hate to say it, but there was nothing to do. I know that statement sounds absolutely absurd considering that I was in New York City— a city widely regarded as the greatest city in the world. But given the inclement weather, there was no reason to go to the courts and watch the rain fall, and all other activities were out of the question because I was sick. The only thing there was to do was to get on each other's nerves. And that we did. Brilliantly well. Sydney's main gripe was that I wasn't being affectionate enough with her.

Oh, I'm sorry. Should I use one hand to cover my mouth while I cough up this green stuff so I can still pet you with the other? Please!

When we got tired of fighting, we fought some more.

After four days of room confinement (albeit luxurious confinement at the Ritz-Carlton), I started to feel better and we ventured out in the torrential rain to go shopping. Shopping would normally be the last activity I would ever willingly engage in, but anything was better than being stuck in a room that had begun to feel like a jail cell. We hovered under an umbrella together and hurried down Fifth Avenue, ducking inside Façonnable— one of my favorite stores. Sydney disappeared for a few minutes and then crept up behind me, handed me a gift-wrapped box and said, "Love, even though you're sick and the last couple days have been hard, I adore having you here."

As if her plying me with another "bribe"— which was how I was beginning to view her "gifts"— wasn't bad enough, without missing a beat or taking another breath she plowed straight into, "Why don't you travel with me full-time?"

I wasn't sure if my cold was coming back or if it was Sydney's offer that made my skin crawl, but I instantly got the chills and my head began to ache. I turned around and said, "What?"

"Wouldn't it be so great, love? You could take the year off from selling real estate and travel with me."

I took the box she was holding out in front of me and tucked it under my arm. "And, how do you expect me to support myself while I'm off gallivanting around the world with you?"

"I could put you on salary. I'll pay you cash every week." She seemed even more excited by her offer to pay me. Hey eyes lit up and overshadowed the glare coming from her mouth.

"And what exactly would my title be? 'Sydney's girlfriend?' Sounds a little too prostitute-ish for me. Thanks, but I think I'll pass, Heidi Fleiss."

"Oh c'mon! You could be my attaché. It would be heaps of fun!"

I silently laughed at Sydney's attaché idea. She wasn't looking for an attaché. She wanted an attachee. Pure and simple, Sydney just wanted me to be attached to her and she'd go to any lengths to see it happen, including paying her own girlfriend to travel with her.

God, what have I gotten myself into?!

"Sydney, I appreciate the offer and all that you're trying to do, but I can't."

"C'mon…please? Pretty please?"

Apparently, she hadn't heard of respectful declines or respectfully accepting someone else's decision— even when it sounded as definitive as mine. And my patience— compounded by the throbbing sinus headache which had indeed elected to return— was as thin as Lara Flynn Boyle at the Emmy's.

"It's not going to happen. Please just drop it, and let's enjoy the rest of the day."

Blessedly, Sydney didn't mention it again, and we continued shopping in fragile peace.

As we navigated through the masses of pedestrians toward our hotel in Midtown with our Façonnable and Thomas Pink bags in tote, Sydney's offer reverberated in my mind. No matter what I did or how I tried to distract myself, I could not stop thinking about it. *What about me and my life?* I had been around my friends on the Tour long enough to know that everything revolves around them and their careers. To say they are pampered is an understatement! There's always someone there— whether it's a coach, a parent, an agent or a girlfriend or boyfriend— to do almost everything for them. And the worst part is that so many of these women come from a meager existence and learn how to play tennis before they learn how to walk. Once their talent is identified when they're kids, becoming a champion is their sole goal and purpose in life. I have heard the so-called success stories of some players that, once they broke into the Top 50, they could finally move their residence from the backseat of the family car to an actual dwelling as defined by any ordinary person. But forget about becoming a decent human being. Morals, manners and values will not win you a Grand Slam. Becoming a tennis champion changes their lives completely. Some of them have no idea what it means to be thankful for the talent that they are blessed with or the financial security that comes with winning major tennis tournaments. Instead, they have tunnel vision and are blind to anyone or anything that cannot help elevate their stature even further.

Some of these women, most of them still girls, live their lives in the in the shadow of their own ego. Oh, the egos! It's incredible! And it's not uncommon that they don't even enjoy playing tennis once they've reached the top. How sad is that? It's like a syndrome and it's predictable— the "I was a no one a year ago, but look at me now, and oh, can you carry my new Prada bag but don't scratch it" syndrome.

In their defense, I'm not sure how they're expected to be "normal." Tennis players live a really strange life— one that's actually nomadic. They travel in packs to the same places the same time every year. Everyone knows everyone. Nothing and no one is sacred. One week, you might have a best friend, and the next week, after having beaten her the week before, you may have a new enemy. Loyalty is a commodity, not a virtue. I guess it all takes a toll on you, especially if you're not winning.

When I met Sydney, she was demure, reserved and polite. I saw no signs of egotism. Now that she was starting to climb back toward the top of the rankings, I was starting to see her ego, beginning with her outbursts on the court. And now with her offer of putting me on salary, I saw it again. But really, why should my life and my career take a backseat to hers? I guess because in her mind, she's a world-class champion and I'm just a washed-up lawyer turned realtor. Fine, but if she starts standing under a clock and telling me that people are walking by to look at *her,* I won't put up with it for one second!

All of this started to overwhelm me and I decided that I needed a break from the tennis tour— and Sydney— for an evening. Blessedly, one of my college friends lives in New York and she and I have a tradition of meeting for a drink at the Rainbow Room when I am in town. Tonight, my saving grace was a date with an old friend, a cosmopolitan and a booth at the top of Rockefeller Plaza. Silly me, I didn't realize that having a girlfriend meant that I could not go anywhere without her. I thought Sydney was joking when she pouted because I didn't deliver her an invitation to join me. She wasn't. Not even a little. She was devastated that I was venturing out without her. I might have understood this if we had not spent any time together since my arrival. But, the fact was, we hadn't spent one minute apart since I walked into the players' lounge from the airport. As politely as I could, I dismissed her requests to join me, but as I walked toward the door she followed me and begged me not to leave.

"Love, you shouldn't be drinking. You're still sick. Why don't you just stay here with me and have a cuddle?"

Now I was just plain annoyed! "Sydney, I'm fine. Stop trying to mother me!" I scoffed.

"Well, can't you go have a drink and then call me and I can meet you guys?" Her words echoed across the room.

I looked at her like she was crazy. I was shocked at how desperate she was to fuse our worlds. She literally wanted us to become one. "Sydney, I just want to go spend some time with a friend. Is that asking too much? It's nothing personal. I've been with you non-stop since I got here."

"I just don't see why I can't come," she begged.

Aha! And therein lies the root of the problem!

Attempting to entice me further, she added, "Why don't you wear one of the new shirts I bought you today?"

I wouldn't have believed it had I not seen it with my own eyes, but she followed me into the hallway all the way to the elevator dressed in only my favorite Harvard Tennis T-shirt (the one I had specifically told her was off limits!) and underwear, still trying to persuade me not to leave her behind. "I know a really cool bar we could all go to."

I pushed the button and waited for the elevator, trying to remain civil. "Sydney, please. I'm already late. I can't stand here and have this discussion with you. You have other friends. Go hang out with them. Hell, just go down and stand on the corner and sign autographs if you're lonely. Or just stay in and entertain yourself. I'll be back later. I'll see you in a little while."

Ding!

The elevator arrived, I got in and that round was over. Replaying in my mind her pleading with me half-naked in the hallway, I thought, *what was that? I've never seen her like that!*

The door opened to the opulent lobby and off I went, hoping that when I returned there would be a pot of gold at the end of the Rainbow Room— that Bad Sydney had left and her better side had returned.

* * *

I came back pleasantly buzzed and found Sydney sitting up in bed with a magazine propped on her lap— very obviously awaiting my return. She barely glanced over the top of the pages when I walked toward her. I kissed her on the cheek and began undressing.

As I pushed my toothbrush in and out of my mouth, she asked, "Aren't you going to tell me about your night?" with an anxious edge in her voice.

I spit out my toothpaste and answered from the bathroom. "There's not much to tell. We had a few drinks and caught up. I was only gone a couple hours."

I got into bed, wearing my second favorite Harvard T-shirt and a pair of boxers. Sydney had not moved. Her magazine was still on her lap, probably on the same page it had been on since I'd walked in. I leaned over and kissed her goodnight before rolling over to go to sleep. Just as I fell asleep, I was awakened by her stern voice. "We need to talk."

Knowing I was making a big mistake, I rolled over. "What's wrong?" I asked, foolishly.

"What's wrong?" She huffed and exclaimed, "I'll tell you what's wrong…"

Sydney launched into a discussion about how she was not getting enough attention from me and that she needed to feel my love. Stunned, I sat up and leaned against the headboard as she spoke. I massaged my temples with my fingers. She droned on about needing this and wanting that and reminded me, about one thousand times, that this is "the last Grand Slam of the year" and that it was so important for her to have my *full* support so she could do well. I wondered how only giving her ninety percent of my support would affect her results and, further, how she measured what percentage of support I was giving. Was I only giving seventy-five percent if I went out with a friend for a drink and left her behind? Was checking my e-mail three times a day and making a few phone calls to pals outside of the tennis world enough to knock my support down to fifty percent? According to Sydney's standards, was it even possible for me to give her one-hundred percent? For a few seconds, I escaped into my mind and tuned her out. I thought to myself how incredible it would be if life came equipped with a remote control. That way, I could use it to "stop," "rewind," "fast forward," "pause," "mute" or "eject" whatever scene of life that was being played out in front of me. As I was fantasizing about which action I would take with my remote, I returned to reality. Sydney was next to me driving me absolutely crazy and it was almost two o'clock in the morning.

As I zeroed back in on the conversation, Sydney repeated herself over and over again. "I just don't understand why you're so stubborn. We're good together. You just need to let yourself feel. Stop fighting me. Just let me love you."

I had no idea what to do or what to say. I thought we were talking about support, and now she was talking about my opposition to her love? This was so *not* what I signed up for. Talk about intense! Who was this woman I was next to in bed and what had she done with the sensitive, calm, care-free Sydney who I had fallen in love with? I couldn't help but keep score, and this was the third side of Sydney that I had never seen before and didn't care to see again.

When I felt like it was safe to talk, I coolly said, "Sydney, I'm not sure where all of this is coming from, but you're kind of freaking me out a little. I'm sorry if you're upset that I wanted to go catch up with one of my friends. Maybe you're just nervous about your match tomorrow." I turned back over and pulled the blanket over my shoulder before uttering my last non-negotiable words. "Whatever it is, let's just talk about it in the morning. It's late and you need to get some sleep— and so do I." I can't believe those were the words that came out of my mouth. Why didn't I jump on her the way she had just pounced on me?

Answer: I don't like altercations. I never have. Yelling was not a foreign sound in my house when I was growing up, but it always seemed to go away quicker if I just agreed to whatever was being yelled. I'm a pleaser. I never wanted to make my parents mad, so I did everything I could to please them— amazing how these things stick with you. It's funny that I have such a strong personality, yet I cower so easily to people I love in the face of adversity in order to avoid conflict. I'll work on that.

The next morning, I was a little afraid to open my eyes. I wasn't sure which Sydney I'd find next to me. I found none. When I rolled over she was gone. Before I had a chance to wonder where she went, my cell phone rang and the caller ID flashed: MOM HOME.

Yawning, I answered, "Hi, Mom."

"Good morning, sweetheart. Are you still sleeping? It's almost ten."

"No, I'm up. I'm just not moving quickly today." I didn't bother telling her that I'd slept in because I'd been kept awake the night before by my girlfriend who had morphed into a crazy person.

"Well, your father arrived last night. We're getting ready to go play golf so we just wanted to say hi. Hold on. Your father is grabbing the phone."

"Hey, kiddo! How are you?"

"Hey back. I'm fine, Dad. A little tired today, though."

He laughed, "Who can blame you for being tired! Jet-setting to tennis tournaments while working full-time must be exhausting. And you thought being a lawyer was tiring!"

I detected more than just a hint of sarcasm in his voice but was impervious to it. My parents seemed to have adjusted to the idea that I was dating a professional tennis player, which (or rather *who*) would require my presence at various tournaments around the world. Since Sydney was a world-famous tennis player with global name recognition, my travel schedule was somewhat more justifiable to them. But still, neither of them thought I should have given up my law career to move to California to become a realtor only to uproot myself again to travel around the world as a "lady of leisure." Whenever our phone conversations spiraled into "And this is what we sent you to law school for?" my stomach churned anxiously and I generally found an excuse for having to abruptly hang up the phone (like, "Sorry, Dad, there's a mass murderer outside my window. I'll have to call you back if I'm still alive next week."). I knew they both thought I should be focusing on my new career— they didn't have to rub it in.

As I contemplated my escape from the conversation (guilt trip), I heard a key go in the door. Ignoring that I was on the phone, Sydney barreled in, placed the bag that was in her hands on the credenza and leapt onto the bed. I covered the phone and whispered to her that I was talking to my dad, but she again ignored me and literally shoved her tongue into my mouth.

"Steph, you there?" my dad asked.

With Herculean strength, I pried Sydney's mouth from mine. "Uh, yeah, Dad. Sorry. I just remembered I need to e-mail a client I'm working with," I offered clumsily, knowing his appreciation for work ethic.

"That's more like it! I'll let you go. Don't want to stand in your way of making millions," he said approvingly.

"Okay, Dad. Talk to you soon."

I checked twice to make sure I'd hung up the phone before giving Sydney a good morning greeting of my own. "Sydney, what the hell was that?! I told you I was on the phone with my dad and you practically suffocated me with your tongue."

Laughing snidely, she said, "Love, will you relax?! He didn't know what you were doing. But even if he did, he knows we're in love so what's the big deal?"

I stared at her in disbelief and had absolutely nothing to say. My parents had both accepted my "sexual orientation" (as they referred to it) almost immediately when I'd come out to them in college, although they would certainly have preferred to see me dust off the wedding dress I'd worn when I was a debutante and stroll down the aisle in it to meet a nice Jewish boy waiting for me under the chuppa. By now, they knew that wasn't going to happen. But I didn't flaunt my lesbianism and certainly didn't advertise gratuitous displays of affection to them. It had nothing to do with being gay— even when I had boyfriends, I wouldn't have kissed them in front of my parents (or loudly while I was on the phone with them!).

"Anyway, I sneaked out to get us some breakie. The rain's gone and it's a beautiful day!"

She didn't mention one word about her outburst the night before so neither did I. Nerves. It must have been nerves. This wasn't golf, but for the moment I pretended that it was. Everyone gets a mulligan in golf— you know, a second shot off the tee when the first shot is hideously muffed. Just this once, Sydney can have one, too. Okay, it's not exactly just the once, so…forgiven but not forgotten. As my old role model, Grace Van Owen, would say, "Judge, I object to counsel's line of questioning and would like her outburst duly noted for the record." The record so shall reflect.

Later that day, I found myself sitting courtside watching Sydney battle out her third round against the Number 2 seed. After a rough start, she lost the first set. Not ready to concede, she gained momentum in the second. It was fantastic tennis. Sydney looked great. Suddenly, everything was working for her as she held her own in the second set. Her two-handed topspin backhand was like a bullet, her volleys were sharp and her serve forceful. The score was even at six games all, which forced a tiebreak. Sydney opened the tiebreak and served the first point. Her serve was returned into the net. 1-0, Sydney. The next two serves came from her opponent's racket— first to the backhand side and then to the forehand side. Sydney stepped to the baseline to receive serve. The ball sped to her backhand; she returned with absolute authority and then rushed to the net behind it. Classic and perfect tennis, but Sydney got passed down the line. The following point, her opponent served an ace, handing her a 2-1 lead.

Shit.

The next two points were back on Sydney's serve. She served an ace to even the score but then double-faulted for the deficit. 3-2, the other girl. I could feel Sydney beginning to fume.

Oh, no!

Again, two serves from her opponent. Tit for tat. She gained one point and lost one. 4-3, the other girl. Sydney stepped up to the baseline for the first of her two service points. She tossed the ball above her head, arched her back, jumped into the air where her racket met the ball and smashed it over the net into her opponent's service box. A rally ensued between the two competitors with equal shot time shared by both. The ball flew back and forth over the net from racket to racket. *Pop! Pop! Pop!* Each shot outdid the last. Sydney capitalized on a short ball from her opponent and sprinted into the net behind it. When her approach shot was returned, Sydney practically dove into the alley to save the ball from passing her down the line again. Somehow she got her racket on the ball and flicked it over her opponent's head, sending her scrambling back to the baseline. In an amazing feat, the Number 2 seed returned the ball with terrific force down the center of the court, just one millimeter from Sydney's racket. Sydney read the speed of the ball, yelled, "Out! Out! Out!" and jerked her racket out of the way of the ball. It sped by and landed behind her— on the baseline, but Sydney was positive the ball was long. Not a word from the linesman. The ball was called good and the point awarded to Sydney's opponent for an advantage of 5-3.

I felt my stomach drop. I could see it about to happen. Sydney's arms flailed as she walked closer to the chair umpire whose chair was ten feet off the ground in the middle of the court by the net. I thought she was going to climb up the ladder to the chair where she would receive more than a code violation; she'd be ejected from the match. Her veins popped out of her neck and she started screaming at the chair umpire. "Are you blind?! Have you gone bloody insane! That ball was out! It wasn't even *close* to being in! You've gone completely mad! Get off your bum and do your bloody job!" Her tirade continued as the crowd watched in awe, some agreeing with her and others just jeering her.

When Sydney's pleas for a call overrule were met with silence, she dragged herself back to the baseline— her anger far from subsiding. After a few seconds of silence, Sydney pointed directly at the linesman who had neglected to call the ball out and said, "You're the worst! The absolute worst!"

There it was again. Bad Sydney had appeared. And that was the end of the match. Sydney dropped the next two points, handing her opponent the second set and the victory.

As the rest of the crowd was clapping, I stood up and made my way out of the stands to head back to the lounge. I replayed Sydney's outburst and my mind wandered. I remembered the shock I felt when I saw my first gray hair in my head when I was twenty-two. I gasped in horror and immediately snipped it with a pair of scissors (it hadn't sprouted up quite enough for my fingers to grasp it and pull it out), praying it would never return. Sydney's tirade echoed in my head and I wished getting rid of Bad Sydney could be accomplished with a single snip. It's never *that* easy— I have several gray hairs that replaced the initial one to prove it! But still, it would be nice if Sydney would just cut it out— even a little.

I rounded the corner and saw a familiar face walking toward me. "Tough one to watch, huh?" Casey smirked. Obviously waiting to play her match, she was dressed in her new Nike clothing that hadn't even hit the stores yet.

"Who says there are no fireworks in tennis?" I joked.

She took a deep breath and shook her head. "You better get used to it."

"Oh, so this is not a new thing?" I asked, fearing her response.

She shrieked, "As if!" And then excitedly said, "Are you kidding? Sydney's legendary for going nuts on the court! Her attitude is why we're no longer playing together— well, one of the reasons, anyway. She can be an absolute psycho out there, and I just got sick of it."

"She's pretty intense. I didn't realize that. She had words with the chair ump in LA, but now it seems to be par for the course."

She laughed. "I bet I can count on one hand how many matches she *hasn't* had words with the chair ump! She's gotten more warnings and more codes violations than I can remember. I guess she's been on her best behavior, but you just saw her true colors. I'm surprised it took this long for them to come out. She rarely goes on the court without getting into a fight with someone. It used to be me. Intense is an understatement for Sydney Foster." She pointed to my left hand. "Nice ring. How long's it been with you two?" It was clearly a rhetorical question. She smirked and raised an eyebrow. "That's intense."

Shit.

Whether she was being a meddlesome ex or not, Casey had a point about the ring and she had insight that I didn't have into Sydney's behavior.

Despite Sydney's singles defeat, all was not lost. She was still in both the doubles and mixed doubles draws. Another perk of the Grand Slams is that they all offer mixed doubles. Many top players enter the doubles and mixed doubles draws solely to add padding to their paychecks. Not so with Sydney. It wasn't the cash prize that drove her. Sydney salivated over having *three* chances to win a Grand Slam title (although she did enjoy her million dollar paychecks, as well!).

But immediately following her singles debacle, Sydney wasn't thinking of her future success possibilities; she was too busy dwelling on her loss. For the entire drive back to the hotel, she stared out the window in silence while gripping my hand. Occasionally, she'd squeeze my fingers tightly and clench her jaw, and I knew she was replaying a point she had lost. Even she admitted after her first-round loss at Wimbledon that "you win some, you lose some," but I didn't think consoling her with those words would be warmly accepted at that very moment. The only voices that spoke during the forty-five minute drive were the ones yammering over our driver's walkie-talkie.

The first words that escaped Sydney's lips were to the room service waiter. After feasting on her favorite comfort foods— a grilled-cheese sandwich with a double order of well-done fries and a large bowl of tomato soup extra hot— her spirits were lifted. French fries can brighten even my darkest day, so order seemed to be restored all around. Before we got into bed, she smiled widely and made an announcement.

"Love, I have a surprise for you." She retrieved a piece of paper from her bag.

Jesus Christ! Another surprise?! I still hadn't gotten over the surprise of the braces one week earlier.

"For our three-month anniversary, I got us tickets to a concert. I'm taking you to the John Mayer concert in Palm Springs in a couple weeks." She proudly displayed the tickets she had obviously printed from the Internet.

Okay, first of all, on account of its very definition a "three-month anniversary" is impossible. I hate when people do this. I was fifteen the last time I celebrated a relationship on a monthly basis. I was a sophomore in high school, going steady with Tim Carlyle. Our monthly celebrations back then were cute, but I had long since outgrown such "anniversaries." Second, Sydney and I had not made plans for her to visit LA and I was quite certain that she was not going to fly across the country for a concert and then just go back home. Suddenly, I felt as if the room were getting smaller. I took a deep breath. "Ummm, that's a really nice gesture, but I'm not quite sure I understand."

Sydney explained, "I have a couple weeks off after the Open before we leave for Germany, so I thought I'd come back to LA with you to hang out, and we can go to the concert together."

Looking at another ticket she had purchased without consulting me, I didn't know how to respond. "Sydney, this concert is on a Friday and it's at least four hours away in Friday traffic." Apparently, this tennis all-star wasn't well versed in the horrific traffic patterns in and around Los Angeles that make the highways look more like concrete Christmas trees than passable roads.

"So, you can just take Friday off and we'll make a weekend out of it. I'll make reservations for us to stay at Le Parker Meridien in Palm Springs. It's totally stunning!"

I was starting to feel like a bird in a cage. And I never did like Tweety, so I wasn't liking this, at all. "Sydney, again— I feel like I keep saying this— I really appreciate the offer, but by the time I get back I will have been gone for two weeks and, as it is, I'll only be home for a couple weeks before I leave again. I adore you, but I need to be home alone and do my own thing."

"Don't be silly, love! What's the problem with me coming to LA for a couple weeks? I need a vacation. I won't be in your way. You can go to work everyday and I will entertain myself and just wait for you to come home every evening."

Ahhhh! Suddenly I can't think of *anything* worse. Somehow, I remained outwardly calm and delivered a non-negotiable rejection. "Sydney, I think it would be better for us both to have some downtime. Plus, I may be going to a conference for real estate the weekend of that concert, so I can't go anyway." Good thing I remembered that conference, even without my Palm Pilot. For good measure, I added, "You should check with me before you go buying anymore tickets."

And that was the end of *that* conversation! But, Sydney wasn't happy.

Hoping to escape further discussion, I slid into bed and said goodnight. Sydney tossed and turned and huffed and puffed behind me. Anyone who has ever grown up with an annoying sibling has played the "Not Touching, Can't Get Mad" game. You know, when someone (usually a younger sibling) is sitting next to you doing something that is annoying the hell out of you, like pointing a finger at your face, but not actually touching your face. You go to swipe their finger away and they snicker, "Not touching, can't get mad!" Well, Sydney was bouncing around in the bed essentially playing this juvenile game, waiting for me to roll over and engage with her. I wasn't five anymore, so I wasn't playing.

Finally, she stopped moving her body. But she started moving her mouth.

"I don't understand you! I don't understand why you're so resistant to us spending time together," she blurted.

Shit, here we go.

I had a feeling I wasn't going to be sleeping anytime soon.

I rolled over and calmly said, "I'm not. I just don't think we should spend every waking moment together."

"Why not? That's what new couples do!"

Oh, no! This is worse than I thought! I was really starting to fear that Sydney was going to pound on her chest and yell, "Me, Tarzan! You, Jane!" in order to get her way. "Sydney, since we met we've practically been together non-stop. It's been a lot of fun. But at some point we need to get back to reality and have our separate lives, too."

"What for? We're in love! I'm happiest when I'm with you! What's wrong with being together all the time?"

I couldn't help but think of Bad Sydney on the tennis court. I was in trouble. I was in bed with Bad Sydney and there was no chair ump to silence her with a code violation! "Sydney, we've only been together a couple of months. We should still be dating, but I feel like we're married. I've made that mistake before… "

"With who?" she interrupted.

Uh-oh. Here comes her favorite topic.

"Not that it matters, but with Paige. I was totally addicted to her and I never want to be in that position again." Sydney hated hearing about Paige (although I had to constantly listen to her blather on about Casey). Paige was my first real love but, again, in the brilliant clarity of hindsight, I'd come to realize that my relationship with her had been unhealthy. I lost myself in her and had no idea who I was without her. I didn't want to make that mistake again. I wanted to be in a healthy relationship and it was becoming clearer and clearer— even to me— that this wasn't going to be it.

"My feelings are hurt that you're not addicted to me the way you were to Paige."

Your feelings are hurt that I'm not addicted to you?!

I was absolutely flabbergasted as her words echoed in my mind. I truly couldn't believe what she had just said. Doesn't she understand that an addiction is a *bad* thing?! This is not a tennis match. I'm not a prize to be won! Well, I am a prize, but this is not a tennis match! I didn't know what to say. What *do* you say to something like that? Glad to know you're into addictions, please pass the crack?

I rolled back over onto my side. Already stunned, rage was growing inside me. "Sydney, it's late. Can we please not have this discussion now? We're both tired. Let's just go to sleep."

Bursting with frustration and almost yelling, Sydney launched, "I don't know how you can sleep when I'm so upset. Do you have a heart at all?! Why are you being so cold? Can't you just wake up and talk to me?"

"Sydney, honestly, I really don't think it's fair for you to be making these kinds of demands on me."

"You're my girlfriend…"

Clenching my pillow in frustration, I snapped, "Yes, I am! But I'm not your possession or your goddamn good-luck charm!" I raised my voice to match Sydney's.

Okay, so every once in a while I can spew out a direct hit. Unfortunately, it apparently just ricocheted off Sydney's protective force field and careened out into the ozone!

She yelled, "I'm not asking for much. Only that you give to me and support me!"

God, this is intense. Too intense for two-and-a-half months! "This is exactly why I told you I thought we should slow things down! I feel like you need more than what I'm giving you in this relationship. The thing is, I love you, but I think we moved too fast. This is getting out of control. We should be having fun with each other, not making demands. I feel like all you want to talk about lately is our relationship. It's too early for that."

"I just don't understand why you don't want me to come back to LA with you."

That's it! I've had it! I'm tired and I can't deal with this!

I lost my temper. I do that sometimes when I feel cornered. Strike that. I do that frequently when I get cornered.

"Sydney, all I'm hearing in this conversation is that I'm not giving you what you need. I got it! But I don't need this! Maybe we moved too fast and now we've worn this relationship out!" I was tired of fighting so my only other option was flight. I got out of bed and stomped over to the closet.

"What are you doing?" Sydney yelled.

"Packing my things. I'm going home tomorrow," I announced, fully enraged.

"Love, calm down. Please don't leave. I need you. I need you here. I'm sorry. I don't want you to go. Please don't go!" She sat up on the edge of the bed and began sobbing and begged me not to leave. I watched as sounds came out of her that sent chills up my spine. Her shrieking sounded like an animal being sacrificed. I could not believe that a world-class athlete who had won every tennis tournament there was to win and who was supposed to have incredible mental fortitude was reduced to a crying, screaming, blithering idiot. She begged and pleaded with me not to go.

I ripped my clothes off their hangers in the closet and haphazardly threw them into my Tumi duffel bag. *Where the fuck is her game face? Did she leave her backbone on the tennis court? This is pathetic!* I never imagined that she would act like this! Sydney Number 4 had just entered the building and was now hovering over me as I packed. Moving on to the shelves, I grabbed a handful of T-shirts, starting with my favorite Harvard Tennis T-shirt that Sydney had claimed as hers. As I crammed my clothes into my bag, Sydney started taking them out.

"I don't want you to leave. Please don't leave me."

Successfully winning round one of the tug-o-war, Sydney relinquished my now wrinkled and stretched Seven jeans and I continued packing while she continued sobbing. Trying to reason with her, I insisted, "Sydney, take a deep breath and clam down. Please stop crying."

Sniffling and practically hyperventilating, she said, "I...I just can't lose you. You have no idea how much you mean to me. Please stay," she pleaded, as she plopped down onto the bed.

If there'd been a paper bag in the room, I'm not sure if I'd have given it to her to help her breathe or if I'd have wrapped it around her head to keep her from breathing!

It was after two o'clock in the morning and I was utterly spent. Sydney continued to sob and my anger was rapidly replaced by guilt.

Shit! Goddamn Jewish guilt! I know I should leave, but I can't. Watch, if I leave, then she'll lose and blame it on me and this fucking fight. I just can't deal with this on my conscience.

I emptied my hands of my clothes and, in a more civilized tone, said, "Sydney, I don't want you to be upset, but I also don't want to talk about this anymore tonight. I just want to go to sleep. I'll stay if you promise not to talk about this anymore. Can we please just go to sleep?"

Wiping her tears on the sheets and taking quick, shallow breaths, she said, "I just want you next to me. I promise not to talk about it anymore."

I got back into bed and not one more word was spoken. Several minutes later, my pulse finally slowed down. I lied motionless, staring at the ceiling. *If she opens her mouth one more time, I swear I'm gonna shove a tennis ball down her throat and leave her for dead. The only hope this relationship has for survival is if she lets go of me a little. Please, God, make her let go.*

Sydney fell asleep quickly, but I could not escape my thoughts and lull myself to sleep. I feared I'd done it again— that I had fallen prey to false intimacy. Maybe straight women are guilty of it too, but I can't speak for them. Lesbians are famous for jumping into bed with someone immediately and mistaking sex for love, thus, being falsely intimate. It's next to impossible for a woman to have "no strings attached" sex. Put two women together and forget about it! There's no such thing as a one-night stand in the lesbian world, at least not in the lesbian world I know. Two women sleep together without knowing each other and go from being complete strangers to girlfriends with unwarranted familiarity toward each other. It's all downhill from there. Intellectual reasoning gets thrown out the window.

Is this what I had done with Sydney? I mean, how is it reasonable, after knowing someone for a few days to contemplate trips together or, even more ridiculous, a life together?! What's next? Oh shit! What am I doing?

My chest was moving up and down swiftly and my pulse was pounding in my temple.

Calm down. Just relax and go to sleep. Everything will be fine.

The next morning my head was spinning and throbbing as if I were hung over. I couldn't stop thinking about the night before and about the change I was witnessing in Sydney's personality. Just like after her mulligan the other night, Sydney acted as if nothing had happened the night before. I was sensing a pattern. I just wanted to make it through the rest of the tournament and get back home to clear my head.

Because the rain had postponed match-play for almost a week, the tournament officials were still scrambling to get the schedule back in order and Sydney had to play both of her first-round doubles matches back-to-back on the same day in order to accommodate the schedule.

Despite some rather close line calls, she remained astonishingly level-headed throughout both matches, with a few minor exceptions. Unfortunately, she didn't emerge victorious from either contest. I nervously waited for her outside the locker room, anticipating that she'd appear bitter and surly. Surprisingly, she met me with a warm smile on her face, and seemed relieved to be free of the pressure of the Open. In an unexpected twist, I suddenly found myself in the company of the Sydney I'd met at Wimbledon, and it was a welcomed reunion.

Sydney wrapped her arms around me and said, "Not quite the result I was hoping for, but all's not lost...I still have you, love." She smiled even wider and said, "Casey's out, too. She just lost. I saw her in the locker room. The whole lot of us are going to have dinner tonight."

"The whole lot of us?" I said, puzzled.

"Yeah. You, me, Casey and Trish."

Surprise, surprise. Trish had made an appearance at a Grand Slam! I had occasionally seen her in the players' lounge and also meandering through the crowds toward the courts (one time I even saw her sprinting after Tommy Haas and his entourage), but I had not cultivated a friendship with her. Sydney, on the other hand, had made amends with Trish and Casey and they had all become friends again. At first, I didn't understand why Sydney talked to her ex-girlfriend on a daily basis. But I came to understand their comfortable dependence on each other was the result of them working and traveling together. Since I had been traveling so much with Sydney, I was starting to get to know her ex-girlfriend as well. I found Casey disarming and genuine and felt bad for judging her so harshly at Wimbledon. I was now forming a friendship with her.

Sydney paused as she checked an incoming text message. Grinning, she announced, "Our dinner party has grown. Conchi, Ribi and Erin will be joining us as well." Pleased, she snapped her phone shut and we continued toward the transportation area.

Later that evening, our group stumbled into the Palm Restaurant together. Sandwiched between Sydney and Casey, I sat amid caricatures of famous faces on the walls, while dining in the company of tennis celebrities as we embarked upon a carnivorous joy ride. Bad Sydney had disappeared and Good Sydney was back! When Casey wasn't ogling over her straight best friend on her other side, she was bending my ear as if I were her new best friend. She nudged me with her knee and whispered, "So, how was she after the matches today? Intense?"

Smirking subtly, I said, "Actually, no. She was surprisingly mellow." I was happy to give Casey a positive review but refrained from regaling her with the sordid details of how Sydney was so relaxed after her losses that we actually spent the rest of the afternoon in bed, enjoying each other.

"Looks like you're doing a good job of hanging in there. Maybe you're actually having a calming effect on her. God, knows I couldn't tame her!"

Shaking my head, I admitted, "Sometimes it's really tough..."

"Oh, you don't have to tell me. I know. Trust me, I know. We didn't make a good couple, but I do love Sydney, and I'm glad we're still friends." She sipped her wine and said, "You're good for her. You seem like you ground her. I'm glad she has you." Casey's tone was sincere and honest and, instantly, I liked her even more. Hearing her words brought me comfort— both in the fact that Casey's romantic interest in Sydney had definitely faded and that she valued her friendship. Such reassurances from an ex are always nice to hear.

Sydney yelled across the table, "Trish, that's about thirty bucks worth of wine in your glass. You gonna drink it?" She extended her open hand before Trish answered.

"No, you can have it." Trish handed Sydney her full glass. "My lips feel a little dry. I need to excuse myself and go reapply. You never know when Mr. Right is going to appear and I don't want to meet him with, like, naked lips." She was right. The dark brown Iced Mocha sheen had faded, leaving traces of pink on her very obviously collagen-injected lips.

Sydney happily accepted Trish's wine and poured some of the precious red liquid into Conchi's and Ribi's empty glasses. As soon as Sydney finished pouring, Conchi lifted her glass and said, "I cannot believe the shit luck we all have this year! None of us make it pass the third round! *Ay la puta madre!*" She sipped her wine and laughed.

"Conchi! Is not important, the win all the time!" Ribi added sarcastically, waving her index finger in a chiding motion and hissing like a stuttering snake.

"Tu callate, tonta!" Conchi jokingly snapped.

Although I don't speak Spanish, I had become quite familiar with this phrase which translates as "you shut up, dummy." I'd been on the receiving end of it many times.

Sydney, Casey and I laughed as Ribi and Conchi engaged in a friendly verbal spar.

Oblivious to the joke, Trish chimed in, "I agree with Ribi. What's the point of playing if you're not going to win, right?" Instantly, as if there'd been a power surge, the laughter stopped and a hush fell over the table. Five pair of eyes stared at Trish. Unaware of the incongruity of her ridiculous comment, she retrieved a piece of paper from her Louis Vuitton purse and continued, "I've tallied all of Casey's points. Her early departures here at the US Open are, like, really going to hurt her rankings." She shook her head disapprovingly.

Before the silence became painful, Sydney smiled and in a derisive tone said, "Trish, mate, weren't you on your way to the powder room?" She mimicked putting on lipstick. One emaciated Trish, tossed her long black hair over her shoulder, clutched her purse and excused herself from the table. I watched in awe as she sashayed effortlessly in her black strappy heels (Christian Louboutin, judging by the signature red soles) across the room.

I had never spoken to Casey about Trish— never even mentioned her name. Once Trish left the table, I asked, "Is she okay? She's barely said a word all night and hasn't touched her food or taken one sip of her wine." The rest of us, however, had been quick to raise a glass, use a knife and fork and spew laughter. For the life of me, I didn't see what Casey saw in her!

Shrugging her shoulders, Casey answered, "Yeah, she's fine. She's taking my loss today harder than I am. She does that. It's part of her charm. That and constantly talking about her search for 'Mr. Right'." Casey laughed and swallowed the rest of her wine. She raised her empty glass and announced, "Bottle number six? Who's ready for more?"

As if on cue, Conchi, Ribi, Sydney and I all raised our empty glasses simultaneously and Sydney relinquished the textbook-sized wine menu she'd been guarding to Casey. Within minutes, our glasses were refilled and except for Trish, we all looked as if we were having the time of our lives. It was a fantastic ending to the last Grand Slam of the year.

The next morning, I woke up with a splitting headache again, but, at least this time it was from too much vino! Somehow, I dragged myself out of bed and made it down to the lobby, where my car and driver to the airport were awaiting me. Sydney convinced me not to abandon our relationship and to give us some time to work out the kinks. She finally agreed (or conceded) that it might be a good idea for us to have a few weeks to ourselves in our own environments before I joined her in Europe. I felt refreshed. Plus, I now felt like I had an ally— someone who could truly understand my frustrations and concerns with Sydney because of personal experience. After the US Open, I indeed had a new best friend— Casey Matthews.

* * *

My friendship with Casey was solidified a couple weeks later when I flew to Germany for the Munich Grand Prix. After suffering embarrassingly early doubles losses at the US Open, Sydney and Casey decided to recharge by reuniting and playing doubles together again— on a trial basis. Apparently, Casey had a habit of discarding her doubles partners when success wasn't constant. She no longer held the Number 1 ranking and desperately wanted it back. Obviously, she thought Sydney would be a good vehicle to drive her back to the top of the rankings. Regardless of the motivation, Sydney was ecstatic about the reunion. Since their split on and off the court, Sydney was constantly trying to persuade Casey to play doubles with her again. Her persistence finally paid off and the two agreed to step on the same side of the court together for the first time in over one year in Germany.

When I got off the plane I was greeted by a flower-bearing Sydney in the baggage claim area. I had recovered from my experience at the US Open and hoped that things would be different now that we had discussed our needs. I was happy to see her but was surprised that she had not sent a tournament driver to pick me up. The reason for her personal escort became obvious when we stepped outside and she pointed across the street to our hotel. We walked in the cold drizzle across the street. The parking lot of the hotel was filled with brand-new Porsches— Targas, Carreras, Cayennes— convertibles and hardtops. These shiny cars stood out against our rather dingy accommodation, the Mövenpick Hotel. It wasn't at all what I expected.

There was no grand entrance and no glistening lobby. But it was the only hotel close to the tournament site, so it would be home for the week.

Our room was on the second floor, just down the hall from Casey's. A shopping bag in front of the door blocked our entrance. Sydney picked it up and opened the door. "Must be today's gift. I love this tournament. They give us a present everyday." She reached inside the bag and pulled out a reversible blue down vest— the kind that accompany skis and snow boots. Tossing it onto the bed, she said, "This'll look great on you!"

I thanked her as I set my bags down, and then gave her a proper hello. Sydney's lips were still cold from our walk outside, but her mouth quickly warmed on mine. Before our fierce kissing got carried away in our modest and musty-smelling room, we stopped ourselves. She was due at the courts forty-five minutes later to watch Casey play her first-round singles match. I decided to go with Sydney instead of succumbing to my jetlag and diving into bed. We walked through the lobby, out the door and, oddly, headed toward the parking lot. I was confused— again.

Sydney smirked and pulled a set of keys out of her pocket and pressed a button that apparently disengaged the alarm of a silver Carrera parked ten feet in front of us.

"What the...?"

"Beautiful, huh? This tournament is the best! We have our choice of Porsches to drive everyday. Tomorrow I plan to get a Cayenne! And if I win the tournament, I will have my choice of all of these beauties to take home. Don't ever say I don't drive you in style!"

I got in, closed the door and checked out the interior. It smelled like brand-new leather. "These haven't changed much in twenty years," I said. I didn't mean to burst Sydney's bubble, but a Porsche was not a novelty for me. I grew up with them. By the time I was twelve, I think my mom had owned one of every model. My dad liked giving them to her as Christmanukah (since we celebrated both Christmas and Hanukah, this is how we merged them) presents. I remember one December when he came into the kitchen and handed my mom a set of keys and said, "Merry Christmas and Happy Hanukah and all of that stuff. I got you a card. It's in the garage. I just forgot to put the 'd' on the end of it. I think you'll like it, though." There never was a card. My dad has always been spontaneous and wildly generous, but not the most sentimental character.

Although this was not my first ride in a Porsche, it was my maiden journey in a Porsche on the Autobahn. For a second, I thought I was in the car with Mario Andretti. I gripped the handle by the door and my palms started sweating as Sydney swerved around a corner not bothering to reduce her speed by even one kilometer. Right after I swallowed what was probably vomit making its way up to my throat, I barked, "What are you, a fifteen-year-old boy on a joy ride? Slow the fuck down!" She thought it was funny. I wasn't laughing. I was annoyed. *Drive me in style! More like drive me crazy!*

By some stroke of luck, we arrived at the club in one piece. I got my badge and made my way up to the players' restaurant. There was beer on tap, and I couldn't get it into my body fast enough! I planted myself at the bar. I don't speak a word of German, but somehow confidently ordered, *"Ein Bier, bitte."* The man behind the bar spoke English back to me and handed me a cold pint. Before I had a chance to lick the froth off my lips, I heard a voice squawk, "Jesus Christ! It's barely noon, and already you're throwing one back!" I turned to find Casey standing next to me with a huge smile on her face.

She laughed and whispered under her breath, "Is she driving you to drink already?"

I stood from my stool and gave her a hug. "Shouldn't you be warming up or something?"

"Already did. The match before mine is a set and 3-2. I should be on soon. You watching?" She looked over my shoulder. "Where's the wife?"

"Oh you mean Mario Andretti? Probably taking her driving gloves off and getting some balls."

"Oh yes, Sydney and her Porsches. Used to drive me crazy! And now you get the pleasure of it!" As she tied her trademark blue bandana around her head, she looked toward the court, and saw that the match was one game closer to ending. I hurriedly swallowed my mouthful of beer so I could wish her good luck as she quickly scurried back toward the locker room.

Casey won her match with Sydney and me cheering her to victory.

Afterward, Sydney decided to stay at the courts and get a massage since she wasn't scheduled to play until the next day. The only Porsche that was available for Casey to take for the evening was a stick shift. She pouted disappointedly but changed her expression when I volunteered to drive the standard shift Targa (I didn't know they even came in manual) back to the hotel. I think knowing how to drive a stick shift should be a requirement. What if there were an emergency? Yet another example of how pampered these girls can be and how they can expect everything to be done for them!

When we got back to the hotel, I went with Casey to her room. Unlike the musty aroma in our room, Casey's smelled of red currant from the candle she had burnt earlier. Her room was organized and tidy— the opposite of Sydney's and mine. Sydney wasn't the most meticulous person and had a habit of tossing clothes onto the floor, instead of folding them and placing them in drawers. I'd given up trying to persuade her to pick up after herself. Her response was always the same: "My job is to play tennis, not to clean rooms. That's what maids are for." Apparently, Casey didn't share her point of view.

Happy not to have to step over mounds of clothes piled on the floor, I lowered myself into a comfortable chair and Casey plopped down onto the end of the bed. We found ourselves lost in conversation for hours without any awkward lulls. We talked about life on the Tour, what books we were currently reading (she, the *Da Vinci Code* and I, *The Kite Runner*), what music we enjoyed (she cringed at my love for country music and I balked at her love for rap) and our "dream vacation" spots (hers, Hawaii in the spring and mine, Venice in the winter). We laughed often— the full-bodied kind of laughing that made our stomachs hurt and our eyes tear. Spending time with Casey was effortless, and a part of me wished Sydney was more like Casey. I caught myself looking at my watch, hoping that somehow the minutes would pass by slower or that time would find a way to stand still.

Gradually, we made our way to the topic of love. Casey chose to ask me about my past relationships— specifically, my relationship with Paige— because she knew it was a source of contention between Sydney and me. I confided in Casey about the bond I once shared with Paige because of her beauty inside and out. I never considered Paige my soul mate, but she was the closest thing I had ever felt to one.

Despite our drastically different upbringings and desires in life, we had a symbiotic relationship that ended abruptly because Paige has a habit of sabotaging good things (having an affair with someone *does* tend to bring a relationship to a screeching halt!). But Paige was the first great love of my life. I admitted to Casey that sometimes I wondered if Paige and I would still be together had she not had the affair. When I felt the nostalgia of discussing my past love beginning to somber our lighthearted mood, I shined the spotlight on Casey and asked her about Trish.

I listened intently as Casey described her love for a woman who could not love her the way that she so desperately wanted. She described a closely-knit friendship based not on tenderness or love but on dependence and obsession. It was as if Trish were Casey's most sought-after prize that she could never win. Casey admitted that while the thought of being with another woman disgusted Trish, she still held out hope that Trish would someday have a change of heart. Instantly, I had insight into all of the rumors floating around the Tour about the nature of Casey and Trish's alleged romantic relationship: there wasn't one, hadn't ever been one and would never be one. The more I learned about Casey and Trish, the more I realized how extremely dysfunctional their friendship was. In fact, they put the "fun" in dysfunctional. Casey and Trish went everywhere together and did everything together. They were each other's first phone call every morning and the last one at night. But this wasn't *When Harry Met Sally*. These two were not *destined* to end up happily ever after, they were just consumed with each other.

Inevitably, we talked about Sydney. Casey and I both had relationships with Sydney. Granted, the difference was that Casey had extricated herself from her romantic involvement with Sydney, and I was still "caught in the web," as Casey jokingly put it. Since Casey had spent several years with Sydney, she could understand my frustration with certain aspects of our relationship. Most of all, Casey understood my intense craving to have a friend who empathized about my dilemmas with Sydney and who would not accuse, judge or analyze me.

Losing track of time, we opened up to each other, exposing our most intimate and private thoughts, as if we had been friends forever. Needless to say, we bonded. And when Sydney knocked on Casey's door to retrieve me, we parted like two young girls who'd just exchanged vows of being best friends forever, looking forward to the next time we could share more cherished information.

It was in Munich that the connection between Casey and me grew and our friendship transcended the boundaries of casual to connected. We felt a deep affinity toward each other and found ourselves speaking a secret language of smirks, laughter and innuendos to whose translation only we were privy. The three of us— Sydney, Casey and I— began to spend every waking moment together, but Casey and I relished even thirty seconds of privacy where we could confide in each other. Even better was whenever a chunk of time fell into our laps allowing us to sit and talk for hours about everything and nothing.

As the week progressed, both Sydney and Casey collected victories. Sydney fared better in the singles draw than Casey, who lost in the second round. Sydney didn't come home with a Porsche, but only because she lost in the finals. Unfortunately, her doubles results mirrored her singles. She and Casey made a gallant effort but lost in the finals, just short of capturing the doubles title in Munich. Bad Sydney showed up to play in the championship match and it was a total and complete disaster. Her temper got the best of her and she went on a crusade against Casey, the chair umpire and two of the linesmen. Casey walked off the court riddled with embarrassment and disgust, and Sydney departed with a code violation from the chair umpire for unsportsmanlike behavior. The Matthews-Foster reunion was short-lived, but the Matthews-Alexander friendship looked like it was going to be permanent.

5

$\mathcal{H}$eadline: Sydney Foster suffers devastating early embarrassment

"I can't wait to meet your mom, love. She's gonna love me!" Sydney oozed with confidence while glaring into the rearview mirror and adjusting her new Gucci sunglasses.

I smiled indulgently as I closed the passenger-side door to her shiny black BMW X5 (my least favorite of all luxury SUVs). It was Thanksgiving morning and I was beyond nervous. I fastened my seat-belt and hoped that the three-and-a-half hour drive from Sydney's house in Miami to my mom's house on Longboat Key would calm me. My anxiety was compounded by Sydney's insistence on wearing the same outfit that she'd worn the night our romance began at Wimbledon— that white Hollister Co. miniskirt and flimsy black tank top. She thought it was feminine and flattering, and in response to my skeptically raised eyebrows when she'd stepped out of her walk-in closet, she boasted, "This impressed you. Let's see if it impresses your mom." She then winked and smirked suggestively. I cringed at her stupid and childishly inappropriate implication. Admittedly, I once ogled over Sydney in that ensemble. But now I couldn't decide whether I thought she looked more like a tart or a transvestite. I bit my tongue and decided not to take issue with her attire.

Sydney and I had been together for almost five months and for our five-month anniversary (she still insisted on monthly celebrations) she gave me a card and a promise to love me forever. In return, I invited her to my mother's house for the most sacred and special of all holidays in my family— Thanksgiving. This was a big deal. I had never taken any of my girlfriends home for Thanksgiving.

This year I didn't have a choice, though. Even if I didn't want to include Sydney, there was really no way that I could fly all the way across the country to celebrate Thanksgiving and indulge in a fabulous feast on Longboat Key, and leave Sydney sitting home alone a few hours away in Miami defrosting a TV dinner. Instead, I flew to Miami the day before Thanksgiving so I could accompany her to my mother's house.

We arrived on my mother's doorstep just before ten o'clock. I held my breath as we walked through the door. The dining room table, in true "mom fashion," was decked out with glimmering crystal, shining silver and three generations of china. Thanksgiving is a formal holiday for my family. I have no memories of eating turkey in front of the TV watching football, which, I have heard happens in some people's homes. I hate football, so I have never felt like I was missing out.

From the entryway, I could see directly into the kitchen. My mom, as usual, was doing eighteen things at once. She balanced her phone against her head as she reached into a cabinet for a pot. *Clank!* The kitchen faucet was running, and just as she turned it off, she must have heard the front door shut. Judging from her tone, she was conversing with a client. Thanksgiving was never complete without a crisis caused by one of her clients requiring her immediate and prolonged hand-holding. She smiled and waved a frantic hello but then continued with her call.

I ushered Sydney away from the kitchen and gave her a tour of the house. She marveled at my mother's impeccably decorated living room. Inspired by the modern decor, she said, "These built-ins are fantastic! I should have done something like this in my house— to show off all my trophies."

As if the numerous custom-made glass shelves which prominently displayed her countless tennis trophies in her own living room wasn't impressive enough! Admittedly, Sydney's house in Miami was quite remarkable. Though not a waterfront property, her house was a beautiful piece of real estate, no doubt decorated by an interior designer with exquisite modern taste and flawless attention to detail. Not exactly homey or well-lived in, I somehow managed to comfortably laze on her sleek black leather living room couch, in front of the room's pièce de résistance— the fifty-inch plasma TV that hung above the fireplace.

When my mom finished her phone call, she found us in mid-tour. "Hi, kids. So sorry. It *never* stops. Not even on Thanksgiving!" She greeted me with a kiss and a hug hello and then turned to Sydney. "It's a pleasure to meet you, Sydney. Steph has told me so much about you."

Sydney pushed my mom's extended hand out of the way and threw her arms around my mom's back. She hugged my indulgent mom as if they were old friends reuniting. "It's nice to meet you, too, Blythe."

BLYTHE?! Who said you could call my mother by her first name?

The headache that I'd talked myself out of having in the car suddenly returned. I'm sure my mom would have refused to be addressed as Mrs. *Anything,* but Sydney didn't even give her the chance to politely decline the formality. *Way to go, Sydney! Can't undo that first impression! You just embarrassed yourself and me. And you just got here!*

Unfazed (at least outwardly), my mom smiled at me. "I'm so happy to have my baby home for Thanksgiving!" Putting her hand on my shoulder, the smile quickly disappeared from her face. "Sweetie, I have some bad news— your father won't be joining us for Thanksgiving. There was a horrible ice-storm in Tulsa, and the airport is closed." She sighed and shrugged as she mumbled something under her breath about having told him to take a flight earlier in the week and that he "never listens."

Sydney boomed, "Well, that just means more food for us! I hear you're a fantastic cook, Blythe. I thought you might enjoy a nice bottle of Cabernet." She reached into her bag and proudly displayed a generous bottle of Opus One 2002 Cabernet Sauvignon. She winked and said, "This is a *really* good one. We should probably open it now and let it breathe." She nodded her head toward the kitchen as if she were the master of that domain.

It was all I could do not to hit her over the head with her stupid bottle of wine. Who does that? Who hands a hostess a present and then tells her what to do with it? I had half a mind to tell Sydney what she could do with her wine. I had a feeling my mom did, too. I was afraid. Really afraid. We had only been there for fifteen minutes and already Sydney had two strikes against her in my mind, but who's counting? The apple doesn't fall far from the tree, so I think it's safe to assume my mom was.

My mom's few minutes of reprieve from her phone quickly ended as she skirted out of the living room to answer the ringing phone.

One of my favorite parts of Thanksgiving has always been standing next to my mom in the kitchen, helping her cook. She makes everything from scratch. Not even her breadcrumbs are store-bought. But no one could ever accuse this "Type A" personality of being an overachieving perfectionist! All of her secret recipes were handed down to her from her grandmother whom she absolutely worshipped. People have begged and pleaded for the recipe to my great-grandmother's legendary cornbread stuffing, but to no avail. I remember Thanksgivings at her house in Texas when I was a young kid. My great-grandmother is no longer with us, but Thanksgiving is never complete without her. Carrying on the Thanksgiving tradition with all of the original recipes is my mom's way of paying homage to her.

The oven was warming and the house was starting to smell like Thanksgiving. The incredible smells that emanate from the kitchen are indescribable. Poultry seasoning was in the air and sautéed onions and celery were on the stove. Potatoes needed peeling and this was my cue to join my mom next to the sink. As a kid, it was always my job to peel the potatoes because it was one of the only jobs that she was confident that my young hands could not blunder. Twenty-some-odd years later, I still had not graduated from potato-peeler. We stood side by side as I peeled the potatoes and my mom rinsed out the bird's cavity. I volunteered to massage the breasts, but I wasn't going anywhere near the cavity! I hadn't peeled three potatoes before my mom's phone rang and Sydney's separation anxiety compelled her to seek my attention. Sydney came into the kitchen gripping her bottle of wine, still not satisfied that it had not been decanted.

"Love, where does your mom keep her decanter? We need to open this well before dinner."

First Blythe and now 'love!' What is wrong with her! Don't call me 'love' in front of my mother. What kind of an idiot sexualizes someone in front of her mother just after they've met?

I pretended I didn't hear her as she walked past me and motioned to my mom, pointing to the bottle and mouthing the word "decanter."

My mom tried to act polite. *Tried.* Covering the mouthpiece of the phone with her hand, she curtly asked, "What? What is it that you need? I'm on the phone. With a client!" Normally the consummate gracious hostess, I could hear the annoyance in my mom's voice clear as day as she somewhat politely acknowledged Sydney.

Sydney, now actually speaking audibly, repeated, "Where's a decanter? I'll decant this for you."

I was speechless. I felt like I was watching a train wreck in super-slow motion. Cardinal Rule Number…something: *Never* interrupt my mom when she's on the phone unless you want to be a permanent fixture on the wall. If the house were on fire, I'm not sure I would interrupt her to tell her. My mom didn't deign to acknowledge Sydney's request with words. Incredibly articulate, my mom is an expert at communicating, even without speaking. I'm not talking about silent hand gestures that universally mean "fuck you." In my life, I have never known words to fail my mother, but she has the distinct talent of having the option of whether to use words or just her glare when she wants to make a point. My mom is famous for "The Glare." I was born with the same "go to hell" look on my face that my mother had perfected after years and years of practice. I must have been able to see through her womb to her face because if this doesn't epitomize learned behavior I don't know what does. Unfortunately, my glare works on everyone but my mom and hers works on everyone— especially me. As she turned her attention back to the phone, I saw The Glare and she merely waved her hand in front of her face pointing to a cabinet near the bar. Translation: "Stephanie, find her the fucking decanter and tell her not to bother me again!"

Sydney decanted the wine and I suggested that she might want to watch a football game in the TV room. She, of course, declined my suggestion and lingered on the other side of the kitchen.

When my mom hung up the phone, Sydney was swirling the wine in the decanter. I had seen her do her pretentious wine routine— swirl, smell, observe, swish and swallow— many times. Granted, she was something of a connoisseur and probably could detect the faintest hint of black licorice and tobacco leaf, but it was still annoying to watch. Barely removing her nose from the decorative crystal bottle, she flippantly said, "Blythe, it's a holiday! Take the day off, for God's sake! Why don't you just switch off your cell phone?" And that was it. In less than one hour, Sydney had sealed her fate with my mother.

My mom does work a lot. It's who she is and what she does. It has always been that way and it always will be, and I can guarantee that Sydney's "suggestion" to my mother was not warmly welcomed. There are two sure-fire ways to get on my mom's bad side: 1) question her usage of time; and 2) fuck with her daughter (this list, by the way, is by no means exhaustive— these are just two of her favorites). Do one of those two things and it's pretty much a guarantee that you've terminally offended my mom. There's a running joke that if you piss her off, you can do one of two things: leave town or die. At this point, I had a feeling that Sydney's stay on Longboat Key would be short-lived.

I didn't dare look at my mom after Sydney's suggestion that she cut herself off from the outside world because it was a holiday. My mom walked toward me, her brow so furrowed that her eyes were barely open enough to squint, and I knew the inevitable was imminent. I was on the verge of seeing the dreaded glare— the one I had spent my entire childhood trying to avoid. Hell, I was still trying to avoid it. Thanks to Sydney, before I had a chance to take cover, my mom directed The Glare at me, and I feared lasers were going to shoot from her eyes.

My mom's jaw muscle was still clenched when she joined me by the sink. Sydney was done swirling the wine and announced that she was going to put her cherished decanter on the table so it could continue to "open." Under her breath my mom whispered, "I know we're from Oklahoma, but does she think I've never seen a bottle of wine before? Moonshine is not exactly my table beverage of choice. It's not like I drink wine out of a box. I do know how to decant wine. If she knows so goddamn much about wine, why is she bringing me a complex, spicy Cabernet to pair with turkey? Just get her out of my kitchen, and do it now before I stuff her inside this bird!" Her jaw barely moved as she spoke. Her delivery was perfect, though. Brilliant, in fact. She smiled as she discretely and, in the most dignified of manners, shredded Sydney into one million little pieces.

A few hours later, after much scurrying around in the kitchen, the table was set, the candles were lit and the food was ready. As we sat down, I hoped that dinner would be less eventful than the afternoon had been. My mom sat at the head of the table and Sydney and I sat across from each other on either side of her. The food was so bountiful

I didn't know where to start. After all of the dishes, platters and gravy boats had been passed around, my mouth was salivating with the anticipation of creating my first "perfect bite"— a well-salted and peppered mixture of mashed potatoes, stuffing, gravy and turkey breast. As I lifted my fork to my mouth, I looked across the table at Sydney. Her perfect bite was different than mine. She had just shoved a snowball-sized wad of mashed potatoes and turkey into her gaping mouth. I saw a mixture of pink and white swishing around in her mouth as she chewed with her mouth open. Her foul eating habits had annoyed me before, but this time I was truly disgusted. She smiled at me after she swallowed. Her braces were filled with Thanksgiving delights. I lost my appetite. So much for my perfect bite.

Sydney didn't put down her knife and fork until she had cleaned her plate of every last morsel of food. And, speaking of clean, she didn't bother to use her napkin once during the meal. Apparently, she thought the white, freshly-ironed linen napkins neatly placed under her fork were *objets d'art*. Or maybe she recognized them as napkins but thought that they were merely optional. Sydney ate her entire meal taking a fraction of the bites that a normal person would take. My mother may have taken three bites of her dinner and I had barely put a dent in mine by the time Sydney was done hoovering her plate. I made fun of her once for wolfing down her dinner so quickly and she explained that she had eaten that way her entire life because when she was a kid, the food was put on the table and if she didn't dive in and grab what she wanted immediately, before her brother or father, there would be nothing left for her. At the time, her explanation sounded reasonable and I bought her story. But I looked around our table at that very moment. There was enough food to feed a small army and only three of us sitting at the table. It's safe to say that Sydney could have taken a breath between bites and after exhaling there would still be food left for her.

After dinner Sydney and I planted ourselves in front of the sink to do the dishes. My mom is very particular about how the dishes are washed after Thanksgiving dinner. The Bacarat crystal *never* goes in the dishwasher. It gets washed and dried by hand with a special cloth. The gold serving pieces are never to be placed next to the sterling. And the china is to be spaced far enough apart in the dishwasher so the plates don't rattle against one another during the washing cycle. It took us almost two hours, and we were nearly finished cleaning when I realized water was dripping out onto the tile floor from under the sink.

Shit, this is all I need right now!

My mom doesn't deal well with little surprises like this, especially after being on her feet all day and doing her best not to kill her houseguest from New Zealand. Too late. My mom noticed the puddle on the floor. The sky was falling. Immediately.

No problem! Sydney to the rescue! As my mom's eyes widened at the sight of the small lake that was accumulating under the sink, Sydney swooped in and offered to save the day. "Blythe, it looks like you have a minor leak. No worries. I can fix it."

My face contorted with confusion. In unison, my mom and I said the same two words quizzically. "You can?"

"Sure! No big deal. I've seen my dad fix a sink a million times."

Right. No big deal.

An hour later, Sydney lifted herself up from under the sink.

"I think we might need to call a plumber." She half-smiled and placed some metal pieces on the counter that I recognized as parts of the drainage system that was once intact under the sink.

I stared at her. *God, why me?! Do you want to guess how easy it will be for me to find a plumber on Thanksgiving night? How about my mom's reaction to this mess? Want to take a stab at that one?*

I grabbed the Yellow Pages and flipped through, pretending to have everything under control. I shrugged Sydney off and sucked on my index finger to stop the bleeding from the papercut I had just gotten and eventually found a plumber willing to make a last-minute house call.

After the plumber left, it was my turn to get on my hands and knees under the sink. I sopped up every last drop of water and couldn't wait to get into bed. When my mom learned that I was going to have back surgery, she personally tested every bed model from every mattress manufacturer and found, without a doubt, the world's most comfortable bed. I always looked forward to going home if only just to get a good night's sleep in this bed. When I walked into my bedroom, it was like standing on a diving board over the most gorgeous and inviting pool you can ever imagine. All I wanted to do was dive in and float away to a deep sleep. I pulled the fluffy duvet back and prepared for my triple gainer, but instantly my dream pool turned into a nightmare. I wasn't diving anywhere. Sydney was lying there…naked. Yes, naked! In my bed! At my mother's house! Can you imagine?

As far as parents go, my mom's liberal and cool. My swearing has never offended her (and trust me, there's lots of it!). My occasional beer when I was in high school was always overlooked (and by occasional I mean frequent!). Bringing girls home and sleeping in the same room with them was allowed. My mom respects me and my choices, and I, in turn, respect her. That means, under no circumstances, will my girlfriend sleep naked in my bed at my mom's house! Isn't that a no-brainer? I was mortified that Sydney even thought she could. I was exhausted and it was all I could do not to explode at her. Instead, I threw the duvet back over her and calmly asked, barely moving my jaw, "Sydney, what are you doing?" There was a time when I used to pull back the covers of a bed and take delight in seeing Sydney's naked body waiting for me. Right now, all I wanted to do was take a Valium!

She answered with surprise, "Huh, I'm waiting for you to get into bed. What's it look like I'm doing?"

"Your clothes. Where are they?"

"What do you mean, my clothes?"

"I mean your pajamas!"

"You know I don't sleep in pajamas. What are you talking about?" She had the audacity to take an annoyed tone with me.

"Uh, I'm talking about that you're in my bedroom, under my mother's roof, and as if those two things need explaining, pure and simple, here you wear pajamas!"

"Why?"

"What do you mean, *why?* Because it's disrespectful not to! This is not a hotel, Sydney! This is where my mom lives. You can't just come here and treat her home as your own."

"Steph, c'mon. We're adults."

"Adults or not, we…*you* are a guest in this house, and guests go to bed clothed! What if she comes in here in the morning?"

"She wouldn't do that. She respects me and our relationship more than that."

Is she kidding?! My mom doesn't give a shit about this fool, and she certainly doesn't have regard for our relationship after her behavior this afternoon! I can't handle this! Surrender me now! I mean ASAP! This girl's got a lot of nerve! What does she think? I'm going to strip down to my birthday suit and jump in bed with her and pretend that we're at a nudist colony? Get a fucking clue!

"Sydney, I'm dead-tired and this is not open for discussion. You have two choices— put your clothes on and stay here or put your clothes on and go home. You choose, but by the time I finish brushing my teeth you better be clothed. Period."

* * *

I woke up the next morning and walked out of my room fraught with nerves. I found my mom in the kitchen. It wasn't even nine o'clock and she was decked out in some version of Armani, accessorized by Chanel over her shoulder and Prada over her eyes (my mom's an indoor sunglass wearer). She was collecting some papers and getting ready to leave. I walked over and cheerily greeted her, "Good morning, Mom. Thanks for everything last night. As usual, it was fantastic!"

"I'm glad you enjoyed it. What are your plans for the day?"

Uh-oh, here it comes!

"Not really sure yet. I haven't talked to Sydney."

"Is she planning on staying again tonight?" she asked coolly.

Her dark glasses covered her eyes, but I was certain that she was squinting and doing her best not to speak her mind. She tucked the papers into her bag and slid her glasses down her nose. *Bam!* And there it was! The Glare. If Sydney had planned on staying and relaxing by the pool or sipping a fruity drink with an umbrella in it with my mom and me at the country club, her plans had just been changed for her. Apparently her invitation had just been rescinded. Trying to avert The Glare, I sheepishly answered, "I don't know. We haven't talked about it."

"Well, I have a bunch of things I could use your help with, so maybe Sydney can go back to Miami today and you two can meet up after the weekend. Besides, I don't get to see you that often, so it might be nice to spend time with you…alone."

I love it when my mom phrases things that are really not open for discussion as a question, like "Steph, do you want to run to the grocery store and pick up a few things for me?" or "Steph, I know you despise the Rosenblums, but do you want to do me a huge favor and be my date to their dinner-party next week?" or "Steph, do you want to ask your girlfriend to get the hell out of my house?"

Point taken. No more "questions" needed to be asked. Dutifully, I responded, "Sure. I'll talk to her when she gets up."

"I'm running to a listing appointment. I love you." As she walked by the empty wine bottle that Sydney had left on the counter as a trophy, she picked it up as if it were hazardous material and extended her arm toward me. "Please put this in the recycle bin."

I freed her hands of the wretched bottle.

She pushed her glasses back onto the bridge of her nose and before she turned to leave, she did the Northeastern all girl's school talk-through-her-teeth-without-moving-her-jaw routine and said, "Stephanie, please don't *ever* bring someone home to me again until you have been dating them for *at least* a year."

My mother never calls me by my full name unless she's thoroughly annoyed. I gritted my teeth. *Nice going, Sydney. You fucked things up for both of us!*

Three days later, Sydney and I boarded a plane in Miami for LAX. She was flying through LA on her way home to Auckland, New Zealand for the holidays. I was almost at the end of my rope. Sydney hadn't received my mom's endorsement and that was weighing heavily on my mind. Not even the charming thank-you card that she sent impressed my mom. Oh wait. That's because she didn't send a thank-you card! Major, major faux pas! Who doesn't thank someone for graciously opening up their lovely home and including them in their most sacred family holiday? Apparently, Sydney Foster doesn't. This only enraged me further. But let's be honest, Sydney was causing me to pause even without the assistance of outside influences. I was pretty sure that our relationship was on its way to being a thing of the past.

Sydney's last words to me before she left for Auckland were that she thanked God for the flexibility I had in my schedule to travel with her because without me by her side, it would be impossible for her to go on the court. That's what I was left to mull over and over and over in my mind for the next three weeks while she spent Christmas in New Zealand. What I was really left with was a turning point.

6

*O*ne last shot to get the round ball into the square box

"United Flight 197 to Sydney now boarding through Gate 52."

I was waiting in the United Airlines lounge of the Los Angeles International Airport when I heard my flight being called. I stood up, straightened my sweatshirt and threw my bag over my shoulder as I gulped the rest of my beer. I laughed to myself when I looked at the ratty Asics running shoes on my feet. My sneakers were accompanied by a pair of men's Lucky Brand jeans that could not quite be considered "flattering" and a sweatshirt that could most aptly be described as "comfortable." I wasn't exactly a picture of stylish couture, so I was fairly confident that the photographers from *Vogue* would not be contacting me to coordinate a shoot for their cover. But hey, people don't dress up to get on planes anymore. It used to be that airline passengers looked more like church-going individuals than paying customers (although some would argue that there is not much of a difference!). I'm not as casual as some of the people I see rolling onto the planes, but I don't remember the last time I donned a seersucker suit and Mary Jane shoes in my window seat. Generally, I take great pride in my appearance, especially when I'm on my way to see my girlfriend. But not this time. Long gone were the days that I dressed to impress Sydney Foster. I was wearing sneakers with jeans for Christ's sake! It's a good thing the TSA security screeners don't profile professional female golfers. Add a sleeveless polo shirt and a visor to my outfit and I'd certainly be detained!

I sat down, buckled up, kicked off my Asics and prepared myself for the fourteen-hour flight. I was on my way to Sydney, the city, to ring in the New Year with Sydney, the girlfriend who might soon be no longer. Australia and Japan were the last legs of the ticket Sydney had handed me during the summer— the first class one with "no strings attached." Sydney asked me to fly over one week before the first tournament started so we could spend some time together away from the courts. I vacillated between going and not going but decided to go and give our relationship one last shot. I knew that this trip would either make or break us. Finally, I agreed to go and landed in Sydney on New Year's Eve morning.

Sydney is one of my favorite cities in the world. I lived there for a term when I was in college and took full advantage of my semester abroad. But it had been six years since I left, and I was eager to revisit this great city. I cleared customs and found Sydney waiting for me outside the baggage claim area. She was grinning from ear to ear and so was I. The only difference was that mine was forced. *Uh-oh.* Not one single butterfly in my stomach at the sight of my girlfriend whom I had not seen in three weeks. This was not a good sign. *Shit.* I felt bad for my lack of enthusiasm but then pardoned myself when I realized that maybe jetlag had stifled my excitement.

Sydney had grand plans for our first New Year's Eve celebration together. First we would go to dinner at a gorgeous restaurant on the Harbour and then back to a friend's apartment that she had borrowed for the night. It was a stone's throw from the famous Harbour Bridge, and Sydney planned for us to ring in the New Year with a bottle of Dom Perignon as we watched the fireworks explode and light up the sky above this glorious city. Try as I might, I could not muster the excitement to make it past ten o'clock and Sydney rang in the New Year alone. Despite my exhausting journey to the Land Down Under, I don't think I was suffering from jetlag.

I wanted so desperately for the feeling, or lack thereof, to pass and for my excitement toward Sydney to come back and overwhelm me. I knew it was only a matter of time before Sydney reacted to my apathy and the thought of another dreaded relationship confrontation sent my heart into palpitations. I felt like a child who was running through the house with a pair of scissors. At best, I would be reprimanded. At worst, I was going to impale myself on the sheers. I didn't like either scenario.

Thankfully, after our first night in the borrowed apartment by the Harbour, Sydney and I went to stay with her brother, Russell, in Bondi Beach. This excursion offered a much-needed reprieve from the one-on-one time with Sydney. Sydney and Russell were extremely close and he generally vacationed in Australia from Auckland each January so he could watch his little sister play tennis. Russell was laid back and very agreeable, and I liked him instantly.

To Russell, Sydney introduced me as her girlfriend. She had only recently come out to her family, but they all knew she dated women, and only women even without her saying so. She wasn't fooling anyone. Sydney walked like a man and talked like man— there was no way she was dating a man. There's a saying: "If it looks like a duck and acts like a duck, it's probably a duck." In the lesbian community, we substitute the word "dyke" for "duck."

Part of the way I have always gauged whether or not I thought I would have a future with a girlfriend is by imagining our two families melding— a litmus test of sorts. Although I enjoyed meeting Sydney's brother, I could not see myself joining that family. More to the point, I had absolutely no desire for Sydney to become a member of my family. I had been questioning my feelings for Sydney for some time but had really hoped that maybe she was right and some real "family time"— time away from the whole world of tennis— would shed a different light on our relationship. But it didn't help matters much that Sydney was already picking out china patterns between practice sessions. She was ready to have a wife and she was dead set on me. I tried to smile and shrug off her fantasies of us living the lesbian equivalent of the Cleaver lifestyle, but my spark for her was gone. The light that lit my fantasy world with her had burned out, and I knew it the second I set eyes on her in the Sydney airport. I just wasn't ready to admit it.

After our first night at Russell's apartment, I woke up in the morning and rolled over. I realized that I had stopped cuddling with Sydney. In fact, I had stopped touching her altogether. Our sex life had dwindled to the point that it was teetering on non-existent. Sydney had noticed it too and instantly began putting pressure on me. She would press her lips hard against mine, hoping it would lead to foreplay which would lead to sex. It didn't. And when she was rebuffed, she'd launch into a discussion and all but insist that I have sex with her. If I haven't appropriately communicated by now my fervent disdain for being told what to do, let me express it in unequivocal terms: I hate, loathe, despise being told what to do!

I felt trapped, and I was starting to boil inside. As the days passed, what initially drew me to Sydney was now a distant memory. I watched her naked body cross the room and the thought of being physical with her didn't even cross my mind. Although I couldn't admit it then, I can now. There were times when I would rather have gnawed my own arm off than extend it to touch her. I was getting to the point where even being nice was an effort. The more I tried not to be annoyed or not to argue with her, the harder it was to be pleasant. Anyone who has ever been in a failing relationship understands the extreme difficulty of trying to put on a "happy face" when the thought of that person just starts making your blood boil.

* * *

The view overlooking the Harbour from our hotel room was breathtaking. Sydney and I moved from her brother's apartment at Bondi Beach to the Four Seasons Hotel in Circular Quay a few days before the tournament started. While unpacking, I stared out the window and got lost in the panoramic view of the city from our room. For a moment, I forgot where I was and with whom I was, until Sydney emerged from the bathroom.

"It's a gorgeous view, isn't it?" She could almost pass for an Australian with her New Zealand accent.

I turned toward her and agreed, "I could never get tired of looking at that opera house."

"I didn't mean *that* view. I meant *this* one." Dripping wet from her shower and wearing only a towel around her waist, she pointed to her half-naked body.

A pair of pliers couldn't pry my lips apart to form an indulgent smile, but Sydney didn't seem to care. Instead, she removed the towel from her waist and began to pat herself dry.

"Love, I've come to a decision about something."

You're sending me home early? No, I wouldn't be *that* lucky!

"I feel I'm on the verge of a breakthrough with my singles, and I've decided to focus my efforts solely on that."

Does that mean she no longer has time for a relationship? Filled with hope, I listened curiously. Her cadence indicated that there was more to her decision.

"So, no more doubles— at least not on a regular basis. I'm only going to play doubles recreationally."

I had absolutely no idea what playing doubles "recreationally" meant and asked as much. "What does that mean?"

"Just that I'm tired of torturing myself on the doubles court. Doubles should be fun for me— something I can do to take my mind off of singles." She grimaced and then continued as if I were not sitting two feet from her. "Shit, I forgot that I already committed to playing mixed doubles at the Australian Open next week. Ah, no matter. I can just bail on my partner. God knows it's happened to me more times than I can count. No. I shouldn't do that. Okay, fine. I'll play mixed there, but then that's it for a while." Seeming to remember that I was in the room, she glanced at me with a smile. "And you know what the best part is? I'll have much more time to spend with you."

Great. Sydney had decided to stop torturing herself on the doubles court, and I couldn't help thinking that now she'd have more time to torture me. I looked toward the window that separated us from the city below. If there had been a way to open it, I just might have jumped out.

Casey and Trish checked in the day after we did. Yes, I did say Trish. Surprise, surprise! Casey's still-non-girlfriend-best-friend had made the journey to Australia. Unfortunately for Casey, Trish had no intention of going down under on her. Anyway, I ran into the non-couple couple in the lobby upon their arrival. I spotted Casey from across the reception. Immediately, I got a skip in my step and butterflies swirled in my stomach. I never asked myself why. More of that "Don't Ask, Don't Tell," I suppose.

Much to Sydney's chagrin, Casey arrived in Australia with a new doubles partner, Marisa Davis (whose husband traveled with her full-time— see, there *are* husbands and boyfriends on the Tour!). Although Sydney and Casey had managed to regroup from their brief re-teaming and were back on friendly terms, Sydney was not altogether supportive of Casey's new partnership. Marisa, another Tour veteran, had formerly held both the Number 1 singles and doubles rankings. Casey saw an opportunity to reach the pinnacle of the rankings with Marisa. The Davis/Matthews team was predicted to produce greatness and capture the Number 1 ranking by year's end. Ironically, Casey had decided to go on hiatus from singles so she could focus on doubles and that World Number 1 ranking.

Both Sydney and Casey made their debuts at the Sydney Open with their respective new resolves, and one week later, they both exited with success. Sydney fought through the draw to the singles final and added another champion's trophy to her collection, while Casey and Marisa claimed the doubles title adding new trophies to their own hearty collections. Hooray for Sydney! Drinks all around! Was that convincing?

* * *

We all reconvened in the lobby of the Crown Towers Hotel in Melbourne the next week for the first Grand Slam tournament of the year— the Australian Open. Sydney had climbed back into the Top 20, but just barely. As the World Number 20 ranked player, she secured herself a prestigious seeded position. She held the distinction of being the Number 20 seed at the Australian Open as well as the not-so-prestigious distinction of being the first seeded player to be eliminated from the singles draw. Her loss came in the third round. The match was rather unremarkable and was over very quickly. Basically, Sydney could not hit a return of service in the court to save her life. She was equally challenged to place a serve inside the service box. She lost her temper a few games into the match and I feared for the linesmen, the chair umpire and anyone else who didn't see things her way. Sydney came off the court pouting and cursing. I did my best to cajole her out of her mood so she'd be prepared to play mixed doubles.

Somehow pushing her early singles loss to the back of her mind, Sydney and her male counterpart rallied through the mixed doubles draw to the finals, leaving pairs of victims in their wake. After a quick warm-up, Sydney sneaked up behind me in the players' lounge. I could literally feel her breathing down my neck.

"Who are you texting?" she asked firmly.

"Paige. Why?" I said defensively.

The smile on her face disappeared. "What are you texting her?"

I snickered and said, "Sydney, remember? We talked about this. Boundaries. I got 'em. I like 'em. I need 'em." Paige was a huge source of contention between us. Sydney hated that I had become friends with the ex-love-of-my-life, despite the fact that Sydney and I spent practically every waking moment with her ex-girlfriend. Apparently, Sydney thought it entirely normal to demand that I share the contents of any incoming texts, voicemails or e-mails from Paige with her. It would be an understatement to say that her demands were unwelcome.

Obviously not persuaded by my request for privacy, she persisted, "If you have nothing to hide, I just think you should let me read them."

Just then, the Tour massage therapist appeared and asked Sydney if she were ready for her rub-down. Thank God! Her timing was perfect. I knew Sydney wasn't about to give up grilling me about Paige— despite that she was due to play in the Australian Open mixed doubles final shortly. I relaxed my jaw and said, "Lucky you."

"Actually, lucky her! She gets to put her hands all over my body. Jealous?"

I rolled my eyes. "Oh yeah, terribly."

It took me a while, but as soon as I had recovered from my blinding jealousy, I walked out of the players' lounge into a sea of people swarming to watch the final matches. I meandered through the crowd and then found my way into the small stadium court next to the Rod Laver Arena, which housed the much bigger stadium court. Sydney and her partner were about to square off against the Number 1 seeds. Finally! Sydney had gotten a draw where she faced the top seeds in the final and not the first round!

The stadium was filled to capacity and I took my seat in the players' box. Just after the warm-up began, Sydney sprinted over to me. She raised her clenched fist toward me and said, "I forgot to take this off in the locker room. Be a doll and keep it secure for me while I bring home another title." She opened her hand and passed me her sterling silver Cartier Roadster watch. "You should wear it— it goes much better with the ring I bought you than that old one you're wearing." She winked and, drawing even more attention to herself, loudly said, "Cheers, love!"

as she backpedaled toward her changeover chair.

I looked at my wrist. *That old one I'm wearing?* Sydney was referring to the two-tone yellow gold and sterling silver Rolex that my parents had surprised me with for my thirteenth birthday. Her voice was filled with such condescension that for a split second, I actually considered doing as she'd instructed. Mentally slapping myself across the face, I quickly came to my senses, wiped the crystal face of my "old" Rolex with my shirt until it shined and deposited her watch into my pocket. As I repositioned myself in my seat, I rolled my eyes and wondered why Sydney hadn't simply put her precious Cartier in her racket bag for safe-keeping. I concluded that it was probably just one more way for her to mark what she considered to be her territory.

I had the displeasure of sitting a few rows over from a group of people I would not exactly call Sydney's biggest fans. Tennis, like golf, is known as being an extremely civilized sport. Silence is demanded before play commences. Clapping and cheering are contained. It's considered bad etiquette to clap or cheer at the mistake of a player. Just like burping at the dining room table in the middle of dinner (or handing a hostess a present and telling her what to do with it), clapping at an unforced error is just not done. The people sitting next to me were clapping every time Sydney made a mistake, and it seemed like their euphoria was going to launch them out of their seats. I knew that Sydney didn't have the best reputation on the Tour. She was never going to win the prize for being "The Most Loved," but I had no idea just how much she was disliked until then. It's one thing for her to have a reputation for being explosive and intense among her fellow players and opponents, but it's an entirely different thing to invoke such glaring disdain from strangers in the crowd. A part of me wanted to tell the boisterous blokes next to me to shut the hell up as they jeered and laughed at Sydney's double faults or missed shot opportunities. But just as I was about to come to her defense, Bad Sydney would appear on the court and silence me. And then I would think maybe they had a point.

The past year's champions denied Sydney and her partner the Australian Open mixed doubles championship. They claimed a consecutive victory by defeating Sydney and her partner in a nerve-racking three-set match. Sydney was incensed— especially since Casey and Marisa were on the stadium court in the Rod Laver Arena accepting their trophies for winning the women's Australian Open doubles championship. Fiercely competitive, Sydney was outraged by the blow to her ego.

After the match, Sydney was silent for most of the drive back to the hotel. We walked into our suite and I opened a bottle of wine. As I poured a glass, Sydney approached me from behind. Every hair on my body stood on end and not because I was excited. I subtly shrugged and slipped to the side. She didn't understand how I didn't think she was God's gift to me. She assumed that her touch would send electricity through my veins and that I would rip my clothes off and dive into bed with her. But I had reached the point where closing my eyes and hiding behind fantasies that Sydney was not the person actually touching me could no longer carry me through sessions of intimacy with her.

Once I escaped her grasp, I poured myself a glass of wine. Before I had filled the glass, Sydney exploded. In a fiery display similar to her outbursts on the court, she erupted behind the closed doors of our room. As she yelled, she burst into tears. Through her tears she screamed that I wasn't giving her enough, that I didn't love her enough, that I didn't make her feel loved, that I was stubborn, that I was cold, that I was insensitive and that I was inflexible.

And the truth is, at that point I may have been several of those things. I had lost count of how many arguments we'd gotten into in Melbourne, but I was determined to make this one our last. As she spewed profanities at me, I sat in silence. I had lost all desire to defend myself or argue with her. Clearly, our relationship was over. Well, it was clear to me but not to Sydney.

When she completed her monologue, which had reached ear-piercing decibels, I told her she was right. I wasn't giving her enough. But it wasn't because I was stubborn or inflexible. Rather, it was because I felt differently toward her than she did toward me.

Finally! I had *finally* admitted what I had been denying to myself for so long— I was not in love with Sydney Foster. My admission didn't go over so well and she locked herself in the bathroom to sob for an hour. The sounds that came from the bathroom were horrendous. Holy Mary Mother of God! At times like these, even the token Jewess is happy to employ her adopted, religious tongue— wafer or no wafer.

I sat at the table and sipped my wine, not knowing what to do. I was on the other side of the world and I just wanted to go home. The trap of being a lawyer was almost looking like sugar-coated candy compared with this instant replay routine. This was the third time I had tried to break up with Sydney *this week*. Each time I tried to leave, she begged me to stay. Once, she threw herself in front of the door and refused to let me leave. The second time, she sobbed uncontrollably. Both times she persuaded me to change my mind— how, I'm not quite sure. But then, at least for a little while, she behaved herself before getting obsessive again. She was no longer the person she had been when I met her. Now she was just aggressive, obsessive and abrasive. I was not even attracted to her anymore. I had hoped for months that she would revert to the fun, cool girl that I experienced during our time at Wimbledon and that we could somehow get back to being good together. I had been holding my breath and biting my tongue, but all it had earned me was a purple face and a lisp.

I stood outside the bathroom door and between her wails I told Sydney that I thought it would be better if I left and went home directly from Melbourne. To this, she responded, "If you leave me, I'll quit playing tennis. I can't play without you by my side."

How unfair is that? I had been feeling the pressure of holding Sydney's happiness in my hands for a while. She had even recruited her friends to tell me how happy she was— all because of me.

Her words reverberated in my mind. *Do you know how much pressure that is? So if I break up with you and make you unhappy your tennis will go to shit, and it will all be because of me! You want me to be your savior and I just can't do it. It's bad enough that you've driven me to drink almost an entire bottle of wine and have made me crazy enough to sit here talking to myself!*

I know, just leave! Right?

Ha! If only it were that easy. I swear, in some entirely Machiavellian plot, Sydney had arranged my travel itinerary so that if I had tried to leave before my scheduled flights, I would have had to fly from Melbourne to Tokyo, stay a whole day there and then fly from Tokyo to Los Angeles. Truly, I was coming to believe she was diabolical. I could change my ticket and fly directly from Melbourne to Los Angeles for the bargain price of $8,000. I had never been in an $8,000 fight and I wasn't about to get into one now.

When Sydney finally emerged from the bathroom, she had come to a conclusion. She didn't care that we felt differently about each other. She still wanted me and would take me any way she could get me.

Outta the way, sister! It's my turn to hibernate in the bathroom. In the tub. With a razor blade!

Sydney even suggested that I would grow to love her. The thought of it made my skin crawl. This was not some arranged marriage and I was not some thirteen-year-old impoverished farm girl! She refused to take "no" for an answer and once again declined what she apparently thought was a negotiable invitation to break up with her. Remember what I said before about what happens when you run with scissors in your hands? Not only was I yelled at, but I had just impaled myself on them!

My only alternative to throwing down my credit card to escape was to keep the peace for another week and continue on to Tokyo before heading home. That's what I planned to do.

7

*A*dvantage Casey Matthews

Sydney and I almost made it out of the country without exchanging cross words. I bid farewell to Australia, and Sydney took issue with the skip in my step as I made my way toward the plane and a heated argument quickly ensued. Apparently, I appeared just a little too happy about being one step closer to home for her taste. I was in desperate need of a time-out and was determined to take one, despite the fact that Sydney would be sitting right next to me on the plane.

We emerged from the plane in Tokyo after almost nine hours of silence. I still hadn't cooled off enough to want to engage in a mature conversation with Sydney as we collected our bags in the Tokyo Narita International Airport. We pushed our trolleys outside in silence to where a big coach bus was parked. I was expecting an official tournament car to be awaiting our arrival, but there was not a single one in sight. Sydney pointed toward the big Greyhound-like bus and said, "That's us." The directors of the Tokyo Classic chartered coach buses to transport the players and their guests during the tournament. If you're Venus Williams, the tournament provides you with a driver and a Mercedes. But for the rest of the players, the wheels on the bus go round and round. I have to admit, throwing Sydney under the bus *did* cross my mind.

After thirty seconds in the bus looking down at the traffic, I was thankful that we weren't in a car. Driving a car in Tokyo seemed like nothing short of volunteering for a suicide mission. It was a two-hour ride from the airport to the InterContinental Hotel on the outskirts of

Tokyo. To no avail, Sydney attempted to engage me in conversation for most of the second hour. Even her announcement that our suite would have heated toilet seats only elicited a caustic "neat" from my lips.

By the time we checked in and went to our room, I decided to start speaking full sentences to Sydney again, albeit somewhat begrudgingly. Before I was able to squeeze out an entire thought, Casey knocked on the door. Her room was just down the hall from ours, and she had come to collect us so we could all ride the bus to the courts together. After Trish had left Melbourne halfway through the Australian Open, Casey and I took refuge in spending time together as we had done the previous fall. The more time we spent together, I was beginning to think that I was taking more than just refuge in her, and she in me. I thanked God that Casey was in Tokyo. But whenever I'd start to dwell thoughts of Casey, I reminded myself that she was Sydney's ex-girlfriend.

Casey seemed to find me wherever I was and direct a special smile at me. We could dismiss some of our encounters as chance meetings, but coincidence could not explain our express desire to spend time together away from the courts. Just as I had overlooked the numerous red flags about Sydney from day one, I ignored the tell-tale signs that perhaps—no, not perhaps, rather *most definitely*— I was feeling something more than just friendship for Casey. The thought of it seemed so outrageous, impossible, unacceptable, inappropriate and inconceivable that I was blind to the obvious and just enjoyed the euphoria I felt at even the hint of her name.

A few days after the tournament had started, Casey and I chose to steal away on an excursion with some of the other players on the Tour while Sydney was at practice. We had the very distinct honor of being the invited guests of Asashoryu, Japan's Master Sumo wrestler, at one of his private practices. Casey, Marisa and I filed off the bus and sat on the floor of the dojo, Indian style, and watched the gentle giants perform. Casey and I were practically sitting on top of each other as we tried to keep our legs tangled in a position I had not found myself in since my afternoons of mandatory naptime in kindergarten. I laughed at the irony of the situation: there we were, watching in awe as the massive creatures practiced their art in front of us, while we distinctly ignored the "real" huge pink elephant in the room— that

Casey and I had feelings for each other.

Still heatedly envious of Casey's recent victory at the Australian Open, Sydney disregarded her resolution of only playing recreational doubles. She asked for a wildcard into the Tokyo Open the day before the draw was to be released. Her request was granted and Sydney made a last-minute pairing with a young girl named Lindy Brooks whose regular doubles partner had fallen ill. The doubles draw was Sydney's only hope for success in Tokyo since she had lost her second-round singles match. In Sydney's mind, only one team stood in her way— Casey and Marisa, the Number 1 seeds.

The much anticipated Sydney/Lindy/Casey/Marisa match-up came at the end of the week in the semifinals of the Tokyo Classic. I was on the edge of my seat. My nerves were in knots. I could feel my heart in my throat as I gritted my teeth and clenched my fists. I watched nervously as Casey bulleted a forehand cross court. Lindy returned the forehand with great precision, ripping another topspin forehand down the line. Marisa, who was standing at the net, lunged for the ball and punched it back at Sydney's feet with exacting force, making the volley look effortless. As the rally continued, I could not help but think of myself as the tennis ball, bouncing back and forth from Casey to Sydney. Casey anticipated the next shot and rushed to the net from the baseline. Just as she completed her split step at the service line, Sydney pummeled a shot directly at Marisa. She got her racket on the ball, but it popped off her strings and soared over Sydney's head toward the baseline. Sydney had forced the error and the ball was long.

"Shit," I whispered inaudibly.

The chair umpire announced, "Game, set and match, Lindy Brooks and Sydney Foster."

The stadium was filled with disappointed fans, who had been cheering ferociously for Casey and Marisa during the gripping three-set match. Their disappointment quickly gave way to clapping and the audience rose to their feet, applauding the four athletes for their efforts and for the exciting match they had just provided.

My heart sank. Sydney had now secured her place in the doubles final— for the third time in her career, although she had never left with the winner's trophy. She was so hungry for a win that she had been just a little too celebratory on the court, jumping up and down and holding her index finger in the air as if to say, "I'm Number 1!" I was sitting courtside in the players' box as Sydney and Lindy embraced to celebrate their victory. I smiled and clapped when they won the match. No one would have doubted that I was anything but the proud girlfriend of the winner of the match. Secretly, though, there was not an ounce of energy in my body that wasn't willing a win for Casey.

I watched Casey walk to the net to shake her opponents' hands, my eyes fixed on her perfectly round, firm butt, showcased in her tight blue spandex tennis skirt. A hot flush washed over me. My heart filled with disappointment when I saw the despair on her face, which was only exacerbated by Sydney's excessive gloating. Casey quickly collected her things, waved to the crowd, somehow managing a smile, and exited the court.

Not surprisingly, Sydney took great delight in savoring her victory after what she and many others considered an embarrassing result at the Australian Open. She loved the attention and took her time exiting the court, signing autographs on the way out. I had no desire to linger and watch Sydney revel in the fanfare that was meant for Casey and Marisa. As Sydney basked in her glory, I weaved through the chairs and walked down the stairs of the players' box toward the private entrance to the players' lounge. I flashed my badge to the security guard standing in front of the door and made my way toward the lounge, following the sound of Casey's voice.

Our eyes locked, I frowned and sadly said, "Bad luck." I always hated saying that to the players when they lost because I thought it sounded so disingenuous. But a simple "bad luck" was all that was expected and all that was necessary. How unfortunate that I had fallen for a tennis player. Contact sport rituals are so much more gratifying—or at least they would be to me— than those of the more civilized game of tennis. Football players come off the field, win or lose, slap one another on the ass and say, "Good game." The slaps they give are like the little pats you get on your birthday. Oh, how I longed to give Casey "one to grow on" now.

"Your girlfriend's a total disaster," Casey muttered. "The good news is that I get to go home tomorrow and don't have to deal with her for a while!" She paused and then snapped, "Have fun having congratulatory sex with that nightmare tonight. Too bad you'll be thinking of someone else."

Instantly, I could feel the color vanishing from my cheeks and I knew my face had gone white. I think I had known for months that I was harboring a secret crush on Casey, but I always refused to acknowledge it. Now Casey had made an overt reference to the incessant flirting we'd been doing all week and, hearing it out loud, exploded my fantasy world to life! I was speechless.

Shit, I'm gonna need another U-Haul. But seriously, I didn't see it coming. I didn't! Honestly! Ah, what tangled webs we mortals weave!

Just then, Sydney came bouncing down the hallway, making her presence known with her usual boisterous and obnoxious nature. I felt numb. Somehow I parted my lips to congratulate her, but it took every ounce of strength that I had. I could feel Casey's fixed gaze on my face but couldn't bear to look at her as I congratulated someone other than the person I'd been secretly cheering for.

Casey retreated into the Tour office to retrieve her prize money. I stood in the hallway talking to Sydney but couldn't hear a thing she was saying, as my concentration was now suddenly and completely consumed by Casey. Sydney stood before me with a huge smile on her face. I wanted to rip the braces off her teeth! She was still savoring her victory and decided to start her celebration with a massage. I pounced on the opportunity that had just presented itself to me and quickly formulated my escape so I could leave immediately— with Casey.

When Sydney turned and headed down the hallway toward the training room, I saw Casey coming out of the Tour office, walking in my direction. She looked at me and smiled as if Sydney didn't exist. It wasn't the kind of smile friends give each other. She winked at me and motioned, ever so slightly, with her head. I could read her mind and knew that I needed to put my plan into action immediately.

Pleased and excited at how easy my escape had become, I quickly ran into the players' restaurant and prepared a cup of trail mix for the road. With the excitement of a five-year-old on the verge of opening a birthday present, I sprinkled some peanut M&Ms into the mix, knowing that this was Casey's favorite snack. Hurriedly collecting the rest of my things from the locker room, I rushed out the door toward the transportation area, filled with happy adrenaline. As I rounded the corner, my harried nature was replaced with a huge smile and a sense of calm. Casey was a few feet in front of me, heading toward the door, loaded down with her Babolat racket bag on one shoulder and a Nike gym bag on the other, trying to maneuver the hallway with filled hands.

I watched her hobble toward the door, unable to lend her a hand at the risk of raising an eyebrow. Unexpectedly, we now had a façade to maintain and people would talk if we appeared too friendly. I was sure that people were talking already. It must have been curious to others that I would leave the tournament site so quickly and not stay with Sydney to help celebrate her win. But at the moment, I didn't care. Time alone with Casey was a commodity and I wanted so desperately to take advantage of it.

Today our destination was not as glamorous as the master sumo excursion, but we got on the bus and happily assumed our everyday positions in seats directly across from each other. It was just the two of us. Casey was, of course, disappointed about her loss, about leaving the next day and about what a disaster Sydney had been on the court. She hated losing. Even more, she hated losing to Sydney. I could see the distress and uncertainty in her eyes. I would do anything to make her smile. I reached across the aisle and handed her the cup of trail mix that I had made to surprise her. Her eyes brightened and, as if on cue, she smiled.

I smiled back— this time with a wide, toothy grin— and thought, *one point for Stephie!*

We were like two giddy teenagers and took turns taking aim at each other's mouths with M&Ms and laughed as handfuls flew across the aisle and bounced off our cheeks, heads, noses and teeth before landing on the floor. We relished the lighthearted aura that had engulfed us after leaving Sydney and such a stressful and unpleasant atmosphere. The bus navigated its way through the narrow streets of Tokyo, toward the hotel and we enjoyed every second of the ride and each other. It was as if we were in our own world.

We arrived at the hotel and rode the elevator to the eleventh floor, where both of our rooms were; the tension between us was palpable. Neither of us wanted to go our separate ways, so we decided to drop off our things and have a coffee at Starbucks. I threw my bag on the floor of my room and looked for paper to write a note to Sydney. She liked to keep me on a short leash and I had become accustomed to scribbling hurried notes to her that I knew would shield me from a barrage of questions when I returned from wherever it was that I had gone without her— on the occasions that I could actually go someplace without her. I hated checking in with the "warden," but this time, I gladly wrote the note because leaving it was a small price to pay for the pleasure of being in Casey's company uninterrupted for a couple of hours. I left the note on the desk and raced out the door. I could feel the huge the-cat's-about-to-eat-the-canary grin on my face. I suddenly heard a disapproving voice in my head snickering and hissing as if it were my conscience. I silenced it. *Get your mind out of the gutter— we're just going for coffee!*

With a combined feeling of excitement and trepidation, I closed my room door behind me. When I rounded the corner near the elevator, Casey was already waiting for me. I tried to ignore the emotions I was experiencing in my stomach, but they almost knocked me off my feet. Maintaining my composure, Casey and I exited the hotel only to feel the harsh winter wind hit us in the face. But we didn't seem to care as we felt protected and cozy in the bubble of our own world.

When we arrived at Starbucks, I instinctively opened the door and held it for Casey. *What the hell are you doing?! You don't open doors! You hate touching nasty, dirty doorknobs. You're a germ freak. You don't even open doors for yourself! What is going on here?*

We walked to the counter and placed our usual orders: I'm a grande-vanilla-latte-with-skim-milk addict and Casey's a simple grande latte kinda girl. Of course, she also sweetens it with packet after packet of brown sugar. So as she stood at the sugar station, I secured two seats in front of the window.

Sitting in a crowded Starbucks in the middle of Tokyo, with the aroma of freshly-ground coffee beans permeating the air, and surrounded by strangers, we couldn't have been more alone or more happy. As people swarmed in for their early evening caffeine fix, we pushed our chairs closer and closer together. Our legs touched and her warmth sent shockwaves through my body. Suddenly, I felt short of breath.

I smiled as Casey sipped her latte and licked the foam from her lips. There was no place else on Earth that I would have preferred to be. It was there, at that very moment, in a crowded Starbucks in the middle of Tokyo, that I knew that Casey Matthews had stolen my heart.

One hour had passed, in what seemed like the span of a few seconds. Casey and I both knew that we had to leave the haven we had found at Starbucks and go back to the hotel, but we kept purposely getting lost in conversation. We had been talking about Paige and Trish and how much we craved the kind of passion we associated with them. Neither of us had felt a connection like that before or since.

Until now.

We glanced at our watches nervously and there was an awkward silence. Finally, Casey addressed the pink elephant in the room that we had both been ignoring. "Stephie, thank God you were here this week. I'm really gonna miss you when I leave tomorrow. Honestly, I don't know what I would've done without you here."

Casey had started calling me "Stephie." It was a term of endearment. When I heard my nickname come out of her mouth as only she could say it, it gave me a special feeling in my stomach. At this particular moment, I was left breathless. There was another awkward silence. We were both thinking the same thing, but neither of us could vocalize what we had not dared to say. I looked at Casey and tried to read her mind as she stared out the window.

A few seconds later she turned back toward me and broke the silence. "I…I don't know if *this*…if *we* are anything, but…"

I interrupted. I couldn't stop myself. I blurted, "Casey, I think you know that this *is* something and that there *is* something between us. I think I've had feelings for you for months. I just never wanted to admit it." Suddenly, there was not a drop of moisture left in my mouth.

Oh, God! I said it! That makes it real. What have I done?

Casey stared at me silently and looked so shocked that a feather could have probably pushed her out of her chair.

I had just broken the seal, so why stop there? I didn't. And then, despite myself, I continued, "Casey I think you're great. I'm attracted to you and I crave your company. I…I can't get enough…" Suddenly, I found myself on autopilot and I began confessing things to her that I hadn't even admitted to myself. Casey reminded me of Paige, although she was physically the exact opposite of clean-cut, all-American Paige with her splotchy hair, numerous piercings and ink-stained shoulder. I never thought I could be as drawn to someone as I was to Paige, but I found myself magnetically drawn to Casey. I was consumed with thoughts of her laugh, her smile, her eyes, her heart. The funny thing is that when I thought about her, I didn't fantasize about ripping her clothes off and jumping into bed. My thoughts transcended the physical and focused on the tenderness. I had lost count of how many times I had been sitting next to her on the bus during the week, wanting to hop across the aisle and sit with her, just so I could be closer to her. Even on the bus earlier that afternoon, I felt like I was a teenager engrossed with puppy love. I wanted so badly to take her hand in mine. But now, at that very moment, I desperately wanted to hold her face in my hands and kiss her.

I didn't take a breath once during my confession. Talking to Casey was effortless. With every word that poured out of my mouth, I could feel my face blush more and more. It was the simplicity of Casey's complexity that was the catalyst of my infatuation. She sat with her hands wrapped around her coffee cup, which was empty, absorbing all that I had confessed. Her intoxicatingly blue eyes were piercing. Quite possibly her best feature.

"I...I have feelings for you, too. You are so different with me than you are with Sydney," she admitted.

Wham! One mention of Sydney's name was enough to make me feel as if I'd run full-speed into a brick wall. I *was* different with Casey than I was with Sydney, and there was a simple explanation for it.

"Casey, she knows I'm not in love with her and she won't let go. She's making it impossible for me to let go either. She needs more than I can give her and she deserves it." I felt a pit in my stomach as her face dropped, presumably from the guilt she felt about our confessions. I refused to let Sydney spoil our mood. "Casey, we don't have much more time alone together. I don't want to waste these precious minutes talking about Sydney and the problems we're having."

"Stephie, I've been trying to hide my feelings from you and everyone else for a while. The truth is, I'm jealous of Sydney because I can't stop thinking about you. In fact, you're all I think about lately. I wake up every morning excited to see *you*."

My heart dropped into my stomach right then and there.

Casey and I traded admissions until we both agreed that it was time to leave. I dreaded that our time together was about to come to an end, but I knew that we had to leave because Sydney was probably pacing the halls counting the minutes I had been gone and impatiently awaiting my return. I would have given anything to be able to sit there longer with Casey and feel her hand in mine.

We gathered our things and got up to leave. Again, I held the door for Casey. I had a skip in my step as we made the short journey back to the hotel but tried to walk slowly so as to prolong our time together.

A few minutes from having to go our separate ways, I stepped into the bay of the revolving door right behind Casey and fell into her. We laughed and continued into the lobby like two capricious kids. I couldn't believe that I had just confided my most secret feelings and thoughts to her. I was smiling inside and out as we waited for the elevator. Our private time together was about to come to an end for the afternoon. The doors opened on the eleventh floor and we whispered our good-byes. Casey turned to the right and I headed to the left toward my room. Our eyes met once more before we rounded the corner as we both turned around for one last glimpse.

I entered my room unable to rid my face of the smile that Casey inspired. It was the first time I had returned to the room all week consumed with happiness. Sydney was sitting in front of her computer and grinned when I walked in to hand her the coffee that I brought her.

"Ah, thanks, love."

"No problem."

Note to self: make sure to thank Casey for insisting that I return to the room with coffee for Sydney. Funny what a little cup of coffee can do!

I struggled to find a nicety to toss to Sydney. "Good job today. Only one more and then you can hold yet another trophy high." Here's the part I had to force out: "I'm proud of you either way." It almost pained me to say it.

When I was in the sixth grade, Michael Schetz called me a name on the soccer field during gym class which, at the time, I found objectionable and offensive. I retaliated by winding up and thrusting my foot with all of my force into his crotch. He fell to the ground gasping for air and crying like a baby. I remember thinking, *who's the bitch now?!* Later that night our doorbell rang and Michael's mother had dragged him to my house demanding an apology. My mother made me apologize, only because she wanted those "damn hillbillies" out of her house. I said I was sorry, but there was not one bone in my body that meant it. No matter how hard I tried, I could not feel sorry for humiliating Michael on the soccer field.

I felt that same feeling of frustration as I stood next to Sydney. Despite really trying, I just could not muster any real excitement for her. Sure, I told Sydney that I was happy for her, but I was about as thrilled as I was sorry for kicking Michael Schetz in the balls. In spite of my best efforts, I was having an extremely difficult time pretending that I felt any emotion toward her.

As she did after every match, Sydney replayed every point and commented on each one. Our room had an amazing view of the Tokyo skyline and I stared out the window at all of the tall buildings, certain that my eyes were glazing over as Sydney yammered on. My mind was back at Starbucks, and was only brought back to the conversation in Room 1101 when I heard Casey's name.

Emerging from the memory, I looked at Sydney. "What?"

"How's Casey?" Sydney repeated.

"She's alright. Bummed, of course. But she's psyched to be leaving tomorrow."

"Of course she is. She can't wait to get home and drool over Trish in person. What's she doing for dinner?"

"I don't know. I didn't ask." It amazed me how easily that lie rolled off my tongue. I never thought of myself as a liar and despite all of our problems, I was not proud of deceiving Sydney. "I don't really feel like changing and going out to dinner. Do you mind if we just stay in?"

"That's fine with me. We should see if Casey wants to order room service with us," Sydney suggested.

I volunteered to call Casey and invite her to join us for dinner. Filled with excitement that I had to contain, I picked up the phone. Casey must have been waiting by the phone because she answered before it finished ringing even once. As if I hadn't planned on asking her to join us for dinner, I casually extended the invitation.

In a hushed voice, Casey responded nervously. "Was she mad that you wanted to stay in?"

"No."

"Was she mad that you were gone for so long?"

"No! Would you just get your ass over here so we can order some food?!"

Ten minutes later, there was a knock on the door. I acted calm and cool— or at least tried to. Sydney answered the door and Casey made her way into the room. I was sitting at the foot of the bed and Casey joined me. Sydney sat back down at the computer with her back to us. Before Casey and I could get lost in each other's eyes silently wondering but knowing what the other was thinking, Sydney turned around and barked, "I'm starving. Let's order."

God, she's like a bull in a china closet!

When the food arrived, we ate together, talking and laughing, as if this dynamic was normal. It was anything but that. I was sitting across from my girlfriend (Sydney), who was sitting next to her ex-girlfriend (Casey), who was sitting next to her ex-girlfriend's girlfriend (me), with whom she had just spent the afternoon confessing her feelings. We formed the perfect lesbian triangle. There were red flags everywhere, and I (again!) ignored every single one of them. I suppose I couldn't be expected to start listening to reason now!

When we finished eating, Casey surreptitiously winked at me and said, "Hey, I brought my DVDs. Do you guys want to watch something? How about *Sex and the City?*"

"No!" I quickly yelled, defiantly. "I'm sick of *Sex and the City.*" Truthfully, I love Carrie, Samantha, Miranda and Charlotte, but I wanted to watch a movie. My reasoning was simple. The longer the movie, the more time I would get to spend with Casey. I would have given anything for a DVD of *The Thorn Birds* to keep us occupied for hours upon hours. Alas, the movie of choice was *Laurel Canyon*, which was no marathon movie, but it was better than a thirty-minute episode of *Sex and the City*. *Laurel Canyon*, a movie about dysfunctional relationships, with delicious sexual overtones, would have to do. I couldn't think of a more appropriate movie, given the situation.

We all piled into the king-sized bed together to watch the movie. I was sandwiched between Sydney and Casey. Our threesome got comfortable as we pulled the covers over our bodies and settled in. Realizing the absurdity of the situation, I rolled my eyes heavenward. *God, help me. Is this really happening or am I in the twilight zone? Am I really sitting in bed in the dark with Sydney and Casey? How cozy! This scenario is an absolute joke. No one could have written a better script. Isn't this what people fantasize about?* Only this wasn't my fantasy. It was only a part of it. I was in bed with them both, but as usual, felt crowded with Sydney next to me.

It wasn't five minutes before I was boiling under the covers, but there was no chance that I was going to extricate myself. The sweatbox that I had placed myself in was not without its rewards. About an hour into the movie, Casey's hand gently found mine. My heart began to gallop when her skin touched mine. A few seconds later, I shifted so my hand covered Casey's. I held on to her hand as if it were my last possession on Earth. I had no clue what was going on in the movie, and I didn't care. The only thing I did know was that I didn't want to let go of Casey. The clock was ticking and as every minute passed, Casey's time in Tokyo and around me was slipping away. The movie ended. Sydney got out of bed and went back over to the computer. She turned the lights on and snapped her head back toward us, sharply glaring at the bed. "What the hell…?"

Casey and I were frozen as Sydney charged toward us. Paranoia began to overtake me and for a brief second, I panicked. I thought, for sure, that Sydney had somehow seen our fingers intertwined underneath the blankets. Suddenly stopping near the foot of the bed, Sydney said, "Oh, it's just a shadow. I thought I saw a cockroach on the wall."

When Sydney turned from us, I regained bodily movement and relinquished Casey's hand for fear of getting caught. We both sat up, still under the covers, my heart pounding.

I heard the infamous AOL voice announcing "You've got mail" as Sydney logged on to check her e-mail. Concentrating on the screen, she pompously joked, "Casey, I can't believe Marisa missed so many easy volleys today. You sure you don't want to give playing with me another shot? No one's got quicker hands at the net than I do."

Casey threw the covers off her angrily and slid from the bed. "Sydney, why do you always insist on ruining a perfectly good time by being such an asshole? Can't you ever just let anything go?"

"C'mon, Casey. I was kidding."

"No, you weren't and I'm too tired to argue with you. I need to go pack." Halfway toward the door, she smiled tenderly at me and I wistfully watched her amble out of our room.

The second the door closed behind Casey, my mood changed immediately. I was stuck in the room with my girlfriend, whom I was not in love with, and the object of my affection was just down the hall— so close, yet so far away. When Sydney joined me in bed, I completed the final part of the plan that Casey and I had concocted earlier. With a shrill of surprise in my voice, I announced, "Shit! Casey left her DVDs here. I better go take them to her before she realizes it and has a meltdown. I'll be back." I sprung off the bed with cat-like speed. I didn't know if Sydney was going to try to persuade me not to go to Casey's room, but I didn't give her the opportunity. As quickly as I announced that Casey had forgotten her DVDs, I was out the door and on the way to her room. Time was of the essence and within seconds, I was standing in front of Casey's door wearing only my perfectly-worn-in white T-shirt and favorite Calvin Klein boxer shorts.

I took a deep breath, and knocked. Casey answered immediately and with an unmistakably nervous look on her face, let me in. As the door closed behind us, our eyes locked and the reality that I had just raced out of my girlfriend's room under false pretenses began to settle in. In fact, it hit me like a ton of bricks and I could feel my heart racing in my chest and in other unmentionable parts of my body. After a few seconds of silence, I smiled, winked and said, "I think you forgot these." I extended my arm to hand Casey the black case holding her DVDs.

"What did you tell Sydney?" Her hand grazed mine when she took the case, sending a surge through my body.

What did she think I told Sydney? That we planned for Casey to leave her DVDs in our room so I could sneak away and bring them to her?

I smiled fondly and said, "I told her exactly what I'm doing— returning your DVDs."

We continued to stare at each other with passion-filled eyes, both of us becoming increasingly more nervous while at the same time exponentially more excited. I stood with my back to the door and my arms folded across my chest, wondering where the next moment would take us. I broke the silence and said, "Well, give me a hug good-bye, then."

Stepping forward, we reached for each other. As our warm bodies connected, it was like a hand fitting snuggly into a glove. Our frames matched perfectly as we embraced for what seemed to be an eternity but for what was certainly only a few minutes. We stood holding each other, not saying a word, but pushing closer into each other. I could feel her heart pounding against my chest. We rocked slightly as we hugged, and it was clear that neither of us wanted to let go. As every second passed, her grip around my back tightened, as did mine around hers, both of us hoping this would somehow stop the clock and shield us from the reality of letting go.

I gently maneuvered around the edge of her collar and caressed the nape of her neck, while softly brushing her left earlobe with my lips. *It's not cheating if our lips don't touch!*

Casey exhaled slowly and whispered, "What are we doing?"

I'm fairly certain it was a rhetorical question, but I answered softly, "Hugging good-bye."

"We're not gonna kiss! I'm *not* kissing you!" she insisted, in a voice slightly louder than a whisper.

"Who said anything about kissing?" It's not like my tongue was hanging out of my mouth as I wrapped my arms around her. My only intention was to hug her, I swear!

We continued to hug and our hands slowly worked their way down our bodies until our fingers found themselves interlocked. As her hands wrapped around mine, she squeezed with desire and I felt a slight tinge of pain in my left hand. She pressed my fingers together so tightly that the diamond ring Sydney had given me pinched my skin. I thought of Sydney for a brief moment and then pushed her out of my mind. Still holding on, Casey met my gaze in silence. There were no words to be spoken. Finally, a few minutes later, the silence was broken. "I don't want you to leave," Casey said.

A delighted smile spread across my face. If a genie had popped out of a bottle right then, as they did in Disney movies, and granted me three wishes, I would definitely have used one of them to spend the night with Casey.

We took a few steps forward into the doorway to Casey's bedroom. Staring into her eyes, I leaned back and rested my head on the wall. She took both my hands in hers and stepped in closer to me. I gently kissed her forehead. She pressed her body into mine and we both closed our eyes. She began to move her face around mine, slowly and seductively. I tried to reach up and touch her face, but she would not let go of my hands, holding them tightly by her side.

I could hear and feel every breath she took. As I inhaled, I smelled the vanilla in her skin cream. I had fantasized about kissing Casey countless times and now she was standing in front of me about to make my fantasy a reality. Fear and excitement seemed to paralyze me. I knew what I was doing was wrong, but I wanted her desperately. I was so conflicted but was certain to surrender to my demons. My willpower was eroding and I could no longer resist the temptation of Casey.

"This feels so right," Casey whispered, as she continued to rub her soft cheek against mine. Slowly, she reached up and parted my lips with her index finger. The sensation was fleeting as she continued past my lips and gently began circling my tongue with the tip of her finger.

Her touch sent waves of excitement throughout my body. I leaned my head back against the wall, stared up at the ceiling and exhaled deeply. With every ounce of my remaining strength, I whispered, "I can't take much more of this. If you keep doing what you're doing, I can't be held responsible for my actions."

She continued circling my face with hers. Suddenly, I felt the closeness of her lips. They were almost touching mine, but we were still not kissing. Not even a millimeter separated our mouths. Her tongue lightly grazed my bottom lip, which then twitched slightly. I'm not sure what kept me from passing out with excitement.

"Is this crossing a line?" Casey asked with a mischievous smile on her face.

"I think so," I muttered, sort of chuckling. "Fuck it! I can't take this anymore!" I tried to take control, but she wouldn't let me. She pushed me up against the wall and my arms reached behind her back. She stared into my eyes and placed her lips on mine. Before I could wonder what she was going to do next, she kissed me. Her lips were soft, full and moist. Her tongue swept inside my mouth and delicately danced on mine. I reciprocated with more passion than I had felt for anyone in more time than I could remember. Enveloping each other with tenderness, our warm, smooth tongues tangled and embraced. I didn't move once, afraid that body movement of any kind would disturb the moment and end the kiss that I so desperately wanted to last forever. It was, undoubtedly, the most incredible and passionate kiss of my entire life, lasting several minutes.

Our lips parted only long enough for our eyes to meet and for smiles to appear on our faces. Our gazes quickly gave way to an enraptured frenzy as she wrapped her arms around me and we plunged our tongues together again. My head was spinning with the euphoria of kissing Casey, combined with the confusion from the countless thoughts racing through my mind. *God, this feels amazing. I can't believe I'm doing this. I'm cheating on my girlfriend. I'm not a cheater. This isn't who I am. I'm Mommy's good little girl. It's too late now. I must be falling in love with this woman. I don't want to leave. What time is it? How much longer can I stay here? Is Sydney gonna knock on the door? What am I gonna tell her I was doing? What does she think I'm doing? She can't have a clue. I'm scared. I'm excited. I'm happy. I don't want this feeling to end. Are we gonna stop at a kiss? The bed is just feet from us!*

Just then, I felt Casey's hand sliding up the outside of my shirt. Her touch was electric and my stomach flinched as her warm hand slowly traveled up my body. A sudden rush overcame me. My knees buckled. With every inch that Casey's hand moved, I became more and more excited. My desire for her intensified and I wanted her hands all over my body. I closed my eyes and pictured her hands, so strong and so perfectly manicured but calloused from years of tennis. My eyes were closed, but I could clearly see her hands as I felt them wander up my body.

She gently, but firmly, squeezed my swollen breast. The heat from her palm seeped through my shirt. As we kissed, I thought I was going to melt. I was aroused to an uncontrollable degree and every hair on my body was on end.

Our lips separated as I inhaled deeply. "I'm dying to take you over to that bed," I confessed.

"Oh no! We aren't going anywhere near that bed. We're staying right here. Just kiss me. I don't want to stop kissing you," Casey said.

Several minutes later and after much moaning and heavy breathing, I reluctantly pulled my lips from hers. "We have to stop. It's the last thing I want to do, but we have to." I had to straighten myself up and return to my room where my girlfriend was in bed waiting for me. Or knowing her, she might be waiting outside Casey's door when I opened it. I felt as if I was eye level to a snail. I knew that what I had done and what I wanted to continue to do was wrong and inexcusable. There was no justification for betraying Sydney like this. As I felt the shame for my actions, I thought of Sydney for one second longer and wondered how she was going to play the finals of the tournament the next day. *Shit, it's going to be next to impossible for Sydney to compete and even win given that her ex-girlfriend and current girlfriend had just stabbed her in the back with a butcher's knife. Certainly, her backswing will be affected by the blade between her shoulders. What the hell am I doing? Can anything good possibly come of this? NO! God, you are such an asshole! You have a girlfriend! Most important of all, Casey is Sydney's ex-girlfriend! What is wrong with you?! This is totally self-destructive!*

Trying to silence my berating voice in my head, I went into the bathroom and washed my hands and face. Casey stood in the doorway watching me. As I dried my face on the towel hanging on the back of the door, I felt Casey's hand on my arm. She reached for me, pulled me toward her and kissed me. My shameful thoughts disappeared. I was overwhelmed by a force vastly more powerful than my conscience.

Stopping briefly, Casey put her hands on my face, her palms on either cheek. She stared into my eyes, kissed me and said, "You are so beautiful." I turned my head to hide my embarrassment. She placed her hand on my face and gently guided it back toward hers. "I mean it. You're so pretty. You're too pretty for her. I thought that from the first time I saw you with her at Wimbledon…even with that stupid baseball hat on your head backwards. Hell, you're too pretty for me."

Savoring one last kiss, I hugged her good-bye. Our hands remained interlocked as I moved toward the door and opened it to peer into the hallway. Phew! No Sydney. I squeezed Casey's palm tightly and began to walk away, not letting go of her fingers. Our hands released from each other and Casey smiled and watched as I made my way down the hall.

I heard Casey lock her door before I turned the corner. I had just crossed over the threshold of my fantasy world back into reality. The reality was that I had just cheated on my girlfriend with her ex-girlfriend and was about to slink into bed next to her. I wanted to walk slowly and retreat to my thoughts of kissing Casey, but I hurried my pace so that, somehow, it wouldn't seem like I had been gone for two hours.

I caught my breath and quietly put my key in the door. Sydney had left the bathroom light on for me but I had a feeling she was waiting for me to return before she went to sleep. I ducked into the bathroom to glance in the mirror and make sure that the scarlet letter I had envisioned on the front of my T-shirt was, in fact, a figment of my imagination. Reassured, I approached Sydney as if I had not just committed an unspeakable act against her. *Please be asleep. Please.*

Sydney turned toward me and growled, "Did you two watch one of those movies you returned?"

Suddenly, I felt swamped with alarm, my armpits dampening. *Did she know? Of course she didn't know! Does she suspect? Oh stop it. Just remain calm and act as if nothing happened.* Trying not to incriminate myself, I said the first thing I could think of. "No, but I did hear all about a drama. That girl's in a lot of trouble."

Ya think? Oh, and what about me?

Confused, Sydney looked at me and asked, "Why?"

Pleased that she didn't dwell on how long I'd been gone, I continued, "She's so caught up in Trish. I feel really bad for her. I don't know how she'll ever get over her and move on with her life."

She turned over and rolled her eyes. "Yep, she's in love with her straight best friend who's a frigid bitch. Trish'll never be able to give Casey what she wants and Casey keeps hoping and waiting. Is that what you guys were talking about that whole time?"

Of course it was. Ex-act-ly!

"Yep," I said and then elaborated upon my lie, figuring that deception was a safer option than coming clean and telling her that I had just spent almost two hours passionately kissing her ex-girlfriend. "She was waiting for a phone call when I got over there. I guess Trish was supposed to call and Casey was bummed that she hadn't heard from her. So, we started talking about it." Sydney was silent, so I kept talking. Every time I opened my mouth, another incredible lie would fall out. "Casey feels comfortable confiding in me. I understand what she's going through but I don't see her trying to extricate herself from her fiasco with Trish. The longer she stays in it, the worse it's gonna get. I feel really bad for her." *Is that what they call projecting?*

My wobbly legs needed a rest and we continued bantering back and forth as I sat on the heated toilet seat brushing my teeth. Trying to prolong the inevitable of crawling into bed next to her, I yelled out from the bathroom that my stomach was killing me. The stomach infliction had become my standard "Not tonight, honey, I have a headache" excuse. There was only one woman I wanted to be in bed with and the only way I was going to be with Casey that night was to meet her in my dreams. I was desperate to fall asleep.

Sydney had her back to me and was lying on her side. I slipped into bed and put my hand on her shoulder. She reached over and placed her hand on top of mine. I had gotten to the point that merely touching her skin casually was a huge effort— even painful. Not more than thirty seconds later, I removed my hand and rolled over. I stared at the wall and replayed in my mind what had just happened in Casey's room. I wondered what I had gotten myself into and what I possibly hoped to achieve by kissing Casey. But then I closed my eyes and felt the kiss and suddenly it was all I could think about. I went to sleep that night with a grin on my face. It had been so long since I had smiled like that. It was pitch black in the room, but I was glowing.

8

$\mathcal{P}$erfecting the backhanded spin

I might have slept for a total of thirty minutes. I woke up before the sun rose and stared at my watch, waiting for time to pass so I could get out of bed. I was engulfed by a mixture of calm and excitement. *Is that possible? Can I be calm and excited at the same time?* If it is, I felt a calm excitement. As the first golden rays glistened through the curtains, I started to stir and whispered to Sydney, "I'm gonna make a Starbucks run."

Desperate to know how Casey felt about the night before, my plan was to get dressed, knock on Casey's door and take her with me to Starbucks.

Still lying in bed, Sydney turned over and reminded me about her superstitions. Most of the girls on the Tour have at least one or two quirky superstitions like not stepping on the lines when changing sides of the court, insisting on staying in the same hotel and the same room year after year or wearing a lucky shirt. Once Sydney won a match, her superstition dictated that she had to repeat her daily routine exactly the same as she did on the day of the first win. Since our arrival in Tokyo, Sydney's daily ritual was to walk to Starbucks to get us our morning dose of caffeine. Since she was in the finals of the tournament later that day, she could not break her week-long routine. She was convinced that if she didn't personally go and get the coffee, this would be the *one* time that breaking her routine would cause her to lose. I didn't argue and suggested that she get a latte for Casey, too.

"I was going to," she barked as she threw an oversized, wrinkled sweatshirt over her head and then smelled the collar of it, presumably to determine if it were clean.

Repugnant. She stepped into the sweatpants she'd worn the day before, after performing the smell check on them as well.

Sydney looked like an unmade bed. Her disheveled hair could more appropriately be described as an oily brown mass than a head of hair. She didn't bother running a brush through the mess atop her head before she ventured beyond the confines of our room. While she claimed that her lackadaisical grooming in the morning was superstitious, I maintain that it was simply a bad habit. She left the one key that we had to the room on the desk and stumbled out the door. Sydney followed her superstition and I followed my heart.

I picked up the phone and dialed Casey's room.

Casey answered and I spat out instructions without even greeting her. "You are to report to Room 1101 immediately, if not sooner," I ordered while snickering.

"Where is she?" she whispered nervously.

"She went to get coffees for us all. Just get over here!"

Not more than a few seconds passed and there was a knock on my door. Surprised at how quickly she had arrived, I scrambled to my feet and opened the door to find Casey's smiling face. Delighted, I reached for her hand and pulled her inside before anyone caught a glimpse of her.

Casey was still short of breath from her sprint over to the room. She threw her arms around me and gave me a brilliant good-morning kiss. *I guess I don't need to ask her how she feels about last night,* I thought as my tongue touched hers. I had spent the night wondering how it was going to feel to kiss her again— indeed, hoping that we would kiss again. I asked myself repeatedly if my feelings the night before were real or if I had simply created them in my mind. As our mouths moved together, I quickly realized that the chemistry we shared could not be manufactured. The incredible knock-the-wind-out-of-you sensation I felt a few hours before was every bit as real as what I was feeling at that very moment.

In a perfect world, I would have restrained myself and would not have engaged any further with Casey until I resolved things with Sydney. But, c'mon— we don't live in a perfect world. My relationship with Sydney felt more like a diet than a relationship, and I had been deprived of what I had craved for so long, completely unsatisfied with my paltry daily nourishment. I was starving for Casey.

Motioning toward the bed, I whispered, "Let's go over there."

"What about Sydney?"

"What about her?" My tone was indignant. Truly, Sydney was the last person on my mind.

"When do you think she'll be back?"

"She literally just left before I called you. Fifteen minutes."

"What if she walks in?"

"She left the key here. The door's locked. She'll have to knock in order to get in. Stop asking me silly questions. You're wasting our time!" I took Casey by the hand and walked her over to the bed. Unlike the night before, she did not resist the idea of getting into bed with me now.

I sat her down next to me and gently guided her head toward my pillow. Before either of us could stop ourselves, I was on top of her.

"Do you think we should talk about what's happening between us?" she asked.

"I do, but not right now. We only have a few minutes and all I want to do is taste you and feel you." I stared into her eyes and smiled before our lips met. Having her in my arms felt so natural, I wanted to hold her forever. I kissed her gently at first but then more intensely until Casey suddenly took control. She pushed me off her and rolled over on top of me. I squirmed but could not persuade her to relinquish control— as if I didn't want her right where she was. She didn't know it, but she already had control— control of my emotions. My protests were merely for effect. I wanted to give to her and give in to her.

Casey held my hands tightly above my head and leaned toward my face. She teased me slightly, heightening all of my senses. The heat she was emanating penetrated my T-shirt and boxer shorts. She tasted like sugar and cinnamon, no doubt already having enjoyed her morning order of cinnamon toast. Her skin smelled of fresh vanilla and Michael Kors perfume. The combination aroused me to the point that my spine started quivering. Blood rushed to my cheeks and I could feel my heartbeat in my earlobes. I couldn't contain my excitement. With all my strength, I playfully threw her off me and positioned my body back on top of hers. I wanted her so badly.

My body was poised over Casey's as my mouth found hers. As I pushed her legs apart with my knees, her breathing intensified and so did our kissing. I slowly slid my body to the left until half of me was lying on Casey and the other half rested on the bed. Pulling her close, my right hand slowly wandered down her body, starting at her left cheek and resting on her left hip. The tip of my tongue left the tip of hers as I flicked it across her lips and gently kissed her. I enveloped her lips and then moved to her right cheek before shifting my body downward so I could caress her neck. Dropping down, I softly licked and kissed the curve just above her shoulder and then opened my mouth slightly to drag my teeth gently across her neck. She breathed heavily. We both began to moan and I became even more aroused. I moved slowly to the middle of her neck and started kissing her throat. I had ignored my urge to move my hand from her hip, but now I could no longer resist the temptation. I succumbed to my urge, my craving.

Nervously, I slowly lifted her shirt, exposing her bra-less breasts. I couldn't even look at her half-naked body. As my hand found her left breast, I felt like I was going to explode. I whispered, "You feel so good." My palm barely covered her full breast. I squeezed her nipple with my thumb and forefinger. She reacted as if I had sent a surge of electricity through her body. I didn't hesitate to move my mouth toward her supple breast and she didn't stop me. I held her breast with my right hand and ran the tip of my tongue across the top of her nipple. It was already rock-hard but became even more erect instantly when my tongue brushed over it. Her skin was petal soft and poignantly fragrant. Her breathing intensified and her moaning got louder. "Ohh…Stephie…ohhhh! That feels so good."

With uncontrollable excitement, I had begun kissing her nipple softly but was now sucking with more force. She put her hand on the back of my head and pushed my face into her breast. I moved my tongue back and forth across her nipple very quickly while sucking. Moans escaped her lips in rapid succession as she exhaled. She reached for a pillow and put it over her face to muffle her sounds of pleasure. Just as I moved back to her mouth and kissed her lips, there was a loud knock on the door. Undoubtedly, Sydney had returned with our coffees.

Great timing. Cold shower, anyone?

Casey quickly leapt off the bed, pulling her shirt back down and smoothing her tousled hair. Her face was red and she was disheveled and nervous.

"It's okay, it's okay!" I reassured her in a hushed tone as I sat up. "She can't get in until we open the door. Just take a deep breath and calm down."

"But does she know I'm here?" Casey was so nervous that she'd forgotten I had told her that Sydney was also bringing her a coffee.

Unlike Casey, I was not worried at the thought of Sydney walking through the door, despite what had just been going on in her very bed. If she hadn't suspected anything after I'd been gone for two hours to return some DVDs, I was fairly certain that my activities during a fifteen-minute coffee run would not arouse her suspicion.

Casey opened the door, Sydney barreled in and I sat motionless on the end of the bed.

"Here's your coffee, you bitches." She was only kidding. Sydney used the term affectionately, but only because she was oblivious about what she had just interrupted. If she had any clue, she would not be handing us coffees— she'd be handing us death sentences.

Casey passed me a coffee with a devilish grin. My mind was replaying the last several minutes with her and I was not ready to join everyone else in the present.

Sydney took a bite of a pastry and motioned to Casey, "You packed?" As usual, she spoke with her mouth full and as she did, a piece of pastry flew out and landed several feet away. Her eating habits disgusted me more at that moment than ever before, even more so than at my mom's Thanksgiving table. Casey nodded and laughed, knowing the source of my repulsion.

I sipped my coffee absently. Uncharacteristically taciturn, I contributed nothing to the conversation that Casey and Sydney were having. My mind was otherwise occupied. I moved slightly and caught a smell of Casey's perfume on my shirt. I smiled and wondered if my sheets and pillow smelled of her fragrance as well. I hoped so. I leaned over, trying to disguise what I was doing and confirmed that the entire corner of my side of the bed smelled like Casey's perfume. I was strangely comforted knowing that a few hours later, when Casey was on a plane heading back to the United States, a tiny part of her would remain with me in Tokyo. My mind could not escape the thought of Casey. Just moments earlier, I had held her in my arms. Now she was sitting a few feet away from me, but her smell was on my clothes and pillow. And her taste was on my breath. My stomach trembled as Dante's famous words burned in my mind: "From a little spark may burst a flame." *And from this flame started a towering inferno! Ah, which circle of hell will I descend into now?*

When Casey finished her coffee, she announced that she was going back to her room to shower and get dressed and that she would be back to say good-bye on her way down to the lobby. Nothing could take away the bliss that I was feeling as thoughts of being with Casey continued to race through my mind. Trying desperately not to appear anxious over her impending departure, I watched her rise from her chair and begin to walk toward the door. As if we were the only two people in the room, she met my gaze and I smiled at her during her five-second trip across the room.

When Casey left, Sydney looked at me and frowned. "It's too bad we haven't been having sex every morning this week. I could use an outlet for all of my anxiety before the match. But, you know me. Can't do something different on the day of the finals."

Yeah. Too bad.

I looked away and rolled my eyes. We hadn't had sex at all in Tokyo. I found it hard enough to be around Sydney with my clothes on. Taking them off wasn't an option.

I went into the bathroom to freshen up after my earlier romp in bed with Casey. I stared at myself in the mirror in silence. There were no voices that could be heard from the bathroom, but there were certainly plenty of conversations taking place in my head. *What in the hell are you doing?! Are you crazy?! You must be fucking nuts!* I posed a number of very difficult questions to myself, the answers to all of which were explained away by the smile on my face. I stood staring at the huge grin in the mirror. I was actually looking at the intangible feeling that I felt the night before. It was now tangible. I touched my lips as if I were trying to hold my smile in my hands. Maybe I was trying to feel the happiness on my fingertips. Or maybe I was just trying to touch the last place that Casey's lips had touched. Whatever the reason, I just wanted to savor that feeling, the feeling I thought I had forgotten how to feel. I welcomed it back with open arms.

I emerged from the bathroom and found Sydney in the same spot in front of her computer that she had been in since returning from Starbucks. I walked back over to the bed and turned on the television. It seemed as if I were watching CNN through my wristwatch because I could not take my eyes off the minute hand in anticipation of Casey's return. My anxiety increased. Unfortunately, fixing my eyes upon my watch did not make Casey return any faster. I rolled my eyes as a voice in my head repeated, "A watched pot never boils." "Boil this!" another voice inside my head snapped back.

Great, now I've been reduced to having conversations with myself in my head in an attempt to make the time pass faster! I'm losing it! God, I need help! After years of Catholic school training, I'm still able to recite various prayers by memory. But I'm not sure that all the Hail Marys in the world could have helped me out of this predicament.

Thankfully, Casey returned quickly. I had no idea how much knuckles rapping on a door could excite me. Sydney abandoned her post and opened the door. Casey walked in with a huge smile on her face. She looked adorable. Never before had I found the "alternative look" attractive, but to me Casey was irresistible. She was wearing torn jeans held about the waist by a black leather belt with silver studs, a long sleeved black vintage T-shirt with the sleeves pushed up haphazardly and Converse sneakers. Her hair was parted in the middle and hung just below her jaw. I could smell her freshly-applied perfume across the room.

Casey and I shared a Diet Coke and flipped through a Japanese *Vogue* while Sydney sat with her back to us reading the *New Zealand Herald* online. The tension in the room grew as the minutes passed. With the passage of every minute, we were closer to the inevitable— the good-bye. It was almost certain that there were no more private moments to steal, so our sayonara would have to be in front of Sydney. I wasn't sure how I was going to give Casey just a friendly hug and wish her *bon voyage,* but I didn't think it would be appropriate to shove my tongue down her throat in front of Sydney. My heart started pounding and my palms were sweating. The moment had arrived. We could prolong it no longer.

"I better get downstairs," Casey announced.

"All right, Casey, have a safe trip." Sydney closed her browser and rose to give Casey a hug. "Call us when you get home."

I got up and was speechless. My entire life, I had had a line for everything, but at the moment, I didn't know how to say good-bye to Casey. "Travel safely," I said and hugged her good-bye. It was probably the lamest hug I had ever given or received. In a desperate attempt not to show any hint of romantic emotion, we went to the opposite extreme. It seemed as if we had just met for the first time. It was one of those dumb sorority girl hugs— not embracing, just quick pats on the back as if we were trying quickly to blot something out of the backs of our shirts.

Before we were done with our pat down, Sydney decided to walk out of the room and call the elevator for Casey. As she stood waiting for the elevator around the corner, unbeknownst to her, she had given us the unexpected present of a few more stolen seconds together. Casey had more courage than I and kissed me. As much as I loved kissing her, I was petrified at the thought of Sydney walking through the door and catching us. I was beside myself and couldn't help but want to go back to the dumb sorority girl hug for fear of getting caught. I didn't want to break the embrace, but I also didn't want to start World War III, which was exactly what would have happened if Sydney had caught a glimpse of us. The kiss was short-lived and Casey and I walked to the door. Casey shielded the door with her body and gave me one last peck on the cheek. She cupped my face with her hands, looked me in the eyes and whispered, "I'm really going to miss you."

I felt a knot forming in my throat and smiled before pulling her toward me. As we hugged, I heard the elevator beeping. Casey and I reached for each other's hands and, much like the night before, held tightly until we reluctantly broke our embrace and the distance separated our fingertips. I was desperate for her to stay but followed her around the corner, where Sydney was holding the elevator doors open. Casey smiled and gave us one final good-bye. A few seconds later, the elevator doors closed, and Casey was gone.

Casey had been my ray of sunshine since I arrived in Tokyo. She was a buffer during an extremely tumultuous week, sometimes even having to broker peace between Sydney and me. And now I just wanted to "fast forward" to landing back in Los Angeles two days later. I calculated the number of hours remaining until I would say farewell to Sydney at LAX: thirty-six (twenty-six hours left in Tokyo plus ten more on the plane). I wondered how I was going to put on a happy face and get through the next day and a half without my buffer. Then I calculated the number of hours until I would potentially hear Casey's voice again: fourteen hours until she landed in the United States and had access to a phone. I literally caught myself counting on my fingers. *How did I get myself into this position?!* I was in trouble. Serious trouble! Where the hell's that damn remote?! I was desperate to hit "fast forward" and get back home.

Our room felt empty. Thoughts of breaking up with Sydney raced through my mind, as did flashbacks of kissing Casey. My breakup with Sydney was imminent but would have to wait. It would have to be strategically planned. After all, each of my numerous past attempts had failed. When I left Melbourne, I decided that I would break up with Sydney when I returned to my own home where she could not block the door or beg me to stay. I know that there is no good time to break up with someone, but Sydney was vying for a championship in a few short hours. Breaking up with her just before the match would be cruel! My mind bounced from Casey smiling to Sydney crying. Leaving Sydney was going to kill her and I truly didn't want to hurt her.

Great, so I'll just cheat on her with her ex-girlfriend. That should make it easier on her.

I looked around the room, desperately searching for an independent activity in order to keep myself sane before Sydney and I headed over to the courts. I began organizing my things so I could pack my bags in anticipation of our departure the next day. When I ran out of clothes to fold I sat down to do a crossword puzzle. I was just about to put a line through the only remaining clue when the phone rang. Sydney's head turned so quickly she was lucky not to give herself whiplash. But I was sitting on her side of the bed, right next to the phone and promptly answered it. Even without caller ID, I had a good idea who was calling. I picked up the phone trying to disguise my happiness, "Hello!"

"Thank God, *you* picked up the phone," Casey whispered.

Playing along, I said, "Hey! Did you make it to the airport okay?" I wondered what the chances were that Casey had missed her flight! I was beaming but tried to temper the effervescence in my voice.

"Is that Casey?" Sydney asked. I nodded "yes" and continued my conversation.

"Stephie, it's just so weird. I know I should feel bad for what we did, but I don't. I really miss you. I can't stop thinking of you. I hated leaving you. I didn't want to say good-bye." Her tone was earnest.

I grasped the phone tightly and pressed it hard against my ear so Sydney could not hear any of Casey's words. I pushed the receiver so hard against my head that I was beginning to sweat and I could feel indentations from it on the side of my face. My heart sank at the sound of Casey's words. I responded as cryptically as I could and said things like, "Uh-huh…I see…yes, yes…of course…oh I know."

"Listen, check your voicemail and your e-mail. But, Stephie…make sure you erase *everything* immediately." There wasn't a hint of laughter in Casey's voice as she issued her directive.

"I know. Of course," I agreed.

"Stephie, I'm serious. You know she's crazy and you know she has a habit of checking other people's voicemails and e-mails."

"Mmmm hmmm. Yep." I was well aware of the perils of archiving messages when Sydney's curiosity was piqued or even if she just had nothing better to do than be nosey. I'm a "saver" and love to re-read old e-mails and listen to old voicemails. But I vowed to delete Casey's messages for fear of a trespass by Sydney. Although she did not know my password (another source of contention between us, because if I had nothing to hide, why couldn't she be privy to my password?), I didn't question her password-cracking abilities. I changed my security code frequently, staying as far away from obvious choices such as names of pets, ex-girlfriends and favorite vacation spots. I even thought about changing my password to "fuckufoster." I doubt she'd ever guess that one.

"Okay, I have to go check in. I just wanted to talk to you one last time before I left. You have no idea what I had to do to even make this phone call. I've never been so desperate for a phone card in my life. God, I must really have a problem! I'll miss you…I already do."

"Have a safe trip, and we'll talk to you soon." I miss you too! That's what I wanted to say, but I bit my tongue.

When I hung up the phone it was time for us to leave, so I got dressed. During the past week, I had coordinated my trips to the courts with Casey's schedule. Today was different. Sydney and I rode the bus to the courts together. I got on first and Sydney followed closely behind. I took my normal seat on the right side of the bus and Sydney sat across from me where Casey normally sat. There was no laughing, no talking and no smiles. It was the exact opposite of how things were with Casey. I got lost in the world of my iPod (*another* present from Sydney), and my thoughts went directly to Casey. Sydney hated when I listened to my iPod in her presence. She thought it was anti-social and rude. I was just anti being social with Sydney.

When we arrived, the singles final had just begun, and since the doubles final followed immediately afterward, I had at least one hour before Sydney's match would begin. Sydney and I separated immediately. She went to the training room to have a blood blister on her foot taped and I headed to the gym. Exercising, once fallen by the wayside, had become a non-negotiable part of my day. Maybe I was trying to lose the fifteen pounds that I had gained since I had started dating Sydney so I could fit comfortably back into my size 8 pants, or maybe I was secretly trying to lose weight to catch the eye of a certain blonde whose name starts with a "C" and ends in a "Y." I could fool others, but I knew the reason I was trying to get rid of what I affectionately dubbed my "winter coat," which was getting heavy with its year-round use. And slathering Nutella on my toast every morning and then sitting on my ass watching tennis all day wasn't going to do the trick, so off to the gym I went!

Today's torture would be the treadmill. Casey always seemed to pop into my mind during the most torturous moments of my workouts— as I gasped for air on the treadmill or grunted while trying to do that last weight repetition. Thoughts of her were interspersed with an acrid cursing at the torture I was putting myself through. *Fuck, I hate this! Why do I do this to myself? There has to be an easier way. Isn't there a pill or a surgery to fix my flaws? Just shut up and run, fat ass, and wait until the next time Casey sees me! She won't even recognize me!*

Now that I had made my confession to Casey, I could admit that images of her smile were what had been getting me up that hill on the treadmill or through the nineteenth or twentieth repetition with the weights when my muscles were already on fire after the tenth repetition.

I turned on my iPod, put on my headphones and stepped onto the treadmill. As I increased the speed, I tried to analyze all that had happened during the last twenty hours. Admittedly, I have always been a drama queen. I have my mother to thank for my flair for the dramatic. Measured by even the most objective, levelheaded, non-dramatic person, this situation gave new meaning to the phrase "dyke drama." It was all-out scandalous!

Thinking of Casey, I didn't doubt the intensity of her kiss or the sincerity behind her actions. As I ran, questions burned in my mind about Casey's feelings for Trish. Despite these burning questions, I knew that Casey had feelings for me. Then Sydney popped into my head. No matter how hard I tried, I could not get Sydney out of my head. It was like a reality check and it was pissing me off! Why does that always happen? Why do the fantasies we enjoy most always seem to get interrupted by "pop-ins?" I just wanted to fantasize for a few minutes about my time with Casey, but Sydney kept popping in. It was as if she were there to remind me that I had committed an unforgivable act of betrayal. I could hear her shrieking, "How could you? With my ex-girlfriend? My best friend!" I turned up the volume on my iPod as if it would magically mute Sydney's voice in my head.

I squinted as sweat rolled into my eyes and stared at the wall as I sprinted on the treadmill. Thoughts of Sydney made me run faster. I had been running, emotionally, from Sydney for months and had finally come to the conclusion that she was not right for me. As I ran, I made a list of reasons why. *She wants to fuse worlds. She wants more than you can give and more than you want to give— to her. Okay, so she's generous, and in many ways, she treated you very well. She'd bend herself into a pretzel to try to make you happy. But her generosity is not without its strings. She expects you to be indebted to her in exchange for all of her material generosity. She wants you to owe her…owe her your love. She gives to get. She's overbearing and possessive and doesn't want you to have your own identity. The more you try to push her away, the more she digs her heels in and clings to you. What are you doing? Run, run, R-U-N!*

I did one last sprint and stepped off the treadmill. Gasping for air and drenched in sweat, I looked down at my watch. *Shit!* I had been gone for over an hour. I toweled off and hurried back to the players' lounge. The singles final was over and Sydney was standing in the hallway with Lindy and their opponents, waiting for their escort to the court. I had gotten into trouble with Sydney on another occasion for not coming down to the "holding area" before her match. She said she counted on me to wish her luck before her matches because it calmed her nerves.

I raced down the hallway to where Sydney was standing. Out of breath, I huffed, "I'm so sorry. I lost track of time."

Bouncing up and down to loosen her muscles, she pardoned me. "No worries. They're presenting the singles trophies right now, so we have a few minutes. Good thing you got here now, though."

Yeah, good thing. Thank God. Phew!

Suddenly, the tournament officials approached. They exchanged a few words over their walkie-talkies with their colleagues on the court who gave the green light to send the foursome down to the court. As a good girlfriend should, I wished Sydney and Lindy luck and they disappeared through the doorway.

I quickly ran into the bathroom and changed out of my sweaty clothes. I then rushed back around the corner to the players' lounge and went directly over to the computers. My hands shook as I nervously logged on. I knew how odd it would look if someone saw me writing an e-mail after my girlfriend had already been dispatched to the court. There is an unspoken etiquette to be followed at tennis tournaments. Badges are commodities and if a player gives you one, you are expected to be courtside before she gets there— especially if you're a coach and most especially if you're a significant other. I hurriedly typed an e-mail to Casey. The badge around my neck kept hitting the keyboard as my fingers instinctively typed the message in my head. The constant tapping of my badge against the keyboard and the silent shimmer of my ring were reminders that as Sydney's girlfriend, my place was courtside at that moment, and not in front of a computer terminal. I pushed "send," logged off and rushed to the court where I planted myself in the front row of the players' box to watch the match before anyone noticed I was missing.

The match was over in less than an hour. It was an absolute blowout. It wasn't a well-suited match for the finals of such an important tournament. Sydney and Lindy barely broke a sweat as they demolished their opponents. Sydney looked like the player she had earned the reputation for being and could not miss a shot. Her serves were like bullets. Her backhand was unbelievable and her volleys were untouchable. It truly was an impressive performance. Still, I had a hard time digging deep within myself to find some excitement to share with her. Dare I say faking an apology to that pain-in-the-ass Michael Schetz was easier than feigning happiness for Sydney.

I don't know which was worse— Sydney playing an amazingly stellar doubles match or a shockingly embarrassing one. No matter how horrifically she played, in Sydney's mind her partner was always responsible for the loss. When she and her partner were victorious, Sydney made sure to inform everyone that the win was due to her on-court excellence. And if she played exceedingly well, the whole world had to hear about it. In my current frame of mind, I simply wasn't in the mood to massage her ego. As I watched the tournament director hand Sydney and Lindy their trophies, I couldn't help but think that it should have been Marisa and Casey receiving those trophies and celebrating that victory. After two previous unsuccessful bids for this title, Sydney held the coveted trophy high above her head, no doubt savoring the championship just a little more since she'd denied it to Casey. I pretended to be happy for Sydney and clapped as she posed for pictures with her trophy.

During the lull of the camera clicking and flashing, I left the court and walked one last time through the doors to the players' lounge to wait for Sydney. When she walked in I delivered my rehearsed congratulatory sentiment and even topped it off with a smile.

Almost teary-eyed at my sincerity, she said, "Thanks, love."

We gathered our things and walked down the hallway together to catch the bus back to the hotel. The tournament was over and I was one step closer to home. It was getting dark outside and the bright lights of the city illuminated the sky as we boarded the bus. I put my headphones on and stared out the window, wondering if this would be the last time I would ever take this drive from the courts to the tournament hotel. I was certain that I would not be returning to Tokyo with Sydney the next year.

* * *

That night, we ate dinner in the hotel restaurant. Between tasting delicate pieces of sushi that the chef specially prepared for me and "Sydney the champion," I distractedly looked at my watch— my crappy old Rolex— in order to calculate Casey's arrival time. She would be landing soon. And when she did, she would have full use of her phone and full access to e-mail. I felt a tingly sensation at the possibility that I would soon hear from her again. Not only was I consumed with thoughts of her, but I was constantly thinking of surreptitious ways to communicate with her. I wasn't proud of it, but I figured all the sneaking around and dishonesty would end in a matter of hours when I got back home.

I sipped my hot sake as Sydney drenched the last piece of yellowtail in the wasabi-soy sauce mixture before popping the entire thing into her mouth. After swallowing, she sat back in her chair and dragged her tongue across the front of her top teeth while making a sucking sound, vacuuming every last bit of food out of her braces. "So, what do you say we go back to the room and have a private celebration?" She smiled suggestively and chugged the rest of her third beer, waiting for my excited "I thought you'd never ask" response.

Fidgeting with the porcelain chopsticks, I absently responded, "It's getting late. We probably should get going."

When we returned to the room, we immediately got into bed. I dreaded the argument I could feel brewing. I just wanted to get through this last night and make it home in one piece. I couldn't remember the last time Sydney and I shared anything intimate that could even remotely be considered tender. I think Sydney realized that we would not be spending our last night in Tokyo making love. Perhaps she thought sex without the tenderness of making love would be more appealing to me, and her hand wandered toward me. After delicately pushing her hand off my stomach, I actually resorted to flicking it as if it were an insect when she returned it to my naval a second and third time. Had that not worked, I would have reached for a shoe to smash it! I had lost that magnetic physical attraction that I once felt for her and I had no intention of engaging in even the slightest sexual act with her— especially since my erotic desires were now reserved for Casey. I wanted Casey's to be the last lips that touched mine. In a twisted way, I thought that abstaining from Sydney was the fairest thing I could do, given that I had already betrayed her by kissing

Casey. I didn't want to exacerbate the betrayal by being physically intimate with them both at the same time. For a second, I thought about patting myself on the back and rewarding myself for my humanitarianism. But Casey or no Casey, there wasn't a chance in hell that I was going to have sex with Sydney Foster ever again.

After being rejected, Sydney rolled over in frustration. As a peace offering, I apologized to her and handed her a lame excuse for refusing her advances. "Sydney, I'm sorry. I'm just exhausted." I spent two years building strong cases for a living, and the most compelling argument I could craft for not wanting to have sex with Sydney was simply that I didn't want to. With only twenty-one hours left until our separation, it was better than telling her the truth, which was that not only was I no longer interested in having sex with her, but I was not even remotely attracted to her any longer.

"You're always tired…or you don't feel good…or you're not in the mood!" Her speech was somewhat slurred from all the beer she had drank at dinner.

Hmmm, that didn't go over so well. Let's try again.

"Sydney, I really don't want to fight. We've been through a lot in the last few weeks and I just need some space. I'm sorry." Sydney abruptly turned her back to me and stewed in silence. A few minutes passed and then she launched into a discussion about our relationship. I knew it was coming. Why wouldn't it? It was, after all, the only thing we ever talked about anymore. Sydney loved to beat a dead horse and dissect every aspect of our failing relationship. She was beating this dead relationship to death.

She droned on and on and repeated the same things over and over again. I could practically recite this speech backwards by now. As she huffed and puffed, I did what I always did during these altercations— I tried to think of a way to end it. The simplest way to end the argument would have been to have sex with her, but that was not even Plan Z in my mind. My options were limited— do something to placate her or get into a huge argument and be up all night screaming. I opted for the former, but not before taking refuge in the bathroom to escape the storm of tension that was hovering over the bed.

I considered, for a brief moment, locking myself in the bathroom, but frightful images of Sydney physically breaking down the door to retrieve me sent my heart into palpitations. Gathering my resolve, I left the safe haven of the bathroom and walked directly over to Sydney's side of the bed. I gently nudged her, slid in next to her and put my arm around her. It was all that I could muster but it was enough for her. She fell asleep on my chest as I lay awake thinking of Casey. I could feel the pace of my heart increase and wondered if Sydney could, too. I watched her head bob slowly up and down as I took deliberately deep breaths, trying to calm myself.

A few minutes later the phone rang. I rolled over quickly to reach the receiver and Sydney's head slid off my chest and plopped onto the pillow.

"Hello," I answered clenching my hand around the receiver tightly.

"Just the voice I was hoping to hear!" It was Casey. I could hear the smile on her face immediately when she heard my voice.

Cryptically, I said, "Me too. Did my best." Again, I was pushing the receiver into my ear with all of my strength. My overly curious girlfriend was not across the room this time, so I had to be very careful not to let Casey's words reach Sydney's ears. "Did you just land in Boston?" I asked.

Out of breath, she answered, "Yeah, I'm rushing down to baggage claim."

"Are you nuts? You're calling Japan from your cell phone?"

Casey laughed and said, "I couldn't be bothered to go hunting for a calling card, so I just called directly from my cell. It'll probably cost me five bucks a minute, but I needed to hear your voice at whatever the cost. It's just a trip to the ATM anyway."

I was beginning to see the lengths to which Casey would go when she really wanted something.

I told Casey about the match and she pretended to be happy for Sydney. "Tell her congrats," she said sarcastically.

I gave Casey's message to Sydney and she barked "thank you" and almost as gruffly requested that Casey call us in the morning so that she and I could enjoy our last night in Tokyo. I'm not sure whom she was trying to fool.

I paid no attention to her and continued talking. I would have given anything to snap my fingers and make Sydney disappear so that Casey and I could have a real conversation.

I heard the buzz from the baggage carrousel and before we got off the phone, Casey reminded me again to erase any and all messages from her immediately. And then she told me to "travel safe."

Safely, I thought. Infatuation or not, incorrect grammar gives me chills and sends prickles throughout my body the same way nails running down a chalkboard do.

I woke up the next morning overly eager to board the plane. My last-ditch effort to make my relationship work had failed and I just wanted to go back home— alone. When we arrived at the departure terminal in the Tokyo Narita International Airport, my excitement was obvious by the spring in my step and the smile on my face. Sydney was the furthest thing from chipper and was taking slow, shallow steps, as if she were dreading an impending doom. I watched as she dragged her feet and wondered what ulterior motive she could possibly have. Surely she wasn't going to kidnap me and keep me with her in Tokyo? Laughing at the absurdity of the possibility, I couldn't dismiss her psychotic and desperate tendencies altogether. When boarding for the first class cabin was announced, I sprang up from my seat with enthusiasm and headed toward the gate with my boarding pass in hand as if it were my most prized possession. Sydney sullenly followed behind me.

As we arranged ourselves and settled in for the ten-hour flight, Sydney asked, "So, are you gonna let me stay with you in LA for a few days?"

I fucking knew it! I knew she had something up her sleeve! Trying to avoid blowing up at her, I responded with every bit of sarcasm I had in me, "Hmmm...let me think about that for a minute." I paused in silence and stared at the ceiling with my index finger pressed against my lips, feigning a contemplative look. I could feel her staring at me. "Wait. Still thinking." A few more seconds passed. "Okay, I got it. Nope." Before she could argue, I held my index finger up in the air and said, "Oh wait. Let me think some more. Yeah. Still no." I bit the inside of my cheek to avoid laughing.

Sydney's expression was stone-cold. "Steph, are you serious? You really aren't gonna let me stop over for a few days and stay with you? C'mon...please?" She was almost pleading.

Annoyed, I responded, "Sydney, we've been over this. No! I've told you repeatedly, when we touch down in LA, I'm going home alone."

"I just don't understand why you won't let me stay with you."

"Because! Jesus! Is it not enough that I put my life on hold and followed you around the world for the past six weeks? Hell, the last seven months for that matter! I told you this right after I got to Australia. I knew then that you were going to try to insist on stopping over in LA on the way back, and I told you "no" immediately. Remember? I said, 'Let's really enjoy our time together while I'm here because after Tokyo I need to go home and concentrate on my life and my business.' God dammit! I can't believe we have to have this conversation! Can't you respect my needs for once? Why does it always have to be about your needs and what you want?"

"It's not just about what I need. I respect your needs, but I think we need to spend some time together away from my environment. We're always together at the tennis tournaments. I wanna be with you in *your* environment, around *your* life and *your* friends."

"Bullshit, Sydney! You just want to be around me all the time, no matter where we are. I fell for your I-wanna-spend-time-with-you-away from-the-courts crap and came to Australia early. Remember? Oh forget it! I'm not having this conversation. This is not the time or the place!" The first class cabin of an airplane really wasn't the time or the place for a breakup, but she was asking for it.

"You're acting like you don't care that we'll be apart for four weeks."

I erupted. "I don't care! It's not tragic! It's the nature of the beast. You live in Florida, and I live in California. We're not gonna be able to see each other all the time, for fuck's sake! What don't you get about that?!"

"I just don't understand...I don't understand. I'm your girlfriend, and you're acting like you don't want me around."

She was right. I *didn't* want her around. I was at the end of my rope, but I knew that Sydney was far from seeing things my way. So I decided to spare the other passengers the drama of my breakup as their in-flight entertainment. "Sydney, I'm done with this conversation." My tone was not exactly "cordial." It fetched stares from other passengers as well as one of the flight attendants. Sydney caught the attendant's eye, knowing that she had overheard part of the conversation, in which I had very obviously berated the passenger sitting next to me.

Sydney leaned in even closer to me and whispered condescendingly, "Love, I'm just trying to have a conversation with you. I don't appreciate how you're talking to me. Your tone is really disrespectful."

Absolutely amazed that she wouldn't just drop it, I smeared a grin on my face and responded, "Fuck you! How's that grab you?? Is that tone better for you?" God, that felt good! I put my Bose Noise Canceling headphones on and leaned my head back against the seat, trying to relax. I was desperate for a respite from Sydney's sonic pollution. Just as I chose a playlist on my iPod, I suddenly felt my right earphone being pulled off my ear. *Is she fucking kidding me?! Is she really pulling my headphones off my head?! I cannot fucking believe her!*

Before I could finish my thought, Sydney had removed my headphones completely. I looked at her with astonishment. "What is your fucking problem?! Are you out of your fucking mind? Wait, don't answer that question!"

"I don't appreciate it when you put your headphones on and tune me out in the middle of a conversation."

"What are you, my fucking mother? I told you I was done with the conversation. Seriously, Sydney! *Seriously!* I'm done. There's nothing more to talk about. I'm sorry if it hurts your feelings, but I'm getting off the plane in LA and going home. You're getting off this plane and getting back onto *another* plane and flying to Miami. This is not open for discussion. It's not negotiable. Period!"

She continued trying to engage me in conversation and all I wanted to do was block out the sound of her voice with music. "Can I please have my headphones back?" I more demanded than asked.

"No. I'm not done talking to you."

That was the last straw! I waved the flight attendant over and asked her for some water. She returned quickly and handed me a full bottle. I wanted to douse Sydney with it but refrained. I had an even better, more civilized way to exact my revenge. I stood up and plunged my hand into my pocket and pulled something out. Displaying the contents in my hand, I smirked. It was a tiny white tablet— a sleeping pill. Without hesitation, and before Sydney could say anything, I popped the pill into my mouth and washed it down with some water. *Thank God for Ambien!* I looked at a completely stunned Sydney directly in the eye and arrogantly announced, "Since you're just dying to have a conversation with me, you can talk at me all you want now. I'll be asleep within twenty minutes and then you'll have a captive audience for hours."

Sydney shook her head in disbelief. I had emerged triumphant from a task that was even more challenging than winning a Grand Slam. I had made Sydney Foster speechless. Taking the sleeping pill was my only alternative to strangling her. I pushed the buttons on my armrest, which transformed the seat into a bed. A few minutes later, I was asleep.

The next voice I heard came over the intercom. "Ladies and Gentlemen, we are about to make our final approach into the Los Angeles area." I hadn't woken up once during the entire flight from Tokyo. I opened my eyes to find Sydney staring at me— more like glaring, unblinking. I winced. The crazy expression on her face was eerily similar to some that Glenn Close perfected in *Fatal Attraction* when she was stalking Michael Douglas.

"Love, I'm sorry. I just really wanted to spend some more time with you in LA," she said as she handed me an envelope the size of a greeting card.

I took the envelope and swallowed my frustration. *God, are we back on this again?!* "I know, but…"

"I just had such a great time with you over there. I don't want it to end." It was incredible to me that Sydney thought we had had a great time together for the last six weeks. Her love for me blinded her to the reality that our relationship had fallen apart. It was blinding ignorance. In a way, I felt bad for her but I refused to let my guilt over her feelings dictate my actions any longer. I was determined to end our relationship later that day.

I put the envelope in my bag and fumbled to find my cell phone. American cell phones are not compatible with Japanese cell phone networks so mine had been turned off since I had left Australia and landed in Tokyo ten days earlier. I was brimming with excitement at the anticipation of retrieving my messages. I flipped the phone open and hammered the "on" button until the screen illuminated. While all the other passengers were collecting their belongings, I gripped my phone as if it were my last worldly possession. Finally, I received a signal and dialed my voicemail.

"You have three new voice messages," the automated voice told me. I smiled and eagerly played the first one. It was not Casey. *Beep.* Let's just bypass that one. "New message skipped," the voice announced. The second message started to play and I heard Casey's voice. "Hi, Stephie…It's me. I can't wait for you to get home. Call me when…uh, when you can…after…uh…well, call me when you're free." Disguising my smile, I erased the message and played the third one. "Hey…It's me again. You're almost home! Fly faster. I can't wait to talk to you!" I obediently deleted this message as well. I was elated to hear Casey's voice and couldn't wait to talk to her. I immediately sent her a text telling her that we had landed.

I gathered my things and walked off the plane staring down at my phone and typing Casey messages. Sydney walked behind me, annoyed.

"You should really pay attention to where you're going." It was killing her that I was more interested in my phone than with savoring our last few minutes together before she left. I'm sure she was even more annoyed that she didn't know whom I was texting. No doubt, she assumed it was Paige, but she knew better than to ask.

"I am. Do you see me walking into anything?" I said, defiantly.

"It's dangerous to text and walk at the same time."

I rolled my eyes and ignored her, refusing even to dignify that one with a response! I continued texting while Sydney signed an autograph for a fan who had spotted her.

Not one word was spoken between us as we followed the signs to the baggage claim area. Sydney walked behind me, as if she were trying to stall. I tried to avoid talking to her because I knew that she had only one thing on her mind and she was running out of time to think of a way to persuade me to let her vacation in LA for a few days. She was desperate. We collected our bags and passed through customs. I breezed toward the exit as if I were on my way to collect lottery winnings and Sydney dragged her feet as if she were walking, shackled, toward a guillotine. As we exited the customs area, I stopped abruptly and turned toward Sydney. She stared into my eyes and this time I could not avert her gaze. She looked crestfallen and I could see the tears accumulating.

Before I gave her a hug, she said, "I just really thought that you were going to ask me to stay with you."

Shrugging off her desperation so as to avoid an argument I replied, "Come on, Sydney. Please don't start this again." Her gaze was fixed, her lower lip almost trembling. *Oh, no! Don't do this now! I can see the finish line. Tears won't change my mind!* With all the compassion I could eke, I said, "Don't be sad. You knew I wasn't gonna ask you to stay. We've been over this."

"I'm just really going to miss you. I can't believe after all we've been through these past several weeks, this is our good-bye. It just feels weird to me."

Of course it felt weird to her. It should have. Her girlfriend was happy that we were going our separate ways.

I combated her sadness with humor and said, "You better go, or you're gonna miss your plane and I'm not falling for that trick."

She forced a smile and I gave her a hug. She turned to walk away and looked back at me with a flicker of disappointment on her face. Not only was she sad to be leaving, but she was even more sad that I had just brushed her off without even the slightest kiss good-bye.

What? She knows I don't like public displays of affection!

I watched the doors close behind her. She had just left a secure area and re-entry was prohibited. As quickly as my fingers could push the buttons, my phone was dialing Casey. The phone rang and I felt dizzy with excitement. When Casey answered, I jubilantly exclaimed, "I'm free at last! I'm free at last! Good God almighty, I'm free at last!" I truly felt like I had just been emancipated.

"It's so good to hear your voice. I haven't been able to get a certain someone out of my head. I've missed you and it's only been a day and a half." Her tone was very girlfriend-ish. Clearly, I didn't mind.

"I've had the same problem. These past thirty-six hours with Sydney have been nothing short of a nightmare. I'm so glad to be home...alone. It was like pulling teeth to get her to leave. I came so close to breaking up with her on the plane!"

"You didn't, did you?!" she shrieked, as if the thought were preposterous. I glazed over it, interpreting her piercing tone to be inspired by incredulity rather than prohibition.

"No! If I had, she probably would have opened the door mid-flight and jumped out, taking me with her!"

"What were you guys fighting about this time?"

I filled Casey in on the heated spat that led to the Ambien episode. She almost choked with laughter and then said, "Listen, Stephie, I really want to talk to you. We need to talk about this. About us." The laughter evaporated from her voice and her tone was serious.

My stomach dropped with a sinking feeling. I feared that I was about to get the wind knocked out of me. Apparently my silence prompted Casey to continue.

"It's not a bad thing. I promise. Really. I just want to talk about things. I can't stop thinking about you…and I don't want to. But I have to go practice. I'm already late. I promise to call you later."

Relieved, I hung up and checked the text message that came through while Casey and I were on the phone. It was from Sydney. *Are you sure you don't want me to turn around and come back? We could have a great time together in LA.* Annoyed, I ignored the text and hailed a cab.

I waited twenty minutes and then sent Sydney a text back. *Safe travels. Call me when you get home.* I guess she got the message.

The second that I walked into my condo, I plopped down on the couch and called Melissa at work to make plans for an early Happy Hour that evening. She had been expecting my arrival and we planned a date with her couch and a bottle of red wine. I hung up the phone and remembered the envelope from Sydney that I had shoved into my bag on the plane. I gasped when I opened the card inside of it to find $500 cash— five crisp $100 bills. I shook my head as I read the note: THANK YOU FOR PUTTING YOUR LIFE ON HOLD FOR ME THESE PAST FEW WEEKS. ITS [SIC] NOT MUCH, BUT GO BUY YOURSELF A LITTLE SOMETHING FROM ME. I LOVE YOU AND I'LL MISS YOU.

I read the card a few times and stared at the money, wondering if my eyes were deceiving me. More like hoping, anyway. When I realized that my girlfriend had just handed me an envelope of cash as a thank-you, I was catapulted into a state of disgust. I stared at the pile of mail across the room on the dining room table but could only focus on the envelope from Sydney. *Please tell me this is not real!* But, as I held the perfectly pristine bills in my hand, I could not ignore the fact that they were real.

Oh, my fucking God! She really is trying to buy me! I really can't do this anymore.

$\mathcal{T}$he rules of the game: silence, please

I landed in LA armed with three goals:

1) Make sure Sydney got on a plane bound for Miami.

2) Call my new girlfriend-to-be.

3) Get to the safety of my home, plant myself in my favorite spot on my couch and plan my exit strategy (which was to break up with Sydney on the phone when she landed on the other side of the country, thereby preventing any histrionics).

I had already placed a checkmark by the first two goals, but Number 3 wasn't going to be quite as easy. I think playing a game of Twister in a body cast would have been easier than breaking up with Sydney. Thankfully, Sydney's plane didn't land until much later that evening, so I had the entire day to formulate and finalize my exit strategy.

A couple hours later, I made the five-minute drive to Melissa's apartment. I was so excited at the thought of sharing my secret with Melissa that I almost drove up a tree. I nearly exploded with anticipation as I skipped up the stairs to her apartment. Before I'd even knocked twice, the door flung open and a smiling face appeared. We threw our arms around each other and I yelled, "It's so good to see you!"

"You, too! Get in here and sit down! I wanna hear all about your trip. Everything...leave out no details!"

I sat down on the couch and took a deep breath. "I'm not sure where to start. Things with Sydney are...not so good." I paused. "And, I have something to tell you about Casey..."

"You guys hooked up, didn't you?" she interrupted, eyeing me circumspectly.

Completely unable to hide my smile, I attempted to weasel away from her question. "I can neither confirm nor deny your allegation, but if I *were* to confirm it, how'd you know?"

"Puh-lease! Sugar, I can see it all over your face. You light up when you mention her name. Don't even, for one second, try to lawyer-ball me with your 'I can't confirm or deny' nonsense! Start talking," she demanded wryly.

My diplomatic non-answer failed miserably. I folded without attempting to splutter a fruitless diversionary tactic and confessed, "Melissa, I'm in trouble. I'm in deep. I can't get Casey out of my mind."

"Wait a minute. Stop. Go back and start from the beginning. I need to know e-v-e-r-y-t-h-i-n-g."

I didn't know where to start and Melissa sat on the floor on the other side of the coffee table, motionless and spellbound as I spent the next hour purging my soul to her as if she were Dear Abby. I confessed my disinterest in my girlfriend and my burgeoning feelings for another woman. Melissa knew that I had been struggling with my relationship for months but that I could never pinpoint exactly what it was that I was feeling or not feeling. I explained that, for a while, I bought Sydney's psychobabble and actually let her convince me that my resistance to her was the result of never having been in a healthy relationship. Wringing my hands nervously, I took a deep breath and admitted to Melissa that after months of not being able to adjust to my new "healthy" relationship, I had finally realized the crux of the problem: I was not in love with Sydney. I had finally acknowledged the truth and had stopped trying to force something that was just not there. Being with Sydney was like trying to shove a square peg into a round hole.

It would take more than one hand for me to count how many times I've been in love before. After the initial infatuation with Sydney wore off, I think I knew I'd never be *in love* with her, but I just kept trying to be. I really wanted to love her— even tried to force myself to because I didn't want to disappoint her. Initially, Sydney fit the mold of what I considered my perfect woman. She was engaging, successful, well traveled, athletic, impeccably sculpted and even accented. She showered me with affection and I lathered myself with the thought of being in love with her. It's happened to us all— falling in love with the idea of falling in love as opposed to feeling the emotion. In the beginning, I think I loved everything about Sydney. As time passed, I still found many of her qualities attractive, except for one small detail I could not overlook— her personality.

Month after month, I continually let Sydney persuade me not to abandon her. I was starting to feel like one of those women in a Lifetime movie who is in a bad relationship, never stands up for herself and then leaves long after she should have. It was time to stop over-thinking where things with Sydney and me went wrong. Although I couldn't or didn't want to see it when my friends pointed it out to me months before, the problem was that Sydney and I had jumped into a relationship before we really knew each other. I spent the last couple of months wanting to kick myself for leaping without looking and committing to dating someone I barely knew. Now I just wanted to commit Sydney.

As soon as I stopped rambling long enough for Melissa to sneak in a question, she asked, "Sugar, do you think you and Sydney are just having some growing pains? I mean, maybe the honeymoon period's over and maybe you're not used to letting your guard down around each other."

I rolled my eyes and sneered, "Yeah, Melissa, I guess it's normal to let your guard down once you start to get comfortable around someone you're dating. But Sydney takes it to an entirely different level. She's the type of person who'd comfortably walk into your house and head straight for the bathroom with a magazine in hand. She'd sit on the toilet with her periodical and take a dump— with the door open— think nothing of it and then flush the toilet and grab the last Diet Coke out of the fridge on her way back out the door. To me, that's not comfortable. It's disgusting. It's the kind of behavior I'd expect from someone whose only form of nutrition comes from savagely ripping meat off a bone with her teeth. Clearly, Sydney and I have very different comfort levels."

She laughed, shaking her head in disbelief. "C'mon, she doesn't really do that does she?"

"Swear to God!"

"Okay, you make a good point. You do have a problem." She wrinkled her nose, and said, "Shit, I think maybe I gave you the wrong advice last summer when she gave you the ring."

Yes, this is all your fault! Some friend you are!

"I should have listened to myself back then. I stupidly ignored all of the warning signs from day one." Hell, I should have listened to Saskia that first day at Wimbledon and then my other friends after that!

"It's hard to look at infatuation objectively," Melissa offered.

"Yeah, but once that initial heat cools off, you become less forgiving and see things for how they really are. When I really got to know Sydney, I didn't like the person I was in bed with. Turns out, she is not the person she was when I met her. When I first set eyes on her at Wimbledon, she was on her best behavior. She was fun to be around, even though her match record had gone from an impressive winning streak to an embarrassing losing streak. Now that she's winning again, I find her absolutely intolerable. I used to love watching her play tennis, but these days, more often than not, when Bad Sydney takes over on the court, I literally bury my face in my hands and try to melt into the stands. Her head has become so incredibly inflated that she looks like a bobblehead doll. If it gets any bigger, that head of hers is going to topple off her skinny body!"

"Do you think this is just a phase she's going through? What do her other friends think of her behavior?"

"As much as I'd love to tell you I think this is temporary, I don't. People keep telling me that I'm just now seeing Sydney's true colors. And as far as her friends go, she thinks everyone loves her and that everyone is her best friend. The truth is, people generally find her annoying and abrasive and many of them talk about her behind her back. I can't be with someone who is not liked by her peers. I can't. Everyone loved Paige. Everyone loves Casey. I'm used to walking into a room with my girlfriend and seeing people smile because we're there. When Sydney walks into a room, people don't smile. They turn their backs." I took a deep breath and let out an exasperated sigh, "What a fiasco! Oh, God, how did I get myself in this mess?" More like embroiled in turmoil.

In response to the distressed look on my face, Melissa asked, "So you're going to break up with her?" She more told than asked.

"As soon as she gets back home tonight. And this time, I'm not letting her talk me out of it. It's going to kill her and I really do hate the thought of hurting her so badly, but I just can't do this anymore. And, when she finds out about Casey and me..."

"Yeah, about that...what exactly is going on between you two?" Melissa interrupted.

"I don't know. We haven't actually talked about it yet. But whatever's going on between us— oh, God, I can't even think about how Sydney's gonna react. She's gonna go postal!"

"She'll be fine. You can't be responsible for her happiness and you can't compromise your integrity by continuing to betray her even though you don't love her. The Stephie I know is not a cheater."

Hearing those words made me cringe. I'm not a cheater. I'm "Mommy's good little girl." Daddy's "perfect angel." A rule-follower.

I sighed and sipped the last of my wine. Melissa was right— I could not be responsible for Sydney's happiness. I needed to take control of my life and free myself from the burdens and obligations that Sydney had placed on my shoulders. I was certain that after our conversation Sydney was going to have to trade in her tennis skirts for either a white straightjacket or a black-and-white striped uniform. Regardless of the consequences or of her feelings, it was time for me to finally end my relationship with Sydney.

I hugged Melissa good-bye and drove home.

Stepping off the elevator, I heard my phone ringing as I approached my front door. I scrambled to put the key in the door and quickly unlock it before the ringing stopped. Racing into the kitchen, I lurched for the phone without even glancing at the caller ID. "Hello," I gasped.

"Why are you out of breath?" Casey asked.

"I just walked in or, rather, ran in from Melissa's."

"You didn't tell her anything, did you?!"

These were the first words out of her mouth? Not "Hello, Stephie!" or, "I've been dying to hear your voice all afternoon!" I didn't want to lie, but I could tell by Casey's tone that I had no choice. *Great, just when I thought all the lying was going to stop. What's one more? At least this one would be harmless.* Trying to avoid a bald-faced lie, I sarcastically responded, "What's there to tell?"

"I'm serious, Stephie. If we're gonna do this, you can't say anything to anyone about us. I'm not kidding. I'll sprint out the door. I won't even put my running shoes on! This has to be our secret!" Her tone was firm, completely inflexible.

A chill ran down my spine. I knew Casey wasn't kidding. A part of me felt bad that I had already dishonored her request for silence about what had happened between us. But how was I supposed to know that I wasn't allowed to tell my closest friend who had absolutely no connection to Casey or to the tennis world? There was no way I could have kept this secret from Melissa! She knew me too well and would have known I was hiding something from her if I even attempted to scrimp on the details. She was my vault and I always told her everything. And besides, I don't kiss and tell, I kiss and yell!

The last thing I wanted was to lose Casey or jeopardize us so I told her a little white lie. "Don't worry. I kept my mouth shut." *What's wrong with me? Why does she get to call the shots? And do I even have her to lose?*

"Good, because no one can know about us! No one!"

When did *we* become an *us*? What exactly *were* we doing? Or more to the point, what was *I* doing? I was getting ready to break up with Sydney so that I could do what? Sneak around and have a secret relationship with Casey? My feelings for Casey had been growing for several months but it never occurred to me that there was a possibility of our being together. And now that it was within my reach, I was sworn to secrecy and silence.

I offered Casey a morsel that I was certain she would devour with delight. "We won't have to be quiet for long. I'm breaking up with Sydney as soon as she gets home and this time I'm not taking 'no' for an answer!"

She shrieked, "No! You can't!" It was the same high-pitched tone I'd heard at the airport earlier in the day— the one I apparently incorrectly interpreted as being inspired by disbelief.

I thought we had a bad connection. I actually held the phone away from my ear to observe it. "What? What did you say? For a second, I thought you said I can't break up with Sydney."

Even more frantic, she squawked, "I did! You can't break up with her!"

Still not believing that she had just told me that I couldn't break up with Sydney, I wanted to bounce up and down on one foot while tapping the side of my head as I do when trying to get water out of my ears after a swim. Maybe clearing my ears would change what I had just heard. "What do you mean, I can't?" I was shocked that Casey didn't embrace my desire to break up with Sydney immediately and that, unbeknownst to me, she had a different agenda.

"You can't break up with her right now. It will destroy her— and her career. She's *just now* recovering from the dive in the rankings she took when we broke up." She reminded me that Sydney had been quick to blab to everyone on the Tour and anyone else who would listen the year before that she was having an "affair" with Trish, which had destroyed her, their relationship and their partnership.

I didn't say anything. I'm not sure if I was silent because I had nothing to say or because I was faint with shock.

Pouncing on my silence to further convince me, Casey continued, "Stephie, I'm playing well now and my ranking is climbing. Marisa and I are practically guaranteed to own the Number 1 ranking by the end of the year— especially if Sydney is no longer playing doubles. The last thing I need right now is to be followed by the stigma of yet again crushing Sydney Foster. I can't have my life smeared all over the locker room walls for stealing Sydney's girlfriend."

Hold it right there, sister! You're not stealing me! I was leaving her anyway!

Finally, I spoke. "Casey, I just don't understand. I don't see how this is going to work."

"Stephie, it's simple. You have to stay with Sydney and come with her to the tournaments so we can see each other. Since the three of us are inseparable, no one will suspect a thing." Casey very quickly rattled off the rules of the game which were non-negotiable. Somehow, it made perfect sense to her that I deceive Sydney and continue dating her, so I could come to the tournaments and sneak around to have a secret romance with her. Instantly, Casey had sabotaged goal Number 3 that I had armed myself with when I stepped off the plane.

Clearly not convinced that her plan was anything *except* ludicrous, I mockingly asked, "And just exactly how long am I supposed to stay with Sydney and keep up this charade?" My voice was mounting with sarcasm.

"Wimbledon will be the finishing line," she matter-of-factly answered.

"W-I-M-B-L-E-D-O-N!" I screeched. "You can't be serious!"

Wimbledon was months away, not to mention the fact that Sydney would be expecting us to celebrate our "real" anniversary then. Had Casey just arbitrarily chosen Wimbledon— the place I'd met Sydney the year before? I transported myself to Wimbledon and envisioned breaking up with Sydney and wondered if she would distinguish our first anniversary from our twelve-month anniversary. I imagined her friends asking her, "Hey, Sydney, what did Steph give you for your anniversary? A breakup? Aww, that's too bad. Maybe you guys'll be back together for your thirteen-month anniversary." *What's the best way to wrap a breakup?*

Casey suggested that waiting until Wimbledon or, even better, until after the US Open would be the least hurtful to Sydney. *The least hurtful!* Sure. What a joke. There was nothing about this that wouldn't be hurtful to Sydney! So why wait? I knew that waiting was only going to make things worse. The US Open was six months away and I had already dragged things out with Sydney six months too long. The problem was that I have lived in the real world my entire life and have played by the same rules that most normal people play by. Casey, on the other hand, has never even set foot in the real world. She has lived in the bubble of her tennis fantasy world since she graduated from high school and has no idea how things are done in the real world. In her world she considers only what is best for her and for her tennis. And my breaking up with Sydney later that night would not be good for either Casey or her tennis.

I was certain that there had to be another way to deal with this sticky situation. I was also sure that I could not keep up this ridiculous charade for another few months and nor could I, in good conscience, let Sydney fly me around the world and foot the bill for a first-class plane ticket so I could secretly spend time with Casey behind closed doors.

When I was a kid, I wasn't that little girl who played with Barbie and sat around fantasizing about my dream wedding to Ken— obviously! But I did have dreams about my future and whom I would spend it with. Sure, I fantasized about the ritz and glitz that I hoped would someday be mine— summers on the Vineyard, winters in the mountains, shows in the City, dinner parties described as "legendary," escapes to Capri. But none of these luxuries mattered unless I had someone to share them with. I would forego all the fanfare for a guarantee that I could end each day with tea on the veranda in a porch swing made for two and occupied by two. I wanted to live my life in the company of the woman I loved. As I got older, I looked forward to falling in love— really falling in love and having a life with someone. I wanted the kind of love associated with stopping and smelling the roses— pure, simple and unembellished. I thought about sharing my life and making memories with someone. The life I imagined was one made up of happiness, romance and true fulfillment.

I never imagined a life of surreptitiously sneaking around to have a dangerous liaison. I wondered what kind of twisted game I was getting myself into. My mind started racing and spiraling with thoughts of confusion and images of Casey and me sneaking in and out of seedy motel rooms like desperate people tiptoeing around for an afternoon romp. Sure, covert romances are had at the Ritz-Carlton, but I imagined a nasty motel room because I was beginning to feel cheap and dirty with all of the secrecy and silence that was being demanded. For the first time in my life, I didn't feel worthy of five stars. As my skin began to crawl at the thought of a sleazy motel, Casey said, "I promise this is only temporary, but we have to do this so we can be together. And that's what I want. I want you."

When I heard her words, my mind cleared. I blinked and the image of the rundown roadside motel under a sign reading: HBO AND FREE A/C! vanished.

Casey relied on the tournament schedule as she explained the method to her madness. "After Wimbledon, I'll play the California tournaments. We'll figure out a way to see each other then. There are more gaps in the schedule for me after Wimbledon heading into the Open so it will be easier for us to see each other between the tournaments. If you break up with her now we won't see each other for months. That's not what you want, is it?"

I was all too familiar with the emotional blackmail card. I didn't think Casey had it in her to play that card, but she just had and barely took a breath as she continued with her explanation.

"After you guys break up and things have cooled off, we can be together and you can travel with *me* on Tour."

She had just reeled me back in and the blackmail was complete.

"Just think, I'll be everywhere you go to see her. We'll figure this out, Stephie. I promise." As I listened to Casey's words, I could tell that she was smiling. Her smile was like a magical elixir to me. It could make me do stupid things that I would otherwise never consider doing, like stay in a relationship with someone I was not in love with so I could sneak around with her ex-girlfriend. That motel sign popped back into my head. I could see it clearly: PRIVATE BATHROOMS. I missed that part before. It was official. I felt like white trash.

As I was thinking about my debut on *The Jerry Springer Show* and recoiling at the audience hisses inspired by my stupidity, Casey reminded me once again of rule Number 1. "No one can know. Not Melissa, not Trish...no one!"

I just heard tires coming to a screeching halt. I was still having trouble digesting all the secrecy and deception around Sydney, but did she just say we had to keep it a secret from Trish? She did. For the life of me, I could not understand why Casey wouldn't want her non-girlfriend-best-friend to know that she had fallen in love and had finally moved on. I thought Trish would be happy for Casey and me. Apparently I thought wrong.

"Casey, I don't get it. Why can't we tell Trish?"

"Stephie, she'll be devastated. Just like I will be when she finds someone else. We're not together, but we've essentially been in a sexless relationship for the past year and a half. She's jealous of you because she thinks you're replacing her in my life. She's really important to me and I want her to be a part of my life."

What the fuck?! Why would Trish give a shit if we're together? More importantly, why in the hell am I still even entertaining any of this? God, this is getting more ridiculous and more complicated by the minute! Who gives a shit if her best friend knows we want to be together?! What's the big deal? Did Trish expect Casey to hold a candle for her forever and just stay in a holding pattern for the rest of her life? Why in the hell is Trish jealous of her best friend, who is gay, moving on with someone else who is gay?! She's straight and she's not stupid— she's known for a while that we've had feelings for each other.

Just then, I remembered a conversation I had had with Trish a few weeks back when we were in Australia. One day she and I went to the beach together while Sydney and Casey were practicing. I think it was Bondi. No, it was Tamarama. You can't even imagine the getup Trish wore to the beach! The article of clothing that just barely covered her ass looked more like a belt than a mini-skirt and her heels sank into the sand as we searched for a spot to unroll our towels. Trish put her towel right next to mine and as we were bronzing ourselves, out of the blue she turned to me and said, "You and Sydney don't seem like you really fit. I can, like, see you more with Casey than with Sydney. I think you guys would make a really great couple. You'd be, like, so great together."

Out of the blue she had said this! A part of me wanted to confide in her then and tell her how much I cared about her best friend because I thought she'd be happy for Casey. As I was about to agree with her wholeheartedly and ask her how she thought I might best exit my relationship with Sydney and jump into one with Casey, something silenced me. Maybe it was that she paused as she glanced into her Bobbi Brown compact while fluffing her eyelashes with mascara (waterproof, I was assured) before reapplying her bright red lipstick (long-lasting *and* fade-resistant)— in the middle of the beach, under the blistering sun. More likely, though, it was that my gut told me not to open up and trust that trashy Trish.

As I replayed that conversation with Trish in my mind, I understood why my intuition had silenced me. That sneaky bitch was digging for information that she could use as emotional blackmail with Casey. She wasn't trying to push us together— she was trying to pull us apart. Casey must have learned how to play the blackmail card from her blackjack dealing, blackmail wielding, straight, non-girlfriend-best-friend! Trish was consumed with jealousy. She had a place in Casey's life and she didn't want to lose it. Up to now, Trish was Number 1 and wanted to remain the most important person in the world to Casey, even though she knew she couldn't be Casey's girlfriend. How could Casey not see how fucked up this whole thing was?

I was lost in thought when Casey mentioned Trish's name. *Speak of the devil!*

"Okay, Stephie, I better go call Trish before she gets suspicious. She just got off work and I was supposed to call her a while ago. I'll call you in the morning when she leaves. Remember, no more phone calls or e-mails tonight."

When she leaves in the morning? What's that supposed to mean?

Oh, r-i-g-h-t... I had forgotten that when Casey was home from tournaments she and Trish pretty much spent every night together, either at her house or at Trish's aunt's house. Okay, two things: why do Casey and her non-girlfriend-best-friend spend every night that they can together? And why does a grown adult live with her aunt? You see, Casey had previously given me the answers to these questions and as I think of the responses now, I find them just as ridiculous as I found them before I had become absurdly and hopelessly interested in her. Answer Number 1: they spent nights together (in separate beds) because Trish can only fit Casey into her schedule at night when she is done dealing the cards. They have dinner or watch a movie and spend the night together so one of them doesn't have to drive back home. And Answer Number 2: Trish lives at home with Auntie Whatever-Her-Name-Is because when her last boyfriend dumped her, he kept their apartment. Living with her aunt helps her save money while she is trying to find a new apartment. Those Louis Vuitton bags teeming with makeup cost her one pretty penny!

Back to the *"No more phone calls or e-mails."* Casey didn't want me calling or e-mailing her after sundown because she didn't want Trish to know that we were communicating outside of the tournaments— and outside of Sydney. Why the fuck would Trish care if we were e-mailing and calling and how would she know anyway?

Casey's answer: "I don't want to have to explain anything about you to Trish. And if she's here when you e-mail, she might see the message from you when I log on later."

Here's my other question: Does Trish sit on Casey's lap when she checks her e-mail?

Casey's answer was even more absurd than the question: "No, but sometimes she looks over my shoulder when I log on."

Oh, of course she does. Naturally! All of my friends read my private correspondence over my shoulder! Makes perfect sense.

I was getting annoyed. I opened my mouth to form an argument and I was sure that Casey could hear the annoyance in my voice. She stopped me.

"Look, I know this is annoying, but we either do it like this right now or we don't do it at all." She truly believed that things had to be done this way. Sydney had told me on several occasions that Casey could not deal with confrontation. She said that Casey would avoid conflict at any cost…any cost at all. I was aggravated, but I guess I'm not really one to talk about avoiding conflict.

I hung up the phone, loving how I felt about Casey but hating the game I was being forced to play. Casey made all the rules. It was as if she had won the toss and elected to serve the *entire* match. Against my better judgment, I decided to go along with her convoluted and flawed logic, despite my extreme discomfort with it. We had just barely begun our romance and I wanted so badly for it not to end. The power of love so easily overrode my power of intellectual reasoning.

So much for doing the honorable thing and breaking up with Sydney immediately so Casey and I could be together.

I have no problem identifying crazy and unacceptable behavior. I have a history of going along with other people's agendas. I've justified doing things I might not want to do in the past in the interest of achieving a certain goal, so why wouldn't I do the same now? Damn those fettering chains of habit!

I didn't break up with Sydney that night, or the next, or the next. I told myself that if I could just make it past Wimbledon I would blink and the US Open would be over. I had a new mantra that I began to repeat incessantly: "No white after Labor Day. No Sydney after Labor Day. Be 'The Little Engine That Could.' I think I can! I think I can! No white after Labor Day. No Sydney after Labor Day. Be 'The Little Engine That Could.' I think I can! I think I can!"

10

*P*laying the angles

The days that had passed since my return from Tokyo were few in number, but the distance between Sydney and me had grown exponentially. She began to have less and less of a presence in my life, although she still called and texted me constantly. I had learned to be selective in my acceptance and response to her messages. There were only so many hours in the day that I could spend on the phone and I just couldn't waste too many of my precious minutes making small-talk with Sydney. Sometimes when she called, I answered in a harried voice and brushed her off with an "I can't talk right now. I'm with clients." But most of the time, I just let the calls go to voicemail.

Secretly, I hoped the distance I imposed between us would push Sydney to break up with me. I mean, I didn't even pretend to be interested in her any longer. Most girlfriends would view an aloof disposition from their significant other as a hint that perhaps the relationship was over. But not Sydney! She refused to admit that our relationship was unsalvageable and seemed to completely overlook my admission in Melbourne that I was not in love with her. I had the misfortune of dating someone who refused to quit anything. Even a bag of bricks falling on her head would not deter her persistence. In fact, Sydney considered my reluctance to open up and truly love her a challenge. She was going to *make* me love her. I wondered what kind of self-esteem she possessed if she could fathom staying with someone who treated her with the indifference that I did.

Gradually, my friends became aware of my disenchantment with Sydney and our relationship. I remembered a time when I would jokingly utter something about Sydney that was not altogether flattering but would then quickly recant my statement. I would mentally slap myself on the wrist because it wasn't nice to say mean things about my girlfriend— about someone I was supposed to love. Now, I didn't even try to negate whatever blasphemy I muttered about Sydney and my friends started to wonder what the hell I was doing. If I were so miserable, why didn't I just leave? I couldn't explain to any of them my reason for hanging on, partly because I was embarrassed but mostly because I had made a promise to Casey that I would not reveal our secret.

Despite my complaints to my friends about Sydney, none of them thought it was serious enough for a breakup because they still noticed excitement when my phone rang and I excused myself to talk to "my tennis pro." Naturally, most people assumed I was referring to Sydney. Others were simply misinformed, as I would often confirm with a white lie that Sydney was on the phone and then creep into a corner to quietly take Casey's call. I became undeniably radiant at the sound of Casey's voice. No one suspected that my enthusiasm was inspired by someone other than my girlfriend. I was becoming a master of illusion and deceit. Fact, fiction and misinformation had all become so entangled that extracting the truth about Casey or Sydney was impossible. Never before had I known that I had such a dark and mysterious side.

Day after day, I was lying to everyone, including myself. I didn't want my closest friends to think less of me. Just like I crave approval from my parents, I seek it from my friends as well. I'm not sure how I convinced myself that any of my behavior was acceptable, but I did. Sometimes I would stop long enough to think about things. *God, I guess I really am becoming that person— that person who could find it so easy to lie in order to get what she wants.* Amid all the deception, my conscience made itself known. It reminded me of the feelings of fear, guilt and shame that I was desperately trying to ignore. But I quickly retreated to thoughts of the overpowering love that was developing between Casey and me and my guilt faded away.

Meanwhile, Casey was going about her life as normally as possible, which included juggling secret correspondences with me while overtly participating in her friendship with Trish all the while maintaining status quo with Sydney. She scrambled from the tennis court to quiet, solitary places to sneak in phone calls to me during the day. When Trish's working day ended, Casey would tuck me away until it commenced again the next morning. I couldn't help but feel like Casey was the one with the girlfriend. She was much more conscientious of Trish's schedule, Trish's feelings and Trish's needs than I was of Sydney's. The vigilance around Trish had become such a menace that even the mention of Trish's name took me back to second grade, when the boys in my class would try to drive the girls crazy by dragging their nails down the front of the chalkboard. My jaw tensed and my fists clenched at the very thought of her. What angered me even more was that I just cupped my hands over my ears and tried to ignore it. Sure, just ignore it— that was sure to make it disappear! I secretly fantasized about taking that Trash out and leaving her by the curb where she belonged!

Just as I was reaching my breaking point with what I considered ridiculous and unnecessary precautions with Trish, I got a week's reprieve. Casey was leaving Boston and going to Atlanta to play in her last indoor tournament of the season before the outdoor hard court season began. Sydney didn't bother playing in Atlanta since it was a Tier 3 event and she felt she was above having to enter such events, which, according to her, "lacked prestige." For an entire week, Casey would be out from under Trish's watchful eye and we would be able to call or e-mail each other anytime, day or night, without having to worry that someone would overhear the call or oversee the e-mail. I thanked God for life's small pleasures!

It was in Atlanta that the magnitude of Casey's feelings for me became undeniably clear. In her spare time, Casey indulged in one of her favorite extracurricular activities— shopping, and not shopping for herself. She shopped for me. She spoiled me. The UPS delivery man appeared at my door once, sometimes even twice per day during that week. Everyday was like Christmas. I got boxes filled with all kinds of goodies that Casey thought would make me smile. When the first box arrived, it seemed bottomless. As Styrofoam packing peanuts spilled out onto the floor, I reached into the box and pulled out one gift after another— a bracelet, a candle, one of everything from The Body Shop and a sterling silver necklace. There was an inscription on the guitar pick-like pendant dangling from the chain. It was a quote from Henry David Thoreau which read: LIVE THE LIFE YOU HAVE IMAGINED. The necklace was representative of a conversation Casey and I had in which I told her that I wanted to live the life I had always imagined— with her. I held the pendant in my clenched fist and stared at all of my presents. Each gift had been thoughtfully selected. This was the type of package that I was used to giving, not receiving.

Casey had just come back to the hotel from her afternoon practice session when I called to thank her. She answered in a child-like voice, "Heyyyy, Stephie-eee, did someone get a special delivery todaaay?"

I was barely able to find the words I was looking for to thank her. Casey's gift-giving was genuine and sincere. Her generosity and thoughtfulness amazed me. Casey's motives for gift-giving were the opposite of Sydney's, who bought me things just for the sake of buying them or just so she could brag to all of her friends about the elaborate gifts she had given me— mindless materialism, as I had begun to think of it. I thought of the generous first-class plane ticket that Sydney bought me. She got credit not only from me, but also from the hoards of other people she bragged about it to. When I was in Australia, if I heard Sydney boast to one more person that she "flew her girlfriend around the world first-class," I think I might have committed an act that certainly would have guaranteed that I would not be returning home in the first-class cabin. Rather, I would have been extradited in shackles.

I fingered the pendant that now hung from my neck. I thanked Casey profusely and told her that such generous gifts were unnecessary. I stammered, "You...you could send me a paper bag in the mail and write on it: TO STEPHIE, LOVE CASEY. I would be just as happy." Truly, I would have been. I didn't need expensive presents from Casey. I'd love anything she sent to me simply because it was sent from her heart.

The next morning, I heard a knock at my front door while I was in the shower. I wasn't expecting anyone, but I quickly rinsed myself off, jumped out, threw on a robe and raced to the door. It was my new best friend, the UPS man, with another package from Casey. This time, it was an overnight envelope. Still dripping wet from my shower, I ripped it open as quickly as my fingers possibly could. What I saw inside commanded a huge smile and rendered me nearly incapable of standing on my own two feet. There was one item inside the envelope— a brown paper bag— the kind I remembered taking my lunch to school in when I was a kid. I knew what it said before I even found the writing. I shook my head in amazement as clichéd reactions of dizziness and heart-sinking overtook me. I lifted the bag out of the envelope and read the words written on it: TO STEPHIE, LOVE CASEY. I smiled as if I were thirteen and had just had my braces removed. I was buoyant with bliss.

I savored my present before opening the trashcan and dropping it in— as Casey had insisted and as I had so stupidly agreed. Another of Casey's rules was that I destroy any and all correspondence that she sent me so no one would be able to connect us romantically. I desperately wanted her approval so I begrudgingly acquiesced to her demands. As I closed the trashcan lid, I shook my head at the thought that I had just discarded one of the sweetest gestures ever given to me. How romantic. The line to kick me in the ass forms to the left. Please take a number.

The week progressed and I sat glued to the Tennis Channel as Casey and Marisa headed toward the tournament finals, demolishing all of their opponents with ease and finesse. Knowing that I was watching, Casey had signs for me during the match that only I would recognize. She would tap her racket twice signaling, "I'm thinking of you, Stephie" or grasp her necklace signaling, "I imagine my life with you." The afternoon of the finals, Casey's special signals brought me to my feet. As she hit winner after winner, I could barely contain my excitement. Sometimes I even screamed at the television as I cheered. *Oh, my God! Are you kidding with that forehand?! You're on fire!* I couldn't help myself. Each cheer was louder than the last. If only Casey could hear me! I watched from my bedroom in LA as Casey and Marisa claimed victory in Atlanta.

Casey now had a gap in her schedule before the California tournaments started. We were desperate to see each other and immediately focused on how to take advantage of her free time. Casey, Miss Paranoid-of-all-Paranoids, wasn't sure how a covert visit could become a reality. For someone who wanted to be in absolute control of our secret romance, she certainly was lacking in her ability to create a plan of action. She had the vision but could not quite be the architect behind the plan. That's where I came in. I had plenty of experience watching masterminds at work while I was growing up, so I adjusted to the roll rather easily. We decided that the only way for us to see each other was for me to make a trip to Boston immediately upon her return from Atlanta. Being the mastermind, I just had to come up with a plan that would fool both Sydney and Trish. Easier said than done!

Time was of the essence. It was Sunday and Casey would be landing back in Boston by Monday evening. I was determined to be on a plane bound for Boston at the end of the week to spend the weekend with her. I ran through the options in my head looking for the perfect angle to exploit. *What's a good reason for me to go to Boston? A doctor's appointment? No. A surprise party for a friend? No. An alumni function? No. You can do better than that! Think, dammit, THINK!*

Suddenly, it came to me. Continuing Legal Education. It was the *perfect* excuse. I could tell Sydney that I had to go back to Boston to finish some classes I never finished in order to stay in good standing as a lawyer. I always hated going to those damn things and finally I had found a way for those boring classes to benefit me! It was an outstanding alibi. I almost jumped out of my skin as I called Casey to inform her of my genius plan.

"We can tell Sydney and Trish that I have to come to Boston this weekend to take a required Continuing Legal Education class to keep my bar admission current!" I yelled excitedly.

"What?" Casey had absolutely no idea what I was yammering on about.

I repeated myself. "I thought of a reason I *have* to come to Boston. Continuing Legal Education…CLE! It's a requirement. Lawyers have to take a certain amount of credits every year in order to stay in good standing and be able to practice law. Only, I don't have to since I no longer practice law. But Sydney and Trish don't have to know that and there's no way for them to find out otherwise."

I explained that I would call Sydney frantically and tell her that I had just received a notice in the mail from the Board of Law Examiners compelling my attendance at a class that weekend in order to complete my annual credits or I would be ineligible to practice law…ever. Sydney would be none the wiser!

"Do you think she'll believe it? I mean, why do you have to take the class by *this* weekend?" Casey was skeptical.

"She'll have no choice! Ms. Know-It-All may think she knows everything about everything, but she doesn't know shit about CLE requirements in Massachusetts. She doesn't even know what CLE is. And I won't call it CLE, so that sneaky bitch can't check up on me."

"But how are you going to explain why you have to take the class this weekend?"

"Easy. I'll tell her that I've been ignoring the notices— which is true— and that I finally opened an envelope and found a letter informing me that I have to take this class, and that this was the third and final notice— which is not true. In fact, it's a total lie!"

I laughed. *Abe Lincoln's fascination with honesty was so overrated!*

"But, what about Trish?"

Rolling my eyes at the mention of her name, I answered, "Obviously, we'll tell her the same thing! Again, I'll be cagey and tight-lipped about the details. I know how to get around questions I don't wanna answer. I was a lawyer, for God's sake!"

I took a sip of my Diet Coke before telling Casey the best part of my plan. I knew that once I told Sydney that the class was outside of the city, near Casey's house (a mere coincidence!), she would quickly volunteer Casey to host me.

Casey was still nervous, but she knew the idea was a good one. We both knew that Sydney would be beside herself at the prospect of my coming to Boston because Paige lived there. The thought of Casey and me doing anything adulterous wouldn't even enter Sydney's mind. She'd be way too preoccupied with the wrong ex.

I bought my ticket to Boston later that evening but decided to wait for two days to call Sydney with my rehearsed story. Sydney has unmitigated gall and I didn't put it past her that she might somehow try to book a flight and meet me in Boston, so I wanted to give her as little notice as possible. I admit that I did feel a bit evil for taking joy in concocting such a devious plan. But I also thought that if Sydney were ridiculous enough to buy into the charade of relationship that we had, on some level she deserved to get walked all over.

Less than forty-eight hours before my scheduled departure, it was time to make the call to Sydney. I took a deep breath, put my earpiece in and dialed. By the disgusted look on my face, you would have thought that I was eating a can of rotting worms rather than calling my girlfriend.

Here we go— it's show time!

Pretending to be exasperated when Sydney answered, I blurted, "Well, when it rains, it *fucking* pours!"

Surprised, even shocked, that she had been blessed with a phone call from me in the middle of the day, she asked, "What are you talking about, love?"

Somehow I made my voice shake and then launched into my explanation. "So, I guess I should pay attention to my mail more often. I checked my mail today and opened a letter from the Board of Law Examiners in Boston. It seems that I failed to complete some required courses. I have to fly to fucking Boston this weekend to take a fucking class that I was supposed to have taken last fucking year. Apparently, they've been sending me fucking notices for the past year. I always thought they were asking for money whenever I saw an envelope from them, so I always ripped them up and threw them right the fuck away." I thought excessive use of the word "fuck" would make my story *that* much more believable.

Sydney was utterly confused. "Uh, okay…so what happened?"

"I opened my mail box and saw a bright orange envelope stamped with the words: URGENT. DATED MATERIALS ENCLOSED. Good thing I decided to open it. The letter said that I had failed to respond to previous notices, blah, blah, blah. And that this was the final notice before my license would be suspended for failure to comply with the fucking state licensing rules. Motherfuckers! I called them immediately to see if I could talk my way out of it, but the second I heard their condescending laughter, I hung up on them. As if I don't have enough shit in my life to worry about right now, I have to somehow get my ass on a plane and get to Boston to take this fucking class so I don't get fucking disbarred! I'm so fucking annoyed right now, I can't fucking even fucking talk about it!" Believable?

"Wait. Where's the class?" Sydney asked.

"In the fucking suburbs, just outside of Boston. Pain in my ass! And, the last thing I want to do is go stay in a hotel room by myself."

"Calm down, love— "

"No!" I interrupted. "You don't understand. This is serious! I could

171

get disbarred." I almost started to believe the bullshit that was coming out of my mouth. I was really getting into the story as I delivered each strategically placed fucking detail. Okay, *you* might not believe it. But, Sydney was most likely an easier sell than the Average Joe. My story was akin to trying to convince someone that tonsillitis was fatal and Sydney was about to rush me to the hospital. I think I just felt a flame from hell again.

Sliding off the white horse she had just ridden in on to save the day, Sydney responded, "It's not a problem. Casey'll be home this weekend. Why don't you stay with her? Just call her and ask her. I'm sure she won't mind. She'd love the company." Bingo! I patted myself on the back for expertly anticipating that she'd suggest that.

Sydney was quick to volunteer Casey because she wanted to limit my housing options. The last place she wanted me to stay was with Paige, so she covertly tried to head that one off at the pass by suggesting that I stay with Casey. It was just one more example of how Sydney tried to control me. *Nice try.*

This is easier than I thought!

Knowing that Sydney would love my request for help, I said, "Sydney, I can't call Casey and invite myself to stay with her. I hate imposing. I'd feel really awkward calling her. Can you do it? I really can't deal with this right now."

"Yeah, yeah. I'll call her. Don't worry about it. Everything'll be fine, love. I'll take care of it. See, what would you do without me?" I could think of about a million things I would do, but I kept my mouth shut. "And, if worse comes to worse, I'm sure you can stay with Trish."

Miraculously, I stifled my laughter and made a mental note to tell Casey about Sydney's ridiculous suggestion.

When I got off the phone with Sydney, I called Casey to tell her the good news. The mission was accomplished and Sydney bought it without question. I deserved an Oscar for best actress in a drama for my performance! As we were talking, Casey's other line rang. I knew it would be Sydney. Casey put me on hold and answered her call waiting. A couple of minutes later, she clicked back over, laughing. I was waiting as patiently as I could to hear the details of the conversation. Casey told me how perfectly my plan had worked— in fact, better than we had anticipated. Not only did Sydney call and ask Casey if I could stay with her, but she also asked Casey to babysit me and follow me wherever I went. She begged Casey not to let me be alone with Paige. Casey nonchalantly agreed to both of Sydney's requests, adding that she'd do her best not to leave my side.

One down, and one to go. Or so I thought. I incorrectly assumed that we only had to convince one more person— Trish. Now that our plan was actually underway, Casey, being the neurotic one, got nervous and still needed convincing. She insisted that we practice our scripts every time we were on the phone until I left for Boston. She bulleted questions at me and wanted to make sure that I had an answer for every possible question asked. She even called me and tried to catch me off guard when I answered the phone, greeting me with, "What time does your class start?"

Giggling, I responded, "Nine o'clock."

"And where is it?" Casey sharply quizzed.

"I don't know. Somewhere near the mall. I have the address and MapQuested it but haven't looked at the directions."

"What's the class on?"

"I don't know…bankruptcy or some boring bullshit like that."

"How do they know if you go?"

"They make you sign in and sign out. I'll go, sit in the back of the room and sleep or e-mail from my phone and sign out and leave when the torture's over."

Completely out of the blue and off the topic, Casey asked, "Where'd you get that necklace?"

Despite the fact Casey could not see me, I pointed to my neck and said, "This old thing? Some cute professional tennis player who lives in Boston gave it to me."

"C'mon! Be serious!"

"Cutie…" As soon as I heard the pet-name slip out of my mouth, it was too late to take it back. Casey didn't seem to mind her new label, so I continued, "I *am* being serious…and…" The tone of my voice dropped and all hints of laughter vanished. "I need to tell you something…something you probably already know, but I need to tell you."

She stammered and stuttered, "No. Wait. Don't. I mean, I already know. I mean, I don't wanna know right now. Not now. Just wait."

Umm, okay. What did she think I was going to tell her? That I loved her? Over the phone? For the first time? I don't think so!

I cleared my throat and said, "All I was going to tell you was that I got the necklace in a store in LA— on Melrose." How's that for serious?

Her voice was still quivering from what she mistakenly assumed I was going to tell her. She added, "Uh, okay. I, umm, guess that sounds good. But, don't wear that necklace in front of Sydney...or Trish."

I rolled my eyes and grumbled, "If I can't wear it, why the hell'd you give it to me? You should have just ordered me to dispose of it immediately after opening it."

"Stephie, please don't get mad. I promise it won't be like this forever." There was an anxious edge in her voice.

"Fine. Do we have any other questions to go over?" My voice wasn't anxious, but it was laden with an edge.

"Just a few more."

Even though I answered all of Casey's questions without pause, she was still a nervous wreck. She desperately longed to see me but wanted to make sure that all of our bases were covered. I, on the other hand, was not nervous at all. I had an answer for everything that was asked of me. To me, the question-and-answer session was an exercise in futility. Neither Trish nor Sydney, individually or collectively, was a match for me on their best day and on my worst. I had been trained by incredibly shrewd minds during my formative years and more formally by cunning professors during my three years of law school to be three steps ahead of my most astute opponent. There was no chance that either Sydney or Trish, short of injecting a truth serum into my veins, would shake me and thereby expose me to the liability of the truth.

11

Whose fault is it?

I woke up just before the plane landed in Boston. As we descended through the clouds, I stared out the window as the buildings on the ground became visible. A smile warmed my face at the thought of the familiarity of returning to the city where I used to live and an odd feeling of homecoming swept over me. Ironically, this city was the place where I had last felt the passion that I currently felt. Once at the gangway, I impatiently waited for the door to open.

C'mon, c'mon, c'mon! Open the door already! I was in such a hurry to disembark that I became that passenger who I always despised— the annoying one who bumps into you and breathes down your neck, as if that will somehow make the flight attendant open the door faster. I was standing so close to the man in front of me that I could count the dandruff particles on his white shirt. I felt like handing him a sample bottle of Head & Shoulders! An evil smile forced my cheeks upward. *If I pushed him just hard enough, I could create a domino effect— one passenger falling on top of another. Then I'd be able to dash over the crumpled pile the second the doors opened and be the first passenger off the plane.*

As the door was pushed back, I abandoned my fantasy and calmly exited the cabin. My pace quickened as I entered the terminal and I felt like one of those suburban moms I sometimes see on Metro Park trails speed walking, but not quite jogging. I always make fun of them. Yes, I think it's great that they're out there exercising, but they really do look silly with their arms flailing about and their hips swinging from side to side.

I rushed through the terminal and down through baggage claim, desperately anticipating Casey's smiling face. I ran my fingers through my hair and made sure my pink button-down J. Crew shirt was sufficiently smoothed and fell exactly where it needed to, just below the belt loops of my Sevens. A wave of excitement crashed down on me when I stepped off the escalator and set eyes on Casey, casually snuggled in her fluffy blue ski vest like the one Sydney had given me in Germany. It was the first time we had seen each other since departing Tokyo almost three weeks earlier. The reunion was sweet. We couldn't wipe the grins off our faces.

We greeted each other warmly (but not *too* warmly) with an excited bear hug and then walked to the garage. Before Casey even pressed the button on her key disengaging the alarm to her car, I knew the shiny black Porsche Cayenne with the personalized license plate 10SANY1 belonged to her. During the drive to her suburban dwelling, Casey smiled as I pointed things out to her along the way, both familiar and new— things only a Bostonian would appreciate.

We arrived at her house and she parked the car in the driveway. I was nervous. We had planned the entire weekend down to the last detail. We knew what we would say to Sydney. We knew what we would say to Trish. We scripted everything perfectly, planning for any eventuality. We didn't, however, prepare a script for our first moments alone.

As we entered her house, a nauseous feeling overcame me. Before I could free my hands of my bags, Casey pulled me close and kissed me (only after making sure all the blinds were closed and the door was dead-bolted). My stomach dropped. I wrapped my arms around her body and returned her kiss. Indeed, I felt like I was home again. Casey's passion was every bit as wonderful as it had been a few weeks before and, in my mind, in the weeks since.

She led me by the hand up the stairs and gave me a tour of the second floor, which consisted of two uninspiring bedrooms. On our way back down the stairs, she walked in front of me but stopped abruptly and turned toward me. I was silent. Her expression was serious. I stood with my back to the wall, waiting for her to say something. She leaned in close to me and whispered, "Stephie, I think I'm falling in love with you." Her breath was soft and warm in my ear.

Now it was my heart that dropped— into my stomach. I whispered back, "I don't *think* I am. I *know* I am." We embraced in the middle of the stairs. No kissing. Just hugging. I could have stayed on those steps forever.

But of course, we had to abandon the tranquility of the moment so as not to deviate from our plan. Casey broke the embrace and led me downstairs, insisting that we place our obligatory phone calls to Sydney and Trish. As torturously annoying as it was, I refused to let anything detract from the happiness I felt being in the same room as the woman I loved.

I picked up the phone to call Sydney and did the "voicemail dance"— the ritual chanting and swaying that I had begun to do whenever I called Sydney lately. As the phone rang, I softly repeated, "Please don't be there. Please don't pick up. Voicemail, voicemail, voicemail. Please, please, ple…" Just then, on the third ring, Sydney's voice came on the line. It was her recorded voice on her voicemail. *Bonus!* I sighed with relief and left a rehearsed message. It was the same message that I had become accustomed to leaving for her over the past few weeks. "Hey, it's me. I guess I missed you. If you call back and I don't answer, I'll talk to you tomorrow. Hope you had a good day." There was no "I love you" and no "I miss you." There wasn't even an "I'm sorry I missed you."

As Casey picked up the phone to call Trish, I secretly did the voicemail dance in my head hoping that somehow it would summon Trish's voicemail. It didn't and Trish answered immediately. I knew I wasn't lucky enough to have a voicemail interception! After Casey's short conversation, she looked up with disappointment on her face and said, "Stephie, I'm sorry, but we have to go to dinner with her tonight. I had to agree so she doesn't get suspicious."

Before I left LA, I had decided that I would not let Trish ruin my weekend. Although I was getting really tired of adjusting my behavior in order not to arouse suspicion in Trish, I didn't fly across the country to give Casey a hard time about her best friend. There were two reasons for my trip: first, to satiate my burning desire to see Casey; and second, to spend time with her alone. I needed to find out if there truly was anything between us or if we had just been enveloped in a fantasy of emotions in Tokyo. Very quickly, I realized that my desire to see Casey could not be satiated with just one weekend together and that there was, indeed, something for us to pursue. Because of that, I decided not to tread lightly on the Trish situation. Rather, I didn't tread at all.

Shrugging off my annoyance, I casually said, "I don't care what we do. I'm fine with having dinner with her." I knew that telling Casey this white lie and agreeing to have dinner with Trish would make her life easier— which would make my life easier.

Casey wrapped her arms around me and hugged me tightly. As we embraced, my eyes scanned the room. Truthfully, her house wasn't quite what I had expected. Given how successful she had been and how much money she had made, I thought she would have owned a tasteful, professionally decorated home similar to Sydney's. Not sleek, modern, or possessing any of the latest technologies, her house was rather bland. While the pièce de résistance in Sydney's living room was a huge flat-screen TV, Casey's was a six-foot tall CD tower filled with '80s music in alphabetical order— everything from A-Ha's "Take On Me" to ZZ Top's "Gimme All Your Lovin."

Her living room consisted of two large glass trophy cases, two hunter green upholstered couches, a simple wood coffee table, a TV, a desk and office chair. No art hung on the walls, but the coffee table was crammed with picture frames. She lived in the suburbs in an unremarkable community. I was used to living in the city— Beacon Hill, to be exact, with doormen always on hand. I think I only noticed the color on Casey's walls— beige— because I was in shock that I was actually within them.

Stepping back, she interrupted my mental inventory of the room. "I know this place needs work, but I'm never here long enough to make it my home. I'm going to redo it when the season's over." I shrugged my shoulders and contorted my face as if to say, "What are you talking about? I hadn't even noticed." After all, I didn't love her for her house or her interior decorating skills.

That evening, we met Trish at her favorite Japanese restaurant. She spent the entire meal talking to me about how obsessive and nervous Sydney was acting because I was in the same vicinity as Paige. She told us that Sydney had called her and kept her on the phone for hours talking about her fear of my seeing Paige. I still didn't trust Trish. After all, she's the same sneaky bitch who had tried to walk me into a trap in Australia! My gut had told me not to trust Trish that day on Tamarama Beach and I wasn't about to cavalierly hand her my trust now. Trish knew how I once felt about Paige and she thought we should reconcile. At least, that was what she wanted me to believe. Since I didn't indulge her in Australia when she suggested that Casey and I would make a good couple, she decided to push my emotions elsewhere. What she really wanted was for me to be interested in Paige again so that she would have her best friend all to herself in some sick, twisted non-sexual way.

When we got into the car after dinner, I had already washed Trish from my mind and was focused on the rest of the evening ahead of me. During the fifteen-minute drive back to Casey's house, I fantasized about what would happen later in Casey's bedroom as we shared our first night together.

* * *

Snuggled under the cool, burgundy sateen sheets, I waited for Casey. A few minutes felt like a lifetime as she completed her night-time routine with all her moisturizers and face creams. Finally, she crawled into bed, dressed in a camisole and flannel pajama bottoms and turned off the light. Pitch black and silent in the room, I could hear my own heart beating. The vanilla scent of her skin cream stimulated my senses with anticipation. I felt like a virgin on prom night. Casey sensed my excitement, rolled over and enveloped me with tender kisses. Her tongue softly circled mine and very quickly the silence in the room was replaced with the subtle noises of ecstasy— accelerated breathing and faint moans— that came from us. I exhaled and gasped loudly as she nuzzled my ears and neck. Her hand slid up my smooth body, under my T-shirt until her nimble fingertips found my quivering, erect nipples. As she caressed my taut breasts, she began to lift my shirt over my head. I arched my back so she could slide the shirt from my tingling body. At the same time, I reached for her camisole and slowly pulled it from her chest as if I were unveiling a piece of prized, precious art. She guided my naked torso back toward the extra-fluffy Siberian goose-down pillow. As my head sank into the feathers, she pressed her mouth to my lips. I savored the feeling of her half-naked body on top of mine. It was sheer ecstasy. My body, now beginning to smolder, jolted as she stroked my stomach, teasing me. As her hand traveled past my waist, my hips lifted slightly and she reached under my Calvin Klein boxer shorts and between my thighs. Sliding off me just slightly, she rested herself on her left elbow and kissed me with greater intensity as her fingers sensuously explored me. I almost couldn't take it. I moaned as she ventured in and out, slowly at first but then faster and faster until I turned my head to the side, breaking the kiss and whispered, "Oh God... Please don't stop!"

"I promise I won't. I'm just getting started," she murmured seductively and then lowered my boxers, which were now halfway down my thighs. She tossed my Calvins onto the floor and then slid her pants off.

Jittery with excitement and completely naked together for the first time, I gently pushed her onto her back and kissed her earlobe—earrings and all. Her head rested on my hand and her soft hair fell between my fingers. Pushing her legs apart with my knees, I slowly slid my body down hers. As I circled the belly ring in her naval with my tongue, I paused and looked up at her. Somehow, through the darkness, I could see into her eyes. We gazed at each other briefly before I continued kissing her lower stomach. Unable to wait one second longer, she grabbed the back of my head and gently guided me down between her thighs. My tongue plunged inside her and her moaning increased and intensified. Like fresh honeycomb, her sweetness and warmth created a sense of euphoria throughout my body. I pushed her legs further apart with my arms until eventually her legs were in the air, with my hands under her knees. My tongue darted faster, then slower. Her legs rested over my shoulders as I made love to her. Her hips moved with the same rhythm as my head. I moved my tongue from side to side and then in circles, swirling around her moist folds. Her breaths turned into heavy sighs. My body began rocking with hers. I don't know which of us was moaning louder. As my tongue continued circling her, one of her legs fell from my hands and her heel dug into the middle of my back. Her stomach muscles tightened and her body convulsed as she began to climax. She reached down and put her hand on my head. Suddenly, I heard her faint voice, "Oh, Trish..."

I heard the needle skip on the vinyl record!

Fuck off! Did she just say what I think she said? She did! T-R-I-S-H! I'm in the middle of going down on her and she yells out someone else's name?! And not just anyone else's name. Trish!

I immediately screeched to a complete halt and lost my orgasm that I was certain was imminent. I propped myself onto my elbows and as calmly as I could asked, "Did you just call out Trish's name?"

Casey lifted her legs off my shoulders and sat up. "Stephie, I'm so sorry…"

"I don't even know what to say. This has never happened to me before. Are you thinking of her? Is she the one you want to be with?" I accused, more than asked, still completely stunned.

"No…no. God, no! I want to be with *you*. I'm sorry. I don't know why I said that. I wasn't thinking of her. I guess she's just been the center of my world for so long, I said her name out of habit. God, I'm so sorry I said that."

I still wasn't convinced. "Casey, come on. I thought you were over her, but if you want to be with her, you need to be honest with me."

"I don't. I want to be with you. I want you in my bed. I want you to make love to me."

"But why would you call out her name? Have you been with her before and you just haven't told me?"

"No…no…no! Stephie, her name just rolls off my tongue, but I don't think of her that way. I promise…" She stopped herself, leaned down and kissed me with intense passion.

I didn't pull away. Making love was the panacea for Casey's blunder. But as the passion rekindled, Trish's name was branded in my mind. As our breathing became longer and deeper, I attempted to banish thoughts of Trish from my mind and I made love with Casey. Still, glazing over such a horrible faux pas and pushing Trish out of my thoughts is one of the Top 10 dumbest things a lovesick person has ever done!

Our initial night of *amour* was unbelievably intense and tender— after I had recovered from the initial shock. We explored every inch of each other's bodies. We made love for hours and reached levels of intimacy and euphoria neither of us thought possible. Just when I thought the night had reached its pinnacle of intimacy, Casey catapulted me into another world. As we were embracing and kissing, she, without hesitation, whispered to me, "Stephie, I love you." This time she got my name right. "I love you. I really love you, Stephie." I was lying on top of her, looking into her eyes, her face softened by the warm glow cast by the light.

Saying "I love you" is entirely different than saying "I think I'm falling in love with you" and suddenly I felt faint.

Struggling to push words out of my mouth, I softly said, "Casey, can you please turn on the light for a second?" She turned and switched on the bedside lamp. "What did you just say to me?" I asked, needing reassurance.

She looked into my eyes and said, "I love you. I really love you, Stephie." I was lying on top of her, looking into her eyes. When I heard these words, I closed my eyes, lowered my head, sighed and smiled. For hours, I had relished the physical intimacy in unimaginable ways. And now, with three little words, she had given me a slice of heaven that sent me into a state of emotional bliss.

"I love you too, Casey. I'm so in love with you." She was silent. My body was already pressing down against hers, but she pulled me in closer, tighter. She turned off the light and we made love again.

I didn't sleep at all that night, for fear of missing one second of my time with Casey. Our bodies never separated as we shifted and turned together and as the morning neared, I willed the sky to remain dark. Alas, a new day dawned and Casey woke up smiling. I was ecstatic. But a part of me felt bad for making love to someone other than my girlfriend. Then again, I hadn't "made love" to my girlfriend in months because I was not in love with her. Another part of me was afraid that Casey would regret what we had shared the night before, even though she had initiated it. Before I had a chance to obsess about any number of "what ifs," Casey kissed me with absolute certainty, allaying all my fears.

Not one to dilly-dally in bed in the morning, Casey rose as I studied her naked body; she ambled across the room toward the bathroom to get dressed. I had just spent the night making love to her, but I had never seen her naked body in the daylight. As Casey glided slowly across the room, I stared at the places on her body that I had explored a few hours earlier with my mouth and my hands. My body was filled with a warm, tingling sensation. I wasn't sure if it was an aftershock from the night before or if the sensation was inspired by the thoughts running through my mind. Either way, I was happy to be dusting off feelings that I had forgotten existed.

Staring at the ceiling, I stretched and thought to myself how wonderful it was to wake up next to someone I adored— someone I could not get enough of. Pardon me if I sound like a greeting card, but isn't this what people spend their entire lives looking for? This feeling…this magic…this eternal light? Ever since I was old enough to understand what love is, I have wondered what the point of life is without having someone to share it with. Even as a young teenager, I understood that all anyone can ever hope for is to love and be loved by those they love. What could be more fulfilling than that? What I felt with Casey was the best feeling in the world, incomparable to any other. Images of making love with Casey ran through my mind. I remembered once describing Sydney on the tennis court as "poetry in motion." I was wrong. Casey and I making love— now that truly was poetry in motion.

I yawned but didn't feel the slightest hint of exhaustion. I could smell Casey on my body. I stretched my arms and legs to all four corners of the bed and reveled in my bliss until Casey called to me from downstairs, "Stephie, your coffee's ready!" I got up and raced down to meet her.

We sat down on the couch to enjoy our morning coffee. I looked at my watch and laughed at the realization that I was supposed to be in my alleged CLE class. When I saw the look on Casey's face, I asked her the question that I absolutely despise being asked of me: "What are you thinking?" I never could understand why people ask that question. I find it to be one of the most annoying questions one can ask of another. If I want to tell you what I'm thinking, I will!

"Nothing," Casey said, shrugging off my enquiry.

"Casey, come on…tell me what you're thinking." It's here where I would have invited her to go fuck herself if the tables had been turned. Okay, maybe not *her*, but *anyone else* would have been harangued with a mouthful of expletives. But I needed to know what she was thinking. I had to be sure that she wasn't filled with any regrets.

She hesitated and then launched into a conversation about her performance the night before. Casey had often joked with me about our sexual pasts. She couldn't even look me in the eye when she said, "I just know that you've had so many lovers…you've been with so many women and I worry that I won't compare in bed. I'm sort of out of practice. Sydney was the last person I was with and I'd like to forget that ever happened." She snickered, "I'm a professional tennis player but you're a professional lesbian!"

"First of all, it's not a competition…" As these words spilled from my mouth, I realized that I was not taking the right stance with her. Casey was not interested in hearing how terrific she had made me feel the night before. Of course she wasn't! She was, after all, a woman— and a lesbian woman at that! Women can be absolute paranoid lunatics sometimes— and I know this because I can sometimes be one of them. Put two of us together and it can certainly lead to a fast track to the sanitarium. Apart from my being able to erase my past and reclaim my virginity so that I could give it to her, the only acceptable answer to quell Casey's insecurities was that she was the best "lover" that I have ever had.

I despise that word, "lover," when used to describe a girlfriend or a sexual partner. There are a few words in the English language that I absolutely abhor. Lover and vagina are two of them. Yes, I realize the irony of my disdain for the latter. Just because I'm a lesbian and am intimately familiar with the "V" doesn't mean I have to like saying it. In fact, the sound of it makes me cringe. I could never have taught middle school Sex Ed because I would be more uncomfortable with the word "vagina" than the teenagers would likely be. I'll go to any lengths to avoid using both of these horrible words. I'll talk in such circles to avoid the "V" word, it would make you dizzy. I refuse to say it and I haven't found many acceptable alternatives to whispering "down there" when referring to a "V." One of my Spanish friends pronounces it, "ba-heen-ya" and I find that much less offensive. Enough about the "ba-heen-ya."

Back to "lover." I mean, who thought to use this word? It's a nebulous, old-fashioned word that should be erased from modern usage. Why not just "girlfriend?" Even "partner" sounds better than lover (although not much). Not only does it sound icky (unless pronounced, "lovah," and in which case it's funny and campy, but only if used properly), but I just can't take that word seriously. It makes my skin crawl when people introduce their girlfriend as their "lover." It's synonymous with "sex partner" or "fuck buddy," and who would gladly accept that title in a public forum? I would *die* if anyone ever introduced me as their lover. "Hi, Mr. and Mrs. Such-and-Such. This is my lover, Stephanie. As you can tell from her title, she's that *special* person in my life who performs cunnilingus on me." I would never, in my wildest dreams, introduce my girlfriend to, say, my grandmother as my lover! Gross! I might as well just hand good old Granny an album full of Polaroids of my *lover* and me loving each other in the bedroom just to drive the point home further! On second thought, maybe I would have enjoyed introducing a girlfriend to my grandmother ("grandmonster" as everyone *except* my father liked to call her) as my lover, but only in the hope that it would have shocked her into being a more decent human being. That's assuming she and I were on speaking terms before she passed away, which we weren't. I'll never have the pleasure of exacting that shock value on her.

Casey wasn't interested in hearing that she had taken me to beyond the brink of ecstasy. She wanted to hear that no one had ever taken me to the levels of heightened sensation that she had and that she was the most incredible *lover* I could ever dream of having. I told her as much. "Casey, I've never felt as good with anyone as I felt with you last night. And I have never wanted anyone so much."

"Are you sure?" she asked, looking at me with passion-filled eyes.

"I'm so *sure* that if we continue talking about this, we're gonna have to go back upstairs and get into bed."

With that, her ego was sufficiently massaged and the subject was dropped.

Casey and I did not deviate from our plan. We got dressed and waited until I was supposed to be done with my class before venturing into the city. We spent the entire afternoon ogling over each other like two lovesick teenagers. We said "I love you" often, sometimes smiling intensely and other times giggling childishly. We weren't quite as bad as the consummate cheesy couple wearing skin-tight jeans and attaching themselves to each other with their hands in each other's back hip pockets, but we were close. We roamed through the city together, weaving in and out of shops and taking refuge from the cold, but could not wait to get our hands on each other behind closed doors.

When we returned from the city later in the evening, Casey's phone rang as we cuddled on the couch together. It was Sydney. Casey rolled her eyes and answered the call.

I could hear Sydney's voice through the receiver. She skipped the greeting and frantically asked, "Is Steph still awake? I need to talk to you, but I don't want her to know we're talking."

Before answering, Casey looked at me and shook her head as if to say, "I really don't want to deal with this shit right now."

I raised my eyebrows toward my forehead and shrugged with indignation as if to say, "Hey, this is your game, your rules."

She answered, "She went to bed a little while ago."

Relieved, Sydney said, "Good. Please don't tell her we talked, but I need to talk to you about Paige. I know Steph's having lunch with Paige tomorrow. It shits me to no end and I'm freaking out about it but don't want her to know. Can you please go with her? I don't want them to be alone together."

M-o-t-h-e-r-f-u-c-k-e-r! I had to bite my tongue and suppress my annoyance because my head was so close to the receiver that Sydney would certainly hear even the slightest outburst. I wanted to grab the phone from Casey and smash it on the ground.

"Actually, Steph invited me to go to lunch. I planned on going, but why do you want me to go? What're you so nervous about?"

Still shaking my head, I could not believe how insecure Sydney was about Paige. I had told Sydney, earlier in the day, about my plans to have lunch with Paige and she acted completely fine and secure, as if she didn't think twice about it. In reality, she had been obsessing about our lunch meeting all day, and waited to talk to Casey about it until she thought I had gone to bed. I didn't think it was possible for her to make herself look even more pathetic than she already did, but this stunt proved me wrong.

Sydney proceeded to keep Casey on the phone, trying to pull information out of her. "Has Steph even mentioned me or our relationship to you at all?"

Let me answer that for you, Casey. No, Sydney. She hasn't said anything. But don't take it personally. It's probably only because she couldn't talk and do that thing she was doing to me with her tongue.

I could tell that Casey felt some pangs of guilt as she heard the desperation in Sydney's voice. "No, we haven't talked about it."

Sydney questioned Casey more about the next day's meeting with Paige. "Where are you guys going for lunch? What time? Have you been to the restaurant before? Is it nice?" She wanted to know every single detail.

Casey tried to placate the raving lunatic on the other end of the phone line. "Sydney, I don't know why you're so concerned about this. It's only lunch."

"I just don't understand why they have to see each other."

"Why shouldn't they?" Casey asked, matter-of-factly.

"Because they used to go out and Paige was the love of her life! And, I'm not there!" Sydney was now fully yelling.

"So what?" Don't you think you're being a little ridiculous? I think you're being overprotective. Just relax."

"Casey, you're *my* friend! I don't want to hear this shit! Can you please just do this for me? Just call me after you've met Paige. I want to know what you think."

I could hear the shakiness of Sydney's voice. She was about to cry and Casey could no longer entertain Sydney's insecurities. "Please stop worrying. Everything will be fine. I promise I'll call you tomorrow." Casey rolled her eyes as she hung up the phone.

The second she snapped her phone shut, I exploded, "She's driving me fucking crazy! Why does she need to know every little fucking detail about what I do and who I do it with?!" A part of me empathized with Sydney for being nervous about me seeing Paige. But the other part of me wanted to slap her across the face and tell her to stop being so ridiculous. I hadn't given Paige so much as a second thought since before Sydney and I were together. It angered me intensely that Sydney acted totally fine and normal to me about Paige and then went behind my back and called Casey to cry on her shoulder about it and *then* made her agree to be Inspector Gadget and inform her of all the details. Why couldn't she just be a normal human being and say to me, "Steph, I know it shouldn't make me nervous that you're seeing Paige, but it does. I'm sorry. I'm only human and I'm a little nervous because of your history with her." I mean, really, would it have been so fucking hard for her to admit that she was insecure?! Even Casey wasn't insecure about Paige. She was just curious. Why couldn't Sydney be as normal as Casey about it?! I knew that Sydney's insecurity about Paige was partly my fault because I had let her mind play tricks on her about it. But I would have had so much more respect for her if she would have just been honest with me and told me that she was freaking out about Paige!

Oops, I guess I went a little too far with the honesty argument. Hi, Pot. Kettle calling!

I drew in a deep breath and instantly calmed myself. Yes, Sydney was being overly protective and controlling. But how do I have any right to complain about Sydney's dishonesty with me when I just flew across the country under false pretenses to be with her ex-girlfriend? Time for this hypocrite to simmer down.

"I hated being on the phone with her. I feel bad that she's so upset about you," Casey whined, sympathetically.

"I know. Look, I told you…I'm more than ready to break up with her. Then…"

"You can't! Not yet!" she blurted with exasperation.

"Well then, you're going to have to figure out what to do when you get an attack of conscience. I feel bad for what I am doing to Sydney and I want nothing more than to end this relationship with her and focus on you and us. She's certifiable, but I'm not sure I'm much saner to agree to go along with this. I think we should rethink your plan."

"I don't want to talk about this anymore. Let's go upstairs and get into bed," she said beseechingly.

Of course, Casey didn't want to talk about it anymore. That would mean dealing with reality. And why would she want to deal with reality when she could hide behind a façade of lies even longer? She must have had one dinger of a childhood! An only child, Casey was the center of her parents' world. To them, she could do no wrong as long as she was winning on the tennis court. I wondered if she had ever had to take responsibility for any of her actions.

I take back what I said about accepting the blame for Sydney's insecurities. None of this would have even been an issue if Casey wouldn't have insisted on all of this secrecy. It was not my fault. It was Casey's.

12

$\mathcal{S}$tay on the balls of your feet: be prepared for anything

I spotted Paige's long, thick, brown ponytail immediately when Casey and I walked into the pizza shop that used to be our favorite lunch stop. I hadn't seen her for almost one year, but I embraced her long, lean frame and we quickly lapsed back into a comfortable familiarity with each other. I introduced Casey to Paige, although they felt as if they were old friends after all I had told them about each other. They traded pleasantries but genuinely meant it when they told one another that they were happy to finally meet each other. Despite the ease of being in Paige's company, I also felt an awkwardness as the three of us sat down to eat lunch. Paige had no idea that Casey and I were involved. She, like everyone else who knew us, thought we were just good friends— very good friends. My discomfort of sitting across from my old love and right next to my new love quickly dissipated as we got lost in conversation and laughter. A stranger sitting at the next table would have thought that we were all good friends who had known one another for years.

After almost two hours had passed, Casey peeled herself out of her chair and suggested that we continue our afternoon at her house. Without hesitation, Paige accepted the invitation and wrote down the directions to Casey's house.

Once Casey and I got into her car, she said, "Stephie, she's great. She's everything you said she was."

I knew Casey would like Paige. It's kind of difficult not to like her, although I made a special exception when she left me for that whore

189

who was younger and thinner than I.

We hadn't been in the car for five minutes when Casey's phone rang. I could tell by the expression on her face who was calling. It was the warden. Sydney hadn't heard from Casey and was impatiently awaiting the details of our lunch. She had probably worn out the soles of her shoes from pacing and waiting for Casey to give her the full report on Paige. Casey wasn't ready to be hammered with questions yet and ignored the call, sending it to voicemail. I was *dying* to hear what she was going to tell Sydney about Paige, knowing the slightest hint of positive feedback would send Sydney into an irreversible tailspin. I derived some pleasure at the thought of the conversation that was about to take place. Casey and I both knew that it would only be a matter of minutes before Sydney's obsession would force her to call back, so she gathered her thoughts during our few minute's reprieve. Like clockwork, the warden called again a few minutes later to check up on her prisoner. I truly did feel that I was a prisoner. I was imprisoned by ecstasy with Casey and misery with Sydney.

Casey returned Sydney's calls when we arrived back at her house. She planted herself on the couch and prepared to have a conversation that would, no doubt, be the furthest thing from pleasing to Sydney. I helped myself to a beer and sat down at the dining room table, a few feet away from where she was sitting. I swiveled in my chair and faced Casey. I smirked, lifted my beer bottle and toasted the air in Casey's direction. *Ha ha. Have fun. Better you than me!* Casey grinned back and shook her head from left to right before waving to me, only she wasn't waving with all of her fingers. I only saw one— her middle finger.

Sydney answered and before she could say anything, Casey said, "Hey, sorry. I was on the phone when you called." White lie Number 998,575,001.

Sydney exploded, "Where the bloody hell have you been? It's after three! I've been dying here, waiting for you to call me!" I could hear her across the room as Casey held the phone away from her head and reacted to the noise.

"Calm down. We just walked in the door. We were at lunch a lot longer than I thought."

"Where's Steph?"

"Upstairs. She's on the phone."

"Who the hell's she talking to? Certainly not me! She hasn't called me all fucking day! She's probably talking to Paige!" No doubt, the veins in Sydney's neck were now fully engorged.

"Sydney, calm down. I have no idea who she's talking to."

"Well, how was it? What's she like?"

Casey hesitated. "We had a really good time. Honestly, Paige's great. She's super nice."

"Fucking nice. Great. Whatever. Is she pretty?"

"Very. She looks like she does in all the pictures you've seen of her."

I could hear the aggravation in Sydney's voice. "How did they act toward each other?"

"Uh, like they were happy to see each other," Casey said, rolling her eyes.

"What do you mean?!"

"Huh?"

"Well, did they hug? Kiss?"

"Of course they did."

"They hugged *and* kissed?! Did they look like they were just friends?"

"Sydney, stop it. This is stupid. They were together for a long time. They haven't seen each other forever. They were happy to see each other. I don't know what you want me to say. Do you want me to be honest with you or do you want me to lie?"

Now that was funny! I almost spit my beer across the room. Go ahead, Casey. Tell her the truth.

"Of course I want the truth!" Sydney screamed.

"Okay, well, Paige is very pretty. She's really nice. I like her. It seems like they had a great relationship. I can see how they were together for so long. It's obvious that they're still very special to each other."

Oh, *that* truth. I would have paid money to hear the other truth come out of Casey's mouth.

"Does Paige still want to be with Steph?"

"I didn't ask her," Casey reported flatly.

"Dammit, Casey! You know what I mean!"

"Look, just like we're still close, they're still close. I'm not gonna sit here and listen to you go crazy about this. It was lunch. That's all."

"I just don't understand it."

"You don't have to. You just have to accept it."

I looked over at Casey and gave her a smile of encouragement as if to say, "Yeah, you tell her!" I also encouraged her to wrap up the conversation. She rolled her eyes in agreement. "Look, Sydney, I can hear Steph coming down the stairs. I'm gonna get going. I'll talk to you later." She ended the call abruptly and slammed the phone down.

"God, that was torture! She is such a pain in my ass!" Casey looked like she needed a double shot of something to dull her pain after that torturous phone call.

I took the last sip of my beer, walked over and wrapped my arms around her. "I know. She's the most difficult person that ever walked the face of this earth." I looked at her sympathetically. "She's the reason the field of psychiatry exists. How much longer are we going to have to keep this shit up?"

Casey was almost whining at this point. "I don't know. Can we please not talk about that right now?"

"Can we please not talk about that right now?" I mocked, as if I were a three-year-old petulant child. "The longer we keep up this charade, the more upset Sydney's gonna be."

"She'll be fine. We just have to do it the right way."

The right way! I was starting to wonder if a "right way" even existed.

Before I could argue with her, the doorbell rang. It was Paige. Too bad she hadn't arrived a few minutes earlier, before Casey hung up with Sydney. That would've really sent her over the edge!

Casey's phone rang seconds after I answered the door. Casey and I looked at each other with stunned surprise. We both thought, for sure, it was Sydney calling back. We were wrong. I was actually pleasantly surprised when Casey announced that Trish was on the phone. It's true— there is a first for everything! She answered the phone and motioned that she was going to take the call upstairs. I nodded and sarcastically mouthed, "Tell her 'hi' for me," as I ushered Paige into the house.

Paige immediately noticed Casey's trophies. It was impossible to miss them, as there were so many scattered throughout the room. She was mesmerized by Casey's symbols of athletic excellence. I followed her over to the first of the two large trophy cases. I felt pride for Casey.

Paige glanced in awe at all the silver plates, crystal and silver bowls and metallic statuettes which were randomly housed in the cabinets. Paige was not a tennis player or even an avid spectator, but she was well versed enough in tennis to understand the magnitude and importance of a trophy with a Wimbledon, French Open, Australian Open or US Open engraving on it. She gestured in amazement to all the tennis bling in the room. I could see the excitement in her eyes as she innocently asked, "She won all these tournaments?"

I smiled and nodded my head, "Yes." Casey had trophies evidencing her wins in singles, doubles and mixed doubles. She had won tournaments on every surface— grass, clay and hard courts. Her trophy case was home to trophies from the Grand Slams and every tier classi-fication of tournament. It was an outstanding accomplishment and an impressive collection.

Paige pointed to the Wimbledon trophies. "That is so cool! I had no idea that she won so many tournaments."

"What did you think she does at these tournaments? Knit sweaters?" I joked.

"She just seems so genuine and down to earth for someone who's as successful as she is," Paige added, sincerely.

I couldn't tell Paige, but that was just another reason why I loved Casey so much— because she was an incredibly successful athlete who actually enjoyed playing tennis but didn't live her life in the shadow of an ego. She was one of the few Tour players who had done well but had not turned into a pretentious, pampered, pompous princess. There are horror stories about some of the top players. Some of them are completely two-faced, some are indifferent and just keep to themselves and some are just plain bitches to your face *and* behind your back. Casey was proof that not all tennis players are negatively affected by their fame.

When Casey finally got off the phone and came downstairs, she laughed hysterically at what she saw. Paige and I were dancing around the living room, singing. We had broken into her '80s music collection and were taking turns singing verses of Cyndi Lauper's "Girls Just Wanna Have Fun." As Casey descended the last few stairs, she was howling with laughter. She almost lost her footing and fell right into Paige, who was holding her beer bottle up to her mouth as if it were her microphone and her other hand was positioned on her left hip, which was swaying back and forth as only Paige (and most anyone with the name of Shaneqwa or Latoya) could do. I'm not sure who was singing louder— Cyndi or us.

Paige and I quickly dragged Casey into our impromptu karaoke party and I immediately broke into song and began singing into my beer bottle. Between verses, Casey made her way over to me and whispered, "I've never seen you like this before. For some reason, I can't imagine you and Sydney dancing around in your living room footloose and fancy free!"

I looked directly at Casey and shrugged my shoulders and swayed my body while substituting my own lyrics, "Sometimes *this* girl just wants to have *f-u-n!*" Casey had never seen this side of me. Hell, I hadn't seen this side of me since Sydney had come into my life! I didn't feel I could be myself around Sydney, so I just retreated into my head and closed down.

After our makeshift karaoke session had ended, Casey pulled me aside to apologize profusely for a last-minute change in plans later that evening. Trish insisted that she accompany her to a party and Casey explained that she felt obligated to go because Trish was "acting really strange."

Now there's something new and different!

I had had enough of Trish's interferences but I knew that there was a time and a place for everything and my short weekend in Boston was neither the time nor the place to "take out the Trash." Casey had just delivered a punch to my stomach, but I rolled with it without even gasping for air. "Casey, don't worry about it. You do what you need to do and don't worry about me. Don't forget, this is *my* city! It's Saturday night and the mayor's back in town!" I talked a good game, but making a cameo at the local lesbian bar that used to be my stomping ground was the last thing on my mind. I had no intention of doing anything but stay close to Casey's house so I could take advantage of every second I could squeeze out of the weekend with her.

As my time with Casey was ticking away, I lounged on the couch reading, pretending not to be waiting for Casey when I heard a key go into the door. *Excellent! She's back!* When the door opened, my bubble of excitement burst. *Shit, Trish's with her!* My mood went from light and airy to rather ashy. It was midnight on my last night in Boston and now I was going to have to make pleasantries with Trish.

I cracked a smile as the door opened.

"Hi, Steph!" Trish came bounding in behind Casey, beaming. "How was your night?"

"Uh, it was f-i-i-i-n-e, thanks," I answered shakily. I had no idea what the hell she was so happy about.

Casey was silent and anxiously bit her bottom lip.

Still digging, Trish had a smile on her face and looked like she possessed information about some well-kept secret. "I heard you had, like, such a great afternoon with Paige."

Wow, she hadn't even gotten both feet inside the door before she brought up Paige's name! "Uh-huh. We had a really nice afternoon with Paige. Too bad you weren't able to, like, meet us for lunch." My mocking use of the word "like" that she so ridiculously overused didn't faze her.

"I heard. Casey said she's great. She said you two are, like, so adorable together."

See, I knew I couldn't trust her! I could see right through to her ulterior motives. "Paige is a sweetheart," I said, shooting her a supercilious smile. I knew exactly what Trish was up to and I had her right where I wanted her!

"I heard the three of you are having breakfast tomorrow. I'm taking the day off from work tomorrow and I think I'm gonna come, too. Like, I can't wait to meet her." She winked at me as if she and I shared a secret.

Trish's questions promptly went from suggestive to overt. The rapid-fire exchange about Paige and whether or not I thought the two of us would ever get back together continued for several minutes before Trish finally stopped with the Spanish Inquisition having met with less than enthusiasm from me. She made herself at home on the couch opposite me, giving Casey no choice but to sit next to me. Trish was falling asleep and I furtively eyed my watch wondering when she was finally going to leave. *Oh, c'mon! Leave already!* I quickly grew impatient.

At some point, Trish would have to leave. She wouldn't dare spend the night because if she did, the whole sleeping dynamic would have run amuck. She thought I was sleeping in the guest bedroom, which was her "home away from home." Neither Trish nor I is the "couching it" type. If she invited herself to the pajama party, one of us would have to share a bed with Casey— I would gladly have volunteered so Trish could have the guest room, but somehow, I think Trish would have found a way to reject my selflessness. Since I was already "sleeping in the guest room," Trish would have to sleep in Casey's bed with her and there was no way she would do that! What would the neighbors think? If I could read her mind, it would say: *"Me, straight Trish?! I can't sleep in the same bed with Casey. She's gay. I'm not gay! I'm straight! I just worship my best friend. That has nothing to do with being gay."*

Finally, straight Trish departed. I watched from the window as she pulled out of the driveway in her white Ford Focus. I waited until the headlights melted into the night before turning off the light and walking into Casey's bedroom. She was waiting for me and greeted me with open arms and a toothy smile. We embraced and got into bed to spend my last night in Boston together.

The next morning, Paige drove Casey and me to meet Trish at a local diner for breakfast. I knew Trish would be scrutinizing my interactions with Paige and I was ready. We sat down to breakfast and almost instantly, Trish became Paige's biggest fan. She dropped hints, one after the other, about us getting back together. Trish's diversionary tactics had about as much a chance of working as Arnold Schwarzenegger dressing up like Little Bo Peep to deliver his next gubernatorial speech. Regardless of her desire to play matchmaker with Paige, I had already found my match with Casey.

After breakfast, we had a few hours before my departure. Conveniently, Trish volunteered to spend the day with us and then accompany me to the airport so Casey would not have to drive back alone. *What a relief. The thought of a grown woman navigating a big, bad highway alone that she'd driven thousands of times before is preposterous! How selfless of you to volunteer to go with her and personally see to it that she does not kiss me good-bye…I mean, that she gets home safely, Trish!*

Paige and I followed Casey and Trish back to her house. Emerging from the car utterly annoyed, Casey blurted, "I just spent the last fifteen minutes listening to Sydney yell at me."

Oh phew…only that!

Casey proceeded to tell us that Sydney called her right after we left the diner wanting to know where I was. When Casey told her that I was in the car behind her with Paige, Sydney lost her mind. She was livid that she had not been informed that Paige was coming to breakfast and she was even more furious that Casey had left me alone with Paige.

I was so annoyed I thought I was going to explode. I couldn't even excuse Sydney's jealousy by chalking it up to the fact that perhaps it was misplaced. It wasn't. I might have been a little more sympathetic to her insecurities if I could somehow justify them as being a result of her thinking that I was actually having an affair. She didn't think I was having an affair— and certainly not with Casey. She had been jealous of Paige from day one— months before anything had ever surfaced between Casey and me. Sydney was just plain jealous and wanted to control my every move and I refused to let her. I rolled my eyes and shook my head. My fury heightened by the second, as steam almost floated out of my ears.

"Steph, you should call her," Casey insisted.

"Fuck that! That psychotic bitch can go fuck herself! She's not my keeper and I'm not checking in with her just because she's jealous over nothing. She seriously needs help!" It occurred to me right then that I truly was dealing with a sick individual. In a well-ordered world, Sydney would be in a straightjacket.

I stormed into the house and went upstairs to the guest bedroom to pack my bag. *Oh, this is what the guest bedroom looks like!* I had strategically placed all of my things in the second bedroom, just in case any curious eyes made their way upstairs before my departure, but hadn't spent more than thirty seconds in there since my arrival. I ripped the sheets off the bed and threw them in the laundry before Trish had a chance to examine them with her magnifying glass and realize that they had not been slept in.

As I folded my clothes, I could feel eyes glaring at me. I turned toward the door to find Casey looking in. She immediately put her index finger to her lips, signaling for me to be silent. She tiptoed over to me, kissed me quickly and then stepped back, put her hand on her heart and mouthed the words, "I love you." I was shocked. Both Trish and Paige were just downstairs within earshot, and I could not believe the brazen audacity of Casey— not that I minded it!

When I came downstairs, Trish was sitting alone on the couch. I sat down next to her. Again, Trish began hammering me about Paige. *Great, here we go again…more of this shit?* I was tiring of this charade—not just the Paige thing, but the Casey/Trish thing as well. But Trish kept jabbing at me about Paige. I had had enough and I quickly turned the tables on her and started questioning her about her love life.

"So, I hear you have another date this week. Same guy?" Trish had recently decided to go on a full throttle mission to find a husband (which, by the way, Casey claimed to be fine with).

"Yeah, same guy. I don't think it's going anywhere, but I, like, have to put myself out there if I'm ever going to have that house that I want with a white picket fence." She paused, then leaned in and whispered, "This is going to be really hard for Casey and I hope she's okay with it all. I know she wanted things to be different between us, but they just can't be. I want to, like, get married and have kids and I'm not getting any younger. I'm going to start dating…heavily. My clock is, like, seriously ticking. I just hope Casey can handle it."

Trish had just given me an opportunity and I pounced on it. "Casey will be fine…and so will you. You're both going to meet people and find happiness and as long as you guys respect each other's choices and are supportive of each other, everything will be fine. It's not like either of you would ever get involved with someone who didn't understand and respect your friendship." I wish I could have used that remote, pushed "pause" and patted myself on the back. I had been bouncing around on the balls of my feet just waiting for an opportunity to plant that seed in Trish's twisted psyche.

Just then, Casey and Paige came back into the room and my intimate little powwow with Trish ended abruptly. Nervously, Casey said, "Do you know what time it is?" I had been glancing at my watch and knew that we should have left for the airport thirty minutes earlier, but I wasn't in a particularly huge hurry.

Trish rushed us out the door as if a grenade were about to crumble the house and I quickly said good-bye to Paige. We hopped into Casey's car and as we sped down the highway toward the airport, Trish began to grill me, once again, about the possibility of getting back together with Paige. This girl was nothing if not persistent. But Christ! Enough of the Paige thing already! Casey glanced at me in the rearview mirror with sympathetic eyes, sensing my absolute annoyance toward her best friend. I was more than relieved to see signs for Logan International Airport because I didn't have to talk about Paige anymore— no offense to Paige. I looked at my watch. My plane was scheduled to leave thirty-five minutes later. I couldn't decide which would be more torturous— having to be that jackass who had to make a mad dash through the airport like OJ Simpson in order to make my flight or having to pick up my phone and call Sydney before I got on the plane. Neither option sounded at all appealing.

As we pulled up to the curbside check-in, I leaned forward to give Trish a hug good-bye. Simultaneously, Casey got out of the car to retrieve my bag. I had a quick flashback to a few weeks earlier in Tokyo when I had to say good-bye to Casey in front of Sydney. The difference was that Sydney didn't suspect any misconduct between Casey and me. Trish, on the other hand, suspected an attraction and had been digging for information to confirm her suspicion for months. I knew she'd be watching the farewell like a hawk. I could have sworn that I heard Trish whisper snidely, "Make it short and sweet" as I got out of the car. In the span of a few seconds, I thanked Casey for a wonderful weekend, hugged her and watched from the corner of my eye as she and her stupid straight best friend drove off.

I raced up the escalator and weaved through a sea of people, only to stand in an obnoxiously long security line that led to the metal detectors. I now had twenty-nine minutes before my plane was scheduled to take off. Hoping that I would have something of a reprieve, I looked up at the departure board to see if, by some stroke of luck, my flight was delayed. Mine was one of three flights on time. Although I didn't really care if I missed my flight, there was no point in staying in Boston for another night if I could not spend the evening with Casey. And the chances of that happening were slim to none since she was on her way over to Trish's aunt's house for dinner. So I was determined to be airborne shortly.

Finally, twenty-three minutes before my plane's scheduled departure the line began to move, albeit slowly. As I shuffled forward with the rest of the line at a snail's pace, I picked up my cell phone to make my obligatory phone call to Sydney. I could think of at least one million other things that I would rather have done at that very moment. Eating glass was one of them. I dialed the number, hoping Sydney's cell phone battery was dead.

She picked up immediately. "Hi, love."

"Hey. I only have a minute to talk because I'm in the security line about to go through the metal detector, but I wanted to call you before I got on my flight."

"That's okay. How are you?"

Audibly frazzled but silently biting my tongue, I swallowed as much of my bitterness as I could and answered, "Fine. It's just a bit chaotic right now. The line is starting to move and I'm gonna have to hang up in a minute."

"How was your day?"

How was my day? What the fuck! Did you hear a word I just said? I only have a few seconds to talk to you and you ask me how my day was when I know full well that you've been calling Casey all day, checking up on me and yelling at her for leaving me alone with Paige!

Ridding my voice of any hostility, I exuded effervescence as I responded, "My day was great. I had a great time! It was nice to be back here for a few days." I knew that the excitement in my voice would be unsettling to Sydney, but I also knew that she'd pretend to be fine with my response.

"Good. I'm glad you had a good time. What did you all do?"

I knew it! But in the name of all that's good and holy! How many times do I have to tell you that I cannot have a detailed conversation right now?!

As politely as possible, once again, I tried to convey to my overly curious girlfriend that I had to get off the phone so I could catch my plane. "Sydney, I have to go. I get in late, so I'll talk to you tomorrow."

"Why don't you call me when you get in?"

Why don't you go take a flying leap?!

"I get in at almost three in the morning your time. I'm not gonna call you in the middle of the night."

Obviously unable to take a hint, Sydney further insisted, "I don't mind. Call when you get home."

"I'll text you when I get home to let you know I got in safely, but I'm not calling just to wake you up. If we keep talking about it, I'm not even sure I'm gonna make my flight."

"Why didn't you leave for the airport earlier?"

No more Mister Nice Guy!

"Oh, don't start, Mother!" Realizing that I'd snapped loudly, I smiled awkwardly at the passengers in front of me who had turned around to look at me. I lowered my voice and said, "Listen, I really have to go. I'm about to go through the metal detector and I only have seventeen minutes to haul ass and get on my flight."

"I wish you had called me earlier so we could have talked today."

"Well, I've been busy all day. This is the first chance I've had to call you. Besides, I know you've talked to Casey today, so you've been kept in the loop." I only realized what I had just said after those last words flew out of my mouth. I had not intended to let Sydney know that I was aware that Casey had received phone calls from her throughout the day.

"Yeah, but it would have been nice to be kept in the loop…by my girlfriend."

Trying not to raise my voice again, I replied, "Like I said, this is the first chance I've had to call you. Have a great night and I'll talk to you tomorrow. I have to go."

"But, love…"

"Sydney, I have to get off the phone!" My raised tone couldn't be helped and this time I didn't smile apologetically at the curious onlookers.

"Okay, have a safe flight. I love you."

I accidentally hung up the phone before I had a chance to say, "I love you, too." I rolled my eyes as I shoved my phone into my bag. I didn't have time to dwell on my annoyance toward Sydney. My flight was scheduled to leave in fifteen minutes. After being personally searched by a security guard and her magic wand, I clutched my bag and ran down the hall. Of course, my gate was at the very end of the hallway— Murphy's Law! I raced past the other passengers and arrived at an empty departure lounge. Just as a "fuckin' hell" rolled off my tongue, I realized that my curse was in vain. I had not missed my flight. All the other passengers had already boarded the plane and the attendant was near the door, making final preparations for the flight's departure. I rushed down the ramp and handed the representative my ticket.

I hate being the last one on the plane. I looked at my watch. I had ten minutes to spare, but still, I knew that as I boarded, everyone would be thinking the same thing, *"Oh, how nice of you to join us. Now if you*

would kindly take your seat like the rest of us, we might be able to leave on time."
That's what I would have been thinking, anyway. I made my way down
the aisle to my window seat. The entire plane was staring at me as I
placed my bag in the overhead bin. I stepped over the friendly man
who had volunteered not to get out of his aisle seat to let me in.
Landing in my seat, I glared at the man next to me, smiled sarcastically
and said, "Some people have the audacity to think that the age of
chivalry is dead." *Asshole.* He looked at me like I was speaking a foreign
language. I probably was.

Before my armpits had dried, the plane sped down the runway. As
the engines sent vibrations through the cabin, I found a comfortable
tranquility and escaped with my thoughts of the weekend. I watched
the city disappear beneath the clouds as the plane ascended into the sky
and caught a whiff of Casey's perfume on my shirt. I couldn't help but
think I had been whisked away on cloud nine.

13

The devil wears Nike

I wasn't sleeping much. Between jet-setting to the East Coast to have a covert romance and waking up at the crack of dawn back on the West Coast to good-morning phone calls from Casey on the East Coast, anxiety was yanking my eyelids open in the middle of the night. I didn't mind the early morning phone calls, but I could have done without the anxiety. This morning, my wake-up call came just before five o'clock. I knew who it was and lurched out of my sleep as if my pillow were on fire. Enthusiastically, I picked up the phone. "Only a few more hours until I get to see you, cutie!" Casey now much preferred the nickname I'd given her to her own name. It had been a week since my return from Boston and I missed my cutie terribly.

She sniffled and I sensed that allergies weren't the culprit. Before she could say a word, I immediately demanded to know what was wrong.

Tearfully, she replied, "I know it sounds stupid, but even though I've been doing this since I was a kid, I still get sad every time I leave home."

Tennis players really don't have an "off season" and this time Casey would be away from home for six weeks— two weeks in California, three weeks in Florida and one week in South Carolina. Living out of a suitcase and eating in a restaurant for every meal is exhausting and emotionally draining. I had only been doing it for seven months with Sydney and I was exhausted— and I wasn't even traveling full-time.

After soothing Casey and convincing her that she would be smiling again in a matter of hours, I heard the flight attendant calling her flight over the airport intercom. My eyes were surrendering to my fatigue and I suddenly felt like my eyelids weighed 1,000 pounds. I wished her a safe flight and flipped my cell phone shut but then immediately opened it again to sneak in one last text before her plane departed. As quickly as my fingers could type and with one eye shut and the other one squinting at the tiny liquid crystal display, I typed, *Everything will be fine. I love you and I can't wait to see you!* I then hurriedly typed in a destination number and pushed the "send" button. Just as I hit "send," I realized what I had done. I had accidentally typed in the wrong number. Instead of typing in Casey's number, I had typed in Sydney's number!

Oh, shit! What have I done?! This isn't even Freudian, it's imbecilic!

I was instantly launched into a complete state of panic. My heart started racing uncontrollably. I could feel the pulse in my teeth. My head was throbbing. I sat straight up in my bed and stared at my phone which was clutched in my shaking hand. *Shit, shit, shit! Holy fucking shit! You fucking idiot!* I had to exercise damage control— calmly, rationally and immediately. Only a few seconds had passed and the only thing I could think to do was call Sydney. As I scrolled down my address book to the letter S, I wondered what I was doing. *Oh, now you're leisurely scrolling down the names and before you just dial without thinking. What is wrong with you?! Shit, where's that damn remote control when I need it? God, I'd give anything to be able to push 'stop' and then 'rewind' and just start all over! I can't believe how stupid I am!*

As I waited for Sydney to pick up the phone, I tried to reassure myself that the message was not incriminating and that I would be able to explain my way out of it. Finally, Sydney answered. I held my breath, awaiting her reaction. My face cringed as I pressed the phone to my ear, hearing her voice. "Hey, love, I just got your text. What are you doing up so early?"

No sarcasm. No anger. Phew!

Sydney had no idea that I had accidentally sent her a message that was meant for Casey. *Thank God!* That could have been disastrous. If I'd had even an ounce of food in my stomach, I'm certain my nerves would have violently forced the contents up through my mouth. *Breathe. Just breathe.* I sat in bed, with one arm folded across my stomach. My thumb and middle finger of my other hand were massaging my temples while the phone rested between my ear and shoulder. My eyes were closed and my head was moving slowly from left to right, as I wrestled with my state of disbelief. "Uh, hey. I, uh, just woke up and looked at the clock and realized that you'd be leaving for the airport in a couple hours. I just wanted to make sure that your ticket came and that you're all set to go."

"Yep, got it. The FedEx guy just delivered it. I'm just doing last-minute things around here before I leave."

"Okay. I don't wanna keep you. I just wanted to check on you and wish you safe travels. I'm gonna go to the gym when I get up and then get on the road to Palm Springs. I want to leave early so I don't have to sit in traffic on the freeway."

"Sounds good. I get in around five o'clock. I think Casey gets in around two. You should call her if you get in early and you guys can hook up— maybe get some lunch or something."

Actually, she gets in at one-thirty-seven, which is why I'm leaving so early!

Swallowing the ball of nerves in my throat, I said, "Don't worry about me. I'll find something to amuse myself with. Just call me after you've picked up your car and we'll figure out where to meet. I'll see you in Palm Springs."

"Alright, then. I'll see you soon. Oh, and love…I can't wait to see you, too."

My face cringed again as I realized that Sydney was referring to the text I'd inadvertently sent to her.

I snapped the phone shut before sinking back down into my bed. My heart returned to its normal pace and I stared at the ceiling, thankful that I had just dodged a bullet from a gun I had shot. I was chilled at the thought of what *could* have happened and vowed to be much more vigilant in my text messaging. But not even counting sheep was going to lull me back to sleep. Instead, I prepared to make my debut later that day at the Palm Springs Desert Classic.

Given my utter lack of emotion for Sydney and my escalating obsession with Casey, the thought of spending even one night with Sydney in Palm Springs seemed torturous. But, hey, if my ancestors could survive being in the desert for forty years, I knew I could survive a few days. So I carefully picked out a "desert casual" ensemble, which consisted of flip-flops, a pair of baggy khaki pants that sat low on my hips and a new black tank top that read: I DON'T LIKE YOU on the front and STOP CRYING on the back. Melissa assumed that I'd purchased the shirt with Sydney in mind. She wasn't wrong. I gassed up the BMW, threw my melee of clothes into the trunk and departed for yet another tennis tournament.

Never one to travel out of town without calling my mother, I sank into the driver's seat and dialed her on my cell phone. "Hey Mom, I just got in the car."

"Ohhh, you're heading to Palm Springs today? My little adventure capitalist sure doesn't stay put for long!" That was my mom's new nickname for me. The reference always dripped with sarcasm.

I retorted with, "It's tough being me, Mom."

Not buying it, she mumbled, "Mmm hmmm. Sounds like it. So how long will you be relaxing in the desert sun?" She asked in such a way that I felt guilty— as if I should feel bad for embarking on yet another "vacation" while she was working seven days per week. Truthfully, a part of me did.

Fiddling with the radio stations, I answered, "Uh, I don't know. It depends on how Sydney does. Could be two days, could be two weeks." My mom, like everyone else, had been kept in the dark about my true feelings for Sydney.

"Okay, well keep in touch. Oh Steph...will you see Martina?" My mother adored the fact that I now ran in the same circles as Martina Navratilova.

"Yes, Mom, I'm sure I will," I said, trying not to let her know that I was rolling my eyes.

"Well, if you get a chance, tell her I think it's marvelous that she's still playing!"

Eager to get off the phone, I adjusted the temperature in the car and ended the call. "Okay. I love you. Say 'hi' to Dad."

By the time I reached the top of my street and turned onto Sunset Boulevard, I had finished telling my mother only what she wanted to hear— which was that I was on my way to Palm Springs to hang out with the tennis celebs; not that I was going to the desert to further involve myself in an illicit relationship with my girlfriend's ex-girlfriend. Jesus, just hearing that out loud, makes me cringe! Even though I had become accustomed to selective divulgence, I found it difficult to engage in long conversations with my mom. In my mind, the shorter the call, the less egregious the lie. This particular phone call lasted less than sixty seconds.

Rarely, if ever, did I keep secrets from my mother, but this one definitely fell into the "exception" category. There were times when I was dying to share with her the excitement of being head-over-heels in love, but each time I was about to open my mouth and spew my effervescence, I stopped myself. I knew she wouldn't approve— the same way I knew what I was doing was wrong. I'm not saying my mother is beyond reproach or that she's the poster child for morality. But, apart from the little tiny white lies she's happy to ignore for my benefit, she does believe in honesty and integrity and I knew she wouldn't condone my current convoluted triangle of deceit. Her sole goal for my life was that I find happiness, but somehow I knew that she would find happiness derived this way unacceptable. Despite being raised to value the truth, I avoided being honest with my parents and all the rest of my friends and worst of all with myself.

I don't know how she did it, but somehow Casey had convinced me that collusion and concealment were our only options. Everyone was still on a "need to know basis" and, as far as she was concerned, no one needed to know about our romance. Think of it this way: you know the image of a conflicted person who has inner voices telling him or her what to do and, normally, one voice manifests itself as the devil and the other as an angel? Let's assign my face to the angel and Casey's to the devil. So, I see myself in some flowing white gown with a halo over my head (yes, both the halo and the gown are a stretch, but this is my fantasyland so who's gonna argue with me?), and I see Casey's smiling face in a red devil's outfit complete with a pitchfork. Every time my internal, angelic voice would say, "Go ahead...you can tell her" it was as if Casey and her demonic persona managed to snip my vocal chords, rendering me speechless.

Yup— just when I thought things couldn't get any worse— now I'm in love with the devil.

I tossed my phone onto the console beside me, threw on my Gucci sunglasses (another present from Sydney— she had lovingly given me Gucci sunglasses that matched hers), plugged in my iPod to the stereo and off I went down the freeway toward the desert. I had never been to Palm Springs before. I'm not sure why, but Palm Springs conjured images of huge aerodynamic windmills, golf courses, old women wearing white denim pantsuits with ten-inch zippers and white haired men with cigars hanging out of their mouths wearing oversized black glasses and pinky rings. But I soon learned that the only one that was accurate was the windmills.

During the two-hour drive, I couldn't think about anything except seeing Casey. Nothing. I looked down at my MapQuest directions every two seconds, eager to get there, and prayed I wouldn't get lost. That would have been just my luck. I have a terrible sense of direction. The temperature dial in my car read "100°" and suddenly the road was flanked by those huge white windmills I imagined, so I was confident that I was heading in the right direction.

The drive took less than two hours, but it seemed like eternity. Being one of those Jews who celebrated Christmas, I felt like a young kid who was excitedly awaiting morning the night before Christmas. Finally, I was close. Just as I was passing Palm Springs airport, my phone vibrated. I carefully flipped it open, read the text message while steering the car and trying desperately to read and not drive up a windmill. Both my excitement level and my speed increased as I read the message from Casey. *Guess who just landed?* You would have thought I was competing in the Indy 500 as I raced to the hotel. I was dying to see Casey and make the most of our time alone together before Sydney arrived.

Within minutes and according to our plan, I was parked in the back corner of Le Parker Meridien's lot— the same hotel Sydney had wanted to whisk me away to six months earlier— as far away from the other cars as possible. My phone rang again and I could barely contain my excitement. A cursory check of the caller ID confirmed it was Casey. I picked up and blurted, in an enthusiastic squeal, "Is the cutest girl in the world in Palm Springs?"

Smooth as silk, she said, "Well, that all depends on where you are."

The moisture levels between my thighs began to reach fever pitch.

Sensing it could take me a moment to recover, Casey forged ahead. "I'm at the front of the rental car line."

At some events, even though the tournament provides drivers and transportation, some of the players decide to rent cars at their own expense so they can come and go as they please without having to book a car every time they wish to go somewhere. The Desert Classic is one of those tournaments and both Casey and Sydney opted for rental cars over tournament transportation.

"I hope they give me a better car than last year. Anyway, I can't wait to see you! Where are you?"

"I'm in the back parking lot, according to plan, Captain Concealment. It's fucking Africa-hot here, so hurry up!"

Anxiously, she asked, "Are you walking around?"

What she really meant to say was, "You're not out in the open in plain view are you?" I was so excited I didn't have time to get annoyed with her neurosis. "Hell, no! I'm sitting in my car like a princess soaking up the air conditioning. I'm looking at the temperature dial. It's 107° outside. I'm afraid if I get out of this car, I'll melt!"

"We wouldn't want the princess to melt, so you just stay put and I'll be there as soon as I can."

"Oh, there's Jennifer Capriati. Should I roll down the window and tell her I'm on the phone with you, that you say 'hi' and that you'll be here to meet me momentarily?" I couldn't resist and apparently Casey couldn't resist hanging up on me. The phone went dead.

Thirty minutes later, I was still sitting in my car with the air conditioning blowing in my face. But the second I caught a glimpse of Casey's bright blonde hair and her smile behind the steering wheel of her Jeep Liberty, I waited for her to park and then jumped out and braved the desert heat to greet her. I instinctively threw my arms around her and we embraced for a nanosecond until she mechanically cut the reunion short and insisted that we duck into my car and abscond together from the hotel property in order to reduce our chances of being seen by any other players.

Casey was ridiculously nervous as we drove along the windy road out of the hotel— watching for any familiar face that might catch a glimpse of us. Finally, after we exited the hotel property, she put her head back and rested her hand comfortably on mine. But, still, I could tell that she wasn't fully relaxed. I clenched my teeth. *Oh, for the love of God! Relax! No one can see us! And who gives a shit, anyway?* I felt an uncomfortable pause. A few seconds later, she turned toward me and said, "Stephie, I have to tell you something. You have to promise not to tell anyone I

209

told you, because I really shouldn't be telling you this."

I didn't have a clue what was about to come out of her mouth. What more could she swear me to secrecy about? The look in her eyes was eerie and I would have agreed to anything as long as she divulged her secret with haste. But at the same time, I was a tad nervous. My knuckles turned white as my left hand gripped the steering wheel tighter and tighter. I cautiously agreed. "Ummm, okay. What is it?"

She paused once more and then exhaled before the secret kernel fell from her lips. "I think Sydney might be cheating on you," she blurted.

"What?! Are you serious?! With who?! This is fucking GREAT!" Exclamations rolled off my tongue, one after the other.

"You're not mad?"

"Mad?! Why would I be mad?! I'm the last thing from mad! You won't let me break up with her, but maybe she'll do us the favor of breaking up with me! This is perfect! You have to tell me everything you know— NOW!" I could barely contain my elation.

"Well, I'm not sure what's going on, but Sydney's been talking about some girl a lot. And she and Trish were talking the other day, and…Stephie, I'm serious. You can't say a thing about this if I tell you. Trish will kill me!"

"Oh shut up…I mean, go on. Of course I won't say anything. This is fucking genius. Tell me more!" I was nearly salivating in anticipation of the salacious details.

"Well, Sydney called Trish the other day and blabbed to her about this girl she's been hanging out with. Her name is Bonnie and she has a tragic crush on Sydney. She's young and she's an aspiring actress— she does television commercials."

I had to concentrate so I wouldn't drive off the road. "Oh, this is classic! I couldn't have written a better script! Please go on. What does this girl look like?"

"Sydney says she's really cute and young. Twenty-one. Maybe twenty-two."

"Oh, puh-lease! Sydney looks in the mirror and thinks that she's the cutest person who ever walked the face of the earth! What the hell does she know about cute?"

"She thinks *you're* cute," Casey snapped.

"Okay, I'll give her that one. Anyway, so basically, this kid…this lesbian thespian worships Sydney?"

"Yeah, apparently. Bonnie has a huge thing for Sydney and Sydney admitted to Trish that she likes her and is attracted to her."

"Has anything happened between them? Oh, please say 'yes'." I pressed my palms together and looked heavenward, hoping that a "yes" would fall from Casey's mouth.

"I don't know. If they hooked up, Sydney didn't tell Trish. And, really, Stephie, you can't say a word. I mean it!"

"Okay, okay, okay! I won't. But you do realize that this is the best thing that could happen to us, don't you?! Is it possible that I'm getting a Christmas present early? Do you think Sydney will break up with me?" My mind started considering the possibility of a breakup initiated by Sydney. I began to get lost in my fantasy when the car behind us jerked me back into reality by honking to let me know that the red light was now green.

There was no chance that Sydney would break up with me. That would have been too good to be true and I wasn't *that* lucky. Casey quickly reminded me that it was only March and that I had virtually no chance of getting the early Christmas present that I wanted from Sydney.

I was still digesting the possibility that Sydney was cheating on me when Casey insisted that we stop at the nearest Starbucks. I was neither concerned nor jealous because the mere possibility of an affair by Sydney represented a most fortuitous exit strategy. I was jubilant and, despite my promise of secrecy to Casey, I had a suspicion that it was only a matter of time before I would somehow use this new piece of information to my advantage.

As we pulled into the parking lot, I laughed to myself at the sight of a Mercedes displaying the tournament logo. It was an "official tournament car." I didn't have to look at Casey to know that she was about to have an anxiety attack. I nonchalantly parked in the only available spot in the entire lot, which was, coincidentally, right next to the Desert Classic Mercedes. I had to bite my tongue as I pulled the key out of the ignition and saw Kim Clijsters, the then-Number 3 player in the world, walking toward the Mercedes. There was no way we could avoid her. A quick getaway was out of the question. Kim was one of the exceptionally nice players on the Tour, so a superficial nod as we walked past one another was not a possibility. I didn't see what the big deal was, anyway. Casey and I had been seen together at virtually every tournament for the last six months. In my mind, Kim would see two friends grabbing a cup of coffee. But, in Casey's mind, Kim would see two lesbians sneaking off to have an *illicit* cup of….gasp…coffee!

Of course, our Kim sighting was a non-event and we made our way to the entrance. Before I had a chance to make fun of Casey, her phone rang. I playfully rolled my eyes and held the door for her (not considering, for a moment, the germs I'd just encountered) as she walked into Starbucks gabbing on her phone. Casey was even more of a phone whore than I. She was never one to miss a call. God forbid. I assumed that she was on the phone with Trish. Why wouldn't she be? It had been nearly an hour since they had last spoken (assuming Casey had called her after arriving). I was doing my best not to be annoyed. After all, Casey was here with me and Trish, her straight but obsessive best friend was across the country back in Boston. Look at how good I was at justifying odd behavior!

Casey was tucked in a corner near the window finishing her phone call when I handed her a latte packed with sugar, just the way she liked it. She nodded a "thank you" and said good-bye to whomever she was talking and flipped her phone shut. "Sorry about that. That was my coach. I had to talk to him about my practice schedule and my hitting partner for the week."

"Oh, God, don't worry about it! I'm not your keeper. You know I don't care when you're on the phone or who you're on the phone with." A snicker echoed in my head as I smiled at her and sincerely told this white lie. In truth, her incessant text messaging and acceptance of incoming phone calls in my presence was beginning to wear on my nerves since our time together was rather limited. But I didn't find her addiction to her phone nearly as egregious as her addiction to her best friend. I was beginning to think of Trish as if she were a piece of gum on the bottom of my shoe. No matter how hard I stomped, I just couldn't get rid of her.

"Can you believe that the first person we saw was Kim?" Casey looked a tad nervous.

"Yeah, and you saw what a big tragedy it was, didn't you? I bet she skipped practice this afternoon and is on her way to the ESPN booth to break the news to Mary Carillo and Bud Collins that she had just spotted two friends heading into a local Starbucks for an afternoon coffee. Do I look okay?" I playfully ran my fingers through my hair as if they were a comb and puckered my lips into a posed smile. "I bet the camera crews will be here soon to get us on tape for the evening sportscast. By the end of the day, everyone on the Tour is going to think you're the devil for stealing Sydney's girlfriend. And, shit! You're not even wearing a single item of Prada! They're going to have to change tomorrow's headline from *The Devil Wears Prada* to *The Devil Wears Nike.*" I put my hand over my mouth to silence my laughter.

"Very funny, you ass! I know I'm being a little ridiculous, but I just don't want to get caught."

"Well, if you'd just let me put an end to this charade, there'd be nothing to get caught doing," I said, patronizingly.

She acknowledged with a smirk, sipped her latte and stared silently at me as only someone who had seen me naked could do.

"What?" I coyly asked, feeling my cheeks turn fiery red.

"Nothing." She smiled and whispered, "It's just so nice to be sitting across from you right now. I've never seen a prettier face than yours. I could stare at your face for hours and never get tired of it."

"Aww, stop," I said, smiling bashfully. "No, don't. Tell me more." Now this obsession, I didn't mind.

"Nope, that's all you get. So, tell me something I don't know about you— I wanna know every single detail." She pushed her cup back and forth between her hands and said, "Tell me about your sister."

Ugh. She had to pick my *least* favorite subject— one that I generally spoke of to no one. But, with Casey, I was willing to talk about anything. "My sister. Hmm. Not a very pleasant topic. She's a total bitch." There! I said it! "Actually, she and I used to be really close. When I started playing tennis at Bollettieri's, she got uprooted to Florida, too. She wasn't happy about that, but she eventually forgave me. We're only a year apart, but my big sister decided when we were in high school that she no longer wanted to be under the watchful eyes of our 'control freak' parents. She took that to an extreme and rebelled against everything they told her to do and everything they stood for." Casey stared at me intensely, soaking up every word I said.

"Essentially overnight, she decided that my parents were evil for wanting her to graduate from high school and go to college to make something of herself and she hated me because I didn't adopt her views. She turned our house into an extremely acrimonious place, but we all thought she was just going through a phase and that she'd calm down when she went to college. She didn't. Her wild streak just got worse when she moved out of the house. When my parents refused to pay for her 'party-girl' lifestyle, she basically divorced herself from us. I haven't spoken to her in almost ten years." I sighed and drained the last drop of my coffee and said, "And, that's the riveting story of my crazy sister."

Shaking her head subtly, she said, "I think she's crazy for not wanting to have you in her life, but people react strangely to pressure—especially pressure from parents. I know all about rebelling." Casey smiled quirkily, and gestured to her head. "This is my way of rebelling."

I wasn't following and she could obviously see the confusion in my eyes.

"I've spent everyday of my life since I was old enough to hold a tennis racket, trying to stay 'within the lines.' My 'left of center' style—my crazy hair, earrings, and tattoo— are my way of rebelling against all that my world and my parents stand for. It's my way of living 'outside the lines' and creating a little individuality."

Aha! I knew there had to be an explanation for her strict departure from pleated tennis skirts and preppy ponytails.

She inhaled deeply, clenching her hand tightly around her coffee cup. "I know what it's like to constantly try to please parents. My mom grew up in San Juan and was one of the best female tennis players in Puerto Rico. She tried to play professionally but didn't make it. When I was old enough to hold a racket, my dad started giving me lessons and my mom put all her hopes and dreams into me. I was born with this talent to play tennis, but it's been a blessing *and* a curse. Sometimes I wonder if my parents would love me if I never hit another tennis ball again for the rest of my life..."

Having never met either of her parents, I presumptuously spoke for them. "Casey, of course they would!" I said robustly.

Pursing her lips and shaking her head, she said, "Sometimes I really wonder. Both of their lives revolve around my tennis. My dad was my coach for years until we spent more time arguing on the court than actually practicing. Now he's a coach at a country club in Wellesley, but he still tries to give me 'helpful tips.' My mom's a teacher at the high school I went to, and let's just say, without her 'special help' I might have had to wait an extra year to graduate— which would have postponed my tennis career. My entire life, they've encouraged me to do whatever it takes to be the best." She bit her bottom lip and rolled her eyes. "You know what they were most upset about when Sydney and I broke up?"

I shook my head with uncertainty.

"My ranking. My career. They were worried that my tennis would suffer." She laughed. "I guess I showed them! It was Sydney's career that suffered, not mine." She raised her eyebrows and inhaled deeply, "Anyway...that's the story of *my* crazy life."

Wow. Casey Matthews had just willingly volunteered information about her family to me— something that Sydney claimed she guarded ferociously and *never* spoke about.

As we traded stories about our families, I looked at my watch with disbelief. For more than sixty minutes we had not once been interrupted by a cell phone or an unexpected visitor. It was a double-edged sword— it was heaven to be alone with Casey, but it was hell that our private time together would soon be broken up by Sydney. We had less than two hours.

"Let's go back to the hotel," I suggested.

She looked around nervously and whispered, "What if someone sees us in the hotel together?"

"Oh, shit, are we really gonna start this again?" I had neither the energy nor the inclination to humor her neurosis. The clock was ticking and I didn't want to waste my time playing the "what if" game. "Casey, here's the deal: we're gonna drive back to the hotel. If you want me to drop you off at the front, I will. Otherwise, I'll drop you back at your car and we can walk to the reception area together or separately. Either way, we're gonna end up at the same place at approximately the same time. Sydney's plane lands in less than two hours. She expects me to already be here and, for sure, she would expect me to be hanging out with you. So, would you please stop acting like a psychopath and be a normal human being?!"

Thankfully, Casey saw that I was right. Otherwise, I might have had to take her by the hand and forcefully drag her out of Starbucks.

When we arrived back at the hotel, the reception area was teeming with tennis players and it looked like Prince, Babolat, Nike, Wilson and Head bags had been vomited all over the floor. The bellmen were busy loading over-sized duffels onto the trolleys and throwing racket bags over their shoulders, showing various players to their suites. I followed Casey to the front desk and waited while she checked in. Once the receptionist announced Casey's room number, I quickly interrupted and asked, "Can you also check and see if there's another room available on the same floor?" The receptionist stared at me blankly and so did Casey. I explained, "We have a friend checking in later this evening and we'd all like to be on the same floor if that's possible."

Nodding her head in acknowledgement, the receptionist looked down at the hidden computer screen in the counter and I heard the sound of her press-on nails tapping the keyboard. She didn't look up from the computer screen as the clicking continued.

Is this something that they teach in travel school? It seems to be an unprecedented skill required of all airport, car rental and hotel personnel. How to look incredibly earnest while taking the longest possible amount of time to determine the answer to the simplest of questions. I wondered if Ms. Helpful was actually doing anything or if she was just staring at the computer screen and playing Pac-Man or Space Invaders? And, regardless, can she please hurry the fuck up so I can get behind closed doors with the woman standing next to me?

Finally, she looked up and informed me that there was only one room left on the same floor and that she would be happy to put it on hold.

Of course there was only one room left. Isn't that always the case? Thank God you tapped away on your keyboard and worked your magic! You're such a saint for doing your job and accommodating us!

Once she secured the room for Sydney, she handed Casey the key. I graciously thanked the woman. Hearts palpitating, Casey and I rushed to her room. The clock was ticking against our favor. Oh, how I wanted to savor those last delicious moments together before the Control Freak arrived.

14

The new "tennis turn": look left, look right, proceed with caution

"Would you please stop acting like such a psycho?!" I jokingly requested— again.

"Shh! Keep your voice and your head down! Don't make eye contact with anyone," Casey snapped back.

Casey nervously stepped out of the elevator as if she were trespassing in forbidden territory and walked ahead of me down the empty hallway toward her room. Sliding the key in the door, she looked in both directions to make sure that we were still the only ones in the hallway before ushering me inside. Laughing silently, I decided to placate her paranoia for the moment. I could hear the suspenseful music from *Mission: Impossible* in my head and envisioned two weeks of hiding behind doors and camouflaging myself as part of the wall in order to sneak into Casey's room undetected. Once inside, we embraced as if we hadn't seen each other in years. It felt like an eternity since our lips had last made contact and I was jittery with anticipation. I had been desperate to savor her soft, sensuous kiss since we parted in Boston a week earlier, and spending the afternoon after only the slightest peck on the cheek in the parking lot had been torturous.

I sighed happily after my craving for a tender kiss had been satiated. Casey smiled for a second before she broke the embrace and quickly traversed the spacious suite to the sliding glass door, which led to the balcony. Her view overlooked the entrance to the hotel and, apparently, she could see countless tennis players checking in and others just milling about the grounds. She closed the curtains immediately in order to shield us from any wandering eyes— as if someone might happen to look directly up from the entrance area to her room, on the second floor. Jesus! I made myself comfortable on the couch as she closed the curtains. Just then, my phone vibrated. I read the message: *Where are you guys and why aren't you answering your phones?* Simultaneously, Casey received the same text message. Instantly, the smile on her face was replaced with a "what do we do?" look.

Sydney's flight had arrived early. I assured Casey not to worry and that everything would be fine. I dialed Sydney's number and grew more irritated with each ring. I knew that my time with Casey would be ending shortly. Sydney answered and I could hear her annoyance as her voice tightened. "I've been trying to call you guys, but both of your phones are going straight to voicemail. Where are you?"

Truly, neither of our phones had rung. I was beside myself that I even had to entertain this instant barrage of questions, but I knew I had to answer. I got myself into this mess and I had (foolishly) agreed to the rules of the game. As calmly and pleasantly as possible, I answered, "Oh, sorry. I guess we don't get great reception here. We're in Casey's room just hanging out waiting for you. Where are you?"

"I'm waiting for my car. Of course, I got here and the fucking assholes didn't have my booking, so I'm just waiting here until these fuckwits get me a car."

Charming. She certainly has a way with words.

Sydney's misfortune was my good luck and I smiled as I realized that her arrival would now be delayed. I feigned disappointment. "Oh, shit. I'm sorry. You should have called me and I would have come and picked you up." That blatant lie flew out of my mouth on autopilot. God, I hate this!

"Well, that's why I was trying to call you. But, it's too late now. I've arranged for another car. Hopefully, I'll be there soon."

Oh, yes. Hopefully. With any luck at all. I pulled a sarcastic face and crossed my fingers.

"Obviously there's no reception problem with text messages so just text me when you get here and I'll meet you in the lobby."

As soon as I pushed the words "drive safely" out of my mouth, I ended the call and approached Casey who had been anxiously pacing the floor. Assuring her that everything was alright with Sydney, we sat down on the couch. Tenderly, Casey looked at me and said, "You know I love you, don't you?"

I smiled while simultaneously crinkling my nose. "Is this a trick question?"

"No."

"And, I love you, too."

"All of this is going to be worth it, right? You're sure this is what you want— that *I'm* what you want?"

I had to entertain Casey's insecurities on a daily basis regardless of my constant pledges of love and devotion. How much more assurance could I give her? After all, I had agreed to go along with her plan of dishonesty and deception and sneak around behind Sydney's back in order to pursue my love for her. I wouldn't have agreed to all this nonsense if I didn't think it was worth it! "Casey, I love you and I want to be with you. *Never* doubt that."

She smiled and said nothing in return. Instead, she leaned over and kissed me. Before I could get lost in its warmth and happiness, her tongue went from decidedly explorative to curiously limp. I opened my eyes to find hers staring toward the palm trees on the drawn curtains. Abruptly pulling her lips from mine, she jumped off the couch and scurried toward the balcony door.

I remained still, with my mouth agape. "Uh, Casey, am I missing something? What are you doing?" I asked, speaking to the back of her head as she nervously peered through the curtains.

"I'm sorry. I just wanted to make sure she wasn't already here."

I looked at my watch. A total of six minutes had passed since I'd hung up with Sydney. Unless she was riding in on a broomstick, I was fairly certain that she was still stranded at the Palm Springs airport torturing the car rental employees who were no doubt scampering around trying to prepare her rental car while simultaneously being lectured by her about who she was, how she couldn't believe she was not receiving the red-carpet treatment and that "somebody" would most assuredly be hearing from her about the terrible inconvenience she'd suffered due to their inability to perform their job properly.

I watched as Casey's head frenetically jerked from side to side as if she were a puppy whose eager eyes followed a biscuit being waved in front of its face. Knowing that our precious time together was slipping away, I decided to take matters into my own hands. I stealthily retrieved a Tourna Grip from Casey's racket bag and grasped her hand, pulling her toward me. She turned to protest. "Wait. I think I see… "

I smiled and whispered, "Shh. You don't see her. She's not here yet."

I led her back to the couch and gently pushed her onto the cushion she had abandoned just minutes before. She spotted one of her blue overgrips in my hand as I kneeled on the floor by her feet.

"What are you doing?"

Unrolling several feet of the long, thin, sponge-like grip, I coyly smiled and said, "Desperate times call for desperate measures." I smirked as I began wrapping the grip around her ankles. After the fifth rotation, I tied a knot and hopped onto the couch next to her. "There! That should keep you still for a few minutes— which is about all I have left with you now." In one fluid motion, I lifted her bound legs onto the couch, pulled her toward me until she was fully reclined and positioned myself on top of her. Still smiling, I looked into her eyes and playfully said, "I believe we were in the middle of something before, which was very rudely interrupted by your psychotic tendencies. Would you like to start again?"

She did, and instantly I felt the tenderness and moisture of her mouth on mine. I caressed her hair and could smell her lavender-scented shampoo. My fingers trailed nimbly down the outside of her ear and over her neck. I inched her shirt up and my thumb lightly traced the dolphin tattooed on her shoulder. Not bothering to unbutton her jeans, I slid my hand beneath her silk panties, in between her thighs. Without freeing her legs from the restraints, she widened her knees, invitingly. Her moistness covered my fingers and it felt as if I had submerged part of my hand in warm, liquid silver. Slowly, I slipped one finger inside her. As her pelvis rhythmically thrust toward me, she reached down my back and lifted my shirt over my head. Just as my flesh touched hers, the phone vibrated, signaling another text message. "Her fucking timing is impeccable!" I growled, refusing to let Casey get up.

"We have to stop. What if she's here?" She spastically pulled my hand from her pants.

"So what?!" Casey found a way to worry about everything, even though most of her angst was a terrible waste of energy. After all, how realistic was it that Sydney would immediately be knocking on Casey's door the minute she arrived at the hotel? The overly helpful and friendly receptionist at the front desk certainly wasn't going to clue her in on the room number. Unless Sydney just *happened* to take a wild guess and randomly pick the door to Casey's room out of the hundreds of other doors, she could not possibly know what room we were in, much less what we were doing behind that closed door. See? Wasted energy.

I had a hard time accepting Casey's neurosis. Trying to reason with her was about as much a waste of time as trying to inflate a balloon with a hole in it. She had ripped the overgrip from her ankles, disentangled herself from my half-naked body and was now on her way over to the sliding glass door to peer down to the hotel entrance. As she hid behind the curtain trying to identify Sydney in the pool of people below, I put my tank top back on and read the text, which confirmed that Sydney had arrived. "Yep, she's here. I guess I better head to the lobby to meet her before she fills up my inbox with 'Where the hell are you?' texts."

I knew that when I kissed Casey good-bye a few seconds later, it would be the last one for the night. I was certain that I would have to spend the evening with Sydney alone and I feared she would be expecting a sweet reunion. It had been almost one month since we had seen each other and Sydney was overly eager to get her hands on her girlfriend. Little did she know, the reunion would be anything but sweet. I straightened my shirt and combed my fingers through my tousled hair as Casey clasped my hand and led me to the door.

She pouted, "I hate the thought of you being down the hall with *her*. I want you in here with *me*. Try to come back over tonight for a few minutes, if you can." She knew that in a few short minutes Sydney and I would be walking past her door on our way to our room, which, unbeknownst to Sydney, was two doors down from hers. Casey despised the thought of Sydney and me behind closed doors, regardless of my assurances that I would do everything in my power to thwart Sydney's advances.

Casey motioned for me to stand back and remain quiet as she opened the door and looked in both directions to ensure that the coast was clear for me to leave without being seen. Before I had a chance to comment on her lunacy or tell her that there was a piece of overgrip stuck to the side of her leg, she nudged me into the hallway, smiled and whispered instructions for me to call her soon. I quietly laughed and nodded in agreement.

Begrudgingly, I rode the elevator down to the lobby. Stepping out, I tried to appear nonchalant as I rushed toward the reception area. Several minutes had passed since Sydney's text came through stating that she had arrived. When I reached the end of the hallway, I surreptitiously glanced over to the reception desk and saw Sydney standing in front of the same helpful receptionist that had checked Casey in earlier. In a split second, I decided that the best course of action was to sneak up, surprise Sydney from behind and give her a giant hug. Even this minor display of affection would be difficult for me— but could gain me valuable points when I needed them— later. I took a deep breath and set off to do what I knew I had to do.

I could feel Sydney's excitement as I wrapped my arms around her. She turned around with an eerily toothy grin on her face. Of course, she tried to push her luck and plant a kiss on my lips. I turned my head just in time for her lips to land on my cheek. The moistness on the side of my face nearly made me physically recoil. Ick! It reminded me of the wet, sloppy kisses my grandmonster used to give me when I was a kid. I feigned an itch and ran my fingers across my cheek, wiping away the saliva. Sydney tried once more to kiss me on the lips but only got cheek, as I disguised my disgust with an excited and spastic bear hug. I thought of my favorite scene from *Top Gun* when Maverick requests permission for a victory "flyby" of the aircraft carrier tower before landing his jet. His request was quickly denied. Sydney's request to land her lips on mine was dismissed just as swiftly. But, to an objective eye, I appeared happy to see her. Appearances aren't everything. Sorry, Mom, but they aren't!

15

$\mathcal{L}$adies and gentlemen, Ms. Alexander has called for an "injury time-out"

I wondered if Casey was watching through the peephole as Sydney and I walked past her room. I would have given anything to lock myself with Casey in her room. Instead, I continued two doors down the hallway to the room I would share with Sydney. Dreading the inevitable, I knew that once the door closed behind us, Sydney's hands would be glued to my flesh. The thought of it was unbearable, and I was still savoring my afternoon together with Casey as Sydney and I entered our room. Not knowing how I was going to avoid Sydney's advances, I was in a terrible spot of bother.

I tried to find comfort in my "Happy Pill Plan," a scheme I'd devised the week before in order to avoid having sex with Sydney. You see, Sydney's propensity for psychoanalyzing me had surpassed psychobabble and she was now actually doling out diagnoses. According to her, my inability to be fully present in our relationship was a direct result of two things: 1) my relationship with my mother; and 2) my mounting depression (which, according to Sydney, needed to be addressed by a different therapist than the one I'd been seeing, because *obviously* she wasn't treating me correctly). Needless to say, I always ignored her bullshit couch therapy and would never even entertain the validity or audacity of her first hypothesis. There was, after all, a reason for the little saying about the two things that you can do if you piss my mother off— leave town or die. Suffice to say that if Sydney's diagnosis about my relationship with my mom would have reached my mom's ears, it would have been the nail in Sydney's coffin. I didn't want my mother going to jail over Sydney Foster, so I neither mentioned it nor gave it much consideration. However, when it became convenient, I decided to use her depression diagnosis to my advantage.

I sided with Brooke Shields and not Tom Cruise on the issue of anti-depression medication. When I was teetering on the verge of pushing my partner out a window in my Boston law firm and anxiously waiting for Paige to call me when she was too busy chasing some other skirt, my doctor prescribed Prozac. It helped my depression, but it killed my sex drive. It wouldn't have mattered if Sharon Stone had burst into my bedroom and told me that she'd been waiting her entire life to have sex with me (hey, a girl can dream, can't she?!). I just wouldn't have been interested. Call me crazy!

It occurred to me that I could use my Prozac experience to my advantage. For months, Sydney had been insisting that I was depressed. During a brainstorming session, it dawned on me that she just may have a point. *Maybe I was depressed.* Yes, in fact, *I was depressed!* So much so that my depression required psychotropic, mood-altering drugs. Sydney had been badgering me constantly to go back to the doctor and get on the "Happy Pills" and my standard response was, "Mind your own business and swing at a tennis ball before I take a swing at you!" But now I was going to feed Dr. Foster's ego with another white lie and tell her that I was back on the "Happy Pills." Tennis players take "injury time-outs" all the time and I was certain that I could use my Happy Pill Plan to convince Sydney that just as she occasionally had to call the trainer to the court in the middle of the match to nurse certain ailments, I needed a time-out to mend my psyche.

My resolve to stay as far away as possible from Sydney was strengthened by Casey's adamant desire that I reserve my touch for her. The mere mention of my being alone with Sydney was enough to orbit Casey into space— the prospect of my being intimate with anyone other than her was, apparently, her mood-altering drug. Whenever the topic came up, I was always quick to remind her that if she would just let me break up with Sydney, neither of us would have to worry about such preposterous possibilities. Alas, I had agreed to her plan. I had made my bed, now I just needed to figure out a way not to sleep in it. That's where my Happy Pill Plan would come in. I could simply explain my lack of sexual desire as a result of being back on anti-depression medication. After all, Sydney would have written me a prescription with her racket stencil as easily as she handed out autographs if she could. And I thought the Boston CLE plan was genius!

The second the door shut behind us, I felt like a lamb in a lion's den. I could tell by the look in Sydney's eyes that she had only one thing on her mind. Sure enough, as soon as she set her racket bag down, she wedged against me. I was assaulted with nervousness— and, not the good nervousness when something great is about to happen and the anticipation of it is overwhelming. It was the kind of nervousness that I remembered feeling when I couldn't decide between answer choice "A" or "C" on the SATs with only a few seconds left to answer, although neither choice felt right to me. If I selected the right answer, Harvard, Princeton and Yale would await my decision. But if I chose incorrectly the doors to all universities— Ivy League and otherwise— would slam in my face. I had to make up my mind quickly, as Sydney's open mouth was closing in on me. *Shit, shit, shit! What am I going to do? I can't just put my hand up and say, "Stop! Don't come near. I'm on Prozac!"* I was paralyzed with indecision.

Too late.

I waited too long and could not escape the tentacle-like arms that were reaching around me. I surrendered and put my arms around her to hug her. I squeezed her with all my strength, picked her up and tossed her onto the bed. I then stepped back and in an act of jack-assery, lifted my arms and flexed my biceps— as if I were some superhero and my flexed biceps were going to protect me from the forces of evil. *What am I? Twelve? I wonder how she is going to react?* Before she had a chance to murmur a single word, I hoisted my bag onto the bed and started unpacking. Crisis averted…at least for the time being.

As Sydney began to unpack, she told me to close my eyes. I was hesitant, but obliged her request. After repeating "Not yet" and "Keep 'em closed" over and over again while she prepared my surprise, she finally allowed me to open my eyes. I was speechless. The entire bottom half of the bed was covered in Nike clothing and Puma shoes. She didn't have a contract with either Puma or Nike. Sydney had raided both stores and had bought me samples of all the latest fashions knowing that these were my favorite sports labels. There were bountiful piles of clothes and a row of shoes. Apparently, she thought I needed a pair of Puma shoes in every color. It wasn't my birthday and Christmas was months away. I followed my tunnel vision back to the very first (and only) shopping spree that my grandmonster treated my sister and me to. By the time she was finished selecting something from essentially every rack, she had done so much damage at Miss Jackson's (Tulsa's version of Saks Fifth Avenue) that they had to send a van and a driver to follow us home with all our new clothes. I didn't realize it then, but now I know that these kinds of "presents" always come with strings attached.

I felt a pit in my stomach as I stared at the clothes and mentally calculated how much money Sydney had spent. Obviously, she had felt me pulling away from her and showering me with cards full of cash and lavish presents was her way of trying to reel me back in. Little did she know, I was too far adrift to be pulled back ashore. After trying to graciously refuse the gifts, I finally gave in and accepted them, but I hated that Sydney was so blatantly and unabashedly trying to buy my love.

Once I had meticulously placed the last item of my new wardrobe on the closet shelves, we ordered room service. As we ate, my mind took me even further away from Sydney. I politely smiled or nodded as she spoke to me but was distracted during the entire meal. Suddenly, my phone vibrated in my pocket and sent a surge through my body. I inadvertently jerked, startling both Sydney and me. "Was that your phone? Who's texting you?" she quickly asked.

I knew it was Casey. I retrieved my phone and quickly glanced at the message. *This is torture! Text me when you wake up. I love you.* Without hesitation, I misinformed Sydney. "Oh, it's Melissa asking if I made it here safely." As easily as I disguised the identity of the texter, I glided through my phone's menu and changed the setting from vibrate to silent so I could receive text messages undetected anytime during the day or night since Sydney was like a curious cat, ready to pounce every time my phone made a noise. I sneaked in a quick response but returned my phone to my pocket when I caught an evil eye from Sydney.

I continued pushing my salad around my plate, thinking of Casey until Sydney interrupted me. "Love, where's you're ring? Why aren't you wearing it?"

My pulse quickened when I looked down at my unadorned finger and realized that I'd taken my ring off when I'd returned from Boston and shoved it in a drawer next to the framed picture of Sydney holding the Wimbledon trophy that I had already retired from my bedside table. In my haste, I'd forgotten to put the stupid ring back on before I bolted out my front door to meet Casey earlier. *Shit!* Stalling, I took a sip of wine and desperately tried to think of a creative and believable explanation. Sydney's gaze glared at me. Time was running out. I swallowed and handed her the only excuse that my brain could muster. "Damn! I knew I felt naked. I must have forgotten to put it back on when I came back from the gym this morning." I somehow managed to feign disappointment as I delivered my lame story.

"Oh. Well, no worries, love. Everyone here knows you're mine. But don't forget to put it back on first thing when you get home."

No! I'm not yours, you controlling freak! And the sooner you realize it, the sooner we can end this sham of a relationship!

When we finished dinner, I nervously got into bed and braced myself for the argument that was certain to ensue. I hadn't thought of a clever way to deliver the news to Sydney that I was back on anti-depression medication that had totally suppressed my sexual appetite. I rolled over, trying to formulate an iron-clad story, but hoped Sydney would be exhausted from her day of travel so I'd have time to rehearse it. Feeling her hand on my shoulder struck fear in my heart and I knew I was going to have to deliver my story flawlessly. Before I had time to panic, she rolled me toward her. "Love, I know you've been really stressed lately. But I think you're clinically depressed, as well. I think you should go to a different therapist and get back on depression meds."

Great, here we go.

Before I could hide behind my eyelids, Sydney had strapped on her therapist hat and begun to psychoanalyze me.

No time like the present. Happy Pill Plan, don't fail me now!

"Well, it's funny you should mention that because I changed therapists and *I am* back on the Happy Pills." She left me no choice but to make my announcement.

"What? You changed therapists?" she echoed. "How long have you been going and why haven't you told me?"

I sighed and shrugged my shoulders.

"Well, what have you told your therapist about me? Do you talk about me? About us and our relationship?" She was oozing with curiosity.

"Sydney, you don't really expect me to hand you a transcript of my therapy sessions, do you?"

Apparently realizing her questions were unreasonable, she chose a different course. "I guess you can keep that stuff private, but you need to tell me about your pills. How long have you been taking them?" Now irritated, all traces of compassion evaporated from her voice.

"A couple weeks."

"What are you taking?"

"Sydney, I don't really want to talk about this. It's a matter between me and my therapist."

"I'm your girlfriend! I can't believe you've been on medication for weeks and you're just telling me now!" Her nostrils were flaring and so was her temper.

I hadn't witnessed one of her temper tantrums— her flaring nostrils, bulging veins and shrieking voice— since our Ambien episode on the plane from Tokyo and I certainly hadn't missed any part of them.

She continued, "Don't you think I have a right to know what you're taking?"

A right to know what I'm taking? I did not like the direction this conversation was heading. "No. I don't. What does it matter what I'm taking?"

"It just might help me understand what's going on with you."

"Sydney, as much as you'd like to pretend that you're an expert on these things, you don't know shit about depression drugs. Knowing which one I'm on will mean nothing to you! Newsflash: You're a tennis player, not a physician!" I said triumphantly and continued, "And, I know you. If I tell you what I'm taking, you'll go and blab about my personal business to your friends and I don't need that shit."

"That's crap! I would *never* talk to my friends about your problems!"

"Oh. My. God! Are you really gonna look me in the eye and lie to me with a straight face?"

Okay, that was a low blow from the pot calling the kettle black again, given that I'd handed Sydney one prevarication after another for weeks. But I was playing to win this round.

"What in bloody hell are you talking about?!"

"Sydney, for Christ's sake! You've offered to have your friends write me scripts for depression medication."

"I told *one* person!" she yelled.

"Yeah, well, that's one too many."

I purposely withheld the name of my medicine from Sydney because I knew it would infuriate her. Okay, so that was a little mean-spirited. But I despise being forced to do things. God forbid she not have full disclosure and total control over something that pertained to me. I had no doubt that she would fight ferociously to find out what medication I was taking. I was one step ahead of her and my resolve was firm. What she was not privy to was that after Prozac, my doctor put me on a different drug that did not curb my sex drive. I took this drug, Wellbutrin, for a while before my doctor graduated me from it and all other depression medication. When I devised my Happy Pill Plan, I remembered that I had half a bottle of these pills in my medicine cabinet. Before I left LA, I poured my remaining tablets into the vitamin bottle with the rest of my daily vitamins. I had a haunting suspicion that there was a very good chance Sydney would scour my belongings for my mystery medication. I wanted to make sure that she found a prize when she went on her treasure hunt. What I really wanted to do was booby-trap my toiletry bag so that her hand would be treated to a little surprise when she reached into a bag that wasn't hers. But I suppressed my urge. Lying about being on anti-depression medication so I would not have to have sex with my girlfriend was one thing, but walking Sydney into a mousetrap was just plain cruel! I think I just felt that flame from hell again. I was starting to get used to it.

Sydney refused to accept that she was not being provided with the information she wanted and she continued to badger me. No matter how I tried to end the conversation, she refused to graciously concede. She was driving me so insane that I was afraid that, by the end of the night, I really would have to start popping those Wellbutrin— like candy!

I decided to repeat myself one last time. "Sydney, I'm not going to discuss this with you. I've told you everything you need to know. I'm dealing with this, and unfortunately, I'm also dealing with a sex drive that's nonexistent because of these pills." Finally! I had delivered the crucial part of my plan to her.

"Oh, that's brilliant! So you don't want sex? What about me? What about my needs?!" She was now officially irate.

Shit, that didn't go as well as I had hoped.

"Look, I'm sorry. I just don't have the slightest sex drive."

"Yeah, but I do!" Her yelling became even louder.

I argued, "So what do you want me to do? Have sex with you and just go through the motions? You've been bugging me for months to go back on the pills and, now that I have, you're giving me a hard time about it? I can never win with you! I'm sorry if it hurts your feelings, but I'm not interested in sex and I really don't want to talk about this anymore. You're gonna have to go express your primal urges somewhere else!"

It was after midnight and I was exhausted. I wanted nothing more than to roll over and go to sleep and wake up to a new day. Still, Sydney kept beating the dead horse. Not only did she beat the dead Happy Pill horse, but she had worked herself into such a tizzy that she unleashed on me about everything that had bothered her from the past month. I got a verbal bashing about not letting her stay with me in LA for a few days after Tokyo (because apparently, we hadn't talked about that issue enough!), about what an asshole I was for not calling her more while I was in Boston and for spending so much time with Paige and, of course, about how she has physical needs.

After going around in circles for two hours, I reached my limit. I could not spend one more second being badgered by her. I thought I could do it— I thought my Happy Pill Plan would work perfectly and buy me some more time toward Casey's goal of reaching the US Open. As she continued with her tirade, I finally exploded.

Throwing Casey's concerns and wishes out of the window, I jumped out of bed and yelled, "Sydney, this isn't working. *We* are not working. Nothing has changed since Australia. We need to break up. I'm not making you happy and I'm certainly not happy. I can't deal with this anymore." I stumbled across the room in the dark to the closet, molesting the wall until I found the light switch. I was fuming as I tossed handfuls of clothing randomly into my bag.

Sydney got out of bed and followed me. She couldn't contain her anger or frustration and her voice was now so loud it was actually piercing. "Oh, so that's it?! This is your answer? You're just gonna leave? You're such a quitter!"

I continued to pack as calmly as I could. "Sydney, we've been trying to make this relationship work for months. It's just not working. I can't give you what you want and I'm tired of feeling bad about it. Let's just stop trying. This is not a tennis match. Not matter how hard you hit the ball or how much spin you put on it, it's just not landing in the court!"

I saw the same possessed look building in Sydney's eyes that I had become all too familiar with in the middle of the night six months earlier at the US Open. But this time, instead of weeping and cajoling, she exploded. As I removed a shirt from a hanger in the closet, she violently grabbed it and screamed at me to stop packing. "Stop! Just stop fucking packing! You're not going anywhere!" Veins were popping out of her head and she was foaming at the mouth. I'm not kidding; an image of *The Hound of the Baskervilles* popped into my mind.

She repeated herself, "You're not going anywhere— you're not! I won't let you." Her eyes were filled with crazed determination.

I reared back. "Oh, you're not gonna *let* me leave?" My voice was dripping with condescension. I smirked and laughed sarcastically, taunting her.

"Don't fucking laugh at me! You know I can't stand to be laughed at!"

I think we just touched upon an issue she just might need to address in therapy.

She was holding the shirt that she had savagely yanked from my hands. It was my favorite Thomas Pink button-down and she now had it in her clenched fist waving it as her arms flailed wildly while she screamed some more at me. I could see her mouth moving and her veins pulsating, but her words went in one of my ears and out of the other. All I could concentrate on was the fact that my favorite shirt was being held hostage, abused and wrinkled by a crazy woman shouting nonsense and foaming at the mouth. My pleas for the release of my innocent pinstriped blouse were all systematically ignored. As she continued to yell, I laughed weakly when my mind took me to the *Charlie Brown* episode where the teacher's voice was completely inaudible and muffled. Sydney was shrieking about something, but all I could hear was, *"Wa, wa, wa, wa, wa,"* the same way the teacher spoke to the Peanuts gang. I couldn't help it. I chuckled out loud. My laugh didn't help matters much, but I attempted to continue packing while ignoring the verbal vomit that was being projectiled at me. Sydney's screaming fell upon my deaf ears, but apparently not on our neighbors'.

As Sydney yammered on with her tirade, we heard a pounding on the wall. Obviously, our next door neighbors didn't find our middle of the night catfight as compelling or urgent as she did. I was mortified that her piercing hysteria had woken up the neighbors and that it had continued long enough to cause them to strike the wall to demand silence. In a hushed but seriously stern voice I said, "Are you fucking kidding me! This is so embarrassing. You've gone absolutely berserk and the neighbors can hear! Get a grip and shut the fuck up!" My tongue was razor sharp.

Adding to the popping veins and foaming mouth, Sydney was now shaking and starting to cry. In a more civilized voice, she pled, "Steph, it's the middle of the night, please don't leave. Let's just go to bed."

Leave? Who's leaving? Not without my shirt!

"Can I please have my shirt back now?"

She relinquished her prisoner of war and through her sniffles said, "I just love you so much. I don't want you to leave. Please come back to bed with me."

I know I should have stood my ground and left but that would have meant foregoing spending the next two weeks with Casey. I had no idea how I was going to make it through the end of the tournament but, until I figured that out, I acquiesced to Sydney's pleas to stay.

A ball, a net, a court and a heavy racket

It was just before five o'clock in the morning when I woke up. I'd barely slept at all. I watched the clock as each minute slowly passed by. After forty-five minutes, I crept out of bed into the bathroom to slip into a pair of sweats. I approached Sydney's side of the bed and whispered to her that I was going to get some coffee and I'd be back in a little while. I didn't define "a little while." The monster barely moved. She was obviously still exhausted from the tirade she had unleashed the night before.

With my cell phone in hand, I tiptoed into the hallway. Surreptitiously, I made my way to Casey's room and lightly tapped on the door. Casey's paranoia had started to become contagious and my eyes bounced from her door to my door to make sure that Sydney was not following me. When there was no answer, I flipped my phone open to call her, forgetting that I had no reception in the hallway. I turned and walked toward the elevators, fixing my gaze on my phone and hoping to get a signal. Suddenly, I heard a "psssst" and nearly had a heart attack, fearing I'd been caught by Sydney. Before I found myself in desperate need of a defibrillator, I looked up to see Casey walking toward me with a Starbucks cup in hand and a smile on her face.

"Where's Sydney?" Casey asked softly.

"In bed…asleep."

"Does she know you're gone?" I could hear the nervousness building in her voice.

"Sort of. I told her semi-comatose corpse I was going to get coffee."
I followed Casey into her room and told her about the fight Sydney and
I had had the night before and that I wasn't sure how much longer I
would be able to maintain the charade that we (she) had planned. I
sighed, "Cutie, I have to break up with her. I thought I could do this,
but I can't. It's too hard."

"You can't break up with her! You have to stay with her so we can
see each other. Believe me, I hate it as much as you do. I can't stand
the thought of you in that room with her…of you touching her." She
paused and after an extended silence asked for more details from the
night before. "Did you…?" She stopped herself and looked away. "Did
you have sex with her?" she asked.

I shook my head and shrieked, "God no!" I felt deflated and tried to
express as much. "I really don't think I can do this. Don't you
understand? This is hurting me and, as much as I can't stand Sydney
right now, I hate doing this to her. It's not right."

"Stephie, I promise you this is temporary. Just please do this for me."

Casey knew I'd do anything for her— anything to be with her. I just
wish I knew why. Maybe then I could have saved me from myself.

I pursed my lips and drew in a deep, contemplative breath. My
doubts were then silenced by Casey's mouth on mine. She broke the
passionate kiss only to lead me to her bed. Before we could get lost in
the bliss of savoring each other, Casey's nerves got the better of her and
she abruptly stopped our foreplay. She insisted that I get Sydney some
coffee and head back to our room before my presence down the hall
was missed. Once she determined that the coast was clear, she rushed
me out of the door. I bit my inside cheek in frustration.

Next stop— Starbucks for two coffees. One for me and one for my
girlfriend.

Sydney was still sleeping when I returned almost an hour after
departing on my coffee mission. With java and crossword puzzle in
hand, I took refuge on the balcony. Within minutes, Sydney was by my
side. I was still seething about the argument from the night before, so
my greeting to her was rather cold. She sat down next to me and acted
as if nothing had happened. No surprise. She always acted as if
nothing had happened the morning after she'd blown up at me. It was
eerily similar to when a former girlfriend of mine would pick a fight

with me after a few too many Chardonnays and conveniently forget the whole thing the next morning. Sydney had the bravado to shout words at me during an argument, but her thick skin and tough words evaporated with her tears. However, I knew that when I least expected it, she would bring up the fight and beat it to death until there was nothing left to talk about.

Not surprisingly, Sydney's topic of conversation was her itinerary for the day and not the fight. She explained that she was scheduled for a morning practice at eight, which was extremely early, but most practical in order to beat the desert heat. I agreed to go with her to the courts for her morning session. She was pleased and, of course, pushed her luck. "Will you shag balls for me?" she asked, with a monstrous grin on her face.

I looked at her with both shock and disgust. "I know you must be kidding! First of all, in my world, the words 'shag' and 'balls' aren't used in the same sentence. And, second, I'm not the hired help. You can pick up your own damn balls. Do you think I have nothing better to do than follow you around like a puppy dog with a yellow tennis ball hanging from my mouth?"

She thought I was joking and laughed before asking me to reconsider. "C'mon, love, please? Other people's girlfriends do it," she said beseechingly.

"Good. See if you can commission one of them to pick up your balls! Whine all you want, but it's not gonna happen!" She stared at me silently. In my best *Will & Grace* "Karen Walker" voice, I said, "Are we done here, poodle?" Sydney, still silent, shrugged her shoulders with indecision and confusion as to why I was calling her "poodle."

Continuing with my high-pitched, nasal impression I said, "Okay, good, honey. Glad that's settled. Now go get yourself cleaned up and try to do something with that hair of yours!"

Once I had made my desire not to play desert ball girl clear, I drove Sydney to the tournament site. We stopped at the first security point and the guard asked us for our credentials. In her typical "let me handle this" form, Sydney leaned over from the passenger side with condescension smeared all over her face and said, "Hey, mate, I'm a player. I've won this tournament before but don't worry, I'll forgive you for not recognizing me this time. We're just on our way to get our badges." Both the guard and I rolled our eyes, presumably having the same thought: *You egotistical asshole! We couldn't care less who you think you are! So shut up and quit embarrassing yourself!* The guard waved us through.

Players, famous and unrecognizable, were patiently waiting to get their badges— even Martina Navratilova has to wait in this line. By now this routine was old hat: take an ugly mug shot, which is printed on a piece of plastic and then worn at all times on the tournament grounds. Apparently, Sydney didn't see the line of players and guests when she entered the room because she strutted straight to the front of the queue to one of the women sitting behind the desk and made small-talk with her before asking for her badge. Because she was a returning player, her picture was already stored in the computer and she didn't have to pose for another one, which might have been her reasoning for cutting to the front of the line. That or she's just an asshole who thinks that her time is more valuable than everyone else's. I'd like to give her the benefit of the doubt, but I know how important she thinks she is. I, on the other hand, chose to wait my turn and refused her invitation to jump in front of everyone else.

Ten short minutes later, I walked into the players' lounge with my badge around my neck. I was pleasantly surprised to see Casey, who greeted me with a smile.

"How'd it go this morning?" she asked.

"Oh fine. She acted as if nothing had happened."

"Well, I guess that's better than more fighting. I saw her in the locker room a few minutes ago and she didn't say anything to me about the fight. But...and don't get mad...she was busy texting someone." Casey contorted her face as if she had just delivered ghastly shocking news. I think she expected my expression to match hers— which it didn't.

"Well, she wasn't texting me. Let's hope she's texting that thespian she has a crush on." I laughed and mumbled suggestively, "She'll have much better luck with the lesbian thespian than with me. She might even win an Oscar for supporting that actor!"

I heard the locker room door open and saw Sydney walking down the hall toward us. She was carrying a big cardboard box full of balls and was accompanied by her hitting partner. She barely slowed down to say "hi" to Casey, but made puppy-dog eyes at me and, in a pathetically whiny voice, asked if I were going to watch her practice. Annoyed, I shot her a frosty look and responded, "Well, I said I would, even though I've seen you hit a million tennis balls. Stop asking me already! Go practice and don't worry about me." Apparently, she thought her pleas were cute and she pouted some more, protruding her lower lip and contorting her face like a child who was about to cry. I was not moved, nor was I amused. I ignored her and continued my conversation with Casey until she left for her own practice.

After both of their practices were over, I waited for Casey and Sydney outside the locker room. Freshly showered, Casey emerged from behind the guarded doors. "Where's the beauty queen?" I asked smugly.

She responded with a smirk on her face. "She's still in there. She's texting someone again. I'm not getting any new messages. Are you?"

I looked at my phone which didn't indicate that I had any new text messages. "Wait, let me change the setting and turn the volume up," I joked to Casey and adjusted the text message indicator from silent to full-blown ring— purely for dramatic affect. I gave it a minute, but still nothing. Most girlfriends would probably be jealous over something like this, but not me. I was happy and hoped that my silent phone was a precursor to a bang of a surprise breakup by Sydney. I displayed my phone and announced, "Nope. I got nothing. It's all quiet on this western front!" I chuckled as I switched the setting back to silent.

Neither Casey nor Sydney was on the schedule to play that first day, so Casey and I decided to spend the afternoon sitting by the hotel pool. Lounging in the sun was one of Sydney's least favorite activities, so she chose to fill her day with shopping, followed by a second practice session, and then a massage. I found it curious that Sydney so willingly lengthened my leash and let me roam about without her supervision. It only further impressed upon me that her interest had been piqued elsewhere. Regardless, she'd be gone for at least three hours. Casey and I luxuriated in tanning our bikini-clad bodies in the desert sun until we figured enough time had passed since Sydney left the hotel and then we left the pool and proceeded directly to Casey's bedroom— we did not pass "Go" and did not need to pick up $200. We spent the rest of the afternoon making love and savoring every minute we had until Sydney's return.

* * *

The first day of the tournament was indicative of how the next several days would go. Surprisingly, Sydney was uninterested in recreational doubles this week. She stuck to singles and hoped to parlay her Number 9 seeding into a championship. Similarly, Casey focused on doubles— she and Marisa held the prestigious Number 1 seeding. Sydney and Casey had both received byes in their respective first rounds and neither of them would take to the courts until the end of the week.

Each day was a mirror of the first. As I had done since I arrived, every night before I went to bed I would set some clothes out in the bathroom that I could easily throw on with my eyes half-closed in the morning. Just as the sun came up, I'd quietly tiptoe into the bathroom and get dressed. As I brushed my teeth, I made sure to dispose of one Wellbutrin tablet, just in case "someone" happened to be counting how many pills I had with me. Then I would whisper to Sydney that I was leaving to get coffee as I quietly exited and sneaked down the hallway to Casey's room. After some good-morning kisses and hugs, I would venture down to the Starbucks in the lobby. While I delivered coffee to Sydney, Casey would make her obligatory morning phone call to Trish, which she now described as an obligation rather than a desire— and that was good news to me.

Although Casey and Sydney did not practice together, they booked courts around the same time every morning, which was conducive to a breakfast threesome immediately after practice. Sydney would spend most of the afternoon at the courts, either practicing or having a massage, which would leave plenty of time for Casey and me to satiate our sexual desires for each other. After spending as much time together as we could, I would go back to my room, shower and wait for Sydney to return. From there, the three of us would either order room service together or go out to dinner. The end of the night was always the most difficult for Casey— not because we would be away from each other for several hours until morning, but because her mind tortured her with thoughts of the very remote possibility of Sydney and me being intimate. For me, the nights were hardest because that was when I faced one-on-one time with Sydney.

Finally, on the fourth day of the tournament, Casey and Marisa were scheduled to play doubles. As Casey waited for her escort, she asked me for a favor. She prefaced her request with, "I know it's annoying, but…" Then she asked me if I wouldn't mind texting Trish during the match so she'd know what was going on. Apparently, turning on her computer and following the live scores online was not good enough for Casey's best friend because the live scores were sometimes sixty to ninety seconds behind actual live time. Casey was right. It was annoying, but I agreed to do her the favor. After all, I would be sitting courtside, just feet from Casey, and Trish would be sitting in her aunt's house three thousand miles away practicing her dealing techniques, trying not to break a nail. Oh, and then there was that tiny little detail that Trish was not gay! So, why be jealous?

I wished Casey luck when the tournament escort arrived to bring the foursome to their court. She turned to me and whispered, "Don't forget." I thought she was referring to my job of texting Trish and I stared at her with a yeah-yeah-I-will look. Judging from the expression on my face, she felt she had to clarify what she meant. She stepped backwards, closer to me and whispered, "Don't forget to look for my signals." She was referring to the signals that she established in Atlanta— only now there was a new one: a quick double pat of her chest meant that she loved me. I assured her that I would be watching for them. I was beaming.

I made my way through the crowd just as Casey and Marisa were starting their ten-minute warm-up. The stadium was quickly filling with fans. The players' boxes were on either end of the court, near the baselines. I preferred sitting on the side of the court and since seating was on a first come, first served basis, I claimed a seat a few rows behind Casey's changeover chair. It was ridiculously hot and I settled in for what I thought would be a rather easy match for Marisa and her. I opened my phone after the first game to text the result to Trish. To my surprise, there was a text from Trish. *Steph, score? What's going on?*

Not even five minutes had passed since the match started! The urgency of the text might have been alarming to an untrained eye, but it didn't surprise me at all because I knew how obsessed Trish was with Casey's tennis. I immediately wrote back, *Held serve. Winning 1-0.* I refrained from tagging on *Get a life!* at the end of the message, despite my burning desire to do so.

For the next two hours, I watched Casey and Marisa battle back after losing the first set to a low-ranked team. During the second set, I reapplied my sunscreen and got as comfortable as I could get in a plastic stadium seat. Only love could inspire me to endure the back pain caused by those unforgiving chairs! My fingers were crossed, hoping that Casey and Marisa's level of play wouldn't falter and that they would capture the third set and soon be through to the next round.

As the two teams traded game for game, I lost count of how many texts I sent to Trish. In the middle of the final set, I got a text from Sydney. *Where are you?* As I often did, I ignored her text. The last thing I wanted was for Sydney to come and sit next to me for the last few games of the match. Just as I deleted the message, I caught an "I love you" signal from Casey as she changed sides. I acknowledged the signal with a smile but was then pestered by another text from Sydney. *Never mind. I see you. I'm on the opposite side of the stadium, near the entrance. Just on my way in from practicing. Who are you texting?* I shook my head and rolled my eyes. I wasn't sure how she zeroed in on me in a stadium filled with people or how she could see that I was texting someone.

Since I had been spotted, I had no choice but to respond. I quickly and curtly zipped back a message without revealing who I was texting. I had no desire to ping pong text messages back and forth with Sydney. Giving my texting thumb a rest, I focused back on Casey and caught another signal from her. I furtively smiled back— careful not to give myself or Casey away to the ever-watchful eyes of Sydney. Surprisingly, Sydney left me alone and sent a simple text back telling me to meet her in the lounge after the match. She hated sitting in the desert sun— but even more, she hated watching Casey play doubles with someone other than her— so I had a few more minutes' reprieve.

I focused on the court for what I hoped would be the last changeover in the match. Casey and Marisa were now ahead 5-4, and Casey was serving for the match. She held the match on her racket. If she could hold her serve, they would win the match and advance to the next round. If not, the score would be leveled at 5-5, and the match would be up for grabs. During the most critical of games, Casey conjured up the form that had previously taken her to numerous victories. She started the game off with an ace down the "T." The umpire announced the score, "Fifteen, love." The next point ended when Casey crushed an inspired backhand winner down the line. "Thirty, love," the umpire echoed. I took a deep breath and hoped that Casey would serve two aces and close out the match. Unfortunately, Marisa dumped two easy volleys into the net and the umpire confirmed that the score was "Thirty, all." Casey served the next point to the deuce court and ran to the net behind her serve. The return was a solid forehand down the line, stopped by a backhand volley winner from Marisa's racket. They were now one point from victory. As Casey stepped up to the baseline to serve, she waited until the echo of "Forty, thirty" coming from the intercom had silenced. Once the crowd was quiet, Casey picked her spot and served the ball. As quickly as the ball rushed from the service box to the backhand side of the court, the backhand return slammed into the net. Casey pumped her fist, celebrating her victory, and looked directly at me. I was already on my feet, clapping as the chair umpire announced into her microphone, "Game, set, and match, Marisa Davis and Casey Matthews." I quickly sent one last text to Trish informing her of the successful result and waited for the next signal from Casey.

I sat back down and watched while Casey and Marisa signed autographs courtside. Casey motioned for me to walk down the five steps to the railing by the court and then asked me to meet her outside the exit on the other side of the court so we could walk back to the club together.

When I reached the other side of the court, Casey was waiting for me but was being mobbed by adoring fans requesting pictures and more autographs. I smiled and watched her graciously sign programs, T-shirts, tennis balls and even an arm, then pose for numerous photographs. Once she had accommodated everyone, she gleefully walked over to me.

"Thanks for watching and for waiting," she said, with an adoring grin.

Casey thanked me for watching after every match. Thanks were not necessary. There was no place I would rather have been. I patted the powder blue Nike shirt on her back that was drenched in sweat and congratulated her as she slid her bandana off her head.

As we strolled leisurely together toward the club, Casey looked directly into my eyes and said, "Stephie, this is how I want it to be. I want you to come to these tournaments with me. I hate that you're here with *her.*"

Without breaking my stride, I replied, "Hey, this is your brainchild. I'm only here with *her,* so I can see *you.* I'm doing all this so I can be with you, Casey." She frowned and rolled her eyes. She hated when I referred to her by name instead of by the pet name "cutie" that I'd given her. I corrected myself, "I mean, I'm doing all this so I can be with you, *cutie.*"

She smiled in acknowledgement. "I know, but I hate that you're part of her world."

I wasn't sure what she wanted me to say. I was doing everything I could to make the situation more bearable for us both. Short of cloning myself so that Sydney could have one of me and Casey could have the other, there was nothing more I could do. As we passed the players' restaurant, Casey saw Sydney through the glass doors. Once Sydney spotted us, she rushed outside. "What took you so long?" she said, glaring at us. I ignored her while Casey explained that she had to stop and sign autographs and pose for pictures.

Politely put in her place, Sydney extended a "Well done" to Casey, referring to her victory on the court. She then looked at me and barked, "You ready to go? I'm exhausted and wanna get out of the sun and the heat."

"Go ahead, then. I have my car here. I'll just meet you back at the hotel later. I might go watch another match." This was not the response that Sydney was looking or hoping for, but she knew that insisting I come with her would only lead to an argument and not one that she could win— particularly in front of Casey.

Sydney left and Casey and I procrastinated as long as we could before leaving the tournament site and going back to the hotel. I sneaked into her room for a few more forbidden kisses and then schlepped the painfully long ten steps down the hall to my room. I found Sydney engrossed in front of her computer. By the intensity of her fixed gaze and the speed of her fingers racing across the keyboard, I happily deduced she was engaged in some sort of communication with the thespian. I left her to her cyber-sex or whatever it was that she was doing and took a hot shower.

When I came out, Sydney looked at me and exclaimed, "Jesus, you look like a lobster!" I looked in the mirror. My face, shoulders and legs— mid-thigh to ankle— were completely sunburned. She was only able to drag her bottom lip toward the top one momentarily to say, "You didn't use sunscreen?" It was more of an accusation than a question.

"Of course…"

Before I could finish my sentence and snap at her to prevent the lecture I assumed she was going to give, she compassionately said, "Shit, does it hurt?"

I paused before I answered. I looked like a dermatologist's worst nightmare and clearly had failed miserably in my efforts to slather my exposed flesh with sunscreen. It dawned on me that, hypothetically, if I were in pain because my skin was so burned, I would have yet another excuse not to let Sydney touch me. *Cha-ching!* I answered, "Actually, yeah it does…and I'm sure it's only gonna get worse." I figured there was no way that Sydney could convince a lobster on Happy Pills to do anything untoward.

Sympathizing with me, she suggested that I drown my skin in aloe and put on some loose clothing. Happy to take control of the evening, Sydney invited Casey to join us for room service. Casey arrived at our door before Sydney had even returned the receiver to the base. With Casey present, laughter blessed our room for the first time since our arrival.

When Casey finished the last of her well-done fries, Sydney invited her to leave. Once she had left, I crawled into bed like a sad child who had been sent to bed without dessert. I can only imagine the frown on my face. Tension was mounting between Sydney and me and I could feel that she was itching to have yet another "state of the relationship" conversation. I didn't have the energy to argue. By some fortuitous twist, apparently, Sydney didn't have the energy either. Maybe it was because she was scheduled to play her match early the next day, or maybe it was because she knew she wouldn't win any fight she started. Whatever the reason, I didn't care. I relished the silence and watched the flickering florescent green colon that separated the hours and minutes on the digital clock on the bedside table near my pillow. I carefully cocooned my tender red limbs in the sheets and closed my eyes. The next time I opened them, it was five-seventeen. I had made it through another night.

* * *

Later that morning, Sydney prepared to step onto the court. She drew a qualifier so I knew there'd be a better chance for pigs to fall out of the sky than for her to lose in the early rounds of a Tier 1 tournament to a "nobody" as she so delicately put it. As expected, I waited with Sydney in the hallway before she and her opponent were escorted to the court. When the time came, I wished her luck and she disappeared into the crowd.

I waited sixty seconds and then tucked myself into a quiet corner, picked up my phone and called Casey. She was not scheduled to play that day and had already practiced and gone back to the hotel. Lost in conversation and several minutes later, I suddenly heard the chair umpire announce, "Ladies and Gentlemen, this is a first-round singles match. Best of three tiebreak sets wins. Sydney Foster won the toss and elected to serve."

Shit! I missed the entire ten-minute warm-up!

I felt like I was late to French class and I didn't have a note from my mom explaining my tardiness. I hung up abruptly and quickly sprinted through the crowd. Serena Williams was playing on the stadium court, so Sydney's match was relegated to one of the numerous outer courts. As I was running, I realized that I didn't even know which court I was racing to find.

I weaved through the hordes of people, following the sound of the umpire's voice, now announcing that Sydney had just won the first game. I found the court a few minutes later, but the second game of the match had already begun. After the first game of each set, tennis etiquette allows entrance to the court only during changeovers, every two games. The qualifier won the second game, evening the score at one game a piece and I could see Sydney gazing into the stands looking for me because my seat in the players' box was conspicuously empty. As luck would have it, the third game was stretched out with deuce after deuce before Sydney finally won it. I slipped into the stands and sat three rows behind Sydney's changeover chair. Apparently, her homing device wasn't working because she spent the rest of the match peering into the stands looking for me, but never found me. I was just feet from her, yet she kept overlooking me.

How ironic that she can't see what's in front of her nose!

In less than an hour the match was over. Sydney had played beautifully and deserved to win. I darted in and out of the crowd and made my way back to the club. Sydney, still in her match clothes, was waiting for me outside the locker room. "Where were you?" she asked, in a sharp, reproachful tone.

We locked eyes and I immediately felt like I was back in high school. I remembered when I was seventeen and had browbeat my mom into letting me go to a party I was just *dying* to go to. In a bold move, Chelsea and I left the party and lost track of time. I somehow avoided being thrown in jail for driving nearly twice the speed limit to get home, but still broke my curfew. I raced into the house only to find my angry mom looking down her nose at me. As Sydney glared at me awaiting my response, I suddenly felt like I was a teenager again. "What do you mean?" I asked, innocently, as if I were completely unaware that Sydney was perturbed.

"I didn't see you at my match." She was annoyed and had that your-father's-fit-to-be-tied look on her face.

"What're you talking about? I was sitting right behind you…three rows up."

She pursed her lips, shook her head and changed her expression to the you-should-have-called look. "Why didn't you do something to get my attention? I was looking for you the entire match."

Oh, come on, Mom!

"Don't be silly. You knew I was there."

"I know, but seeing you keeps me focused. I like to know exactly where you are in the crowd so I can look up at you between points."

You like to know where I am at all times, period— not just in the crowd!

"Well, you knew I was there, so calm down. Anyway, well done. You showering?"

"Yeah, I'll just be a minute."

Hmmm. Only one minute? Maybe the thespian was busy practicing her lines.

As we drove back to the hotel, Sydney looked at her watch and shot me what she considered her most alluring smile. "God, it's so nice to be done early. I just wanna go back and relax and spend the rest of the afternoon with you."

She was looking at me as if I were an all-you-can-eat buffet.

Oh, hell no! Shit! An entire afternoon alone with her! How the hell am I going to get out of this one?! Why doesn't this damn car have an eject button?!

As I panicked, Sydney reached over and put her hand on top of mine, which was resting on the gear shift. *Oh, God!* I started making a list of things that I'd vow I'd never do again— the kind that started, "I promise I'll be good and I'll never…" if only I could make it through the afternoon fully clothed and unscathed. I forced a smile and looked at the clock on the dashboard. My skin had already begun to crawl and I wondered how long I could last before I would find a way to extract my hand from under her clammy, calloused hand.

Less than one minute. Sorry, but I needed my right hand on the steering wheel while my left hand engaged the turn signal.

When we got back to the room, Sydney dropped her racket bag and dove onto the bed. I plopped down on the couch on the other side of the room and picked up *USA Today* to pillage it for the crossword. After trying numerous times, unsuccessfully, to persuade me to abandon the puzzle and come over to the bed, her temper flared and I was besieged by her anger. She tossed and turned and let out several sighs of exasperation. Mount Sydney was about to erupt and soon I'd be engulfed in lava. I didn't even have time to take cover. I had just filled in the boxes for Clue No. 29 Down, when, suddenly, her words came spewing out. "Is it too much to ask for you to make me feel special?!"

Shit! Here we go.

I put down the paper and huffed, "Sydney, I don't know what you want from me."

"I want you to love me and I want to feel your love, for fuck's sake!"

Yeah, well, there are little girls in hell who'd love a glass of ice water, too, but they ain't gettin' it!

I rolled my pen between my fingers and stared vacuously at her.

"Is it ever going to change? Are you ever going to be the way you were when we first met?"

Are you?!

Trying desperately to maintain my composure, I said, "Sydney, I don't have a crystal ball. I really am doing the best I can. Obviously, it's not enough for you."

God, please just break up with me!

"I just don't understand why you can't come over and touch me."

246

I slammed my pen down on the table and yelled, "It always comes back to sex with you. I really can't deal with this."

"It's not about sex! It's about feeling wanted…feeling special!" Apparently, her internal volume switch had broken because the loud shrill that came out of her mouth made my yelled words sound whispered.

The thing is, Sydney did have a point. What she was asking for from me was not altogether unreasonable. She wanted to feel emotion from her girlfriend. The problem was that I had none to give her.

We went around and around in circles. Sydney was yelling about her needs and how they were not being met and I was yelling about how I was doing the best I could and that I could not give any more than I was giving. Our tirade intensified and the decibels got higher and higher until we were interrupted by pounding on the wall. Apparently our neighbors didn't find the noise pollution any more acceptable during the day than they did during the middle of the night. I really couldn't take much more. I was ready to abandon Casey's plan for real this time. September was six months away but it seemed completely out of my reach. I lowered my voice, threw my hands in the air and calmly said, "Sydney, clearly, I'm not making you happy. I can't do this anymore." I got up from the couch and walked over to the dresser where my car keys were.

Even more enraged, she snapped in a demanding tone, "Where the hell are you going?"

I had given all that I cared to give to the fight and now I just wanted to bolt toward the door. I slid my keys and wallet off the dresser. "Sydney, I need to leave."

At the realization that I was going to walk out on her any second, Sydney, as usual, began to calm down and attempted to persuade me not to leave. Her attempts were all in vain. "What do you mean you need to leave? No, you don't. We can settle this. Please don't leave, love."

Gripping the doorknob, I coolly said, "Every time I try to leave, you always persuade me to stay, but this time I'm really leaving. I really need to be alone right now."

She was silent and let me walk out the door without begging me desperately not to. I really was at the end of my rope.

My first call from the car was to Casey. She could hear the exasperation in my voice and immediately came to meet me. Sitting in the passenger seat, Casey held my hand and listened intently while I rehashed the details of the fight. She had been on the receiving end of countless thunderous diatribes by Sydney so she knew how brutal it could be to be yelled at repeatedly for not being good enough or not giving enough. When I finished recounting the argument, I had made a decision. I could no longer continue. I guess Casey could see that I had hit rock bottom because she assured me that she would support whatever decision I made about the future of my relationship with Sydney. She left me alone with my thoughts as she raced to make a PR appearance at the tournament.

As the clock ticked, I sat, thinking.

17

Forcing the error

When I returned, three hours had passed. I found Sydney ensconced in a chair at her computer. She looked up but said nothing. Trepidation filled the air as I moved toward her. I was exhausted and felt even more dejected than usual. I knew what I needed to do, but I did not have the strength to do it at that moment. I looked at her and said, "I don't want to fight anymore tonight and I don't want to talk about us. I just can't."

"Love, I never want to fight with you. And I don't want to talk about it anymore, either." She lifted herself from her chair and strode toward me. "Why don't you just take a shower and then let's go get dinner?"

I merely nodded. Sydney enveloped my listless body with a strong embrace. I barely lifted one arm to pat her on the shoulder before stepping back. I placed my phone and wallet on the corner of the dresser where I habitually left them as Sydney prepared the shower for me.

As I leaned backwards, I closed my eyes and put my head under the pulsating jet of streaming hot water, which relaxed me as it cascaded down my body. Luxuriating for a few moments, I opened my eyes and could not believe what I saw. I had left the door to the bathroom open through which I had an unobstructed view of the room. Sydney was standing in front of the dresser. My phone had disappeared.

Of course my phone's gone! It's in that psycho bitch's hands! Motherfucker! Cocksucker! Son-of-a-bitch!

Every profanity in my arsenal flew through my mind with dizzying speed. I was outraged! My blood boiled as I watched Sydney punch buttons on my phone in an obvious attempt to check my call logs or my text messages. For a second, I was worried that she might find an incriminating text from Casey, but my nervousness returned to anger when I realized that I had erased each message immediately after reading it. But I had forgotten to erase my call logs from that afternoon, so Sydney was probably scrolling through all the calls that I had made over the past several hours.

As soon as she heard the shower stop, she gently slipped the phone down onto the dresser and sat on the bed, pretending that she had not just violated my privacy. Even if I hadn't caught her red-handed, her demeanor was incriminating. Still dripping wet from my shower, I draped a towel around my body and walked directly over to the dresser and picked up the phone, still warm from being in Sydney's hands. She tried to act normal but was very obviously nervous. I looked at my call logs to examine what she most likely had seen.

Sydney started dressing for dinner as I sat on the edge of the bed, seething. On the verge of becoming unglued, I held my anger in check for as long as I could. Thoroughly disgusted, I could not even look at her. If I gritted my teeth any harder, it's quite possible I would have shattered my molars. Barely able to relax my jaw to form a sentence, I said, "What would possess you…?" I was so angry that my voice was only slightly louder than a whisper and I could not finish my sentence. I paused to fill my lungs with air and then finished my thought, "What…would possess you to violate my privacy and check my call logs?"

Sydney had been caught in the act. Her response was proof that not only did she feel no remorse for violating my privacy, but that she was in desperate need of psychiatric evaluation. She shouted, "You never talk to me! Bloody hell! You never tell me anything, so I wanted to see who you were talking to, because you're certainly not talking to me!" The next words that came out of her mouth were almost more than I could handle. "You *made* me do it!"

The height of Sydney's arrogance shocked me. Completely. Unable to control my anger, I burst out, "It's none of your fucking business who I talk to! And 'I *made* you do it?' You sound like a man who has just beaten the shit out of his wife and then uses the 'she made me do it' excuse. You're pathetic!"

She opened her mouth, no doubt to thrust some other absurd justification at me, but I interrupted her before she could form a single word.

"So, let me get this straight. You violate my privacy and I *made* you do it? You're a fucking lunatic!" I paused as the familiar possessed look returned to her face. "Okay, just so I understand this correctly, it's *my* fault that you're a control freak...*and* that you've guilt-tripped me into staying in a relationship that we both know isn't working...*and* that you're so nosey that you couldn't help checking my phone to see who I've been talking to?"

"I just don't understand why you won't talk to me!" she boomed.

"Because I don't fucking want to talk to you about every little detail of my life! If I wanted to talk to you, I would! God dammit! You're driving me crazy!"

"Why won't you tell me what depression medicine you're on?"

"Oh, fuck! Is that what this is all about?! Knowing you, you've already gone through my things and found my pills! So why would I need to confide in you about what I'm taking?!"

Immediately, the look on her face changed from that of a psychotic lunatic to that of a deer-caught-in-the-headlights. The changed expression was enough for me to know that she had, in fact, gone through my things as I had planned and predicted. I shook my head and rolled my eyes. "Oh, my God! You did, didn't you? You went through my fucking bag, looking for my pills."

That's it!

"It wasn't that hard. I know where you keep your pills. I just looked in your vitamin container." She smirked. She seemed proud of herself. Anyone else would have been mortified they'd been caught red-handed, but not Sydney.

Utterly appalled, I yelled, "And that makes it okay? What is *wrong* with you?! I've met your family and they seem perfectly normal, but you act like you were raised by a pack of wolves! Were you switched at birth or were you just dropped on your head one too many times as a kid? What makes you think it's okay to rummage through someone's things without their permission?"

"I needed to know what you were taking!"

"No, you *wanted* to know what I was taking! And now that you do, how are you better off?"

"I think your doctor misdiagnosed your depression, that's how!"

I thought my ears were playing tricks on me, but I knew who I was dealing with, so I knew I'd heard Dr. Foster correctly. "Oh, really? And I assume you know this because your four years of med school, followed by your extensive residency training, have led you to this conclusion? Jesus Christ! You've been watching too much *Dr. Phil*!"

"No, I was talking to Danni, and…"

"What?! You discussed this with Danni?! See, this is exactly what I'm talking about. You can't keep your mouth shut, which is why I didn't talk to you about this in the first place— because I knew you'd call and blab to your friends!"

"Well, I'm glad I know and I'm glad I discussed it with Danni. We both think you're on the wrong medication."

"I don't give a shit what you and your stupid friend think! She's not even a doctor! She's a nurse!"

Even more resolute about her position, she confidently announced, "The drug that you're on is not supposed to affect your sex drive. It's supposed to enhance it."

I knew she was right about that, but I was not going to concede the point. "And you got this information from Danni?"

"No, I did some research on the Internet and I read that the drug you're on doesn't have sexual side effects."

"Wait, you did research on my medicine? You need help! You seriously need help! Did you happen to see that these drugs can have different effects on different people?" I replied haughtily.

Ignoring my explanation, she asked, "How many times a day do you take that pill?"

"Sydney, I'm done explaining myself to you! And, I'm done with this conversation!"

"I counted your pills. There were fifteen yesterday and there are still fifteen today."

Amid my disbelief, I realized that I had forgotten to discard one of my pills earlier that morning, but I was in no mood to continue the conversation. "Fuck off! You know what? I knew you'd go through my things. I fucking knew it! So, I set you up." I stomped over to the dresser and yanked open a drawer. I retrieved a pill container, pouring the contents into my hand. There were a few Wellbutrin tablets mixed in with other vitamins. Sydney was speechless. "You'll never win. Stop trying! The only thing you will ever beat me at is tennis, you crazy fuck!" I slammed back down onto the bed before launching again. "I can't fucking believe you! You've gone through my things. You've checked my phone. What's next? You gonna break into my e-mail account?!"

"Don't be silly!"

I echoed thunderously, "Don't be silly? *Me*, don't be silly?! You've proven that you don't respect other people's privacy. First Casey and now me! I fucking warned you! I told you if you ever violated my privacy like you did hers, I'd be out the door and I wouldn't look back!" I stared at her lividly.

"Steph, I love you, and I'm just trying to understand why you can't give me more."

I was past my breaking point. I truly was at the end of my tether. My internal filter was useless and I couldn't stop myself from dropping a bomb into Sydney's lap. "You know what? I can't. I can't give you more. Maybe whoever you're texting all the time can give you what I can't." She looked stunned but tried to pretend not to be. I knew better.

"What are you talking about?" she asked, incredulously.

"Oh, don't! Don't even try to play this game with me. You're not one to be glued to your phone, but lately it's become an extension of your body. I know your interest lies elsewhere, so why don't you just cut me loose and pursue her?!"

She continued with her little-miss-innocent routine. "I have no idea what you're talking about."

"Whatever. Deny it all you want. I don't give a shit. But don't act so high and mighty and pretend that you are so above being attracted to someone else! I know you're up to something, and I've known it for a while. I'm not stupid. Even though I don't care what you're doing, doesn't mean I don't see it. Just fucking own it!"

Sydney refused to admit that there was someone else. She was so taken aback by my revelation that she, the queen of beating a dead horse, let the argument go without repeating her case more than three times. That, in and of itself, was a victory for me. I was tired of talking and needed to close the deal. "Sydney, I came back here tonight and the first thing I said was that I didn't want to argue or talk about this anymore. And now, we've been fighting and talking about this for an hour. I'd rather go back to LA than continue like this. It's not healthy for either of us. It's time for us to face the facts and it's time for me to be honest with you."

"Love, please. I'm sorry. I'm sorry for everything."

"Yeah, Sydney, I'm sorry, too. But, that doesn't change things."

"Listen, we're both upset. Let's just go to sleep before we say more things we don't mean."

"I mean everything I'm about to say…"

"Steph, please. If you ever cared about me, can we please just talk about this tomorrow? This tournament is so important for me. Please don't do this now."

Oh, God, here we go with the 'don't ruin my career' plea!

"Sydney, I can't be responsible for your career."

She put her hands over her ears, cupping the sides of her head. I could hardly believe it. I thought I would die if she started chanting, "La la la la. I…am…not…listening…to…you. I…can't… hear…you. La la la la." She didn't. Instead, she pled, "Please…please."

"Sydney, we can't do this anymore. We need to… "

"Steph, please. Please don't make me beg you. I really can't have this conversation right now."

"There's never a good time…"

"Steph, I have to be able to concentrate tomorrow and practice. My next match is so important and I need to be ready. Please. Will you please just calm down? Please just stay and we can work this out tomorrow."

I knew it was over and I think Sydney did, too. What's one more night? Melissa popped into my head, hissing. I thought, *oh, shut up! You'd probably do the same thing, too!* I knew I shouldn't have agreed, but talking to Sydney right then was like gluing Jell-O to a wall. Pointless.

18

*T*wo can play at that game

The next morning, as usual, I knocked on Casey's door just after dawn. She looked like death when she appeared.

"What happened to you?" I joked, as I pushed my way past her. She yawned and, without smiling, sarcastically replied, "Your girlfriend."

I was dumbfounded. We sat down and Casey explained to me that after I had gone to sleep last night, Sydney sent an e-mail to Trish enquiring whether she had told Casey or anyone about her crush on the thespian.

Oops.

My jaw dropped as Casey then explained that Trish was up late surfing the Internet when she received the e-mail so she immediately phoned Casey to confront her. Poor Casey had spent the better part of the night trying to convince Trish that she had not revealed Sydney's lustful admission to me. Their conversation snowballed and Trish quizzed Casey about the amount of time she was spending with me. She chiseled away at her about whether or not she was attracted to me. After hours of denying that she had leaked any of the confidential information, as well as vehemently denying any attraction to me, Trish was finally satisfied and Casey was allowed to slump back to bed.

How generous of Trish not to keep Casey on the phone until the sun came up. It's not like she's playing a tournament or anything!

God only knows why, but I always tried to bite my tongue when it came to Trish. This morning was no exception. "So is everything okay now?" I asked tenderly.

"Yeah, I guess. Trish is just really annoying me. We argue all the time. I don't even look forward to talking to her anymore. It's more of a hassle than anything. Every time we talk, we end up fighting…about you."

Yeah, that's normal. Your straight best friend is jealous that you might be attracted to someone else? Newsflash, Trish: I know you fancy yourself the cat's meow, but you're just a sourpuss! You had to figure that, someday, Casey would be attracted to someone else!

Again, I bit my tongue and changed the subject. "Well, if it makes you feel any better, Sydney and I had an incredible argument last night."

I recounted the abridged version as Casey sat, mesmerized— no doubt recalling her own history with this nut job. She was shocked but not surprised and once she had time to digest everything, she stared blankly at me and said, "You're gonna break up with her, aren't you?"

Casey knew the answer to her question. We both knew that I had to break up with Sydney. I couldn't take it any longer. Sydney was acting crazier everyday. She was making me miserable and if she could be honest with herself for one second, she might be able to admit that she was not happy either. She so desperately wanted our relationship to work that she couldn't be honest with herself. I truly did think that, deep down, Sydney was a good person. Although she possessed a number of qualities undesirable to me, she didn't deserve a loveless relationship. And I certainly didn't deserve a life sentence of having to wake up next to her everyday.

My silence prompted a deep sigh from Casey as she asked, "When are you gonna do it?"

"Today. It's been almost eight hours since we last fought, so I'm guessing we're due for another one soon."

"And then what? Are you gonna leave and go back to LA?"

"Nope. There's no way I'm gonna go to LA if you're here."

"Well, if you break up with her, aren't you gonna have to go home?"

"No. I don't *have* to do anything. Nobody puts Stephie in a corner." We both laughed at my *Dirty Dancing* reference.

I had no intention of leaving Palm Springs until Casey did and I was quite confident that her stay would be longer than Sydney's since Sydney was scheduled to play the Number 1 seed the next day. I doubted very seriously that Sydney would prevail. Casey and Marisa, on the other hand, were scheduled to go on the court later that night and they were the clear favorites to win.

Casey anxiously looked at the clock. "You better go. You've been gone a long time. Oh, but wait. Before you go, I have something to show you. Come here." I followed her to her computer and she logged on to her e-mail account. She snickered, "You're gonna love this."

As she clicked on several icons, the anticipation of what I was about to see was killing me. A few seconds later, a picture of Sydney standing familiarly close to an unfamiliar woman appeared on the screen. Casey pointed to the lanky stranger wearing worn-in jeans and a black sweater and said, "That's Bonnie."

I couldn't believe it! Casey explained that Trish had sent her the picture and that it had been taken at a party at the infamous "Dr. Danni's" house a couple weeks before— probably when I was in Boston. Oh, poor Sydney looked so lonely and despondent cupping a Riedel wine glass with one hand and the lesbian thespian's shoulder with the other. I really should have called her more often from Boston to comfort her as she sat at home "all alone." I laughed as I stared at the picture. Bonnie was cute, but she appeared just as manly as I had come to consider Sydney. They looked perfect for each other! I joked that Sydney looked like a transvestite and the thespian was no better. I gestured to Sydney and then to Bonnie and burst out laughing, "Tranny and Manny!"

"Don't be mean," Casey insisted.

She was just mad that she didn't think of the nicknames before I did.

She jokingly pushed me toward the door. "Go before Tranny sends the National Guard after you."

I looked both directions and tiptoed out of Casey's room with a picture of Sydney and Bonnie emblazoned in my mind.

Later that morning, I barely spoke to Sydney before heading to the hotel gym for a well-needed, stress-busting workout.

When I returned from the gym, the room was empty— Sydney was still not back from practice. Savoring the tranquility, I sat down at her computer to write some e-mails. When the AOL "sign on" screen appeared, out of habit, I clicked on "sign on." I then heard a beep followed by a pop-up error message requesting that I enter a password. I stared at the screen for a few seconds before I realized what had happened. Sydney and I both had AOL e-mail accounts and apparently the computer was still set to Sydney's account. This had happened countless times before. But in the past, Sydney had her password stored on her "sign on" screen so she wouldn't have to manually type it in every time she logged on. Usually, when I sat down at Sydney's computer and clicked on "sign on" I'd be greeted by the infamous AOL voice announcing "You've Got Mail" just seconds later— Sydney's mail. And I would have to sign out and then re-sign in using my own screen name and password (unlike hers, my password was not automatically stored!). This time, however, was different and the reason it was different was because Sydney had "unstored" her password.

Ha! She always bragged that she had nothing to hide and that's why she stored her password on the login screen! That stupid, sneaky fucker changed her password because she's hiding something.

I now had all the confirmation that I needed in order to conclude that I was not the only one who had strayed from this relationship. This discovery, however, probably had the exact opposite effect Sydney was hoping for— because instead of being irked or intrigued or upset or having any other freakish obsessive-compulsive reaction, I was elated and picked up the phone to call Casey, hoping that she'd be finished practicing so I could tell her what had just happened.

I was laughing so hard that I could barely squeeze words out when Casey answered. "Cutie, where are you?!"

"Driving back from the courts. What the hell are you cackling at?"

Still trying to catch my breath, I said, "You're... never... gonna... believe... this!"

She waited silently to hear what she would never believe.

I gasped for air and said, "She *definitely* cheating on me!"

Confused, Casey asked, "What? How do you know?"

"Because I just tried to log on to AOL and she changed her password."

"Shut up! No way!" Casey drew on personal experience and knew the significance of this.

"I just wish I could see what the e-mails say."

"You're on her 'sign on' screen aren't you?" Her tone indicated that she was about to bestow upon me the key to unlocking Sydney's e-mails.

Compliments of Sydney, Casey explained to me how to go into Sydney's stored messages, which didn't require her password. Sydney had broken into Casey's e-mail account the year before by employing this very method. In a bragging spell, Sydney confessed to Casey how she did it.

Two can play at this game! I followed Casey's instructions and, voilà, I had access to Sydney's incoming and outgoing stored mail. I felt a tad guilty as I began to read some of the e-mails that Sydney and the thespian had been sending to each other. After determining that, while they'd been sending messages to each other several times per day, they hadn't actually begun a physical affair, I quickly exited Sydney's account. I didn't want to go too far down that dark path myself. It was more than sufficient to know they were emotionally involved.

Miss High and Mighty isn't so high and mighty at all! I just might get that Christmas present early after all.

My high hopes that a breakup would be handed to me were squelched a few minutes later when I found an envelope with my name written on it sitting on the bedside table. I recognized Sydney's handwriting. I hoped that the first line of the letter would read: DEAR STEPHANIE, BY THE TIME YOU READ THESE LINES I'LL BE GONE. But my gut told me otherwise. And my damn gut was always right. The letter was a three-page, handwritten letter in which Sydney repeated what she had been saying for the past several weeks: I LOVE YOU SO MUCH. I MISS YOUR SMILE. I DON'T WANT TO LOSE YOU. Blah, blah, blah. I NEED TO FEEL SPECIAL AND WANTED. Blah, blah, blah. I KNOW YOU HAVE ISSUES AND THAT YOUR [SIC] GIVING ALL THAT YOU CAN GIVE RIGHT NOW. I CAN BE PATIENT. Blah, blah, blah. PLEASE DON'T LEAVE. IT WOULD MAKE IT REALLY TOUGH FOR ME DURING THE TOURNAMENT IF YOU LEFT NOW. I LOVE YOU AND WOULD REALLY LIKE YOU TO STAY. Blah, blah, blah.

That was it! I could no longer delay what I had been putting off for far too long already. Quivering with pent-up emotion, I anxiously waited for my soon-to-be ex-girlfriend to return.

19

*A*ccelerate the racket and follow through

Following practice, Sydney invited me to lunch. As she had done numerously in the past, I presumed her plan would most likely be to persuade me not to end our relationship. She would attempt to browbeat me with guilt until I relented— again. But this time would be very different. She just didn't know it yet.

As Sydney pulled into the parking lot of the California Pizza Kitchen, I gathered my strength and resolve. I was a ball of nerves as I exited the car. It was akin to the feeling I had as my saddle oxfords walked me into the principal's office hours after my arrival on my first day at Monte Cassino in Tulsa. I wasn't called in to meet the welcoming committee but rather got summoned to Sister Mary Margaret's office for telling dirty jokes on the playground at recess. My mouth was washed out with soap and I was allowed to finish the day at school, but my penance was that I had to go home and tell my mother what I had done. Yes, that's right— the little Jewish girl got her mouth washed out the first day of school by a nun and then had to rat myself out to my mother and face my *real* punishment. I can still remember the look of sheer horror on her face when "Mommy's good little girl" confessed my "sin" to her. I shamefully dragged myself back to school the next day feeling like a young heathenness among baptized angels. To this day, I still maintain that the joke wasn't *that* bad. I wasn't wearing saddle oxfords today, nor was I heading to the principal's office, but I had a feeling that I wasn't going to enjoy this experience anymore than I had enjoyed Sister Mary Margaret and her Sudsy Sue.

As luck would have it, and it truly was by coincidence, the first person I saw when we entered the restaurant was Casey. We were both surprised. I had called Casey earlier after I read the letter from Sydney and informed her that, contrary to what we had planned, I would not be able to spend the afternoon with her because I would be spending it breaking up with Sydney. Apparently, the California Pizza Kitchen was the restaurant du jour. Casey was leaving with a take-out order as Sydney and I were about to sit down for our "last supper."

After giving my menu a cursory review, the waiter appeared to take our order, pen and pad in hand. I stared blankly at him. *Yeah, I'll have one breakup, well-done. And can you hold the tears? I hate the tears. Oh, and can I have the drama on the side? And, she'll have a big tall glass of shut-the-hell-up. Oh, and come to think of it, I'm all done here and kinda in a hurry, so can I get that to go?* As I was having this fantasy conversation in my head, the waiter interrupted me after Sydney had ordered and asked me what I'd like. To this day I have no idea what I ordered.

As soon as the waiter left, I tried to figure out the best way to broach what would certainly be a contentious topic. There was no good way to do this. I had a friend who used to say that breaking up is never smooth or pleasant— if it were, it would be called something like "chocolate cake." She wasn't the sharpest knife in the drawer and I always thought that was a dumb comparison, but at that very moment I definitely saw her point. Here goes. "Sydney, I got your letter, and..."

She interrupted me— shocker, "Love, I don't want to talk about any of that right now."

Oh, now you don't want to talk about our relationship? That's a first!

"Well, I do." Gulp. "And we need to."

"Love, I just want to have a fun afternoon with you."

No, no, no! You're not talking me out of it this time! This is a done deal! "Sydney, we have to break up."

Wham!

The guillotine blade just dropped! Yeah, she wasn't going to take this well. Much like my mom when I confessed my sin of dirty joke telling, the color in Sydney's face began to drain, leaving her pale. No words from her yet. Shit. That can't be good. I dreaded what might possibly come out of her mouth. I looked around to find the nearest escape route in case I had to make a quick run for it.

Finally, Sydney spoke. "Are you sure this is what you want?" Her voice was quiet and shallow.

My turn again. "Let's be honest. We've been over this a hundred times. You're not happy and I'm not happy. I'm not giving you what you want. You need more than what I can give you. You're fighting me to give you more and I'm fighting you because I can't. I think we need to break up before we really damage each other." When the last word came out of my mouth I was relieved. I was determined to follow through with what I should have done months ago. There was no going back now.

My feeling of relief didn't last long. Sydney's eyes filled with tears, but I saw her jaw muscles tense. The calm before the storm was over. I knew her quiet demeanor was too good to be true. I could tell that I was about to be bowled over by a tremendous gust of Sydney's rage. She wiped her tears and then, in a slightly elevated voice, said, "I can't believe you're deserting me in the middle of a tournament."

Whack! There it was!

I interrupted her in an attempt to block the rest of the assault. "Sydney—"

She gave me the same consideration and blurted just a little louder, "Why are you doing this? How can you do this to me and to us?"

Uh, let me see, jackass, because when you're not on the tennis court trying to control the pace of the ball, you're going through my things and monitoring my calls, trying to control me. That's not a relationship, it's a fucking nightmare!

It took me a second, but I calmed down enough to be civil, but firm. "Sydney, I'm not walking out of your life and deserting you. I just can't be your girlfriend anymore. It's not fair to either of us. I think if you're honest with yourself, you'll see that."

Next came the drama. I knew I wouldn't get off that easily. As Sydney's anger surfaced, the color returned to her face. She opened her wallet and took out a picture of us, as well as a note I had written to her just after we'd met. "I guess none of this really meant anything to you. I guess I can just throw this stuff away."

Actually, I never really liked that picture, anyway. I look fat and you look twice your age— you really should have started using sunscreen a lot sooner.

It took every ounce of strength within me not to voice my frustration. "Don't be dramatic. If you want to throw that stuff away, throw it away. But don't turn this into something ugly." Just as she was about to hit me with what would certainly be a poignant retort, the waiter arrived with our food, momentarily distracting her.

Sydney pushed the plate away from her. "My appetite is ruined. I'm not hungry."

"Well, I'm sorry, but I'm absolutely starving!" It wasn't my intention to be insensitive, but there was nothing I could do or say to make Sydney feel better. I guess I could have joyfully announced that it was Opposite Day and that I was just kidding about wanting to break up, but clearly that was not going to happen. At one time, for an intense several days, I really and truly did care deeply for Sydney and, at this very moment, I was sincerely sorry for her pain and sadness. But I was finally doing the right thing— for us both. We both deserved more than a loveless relationship.

As she digested the breakup appetizer that I had just fed her, Sydney regained some of her appetite and inhaled a piece of her pizza in two bites. I was thankful that my days of sitting across the table from Sydney and her foul table manners were numbered.

It looked like Sydney might accept the inevitable, but I knew better than to celebrate prematurely. During the ten-minute drive back to the hotel, I was relishing the peace and quiet when my phone rang. It was my mom. I picked up and we had a brief conversation— our tone light and airy. This, of course, angered Sydney, who couldn't wait to whinge about how I could function well enough to have a tear-free conversation after I'd just broken up with her.

The second I hung up, she snapped, "You're so fucking fake with her, it makes me sick!" She then mimicked parts of the conversation that I had just had in an attempt to prove her point.

I wasn't interested in arguing with Sydney, but I couldn't help wanting to goad her a little bit. "Just because you hate your mother and don't talk to her doesn't mean I have to hate mine. I'm sorry if you thought I should have cried on her shoulder over you."

The truth was, had I told my mother we'd just broken up, her response would have been akin to those people on TV who've just received a knock on their door from the Prize Patrol and are informed that they've won the Publishers Clearing House sweepstakes. The novelty of Sydney had worn off for my mother well before we sat down to Thanksgiving dinner. It's safe to say that my mother was thoroughly unimpressed with Sydney within twenty seconds of meeting her— give or take ten. I'm quite certain that the news of our breakup would be cause for celebration and not tears. In fact, I bet if she knew, she'd happily be looking for that decanter that Sydney was so obsessed with at Thanksgiving so she could temporarily house a nice bottle of celebratory something.

Thirty more seconds, we'd be parked and I'd be out of the car, home free— or so I thought. Nope. When we entered the parking lot, Bad Sydney unleashed on me. After several minutes of listening to her rant and rave about how she couldn't believe it was so easy for me to just walk away and telling me, for the third time in five minutes, how the breakup was my loss, I exploded. If my previous eruptions rivaled Mount Saint Helens, I was positively Mount Vesuvius— which, as you may recall, wiped out the entire city of Pompeii. I yelled, "Enough! Don't you get it?! Jesus Christ! I'm tired of your issues and I'm canceling my subscription! Take me off your list!" The gloves were off and I shouted even louder, "Whether this is my loss or not, you and I feel differently about each other and you have to *finally* accept that!" As I turned to get out of the car, she grabbed my arm— her fingers wrapping themselves tightly around my flesh.

She had a look of anger mixed with absolute paranoia on her face. "Where are you going?!" Her eyes were bulging out of her head.

"Away. From you! And you're going to let me because if I don't leave, I'm gonna say a lot of things you won't want to hear. Things I can't take back. Now let go of my arm and respect that I need some space right now."

Thankfully, Sydney released my arm and I exited the car without sustaining or inflicting grievous bodily harm. If she had held onto my arm for one more second, I swear I would have willingly broken my own arm in half and used the severed part to beat her senseless.

I got out of the car without saying another word and slammed the door. Sydney screeched out of the parking lot. She really showed me! When I was sure I was clear from her line of vision, I darted into the hotel. Within seconds, I was inside and in the arms of the woman I loved. For the first time since this whole charade had started, I felt like I wasn't doing anything wrong. I was single and could now legitimately knock on Casey's door without worrying as much about Sydney. We sat on the bed together and I rehashed all the gory details of the breakup. Despite the deviation from Casey's plan, we both felt relieved, but neither of us quite knew how to proceed.

After an hour of my own version of "breakup sex" (where does it say that breakup sex has to be with the person with whom you broke up?), I took a shower and went back down the hall to my room. When I put my keycard in the slot, access to the room was denied. I pulled the plastic card back out and stared at it for a second, confused. Sydney wouldn't possibly have had the lock reprogrammed. Or would she? No, I doubt that. She wanted to lock me in, not out. I tried again and realized my access was denied because the deadbolt was on the door.

That's weird. It's the middle of the day and Sydney never bolts the door in the middle of the day. Interesting.

I knocked on the door and after a moment, Sydney answered it. The sun was shining brightly outside, but when she opened the door the room was almost pitch black. *Shit, is she sacrificing a chicken?* The curtains were drawn and the TV provided the only light in the room. She walked past me and collapsed back down onto the bed next to her phone.

Aha. That's the reason the deadbolt was on the door. She was on the phone with someone and she didn't want me to walk in during the conversation. God, she can't be any worse at this!

I wondered if Sydney's first call was to the thespian or to one of her friends. It didn't matter.

Sydney had just ordered a Pay-Per-View movie and asked me to watch it with her. *Are you insane? I'm only here long enough to pack my stuff and get the hell away from you.* But then I realized it would, perhaps, be more civil to de-escalate the stakes and maybe, talking things through while watching the movie was the most harmless activity that Sydney and I could do together. "What are you watching?" I asked.

"Love Actually."

I rolled my eyes and didn't try to hide it. "Listen, Sydney, we need to figure out some things…"

She pushed "pause." "I'm really upset about all of this and tomorrow I have to go out on the tennis court and win a match. It's my work. I know I don't have the right to ask you this, but it would really mean a lot to me if you would just stay here with me until the tournament is over. I don't expect anything from you. Just your support."

What was I supposed to say? Without a miracle there was pretty much no way Sydney could pull off a win the next day against her tough opponent. Her time in Palm Springs was definitely coming to an end.

When the movie finished, I left to go watch Casey's match. I didn't invite Sydney to come with me, but she wasn't interested in watching Casey play doubles anyway. Unless Casey was playing with her, Sydney was indifferent to Casey and her successes or failures on the doubles court. I disregarded all speeding rules as I raced over to the courts. I found Casey waiting for me outside the locker room. The match before hers had just split sets so we went up to the players' lounge. Marisa was in the training room warming up, so we had the room all to ourselves. Casey's was the last match of the day, so all of the other players had left. Just as we sat down on the couch, her phone rang. I guessed it was Trish.

What the fuck do you want?! Leave us alone! The look on Casey's face confirmed that Trish was the caller. She mouthed the words "I'm sorry" to me as she sat beside me and took the call.

As the conversation intensified, she got up and started pacing in front of me. At the same time, I received a text message from Trish. *Hey, Steph. Sorry about you and Sydney. Are you sad or relieved? Where are you? I hope you know that I'm here if you want to talk.* I read the text a few times. *Wow, this girl's good.* I then sent a strategic message back, selectively responding to Trish's text. *Thanks. Breakups are always sad, but it needed to happen. I appreciate the offer to talk, but I don't want to involve any of our friends.* Pleased with my response, I pushed "send." *She's good, but I'm better. Don't fuck with me, straight girl!*

Casey had no idea that Trish and I were texting each other while she was on the phone with Trish. And Trish had no idea that I was right next to Casey for what could not exactly be considered a "good luck" phone call. Given Trish's obsession with Casey and supposedly her desire for Casey's success, I could not believe that Trish was subjecting Casey to such severe harassment before she was about to go on the court. Casey finally ended the conversation. I could see the frustration on her face and asked, "What was that all about?"

"You."

"Me? What about *me?*"

"Bottom line is that she knows I like you. She keeps asking me and I keep denying it, but she doesn't trust me when it comes to you. She freaked out when I told her that you were gonna stay in town until Sydney's out of the tournament."

"I'm sure. She's definitely fishing for information." I handed her my phone and said, "Have a look at this." I had saved the message from Trish for her viewing pleasure.

She shook her head as she read it. With an exhale of exasperation she said, "Wow. She's really sniffing."

Yes, that's right. The jealous, non-gay, obsessive best friend was sniffing around some more. This was really starting to get old, especially since I had already tired of it in Australia.

I glanced at the scoreboard and saw that the match before Casey's was almost finished. Casey gasped, "Shit, shit, shit!" when she realized that she'd been too busy dealing with Trish and her drama to pay attention to the status of the match on the court ahead of hers. She hurriedly made her way down to the locker room to get her racket bag and meet Marisa. I wished her luck and she reminded me to watch for her signals. As if I needed reminding!

It was after ten o'clock when Casey and Marisa finally stepped onto the court. The match went three sets and lasted for almost two hours before they finally closed it out and claimed victory. I followed the crowd out of the stadium but darted across the pedestrian traffic and slipped into the club. I turned the corner and came to a screeching halt before nearly plowing Ribi over. Through her yawn, she said, "Hola. I'm surprised to see you here this late. What are you doing?"

Suddenly, I was nervous. My eyes darted around looking for Casey as I answered, "Uh, yeah. I just came to watch some doubles." Clearing my throat, I asked, "What are you doing here this time of night?" I hoped my diversionary tactic would work.

"I came to scout the match. We're on the same side of the draw as these girls."

I saw Casey out of the corner of my eye. Clearly not wanting to arouse further suspicion, she exited the door nearest the players' lounge without acknowledging Ribi or me. I subtly watched her leave, trying to quickly wrap up my conversation with Ribi. Apparently, repeatedly averting my gaze from Ribi to Casey was not exactly subtle. Ribi snickered, "You better go. Sydney is probably waiting for you." She raised one eyebrow as if she were proud of her joke, although I wasn't sure if it was inspired by her awareness of Sydney's possessive nature or if it was an insinuation about Casey. A chortle escaped her lips and she patted me on the shoulder as she walked past me.

I smirked and refrained from borrowing the phrase that she, Conchi, and I frequently hurl at one another— *tu callate, tonta!* Had I not been in a hurry to catch up with Casey, I would have happily reported my newfound freedom to Ribi.

Obeying her text, I met Casey in the parking lot of the hotel. I pulled up next to her and saw that she was gabbing on the phone. It was the middle of the night on the East Coast, but the only person she could be talking to was Trish. I gripped the steering wheel and gritted my teeth. *God, this is getting totally fucking annoying! I got rid of my wife today. When is she gonna get rid of hers?*

I'd had enough drama for the day and was too tired to deal with anymore. When Casey finally got off the phone, I walked her to her room, went in for a goodnight kiss and then performed the usual ritual to make sure that the coast was clear. I was exhausted by the time I settled down for the night next to my ex-girlfriend.

20

$\mathcal{K}$eep your head in the game and close out the match

Less than twenty-four hours after our breakup, Sydney marched onto the stadium court for her match against the Number 1 seed. Acquiescing to her request, I sat at the end of the court in the players' box so I'd be visible to her. The stands were packed with fans that went wild when Sydney lost the opening game. Clearly, they were rooting for her opponent. After a point where she almost got her head taken off by a crushing overhead, Sydney looked over at me for support. She caught me texting. *Oops.* She despised not having my undivided attention during her matches. I shot a tight-lipped smile back at her and brushed her off with a thumbs-up before blatantly continuing my text with the other thumb. Sydney wasn't my girlfriend any longer and she had no say in what I did or didn't do!

I had barely started sweating and the match was over. Sydney was dismissed in straight sets and only won a total of three games. My exgirlfriend had now been eliminated from the tournament. And truly, I felt bad for her. Even though I didn't want to be her girlfriend, I didn't wish her ill will.

One last time, I waited for Sydney in the players' lounge. She was taking an unusually long time to shower and collect her things. Naturally, I figured she was on the phone in the locker room being covertly consoled by the thespian. When she finally emerged, she appeared unfazed about her elimination from the tournament, which only confirmed my initial suspicion. Freshly showered and dare I say glowing, Sydney told me that she had spent the last hour on the phone with the airline (because her agent was "too incompetent to get it done himself") and booked the only remaining first-class seat she could get leaving Palm Springs this week. She was scheduled to leave the next morning. I got an early Christmas present after all! I made a note to remember to thank good old Saint Nick later.

I had one more evening to get through with Sydney and she asked if I would have dinner with her— alone. I agreed, albeit with much hesitation and trepidation, but only because in the twenty-four hours since we'd broken up, we had been getting along remarkably well. After all the fears, concerns and expectations of being "found out" and "exposed," followed by scenes of high drama and hysteria straight out of *Who's Afraid of Virginia Woolf,* I was actually able to relax and Sydney and I were able to laugh together for the first time in months. She was on her best behavior. Granted, she was probably holding out hope for a reconciliation, but on the whole, we were ending our relationship as amicably as possible. And that, in the end, was what all the sneaking around and subterfuge had been about— right?

Our dinner was interrupted by a text from Casey, although my silent phone did not alert Sydney to that fact. I had placed my phone on the booth next to me so I'd be able to check for any incoming texts. The message, *Fucking lost,* was surprising— even shocking. I was certain that Casey and Marisa would navigate easily through the draw to the finals.

Slipping my phone into my pocket, I cut short the little Camelot-like scenario and immediately excused myself from the table to go to the bathroom and call Casey. "Cutie, I just got your message. Are you okay?"

Through her tears she said, "I can't believe we lost. I think I made a huge mistake partnering with Marisa. She's just not good enough." For a second, I thought I was talking to Sydney. It wasn't like Casey to so overtly blame losses on her partner.

Casey was distraught and I was determined to swoop in and save the day. "I'm so sorry. I'm gonna tell Sydney that I just got a text from you and that you guys lost and that you want us to come and have some beers with you. Better yet, you text her and tell her that. We'll be there soon."

"Wait! What am I supposed to do about my ticket?" Casey was famous for packing up and leaving on the earliest flight whenever she lost. But this time, she wanted to stay an extra day to be with me. "Both Sydney and Trish will think it's weird if I'm not on a plane tomorrow."

"Cutie, calm down. You don't even know that you could get a seat tomorrow. Just have your agent work her magic and book a seat for the day after tomorrow...or the day after that for all I care."

Thinking outside the box was impossible for Casey. She was the one who insisted on all the dishonesty, but she could never figure out how to cover her tracks. She made a big deal out of everything. Take, for example, her concern about her ticket. Sydney had told us earlier in the day that she was barely able to get a seat on a flight the next morning. Why Casey couldn't parlay that information and use it to her advantage was beyond me, but she just couldn't. She needed me, the mastermind, to tell her to have her agent make her airline reservation for the day after tomorrow and then to just tell Sydney and Trish that she couldn't get out until then. I guess having a law degree comes in handy for solving colossally complex matters such as these. Being charged with the task of thinking of everything really was getting exhausting and annoying and I was glad that it would soon be over.

I assuaged Casey's chronic anxiety as much as possible, but I needed to get back out to the table before Captain Curious worried I had fallen in the toilet and came looking for me with a plunger. I rushed back over to Sydney and found her staring at her phone, reading the text from Casey reporting her loss and requesting our company.

A room service tray with two empty beer bottles sitting outside Casey's room was an odd sight. We knocked on Casey's door and she answered with cash in her hand. "Oh, I thought you were room service. I ordered some more beer for us."

"What happened? Couldn't carry the old lady tonight?" Sydney asked, as she barreled into the room. Leave it to Sydney to cut to the chase.

"Sydney, not now! I don't want to talk about the match! God! First Trish and now you!"

Sydney snickered condescendingly, "Aww. Trish must be devastated that she can't strut into the casino with an air of superiority and brag about her best friend winning another tournament! I bet she's already calculating how many points you're gonna have to make up so your ranking doesn't drop."

I laughed silently, actually agreeing with Sydney.

Casey rolled her eyes and groaned, "You're both pains in my ass! As if losing a match I shouldn't have isn't shitty enough, I have to listen to Trish tell me that I shouldn't be drinking because I need to lose some weight— six pounds, to be exact— and work on my fitness so I'm faster on the court and then you stroll in here and gloat! Ahh!" Exasperated, she threw her hands in the air. "Whatever, I don't want to talk about it anymore!" She sipped the last of her beer and announced, "I got a flight."

"Shocker! That's the first thing you always do. What time are you leaving tomorrow?" Sydney asked.

"I'm not. I couldn't get a flight tomorrow. I got one for the day after. I'll just stay here and practice tomorrow."

See, was that so hard?

I made my way over to the couch, biting my tongue to avoid hurling an expletive at Trish for having the audacity to suggest that Casey needed to lose weight. She didn't. Stupid Trish. She should stick to what she knows best: blackjack and high heels.

"Want me to sell you my seat? My flight leaves at eight in the morning. Direct to Miami."

Casey ignored Sydney and asked me, "What time are you leaving tomorrow?"

"Certainly, not at the crack of dawn! I'll get up with Sydney and then workout before I leave." I shot Casey a quick grin.

Perfect! We had just provided Sydney with alibis. In less than ten hours, Sydney would be on a plane and I would be in Casey's arms— for good.

Three room service calls and a total of twelve beers later, Casey and I were pleasantly buzzed and Sydney was practically passed out on the bed. Casey poked her in the side and instructed her to go sleep in her own room. Sydney perked up enough to grumble something at me. "C'mon. Let's go back to our room and go to bed."

I looked at her like she was an alien from another planet. "You go ahead. I'll be back in a while."

She knew she had stepped over a line and then tried a different approach. She whined, "Oh, please come with me. Aren't you tired?"

"Sydney, go. I'll be there in a while!"

She pouted and left, reluctantly.

"God, I thought she'd *never* leave!" Casey said as she exhaled loudly. Within seconds after the door had shut behind Sydney, Casey lifted her paper-thin T-shirt over her head and stepped out of her yoga pants before pouncing on top of me, quickly and spontaneously removing my shirt and tossing it onto the floor. Luckily, I was wearing a short sleeved polo with no buttons; otherwise, I'm certain several of the plastic discs would have flown across the room. My bra followed quickly after the shirt, although I'm not certain where it landed. Somehow, Casey bent her leg and gripped my loose linen pants with her toes and slid them down my legs to my ankles. As our lips met, we devoured each other with kisses and I kicked my leg, sending my pants and sheer thong airborne.

Casey straddled my waist and pinned my hands above my head on the arm of the couch while she explored my body. Leaning forward to kiss me, her hair gently brushed against my cheek as her hand slowly traveled down my body. I breathed in the floral scent of her freshly washed hair and was deliciously excited. I arched my back off the soft ultra-suede cushion in reaction to her silky touch. Consumed with excitement and desire, my hands broke free and I reached for the opening between her legs and slid one finger inside her. As I felt her warmth and wetness, my panting heightened to the point where a moan would surely follow. Suddenly, there was a knock on the door.

"Shit! Oh, God! Shit!" Casey squealed, jumping off me and almost passing out with fear. She scurried to retrieve her clothes. She only had two items to slip back into. I, on the other hand, was hastily fastening my bra behind my back and glancing behind the couch for my missing underwear while simultaneously attempting to calm her down. We hadn't ordered any more beers, so we both knew it was Sydney knocking on the door.

"Shit! We've come so far. She can't catch us now!"

"Shhh...calm down," I whispered as she threw her shirt back over the top of her head. "She can't get in here. Just answer the door. Everything will be fine."

She caught her breath and composed herself before opening the door. Indeed, it was Sydney. Neither of us realized that thirty minutes had passed since she'd left. But, apparently, Sydney had been vigilantly watching the clock and had come back to collect me. She pushed her way into the room and saw me sitting on the couch, exactly where she'd left me. "C'mon, Steph, let's go."

Without the slightest hint of urgency toward her request, I said, "Sydney, you're not my mother, dammit! I said I'd be back in a while and I will."

Her eyes squinted and her lips tightened. She had no choice but to accept what I said and left. Casey was so traumatized that her entire body was trembling. I went into the bathroom to wash any trace of Casey off my face and hands and then decided it was best, for everyone, to say goodnight. We hugged and kissed, relishing the thought of falling asleep in each other's arms the next night. Even though Sydney knew where I was, I departed and performed the coast-is-clear ritual out of habit before returning to our room.

Hoping Sydney had passed out again, I quietly entered the room and prepared myself for what I knew would be the last night I would ever spend in her bed. The spring in my step was undeniable as I anticipated the excitement for the next day. Luck was not on my side, though, and Sydney's eyes watched as I floated into the room. Of course, she misconstrued the bounce in my step as my desire to hop into her bed. I couldn't believe it! I had thwarted all her advances since she'd arrived in Palm Springs and now that there were only seconds left in the game, she wanted to rush the field. As if her last-ditch efforts were going to make up for all her psychotic behavior and play on my emotions to sweep me back in time to when we actually enjoyed intimacy! She certainly was persistent. Every time she tried to roll over on top of me, I inched my way out from under her. When that didn't work, her hands began to wander under the covers. I lost count of how many times I pushed her creepy hands off me. When I flicked her hand away from my stomach for the last time, I turned my back to her. I immediately felt her chiseled, muscular forearm across my side and her tennis-calloused hand fell just under my chin and onto my left breast. Her fingers lightly caressed my collarbone. I was about to call room service and ask for a butcher knife so I could chop her arm off just under the elbow, but her hand went motionless. She had crashed into an intensely deep sleep.

The alarm went off at 6 a.m., but I was already awake. I shook Sydney out of her sleep and went down to the lobby to get some coffee for her. By the time I returned, she'd showered, dressed and was ready to leave. *Yippee!* I gladly helped carry her bags down to the car.

Once we loaded the luggage, the dreaded good-bye was imminent. She wrapped her arms around me and had no intention of letting go. I thought I was going to need a box cutter in order to free myself from her grip. It was just past six-thirty but she was already wearing her dark Gucci sunglasses so I couldn't see the tears streaming from her eyes. I knew it was only a matter of time before the flow would rival Niagara Falls. As soon as I felt the first tear on my cheek, I broke the embrace. "You better go. I hate good-byes." Her grip didn't loosen, so I wriggled free and said, "Sydney, I know things didn't turn out the way either of us hoped and I'm sorry for that."

Her arms fell to her side. "Are you sure you don't want to reconsider?" She laughed at her desperate words.

"I'm sure. This is best for us both. You're great, but we're not great together."

"But, we could be..."

Jesus Christ! I'm trying to escape gracefully and this woman just won't let me do it! I'm giving her about thirty more seconds before I tell her what an absolute nightmare she has been, scream obscenities at her and physically push her into the car!

"Sydney, I've given this a lot of thought."

"You're about to let the best thing that could ever happen to you drive away."

Ten, nine, eight, seven...

"Sydney, this isn't right or fair for either of us. I'm really sorry."

"But don't you think we could work through this?"

Three, two...

"Sydney, we've both given all we can give." I paused for a second before wishing her a final farewell. "Have a safe trip."

Blessedly, she got into her car. She started the ignition and rolled down the window. "Love, about the ring…"

"Sydney, of course, I'll send it back to you. I'll do it first thing when I get home."

"That's not what I was going to say. I want you to keep it."

"I can't. I'll FedEx it to you."

"I insist…because I don't think we're over."

You will when you see that ring posted for sale on eBay!

"Sydney…"

"Look, just know that I love you and I want us to work this out. I hope you miss me while you're looking for whatever it is you're looking for out there."

Okay, now you're really on my nerves! I'll miss you about as much as I miss the partner whom, in my dreams, I used to push out a twelfth-story window!

I watched as she drove away. *So long, 'lovah!'*

Back upstairs, only a few short moments later, I followed Casey into her bed. Her sheets were warm and smelled like a mixture of her perfume and body cream. I inched up behind her and put my head on the pillow next to hers. I thought I was dreaming as we fell asleep.

When we woke up, we discussed the plan for the day. Anonymity was still paramount. After noon, which was the official check-out time and the latest that I could conceivably still be occupying Sydney's room, Casey instructed that no one could see me in Palm Springs if we were going to play out our little masquerade successfully. Casey decided we could go to the gym and then have breakfast together in public, but after that we'd have to be back in her room and stay there for the rest of the day and night until we both left early the next morning. I had a hunch about how we were going to relish our time all day long in secluded splendor.

Later that morning before the clock struck twelve, I went down the hall to pack my bags and check out of Sydney's room— as if I ever really checked in. When I was organizing my things, I found a card that Sydney had left for me. *Oh fuck!* The text on the card read: I WAS JUST WONDERING…IF YOU'D LET ME LOVE YOU FOREVER AND EVER? And the message that Sydney had printed was more of the same sappy I-love-you-and-I-will-wait-for-you crap that I had heard ad nauseum over the past couple days. I shook my head, buried the card in my bag and piled all my clothes on top of it.

Sure you can love me forever and ever, but something tells me that loving me is not exactly what you're gonna wanna do when you find out that I'm in love with your ex-girlfriend. I can't be certain. Just a wild guess.

I went back to Casey's room and we didn't leave again until the next morning. The rest of the day was ours to simply enjoy. There were plenty of phone interruptions from Trish, but we were not physically separated for nearly twenty-four hours. We spent the entire day talking, watching movies, making love and enjoying the bubble of her room that was our own private world. Our day ended the same way it began— in each other's arms. Neither of us could have been happier.

The next morning, when it was time to leave as the sun was inching up into the sky, I darted out of the hotel to my car and Casey followed behind me in hers. We drove away single-file, making our way toward LA. I felt a frisson of excitement at the thought that she and I were one step closer to spending our lives together. I smiled and waved to her as her Jeep Liberty shot up the freeway toward the exit for the Palm Springs Airport. Soon, she would be on a plane flying to Miami to train for a week before the next tournament started— the South Florida Invitational. And I would be back at home in LA making plans to see Casey again; taking delight in having finally closed it out with Sydney.

21

Game over

Within hours of her arrival in Miami, Casey and I were scheming about how I was going to "conveniently" appear at the South Florida Invitational as her guest, despite my recent breakup with Sydney. Before I knew it, I had boarded a plane bound for Longboat Key, Florida under the pretext of paying my mother a visit. I love you, Mom, but yes, I was using you as a conduit to be with Casey. The plan was for me to visit my mom for a few days and then "spontaneously" drive down to Miami to watch some tennis.

I took a red-eye from Los Angeles and arrived at my mom's house barely able to drag myself outside to my favorite chaise lounge overlooking the Gulf of Mexico. Before I closed my eyes to catch up on the sleep I had missed the night before, I called Casey. Within two minutes I was wide awake— and not because I was thrilled over hearing her voice. To the contrary, I was shaking with so much anger I had to slam down the phone. Casey had just shared some information with me— Sydney had a new girlfriend. Yes, the thespian!

I know what you're thinking, but it's not true!

Just because I didn't want Sydney doesn't mean that I'm one of those ex-girlfriends who didn't want anyone else to have her. On the contrary, I was glad that she had a new conquest, but I was also jealous— but not for the reasons that most ex-girlfriends might be jealous. Casey told me that the thespian picked Sydney up from the airport the night she flew in from Palm Springs and that they had been inseparable ever since. I couldn't believe it! It didn't take her long to move on! Shit, my body was not even cold yet. Her mourning period literally lasted the six-hour plane ride from California back to Florida. I mean, good for her, but if she was so intent on being with the thespian, why didn't she just break up with me earlier or let me break up with her? Why put me through all that nonsense in Palm Springs? The pill counting, the vein popping, the begging and pleading, the tears, the neighbors banging on the walls, the call log trespass, the sappy "I love you" card! I was seething. I clenched my jaw and felt the muscles that had developed under my cheeks, thanks to Sydney. I tried to calm myself by watching the rhythm of the waves as they gently tumbled ashore. I think the only thing that could have calmed me down would have had to come in the form of a prescription.

I abruptly rose from my lounge and launched into a tirade. I spouted, "That fuckin' hypocrite! Asshole! I stayed with her for months as a result of her manipulation. How long have I been trying to break up with her? I put up with her shit and bit my tongue to avoid devastating her so that her precious tennis wouldn't suffer. I've been walking around on eggshells and compromising myself for her benefit and at the expense of my own happiness! Had I not wracked my brain trying to think of a gingerly way to end our relationship? Okay, so I fell in love with her ex-girlfriend. I do realize that's not exactly 'gingerly.' But, that only took place a month-and-a-half ago and I wanted to break up with her long before that. I didn't mean to fall in love with Casey— it just happened. Matters of the heart can't be controlled! I fell in love with someone else, so sue me! And then I stayed with Sydney after I fell in love with Casey so we wouldn't hurt her feelings. Just days ago she was begging me to come back to her and she already has a new girlfriend!"

As the blood rushed to my head and the temperature of my face rose, I could feel my heart beating in my earlobes. Let's face it. I wasn't mad because Sydney had a new girlfriend. I was jealous because Sydney had the freedom to move on and openly be with anyone she pleased. This was a luxury I did not have and one I desperately coveted. Sydney had nothing to hide and regardless of the fact that she had been professing her undying love to me just a few days earlier, it was entirely her prerogative to be with someone else the second we said good-bye. Rebound or no rebound, I was no longer interested in protecting poor

Sydney's sensitivities. She had moved on with her life and I intended to do the same.

Two days later, I packed my bag and got in my car. I raced down Interstate 75 and across Alligator Alley to Miami, to be with Casey. Ironically, as I shifted gears while balancing a Diet Coke between my knees, I felt a sudden déjà vu, as if I were back in high school. Still not providing my mother with full disclosure, I had covered my bases enough with her so that she knew where I was going and whom I was going to be with, but not so much that she knew exactly what I was doing. In fact, I was doing what I frequently did when I was a teenager— bending myself into a pretzel so that no one knew that I was darting out of the house to go and be with the woman I loved. It's funny how the more things change, the more they truly remain the same.

In just under four hours, I pulled into the parking lot of the Loews Hotel, where Casey habitually stayed while in Miami. I followed the instructions that she had given me without the slightest deviation and nonchalantly gave my keys to the valet, grabbed my overnight bag (I was told to bring only that bag so I could carry it with me directly to Casey's room without having to talk to too many people when I got there— for example, a valet *and* a bellman), walked into the hotel and rushed past the reception desk to the elevator bay so as to avoid being seen. Why all of the cloak and dagger still? I had no idea. Anybody's guess is as good as mine. With very little exception, I had done exactly as Casey had demanded for almost two months, so why would I stop now? According to her, it was too soon for us to publicly announce our relationship without it becoming blatantly obvious to Sydney and Trish that we had been involved in a covert romance while I was with Sydney. We had to wait "just a bit longer."

When I learned how to swim at age four, my instructor used to stand in the water and tell me to hold my breath and swim to him. I always found the distance between us daunting and put my face in the water, not knowing whether I could make it. Without fail, every time I was one stroke away from touching him and reaching the goal that he had set for me, he would back up a few paces and increase the distance. It always caused me to panic but, despite all my doubts, I always reached him just before I was certain my lungs would explode. More than two decades later, this same feeling had returned to me. The closer I got to my goal of openly being with Casey, the further it alluded me. I wanted to scream, but I think it would have been as pointless as all the times I yelled underwater at my instructor for backing up. Anyone who has ever tried screaming under water can certainly empathize. Try it— it's utterly maddening.

When the elevator doors opened to the third floor, realizing that I was getting closer to seeing Casey, my pulse quickened as I read the numbers on each door I passed. I exhaled a sigh of relief when I reached her room and then lightly knocked. Almost immediately, the door flung open and Casey pulled me inside. She shut the door so quickly it almost hit me in the derrière.

I took one look at her and thought that her smiling lips were going to come and plant themselves on mine. The sun hadn't set yet, but she was standing in front of me scantily clad in Gap Body sleeping clothes that were practically transparent. I smiled and cocked my head to the left in anticipation, my mouth begging to be kissed. She left me hanging and anxiously asked, "Did anyone see you?"

I laughed it off but was slightly annoyed that her first concern was whether someone caught a glimpse of me as I stealthily made my way from LA to Longboat Key and from Longboat Key to Miami. "Uh, yeah, actually. I ran into Sydney in the lobby. We rode the elevator up together." I pointed to the necklace dangling on my chest and said, "I told her I flew down here to thank you for this. She says you have *great* taste and to tell you 'hi.' She was on her way to visit someone on the fifth floor. I gave her your room number and told her I'd be here for a few days in case she wanted to stop by and visit. You don't mind, do you?"

"C'mon! Be serious. No one saw you, did they? And do you think it's a good idea for you to be wearing that necklace?" She seemed more paranoid than ever.

"Cutie, relax. No one saw me!" I huffed. For the love of God, Sydney wasn't even staying in a hotel since her house was thirty minutes from the tournament! But I'd have shimmied up the side of the building before I'd let any prying eyes catch a glimpse of me. I drew in a deep breath and addressed what I hoped would be Casey's last ridiculous inquiry. "And, as for the necklace, I have no one to answer to about what jewelry I wear or don't wear anymore. Now, will you please calm down and stop asking me such asinine questions?!"

Satisfied, Casey leaned into my body and gently pulled me close. I finally got the kiss that I had flown across the country for.

Within seconds, she led me by the hand through the living room of her suite into the bedroom where candles were lit and music was playing softly in anticipation of my arrival and the romantic night that we would share and enjoy together. She gently kissed my neck and whispered, "Take a shower with me." I exhaled and gasped loudly as she nuzzled my ear.

We had never taken a shower together, but my smile told Casey I would happily join her under the streaming water. Instantly, the ensemble that I had specifically chosen to impress her— a new pair of True Religion jeans and a sexy tight-fitting T-shirt— were balled up on the floor next to her abandoned clothes.

I followed Casey into the dimly lit bathroom and we stepped into the large walk-in shower. We were entering foreign territory together. Steam filled the room as she enveloped me with tenderness. The hot water cascaded down our bodies and splashed onto the tile floor. Savoring the desire that was building within me, I closed my eyes and leaned my head under the nozzle. My senses heightened and my body trembled at the anticipation of Casey's touch. She seductively dragged her tongue from my neck softly down my chest, stopping at my left breast long enough to suck on my erect nipple. Several moans escaped my lips as she slid her tongue down the middle of my gym-toned stomach. My body tingled so much that even my wet hair tickled the top of my shoulder blades, forcing blood to rush through my veins faster.

Pushing the water from my face with my hand, I opened my eyes to find Casey kneeling in front of me. I turned the streaming jet to the side and clenched my fists as she plunged inside me with her frenetic tongue. She licked me with excitement and passion as my body reacted to the ecstasy. We both wailed with pleasure as I grew more and more aroused. Leaning against the cool tiles, I watched the water roll off her glistening back and puddle onto the floor next to her sun-kissed, firm body. I was on the verge of climax. My body jerked every time her fingers climbed up my side and her nails dragged lightly down my back. Suddenly, I unclenched one fist and my hand flew down and landed on her left shoulder which I gripped and squeezed intensely as my entire body began to shake.

She moaned loudly and moved her tongue faster. On the brink of ecstasy, I almost exploded. I bit my clinched fist to muffle my pleasure-filled moans. My teeth seized the top of my knuckle until my orgasm was over and my body had stopped shaking. Several small twitches followed the last orgasmic jolt of my body. My heart was pounding and my stomach and chest were heaving as I tried to regain my breath. Casey lifted herself onto her feet and briefly pressed her lips on mine. As I caught my breath, I wrapped my arms around her and gently kissed her on the forehead and whispered, "I love you."

We toweled off and snuggled under the soft cotton sheets on the king-sized bed. With my head next to Casey's on the same pillow, I inched my naked body forward until my warm chest touched her back so that our bodies molded together, forming an "S." As I wrapped my arms around her tighter, the theme song from *Arthur* played on the stereo. I listened to the words of "Moon and New York" and tenderly kissed the back of her head. The circumstances of our romances were absurd, but Casey had turned my heart around. I fell asleep feeling, for the first time in my life, that I had found my soul mate.

I woke up the next morning, excited to accompany Casey to the tournament. For the first time since we had met, one of her badges was reserved for me and I was going to be Casey's guest. I proudly beamed as my photo was taken. I felt as if it were commencement day— so proud to display that little piece of paper for which I had worked so diligently. Only this time, my badge— which read: GUEST OF CASEY MATTHEWS— was my diploma.

Like most graduates venturing alone into the big bad world, I was nervous. Sure, I had been to countless tennis tournaments over the years, but this was the first one since Sydney and I had broken up and the first one *with* Casey. I donned my badge but was somewhat anxious as I walked into the club. Casey and I went into the players' lounge so she could pick up the iPod that the sponsors of the tournament were handing out as gifts to all the players in the main draw. I waved to the familiar faces but didn't stop to talk to anyone. No one batted an eyelash. Apparently, news of the breakup had not been leaked.

Armed with her goodie bag, Casey went to the training room before her practice. I stayed behind with my friend, Angie, another favorite friend of mine on the Tour. Not Sydney's biggest fan, Angie was slightly more than jubilant when I shared the news of our breakup with her. She thought I was crazy for dating that "nob" anyway. She was even more shocked when I quickly followed the first gossipy newsflash with another that I was certain would burn a hole through the players' lounge like wildfire— that Sydney had a new girlfriend. I strategically dropped that juicy nugget because I figured that people would be too busy chattering about how quickly the teary-eyed but apparently not-so-broken-hearted-Casanova-ex-girlfriend of mine had moved on and found a new playmate of the month, to worry that I was sauntering around the tournament with Casey.

As soon as Casey was out of earshot, Angie leaned in and said, "Alright, what the hell's goin' on between you two?"

I couldn't hide my surprise or my smile. I must have looked like a young child who had been trusted with a secret if she promised not to tell a soul. I never was very good at keeping a secret when pressed, so the smile I cracked certainly was enough of a confirmation that Angie hounded me further.

Playing dumb, I struggled to squirm my way out of answering her questions. "Between who? What're you talking about?" I don't play dumb well.

"Puh-lease! Between Casey and you. Something's up. You're not foolin' me or anyone!"

I wouldn't say "anyone." We certainly fooled Sydney!

I was becoming increasingly more uncomfortable and wasn't sure how to respond. I quickly searched my brain for something funny to say to throw Angie off but came up with nothing. Looking at her with a half-smile on my face, I raised my eyebrows and denied her accusation. "I have no idea what you're talking about." As soon as the words came out of my mouth, I picked up my cell phone to send Casey an "SOS" text. As quickly as I could, I typed, *Help! Being grilled by Angie about us!*

Within seconds, Casey sent a response. *You can tell her.*

I thought my eyes were deceiving me as I read and re-read the text to confirm what it said. I was dumbfounded that after demanding total secrecy for so long, Casey so cavalierly acquiesced and was now allowing me to reveal our desperately-kept secret.

As I lifted my head from reading the text for the umpteenth time, I saw Casey walking toward me with a huge smile on her face. She strode directly over to the table where Angie and I were sitting and plopped down on a chair right next to me and blurted, "So, what're you two trouble-makers gossiping about?"

Before I had a chance to get a word in edgewise, Angie responded, "You."

I could feel my face blushing. Again, I was speechless. Casey smiled and simply responded, "Oh, really? Interesting. Well, I'll let you two get back to it. I'm off to practice." That was it. That's all she said. She didn't give me a look and a wink that I'd recognize to mean "keep your mouth shut" or "whatever you do, deny everything!" Casey merely dropped a boulder in my lap casually and then got up to leave.

Utterly nonplussed, I followed her. There was no way she could leave me there to fend off Angie's inquisition with just that. I didn't want *any* misunderstandings. I wanted to hear it directly from Casey's mouth that I could be honest with Angie. Once out of earshot, I whispered, "Are you serious? Can I really tell her?"

She smiled and said, "Yeah. You can tell her we have feelings for each other, but don't give her any sordid details." I knew there had to be a catch. It was disclosure, but only partial— par for the course with Casey Matthews. Still, I was a stunned. A feather could have knocked me down when the next words came out of Casey's mouth. "In fact, I want you to tell her. I do. I have to go practice, but I want you to tell me all about it when I'm done. Have fun." She looked into my eyes and gave me that special smile that made my stomach churn and continued down the stairs.

I was so shocked that I thought I had forgotten how to walk and nearly keeled over with astonishment. "One foot in front of the other," I instructed myself. Somehow, I made it back across the room to our table without stumbling and falling flat on my face. When I sat back down, Angie greeted me with a hugely mischievous grin.

Even more resolute in her desire for information, Angie smugly asked, "Now where were we?"

Shaking off my shock, I recomposed myself. "Piss off. I really don't know what you're talking about." I tried to maintain my coy façade before I relinquished my secret.

"Oh, whatever! You two can't stay away from each other. It's obvious. Just admit it."

I inhaled deeply and then did just that— confessed. "Okay. We're totally in love with each other, but you can't tell a fucking soul! No one knows and I don't need people talking about this right now."

"I knew it! I always knew there was something going on between you two! I knew it, I knew it, I knew it!"

"Yeah, yeah. You're a regular fuckin' genius. It's not like it's not obvious. I'm surprised more people don't suspect us. Helen Keller could've figured it out, but around here, people are blinder than she was."

"I love it!" Angie exclaimed, so loudly that she attracted onlookers.

Unconcerned about our audience, I fondly joked, "No, you love the gossip and I swear to God, if you open your mouth about this…"

"Oh shut up! I'm not gonna tell anyone. Thank God you got away from Sydney! That made a-b-s-o-l-u-t-e-l-y no sense. You and Casey make t-o-t-a-l sense!"

For the next hour, Angie peppered me with questions. I was in heaven. It was validation. It was as if the swimming coach were walking *toward* me!

By the time Angie was finished with her interrogation, Casey's practice was over and we went downstairs to meet her in front of the locker room. As we rounded the corner, I glanced down the long hallway toward the locker room and saw Sydney coming out. *Shit! This is all I need right now!* She hadn't seen me yet, but I was trapped by concrete on either side of me, as well as above and below me. I could not escape Sydney's gaze. Suddenly, I could hear the ominous *Jaws* music in my head as I slowed the pace of my gait, hoping that this might somehow hide me from discovery. I was sure Sydney still had access to the transponder that she used to track the GPS device she certainly had planted in my ass when we were together. My attempt to camouflage myself with the walls failed. It was only a matter of seconds before the shark would be circling, ready to devour me. The only thing I could do was pivot and subtly turn in the opposite direction. Too late.

I had been made. The voice calling from behind me that I had not heard since I left Palm Springs sent shivers down my spine.

"Hey! Steph!" Sydney called out.

I knew I had to turn around and face the music, but I wasn't ready yet. I kept walking as if I had not heard the voice trailing after me. Sydney's voice had the same effect on me as nails scratching a chalkboard. Again, I heard her call me, but this time louder. "S-T-E-P-H!"

Shit. I had no choice but to acknowledge Sydney. Angie, on the other hand, wanted no part of what was potentially about to be an explosive exchange, so she cringed and gave me an unmistakable sorry-about-your-luck-but-I'm-outta-here look and continued walking.

I felt the weight of the world crashing down on my shoulders as Sydney walked toward me. I would rather have set my own hair on fire than engage in a conversation with her. Alas, she was now standing mere inches from me. For the second time in one day, I had no idea what to say, which was fine in this instance, because I had a feeling that Sydney would do enough talking for us both.

I took one look at her and wished I could vanish into thin air. I knew that pathetic, drawn face of hers all too well. I looked around to see where the dead horse was. It had to be around there somewhere and it was about to get beaten.

Sydney assumed an unsurprisingly dramatic air and said, "I think we need to talk."

And there it was— the dead horse.

Oh, God, why me? Just kill me now!

When I was a kid and got into trouble for doing something wrong, my dad would call me into the study and give me "The Look" (while my mom had perfected The Glare, my dad had mastered The Look). Every kid who has ever gotten into trouble with their parents (and that would be every kid!) knows The Look. Without fail, a lecture from my dad always followed The Look. But, why? The gig's up. What's left to talk about? I always wished that my dad would just cut to the chase and ground me and let me go back to my room so I could sneak in a phone call that I was not supposed to make on the phone I was not supposed to be using for a week.

I met Sydney's gaze and felt a lecture coming on. I leaned my back up against the wall (secretly hoping that my body would trigger some sort of hidden trapdoor that would free me from my concrete prison), folded my arms across my chest before boasting my annoyance and responding icily, "Sydney, there's nothing left to talk about. But just so we're clear, don't think I don't know that you were crying to me, begging for me to reconsider before you left Palm Springs and the minute you got off the plane in Miami, you jumped into bed with someone else." I smiled at a passerby as if I were a politician acknowledging a constituent.

"I didn't jump in bed with her," she feebly insisted.

Oh, shit! Semantics! Maybe they hadn't shared a bed immediately upon her arrival, but there were certainly two people occupying her king-sized sheets now. Anyway, the point is, Sydney had moved on and she was happy. There was not one bone in my body or one ounce of my energy that wanted to dwell on the past with Sydney. People were walking toward us, so I was trying to be as nonchalant as possible. It wasn't a stretch. I really didn't much care whom Sydney was sleeping with. I just wished she would live her happy little life and let me go.

"Whatever." My voice was cold and completely detached.

Tears began to well up in her eyes. "This is really hard for me. I still care about you. This other thing just happened so quickly, and…" She wiped her tears as her voice trailed off.

Kick number two to the ribs of the dead horse. Wait, who's the dumb athlete here? The one thing I am not is stupid.

Did she really expect me to believe that this shit between her and what's her name— the thespian— just started? I knew damn well that there was overlap and that it started before Palm Springs, so I wasn't about to buy the story she was selling. I rolled my eyes and said in a monotone, "Sydney, please don't insult my intelligence."

The tears now streamed down her face. "It's really not what you think. Yes, we were texting and e-mailing while I was in California, but nothing happened while you and I were together. I never would've gone there with her if you had just *once* told me that you wanted me and that you wanted us to work out."

As the conversation continued, Casey walked around the corner. She looked at me and when she saw that I was trapped, she quickened her pace— in the opposite direction. *Chicken!*

"Look, Sydney, I don't really care when this thing with you guys started. Are you happy?"

She lifted her hand, and my heart skipped a beat when I thought she was going to reach for me— and not because the thought of her hand on me excited me! My back was to the wall and I had nowhere to go. Thankfully, she was only reaching to wipe her tears. "Seriously. Are you happy? Does she make you happy?"

Sniffling, she nodded, "Yes. I...I think I'm in love."

Oh. My. God.

It was all I could do not to burst out laughing. A few days earlier, Sydney had professed her undying love for me and claimed to be devastated over our breakup. And not one week later, she was standing in front of me all but admitting that she was in love with another woman. I officially nominate Sydney Foster to be the new spokeswoman for U-Haul. I'm hanging up my shirt!

I don't know why I was surprised at Sydney's newfound love, given that she had given me a diamond ring after knowing me for just over a month. As I looked at her, I realized that there, standing before me, was the world's most ridiculous person! I playfully punched her in the shoulder as if to say, "Good for you, you old son of a gun!" It didn't come out that way. How it really sounded was, "Well then, what're you crying about? You should be happy. You're in love. You deserve to be happy. Enjoy it and stop crying over me!"

"It's just hard. I really wanted things to work out with us." The broken record just skipped again. As she dried her tears, she said, "I just hope we can be friends."

Oh, here we go! The friend thing.

I have never understood the fascination of people, especially lesbians, with insisting on forcing a friendship after a breakup. Certainly, sometimes a friendship can be salvaged, but it is not mandatory. Sydney was the queen of wanting to remain inextricably tied to her exes. She was able to trap Casey, but I refused to fall into the same snare! Did she think we were all going to be friends and sit around a campfire together and sing kumbaya? I'm not the camping type! For a second, I considered placating her by assuring her that we would remain close but decided to be honest instead. "Sydney, I wish you well. I really do. But I doubt we'll be friends. We weren't friends before and I doubt that we're going to be best buds now."

Apparently, Sydney was appalled at my "unmitigated gall." How could I not *cherish* her friendship? She seemed flabbergasted that I didn't want her to remain in my life. "Are you serious?" She started trembling. I couldn't tell if it was from anger or sadness.

"I'm just being honest. It's not like our paths are gonna cross," I said, matter-of-factly.

Trembling with anger, she screamed, "What're you talking about?! You intentionally placed yourself in my world. You're at the tournament! With a badge! In the players' area! You don't expect that our paths will cross?"

Okay, good point. I guess our paths will cross once Casey and I go public.

But I refused to concede.

She continued, "You knew I'd be here and that you'd see me."

"That's true. I figured I'd run into you. But I didn't come here to see you. I came here to see some tennis and hang out with Casey. I ran into you by accident."

"Oh, that's just great! I don't know why you even bothered coming. The only reason Casey's paying any attention to you is because she has no one else to hang out with."

No one else to hang out with! Mmm hmm. Here's a suggestion: go fuck yourself!

I wanted so badly to drop my little bomb on her head just to prove her wrong. I laughed at the thought of her chocking on a mushroom cloud of smoke but decided there was no need for such heavy artillery.

Instead, I shook my head, snickered and said, "Oh, okay. I suspected that, but thanks for clearing that up for me. Do you have any other pearls of wisdom to impart to me, or can I go so I can hang out with the person who has no one else to hang out with?"

"It's not like she considers you one of her good friends," she said, smugly.

Sydney was more clueless than Alicia Silverstone was in the movie *Clueless!*

"She doesn't?" I deadpanned, knowing my blank stare would further incense her.

"No! She doesn't!" she spat.

"Sydney, I don't really care what you think. Go turn on a television because there's breaking news you apparently are not aware of— you're not my girlfriend and I don't give a shit what you say or what you think!" Now I was annoyed and I had a feeling fists were going to start flying. "I didn't care when we were together and I certainly don't care now! What a relief that you don't have to concern yourself with who I hang out with anymore or if someone's hanging out with me because they have no one else to hang out with! Isn't that great?"

Wham! TKO!

As I was about to continue pummeling her, I stopped myself. It was pointless to go round for round with Sydney since in the end, I had already won anyway. Besides, I didn't want my anger to be misconstrued as bitterness— that was the *last thing* I wanted.

I stopped the pettiness before it escalated to pure ugliness. The fact was that I didn't want things to be nasty or uncomfortable between Sydney and me. I just didn't want her in my life anymore. So I extended an olive branch. Golda Meir would have been proud. "Listen, Sydney, this is stupid. Let's not dwell on the past and make this any more difficult than it already is. When I said that you and I probably wouldn't be friends, I just meant that we probably won't be in each other's lives on a daily basis."

She couldn't argue with me. She smiled that crooked, shiny smile that I was so glad I never had to wake up to again. Of course, she had to deliver one last shot to the dead horse. "You know, I wanted to be with you. I really wanted for us to work. I wish you would've been able to give me more. I just wanted a little bit of you."

A 'little bit' of me, my ass!

"Sydney, I know, and I'm sorry. Now stop being so serious and go get your damn iPod so you can give it to your new girlfriend. Isn't that your standard girlfriend present?" She didn't answer but just laughed and rolled her eyes.

And I thought we moved fast! It took her months to give me one and only a few days to hand the thespian the $400 toy.

Before Sydney could justify her outrageously ostentatious gift giving, Casey came traipsing down the hall toward us. She approached with hesitation and gave Sydney the weather report. Suddenly, it was pouring outside and the courts were closed.

Sydney turned and walked away. "Good. I wanna get the hell outta here anyway." When she was halfway down the hall, she lifted her racket over her head and accompanied her wave good-bye with a sarcastic remark, "Later, lovebirds!" She continued toward the parking lot without looking back.

Casey froze. I could tell by the paranoid look on her face that she was concerned about Sydney's remark.

"Before you get yourself all wound up, STOP! She doesn't know anything. If she did, she would have put that racket through both our heads. She's not accusing us of anything. She's just being an idiot. Let's just go before she comes back."

I left with the woman who was just hanging out with me because she had no one else to hang out with.

Whatever, Sydney!

Once we were behind the closed doors of Casey's room, we embraced and Casey said, "You really have no idea how happy I am that you're here. Today made me think of the future— of us together at the tournaments and in life and it made me so happy."

"Casey, I love being here with you and I can't wait…" I stopped, mid-sentence because her cell phone interrupted me.

"Shit. It's Trish." The smile immediately disappeared from her face. "I have to take this. She's been trying to call me since this morning and I haven't spoken to her all day. I'm sorry. I won't be long."

I wanted to throw her phone out the window. The game was over and I was ready to demand that Casey come clean with Trish. She saw me roll my eyes as she answered the phone. She mouthed, "I'm sorry," and led me by the hand to the couch. Before we even sat down, her tone changed from light to heavy. My annoyance got derailed when my phone vibrated with a new text message. It was from Angie: *Hey girls. For the record, Sydney's a motherfucker, and ya'll look much better together. See you at the courts tomorrow.* I smiled and laughed quietly.

Mine was the only smile in the room. Casey's face was plastered with anguish. I could only hear one side of the conversation, but I knew that it wasn't going to end positively. From Casey's responses to Trish, I realized that I was, yet again, the topic of their conversation. Shocker! Trish had called to grill Casey about her "friendship" with me. She didn't understand why I was in Miami. Further, she didn't understand why Casey was spending time with me. She had no idea that I was sitting right next to Casey on the couch, much less that I would be staying with Casey during the tournament. They went around and around in circles. Trish accused and Casey argued.

Out of the blue, Casey reached her limit. She removed her hand from mine, leaned forward, rested her forehead in her hand, took a deep breath and confirmed Trish's suspicions. "Okay. You're right, I have feelings for Steph."

Holy shit! Did she really just say what I think she said? She did! She just came clean about loving me! This is the best news I've heard in weeks!

For the third time in one day, I was shocked and speechless. My heart almost stopped beating when I heard Casey confess her true feelings for me (but not our relationship) to Trish.

The conversation took a turn for the worse and suddenly tears came streaming down Casey's face. Trish had bullied Casey into admitting her feelings for me but, clearly, she was not prepared for the confirmation that she received. Trish had a no-holds-barred meltdown. The call continued for almost two hours and I sat, helplessly, on the couch as the woman whom I loved took a verbal beating from her supposed best friend. Casey had wanted Trish for so long but had been rejected time and time again because Trish insisted that she was not gay and could never be involved in a sexual relationship with a woman.

Casey had finally accepted the reality that she and Trish would never be together and had moved on and fallen in love. Trish, apparently, never thought that Casey would move on or that she would love anyone else besides her and was acting like a jealous ex-girlfriend. She didn't want Casey, but she also didn't want anyone else to have her either.

As I listened to the conversation, I could now hear gasps of desperation in Trish's voice through Casey's phone. I heard Trish tell Casey that she felt as if her world were falling apart. She couldn't bear the thought of losing her place in Casey's life or that she was to be replaced by me. She even asked if I were going to take her place at Wimbledon this year! She was devastated and Casey was distraught that she was the cause of Trish's pain. I couldn't help but think *both* of their reactions were a bit extreme.

I remember the pain I felt when Paige and I broke up. I was so sad that I didn't think I could breathe. Casey and Trish were both crying— more like sobbing and wailing. It was the kind of sadness and desperation I had felt when I closed the door behind Paige for the last time. It was awful. I thanked God I was not in Trish's shoes. Losing Casey would break my heart, too. The thought of it, even for a second, was unbearable, so I quickly dismissed the idea. I didn't really understand what Trish thought she was losing just because Casey's flame for her had burned out. I was sorry Trish was sad, but…let's say it together one more time— *she's not gay!*

I waited patiently for Casey to terminate the conversation (as well as her dysfunctional relationship with Trish). At long last, the conversation ended. Casey was still in hysterics and crying. I put my arms around her and hugged her tightly. "Cutie, I know this is hard right now, but everything will be okay. I promise. Trish's your friend. It will be okay." She buried her face in my shoulder and shook as she cried. As her tears soaked through my shirt, I smiled indulgently as if to say, "Don't worry that you're in my arms sobbing over another woman. It's okay. Really."

When her crying stopped, she dried her tears and looked at me. "Are you sure this is what you want? Please tell me this is what you want— that I'm what you want, because I've just destroyed the person I've cared the most about in my life, until you. Please tell me you're not going anywhere— that you're not gonna change your mind."

I looked steadily into Casey's eyes. "Of course this is what I want and I'm not going anywhere. I love you. I want nothing more than for us to be together."

"Well, she knows now. The game is over and we're free to be together. We can pursue a relationship now."

Instead of hiring a band to play in a parade to celebrate the fantastic news, I spent the next several hours consoling Casey. I knew that in time, Casey would see that her admission to Trish was a good thing and that everything would be fine. Once Trish recovered from the shock that only God knows why she was feeling, she and Casey would be able to put their friendship back together. As the hours passed, Casey realized that she had done what was best for her, Trish and me. After all, she was in love with me, despite her weird addiction to Trish.

I desperately wanted to take away Casey's pain, even if only for a few minutes. We got into bed and tenderly made love. Just before I was about to climax, Casey's cell phone rang and she abruptly stopped what she was doing to answer the phone.

Un-fucking-believable!

Casey rolled off me as if a fire alarm had signaled ordering everyone to evacuate the building. I think smoke was coming from my ears, so it was possible that a fire alarm was about to sound. I exhaled as quietly as I could and bit my lip in frustration, both emotionally and sexually. It was almost midnight and round two of the evening's main event, the Trish versus Casey sparring match, was about to start. I would rather have impaled myself on one of Casey's tennis rackets than listen to them so I rolled onto my side and put a pillow over my head.

I dozed in and out of consciousness and Casey gasped for air between sobs. After another two-hour conversation, which could more appropriately be described as a tearful snot fest, I awoke when I heard Casey say good-bye and snap her phone shut. She sat up beside me crying and sniffling like a wounded groundhog that had just been mauled by a foxhound. Just as I had managed to calm her, a text message rolled in. Casey's eyes were so swollen from all the tears she'd shed and could barely read the text Trish had sent. I got up and filled a bag with ice from the freezer in the kitchen just outside the bedroom and returned to gently help hold the ice on her eyes as she continued to cry. Between sobs and sniffles, she told me that during the second phone call Trish had asked her if it were "too late."

"Too late for what?" I asked.

"She told me that she thought she could do it," Casey said as she blew her nose into a Kleenex.

I was really confused. "Do what?"

"That she could be gay and be with me. She wanted to know if it was too late."

What?! I was silent as she continued to cry.

And then, through her tears she said, "I told her it was. I told her it's too late, because I'm already invested with you. I told her it was too late. She told me she can give me everything I always wanted her to give me and I told her it was too late." The tears continued to stream out of her eyes as I held her.

Another text came in. Casey read it and then repeated it aloud. *"Somehow I will accept this and support you and Steph."* She put her head in her hands and sobbed even more. I held her in my arms.

Jesus Christ, I know this is hard, but how much longer is this gonna go on?! And what the hell was Trish thinking when she told Casey that she could be gay?! That girl is no more gay than I am a card-carrying Republican! Is she crazy? Trish, gay? No fucking way! I really can't take much more of this.

As I wiped Casey's tears, one last text came in. *I love you, baby girl. Good-bye.*

Baby girl? Whatever. I'm not touching that one!

Trish's last text sent Casey even further over the edge.

Oh, God, this straight bitch is an even bigger drama queen than I ever imagined!

I thought Casey was getting up to grab more Kleenex from the bathroom. But instead, she walked over to the window and opened the shade that had shielded us from the rest of the world. She sniffled as she got back into bed and said, "Stephie, now that Trish knows, we don't have to hide anymore."

I replayed Casey's words in my mind. *"Now that Trish knows, we don't have to hide anymore."* Does that mean that we were finally going to go public with our relationship? What else could it mean? English is my first language and a language I know well. I dissected the sentence every way I could and came to the same conclusion each time— Casey and I were finally going to be together and not just behind covered windows and closed doors.

22

The drop shot

The next morning, Casey woke before me. I felt her get out of bed but was too exhausted from the night before to drag my body up from its comfortable position. I was still trying to decide if what had happened was a dream or if it had all really taken place. As I replayed the night before in my mind, Casey lowered herself on top of me. I opened my eyes and met her gaze as she said, "Now that we can openly be together, we have to pick an anniversary date that we can actually tell people, because we can't let them know how long we've *really* been together."

It wasn't all a dream. Yawning, I asked, "Are you okay? I know last night was really hard for you with Trish."

"She's really upset and will be for a while. I hate that I hurt her so badly, but I have moved on. I know she could never be gay— I've known it all along. I was just chasing a dream with her. I had to tell her. I love you."

Casey smiled, rolled off me and swung her feet around to the floor.
"Where are you going?"
"I have to take your ex-girlfriend to breakfast for her birthday."
Oh, yeah. Sydney's birthday. Oh, happy day!

I had forgotten that today was the thirtieth anniversary of Sydney's birth. To me, it was just the second day of April. Casey had taken Sydney to breakfast every year on her birthday. It was one of the traditions with Sydney that, for some reason, she had not abandoned. As long as I didn't have to eat a bowl of porridge with the big bad bear on her benchmark birthday, I wasn't about to insist that Casey break the tradition now.

After getting dressed, Casey walked back over to me and reached for my hand. "I'll be back in an hour and then we'll go to the courts and have the rest of the day to be together. And after that, we'll have the rest of our lives together." She kissed me passionately and rushed to meet Sydney.

Attempting to return to the land of slumber to no avail, I threw on my clothes and excitedly skipped into the living room. I poured myself coffee and bounced across the room to the couch. I was the most relaxed I'd been in weeks. Finally, all the lies and deception had come to an end and all my stealth maneuvers had paid off. I felt like the rest of my life would begin the second Casey returned from breakfast.

As the morning dragged on, it seemed like Casey had been gone for a lifetime. Sipping my coffee, I looked at my watch and realized she'd only been gone for an hour and a half. I sent her a quick text telling her that I missed her. Normally, she responded to my texts within seconds. But five minutes lapsed and no response came. Ten minutes passed and still no response. *That's weird.* I sent another quick text asking if everything were okay. Again, several minutes passed and no response. Trying to quell my neuroticism, I couldn't help but be a tiny bit worried. I wondered if perhaps she had come clean to Sydney and, Miss-I'm-In-Love-With-a-Thespian hadn't taken it so well. When there were no more pops left in my knuckles, I sat on my hands and anxiously waited for Casey to return.

Two hours had passed when I heard a key in the door. My concern vanished immediately and elation filled my face. Casey entered and after taking one look at her for a nanosecond, all of my anxiety returned and the elation drained from my face. Something had happened. I flashed back to my earlier thought and decided that Casey had definitely told Sydney about us. There was an awkward silence as she walked over to me. She approached me with her head held down, but I could see that she'd been crying. She didn't sit next to me. I was frozen on the edge of the couch and she stood just inches from me, intently focused on her feet. After a few seconds, she broke the awkward silence. "I told Sydney…and Trish's flying down here from Boston tonight to be with me."

Be with you? As in be with you?

I felt like someone had just hit me in the stomach with a two-by-four. I had no way of seeing it coming. Casey stood with her arms folded across her chest. With slumped shoulders, she was still looking down at the floor, unable to make eye contact with me. I stared at her as I replayed her words in my mind to ensure that I truly understood the harsh reality of what was happening. Employing yoga technique, in an effort to calm down, I breathed air through my nose as deeply as possible and gently let it spread into my lungs. Summoning all of my strength, my shallow voice shook as I forced out the words, "What? What did you say?"

"Steph, I'm so sorry. I broke down at breakfast. I told Sydney I had feelings for you and she flipped out. She said she'd never speak to me again if I got involved with you. And Trish called and begged me to let her come down here. She told me that I owed it to her to give her a chance…to give us a chance. And she's right. I've loved her since I can remember and I have to give her a chance— I have to give us a chance to see if we can work. She's coming down here tonight and we're gonna figure things out over the weekend."

Steph. For the first time since Tokyo, she called me "Steph," and not "Stephie." *Oh, God.*

With a loss of words, the immediate shock, even worse than what I had felt the day before, sent me into a tailspin. My stomach dropped, goose bumps broke out and nausea began to overtake me. I tried to hold back the tears but couldn't. Attempting to speak, my mouth froze as I fumbled to find words to fill a sentence. Casey just stood there, silently. The words that had so cavalierly come out of her mouth cut right through my skin to my heart and all that was left for her to do was await my reaction. One second I was the happiest person in the world and the next, every ounce of happiness had been vacuumed out of me.

Finally, I found some words and pushed them past the lump in my throat. "I don't understand. I thought you were in love with me."

She stammered, "I am…I was. I…I don't know. I'm so confused. The only thing I know is I…I have to give her a chance. I have to."

"So, what are you saying? We're over?" There was a catch in my voice. As these words came out of my mouth, I could feel my heart beating in my head. The rest of the world immediately went silent. I stared through Casey as snapshots of our time together invaded my thoughts. I couldn't stop the slideshow of vignettes— memories and fantasies— one after the other in slow motion, each one separated by a sound my in head that echoed the snap of a camera. *Starbucks in Tokyo. Snap. Our first kiss. Snap. The UPS man. Snap. Casey's smile. Snap. Making love. Snap. Waking up to each other. Snap. Sitting courtside watching Casey play tennis. Snap. Holding hands. Snap. Uncontrollable laughter. Snap. Walking on the streets of Boston. Snap. Happiness. Snap. Palm Springs. Snap. Wimbledon.* There was no snap after Wimbledon. I could not get the image of being with Casey at Wimbledon as my girlfriend out of my mind. I pictured green grass, white lines, white clothing and bright white smiles— and then Trish popped into my head, sitting courtside. The image was frozen in my mind and suddenly I feared that I was going to regurgitate my morning's coffee.

Casey's words broke the silence and stopped my slideshow. Still incapable of making eye contact with me, she shook her head and said, "We have to be…for now. I have to do this. Please just give me the weekend to hear her out and I promise to call you after she leaves on Monday. I'm sorry, Steph."

I had no idea how I had been thrust from my private paradise directly into the twilight zone in the blink of an eye. Instantly, I was devoid of thought. I was a mental vacuum. I couldn't have spoken even if I had wanted to. For the first time in my life, I couldn't put up a fight. I could not believe this was happening to me. Two hours earlier, I had complete control of my life and my emotions. I had even been thankful the night before when Casey was on the phone with Trish that I was not the one on the receiving end of heartbreakingly bad news. It seemed as if I could feel my heart separating as it shattered. I hoped that Casey would recant what she had said, but I knew she had somehow passed the point of no return by the time she had left the breakfast table. Within one hundred and twenty minutes, she had convinced herself that Trish, and not I, was worth taking a risk for. There was nothing left to say.

Adding insult to injury, Casey had allotted less than half an hour for me to ingest and digest this news.

She had just delivered news that was as crushing as a grand piano falling from the sky onto my head as she was on her way back out the door to tennis practice.

She organized her racket bag and I sat in silence. Tears streamed from my eyes blurring my vision and all that Casey could do was turn a blind eye to my devastation. I don't know why it shocked me since in the face of conflict she habitually looked the other way.

After robotically uttering "I'm sorry" countless times, Casey picked up her bags and walked toward the door. I tried to resist my urge to run after her, but I couldn't. She turned and this time directed her solemn eyes at mine. She made a heartfelt apology before insisting that it was time to leave. I desperately wrapped my arms around her. I was blanketed by an avalanche of sadness. I had just lost the woman I loved from the depths of my soul and with every fiber of my being. My body was shaking from sadness. I loosened my grip to kiss her good-bye. Her soft lips had become familiar to me and my stomach churned at the thought of them becoming foreign. As we kissed, I still hoped that it was not truly a good-bye, but I feared that somehow it would be.

The door closed softly but sent icy shivers down my spine. I returned to the couch, where just minutes before, I had been delivered the incredibly devastating news. In a state of disbelief, I sat in silence staring at the wall, almost catatonically. I remembered my conversation with Trish in Boston when she boasted that she was eager to "start dating heavily" because her "clock is, like, seriously ticking." That straight, jealous bitch had just stolen my girlfriend, and Casey didn't even fight for me. She dropped me without even the slightest hesitation. Unable to even lift a hand to my face, warm tears streamed down my cheeks and dripped onto the floor.

When I was able to garner the strength to get up, I got dressed and packed my things. I closed my bag and wandered like a zombie into the living room gazing at the suite I was supposed to be sharing with Casey for our first tournament together as girlfriends. I knew I would not be coming back to that room, so I placed my key on the table. I reached behind my neck and unclasped the necklace Casey had given me. Running my thumb across the inscription on the pendant, I thought of the hope the necklace had brought me. I clenched the warm metal tightly and then gently placed it near the key on the table. Walking toward the door, I took a deep breath and dried my tears. I stopped with my hand on the doorknob and turned around, once more. I stared blankly at the room and then painfully turned to leave. Out of habit, I looked in both directions before I exited into the empty hallway. The coast was clear. I departed without a soul knowing of my presence, exactly as Casey had demanded while we had been together.

I was dying inside but somehow stopped the tears until I got into my car. The second I sat down, my brave front crumbled and I surrendered to my emotions. I sat in the parking lot for well over an hour before I was convinced that I could safely drive back to my mother's house. The drive should have taken only four hours, but frequent pit stops to dry my tears more than doubled my driving time. As I drove west across Alligator Alley, I tried to make sense of what had happened. I couldn't figure out how something that had seemed so right could go so wrong. I hated the thought of having to bottle up my emotions and the love that Casey and I shared and lock them away in a secret hiding place visited only by tears and sorrow. I tortured myself by replaying conversations in my mind about the life that Casey and I had planned together— about the fantasy we had indulged ourselves with. As I drove, I could still smell Casey on my skin and I dreaded taking a shower and washing her off me, because somehow it would make her absence seem even more real.

I made it back to my mom's house and convinced her that my swollen face was the result of allergies and not a broken heart. If I had admitted the real reason for my red eyes and sniffles, it was quite possible that she would have killed Casey with her own two hands. No one, and I mean *no one,* hurts her baby without having to answer to her. I highly doubt that she would have awarded me a gold star for my part in the whole fiasco, either. Once again, the "Don't Ask, Don't Tell" policy was in effect and I hid in the shower to cry so that the water would muffle my sobs.

I didn't have the strength to call the airline and change my ticket. Blessedly, Melissa did.

The next morning, I boarded a plane and flew back to LA to pick up the pieces of my life. As easily as Casey had come into my life, she was gone. This wasn't my game; it was Casey's. I had dutifully played by all her rules and just when I could taste victory, she handed my cherished prize to someone I didn't even know was on the court. I wished that I could mute the words that traveled through my mind as the plane sped down the runway, "Game, set and match, Trash Avalon."

The agony of defeat

"Ring dammit, ring!" I commanded my phone. When it didn't, I checked the settings to ensure that it had not somehow been inadvertently switched to silent. Then, of course, I'd check to make sure that the volume of the ringer was sufficiently loud enough so that even my neighbors would hear if my phone rang— which it did, but not because Casey was calling. I repeated this routine several times per day. More accurately, several times per hour.

Perhaps I'm the only one surprised that I didn't hear from Casey after her initial weekend with Trish. I was devastated and missed her constantly, but despite my sadness, I had to figure out a way to live without Casey. I had no choice. I had done a number of stupid things when I was with her and if what happened in Miami wasn't a wake-up call, I don't know what is. I told myself I couldn't sit around forever and wait for her to call me and let me know that her weekend with Trish was a success and that the two of them were living happily ever after. Maybe Casey went to Baskin-Robbins a few too many times as a kid and got used to the idea of asking for a lick of whatever flavor tickled her fancy at that particular moment and then tossing it into the trash if it didn't meet with her approval. Rocky Road, I am not!

But still, I could not stop myself from hoping she'd call.

The phone call from Casey came six days later, in the middle of the afternoon. When the phone rang, I barely shifted on the couch, where I had taken semi-permanent residency (the other half of my time being spent in my bed), to look at the caller ID. Seeing her name on the display had the exact effect on me that I had anticipated— rushed excitement, followed by immense fear. By the third ring, I had sufficiently calmed myself and answered without any hint of eagerness in my voice. I greeted her flatly with a simple, "Hi." It felt unnatural to answer her call without enthusiasm in my voice.

"Hi, Steph..." Her voice was somber, as if the words "I'm so sorry to inform you" were about to come out of her mouth.

Still Steph. Not back to Stephie. I felt the knot forming in my stomach. When I saw her name on the caller ID, I had deluded myself into thinking, for a nanosecond, that something good was going to come from the conversation. I now knew I was wrong.

"Steph, I'm sorry I haven't called sooner. I just needed to be sure before I called you. And now I am. Trish and I decided to attempt a relationship together." She sheepishly delivered the news to me, as if her soft tone would somehow lessen the crushing impact of her decision.

It had taken Casey almost one full week to gather the strength to pick up the phone and tell me that she and Trish were now an item. Oh really? As if I couldn't have already guessed it! I don't have fortune telling abilities, but I figured that Trish was going to arrive in Miami armed with all the perfectly correct answers to Casey's prayers that had caused calluses on her knees since they'd met. She would tell Casey anything and everything she wanted to hear and Casey would be an easy sell. I'd be willing to bet the bank that Trish could have sold Casey some swampland in the Sahara without breaking a sweat.

Holding the phone away from my cheek, I quietly wiped the warm tears rolling down my face onto the sleeve of the pajamas that had replaced the rest of my wardrobe. Hearing the news from Casey was like a dagger through my heart all over again. Although I knew she could never take back what she had done in Miami, a part of me was hoping she'd come to her senses and call me to beg for my forgiveness and tell me that she'd made the biggest mistake of her life.

Trying to salvage even a shred of my dignity, I steadied my voice. "Casey, you need to do what you need to do. I'm not mad at you. I will miss you."

Truly, I wasn't angry at her, but I was undeniably devastated. I wondered if she noticed that I called her "Casey" and not "cutie," much like how she had called me "Steph" and not "Stephie." And if so, did the formality hurt her the way it did me?

After a long sigh, she told me she'd miss me too and I hung up the phone. The conversation lasted one minute and forty-nine seconds. I set the phone down on my lap, hoping she'd call right back. For half an hour I stared at my silent phone, feeling completely defeated and utterly empty inside. Casey wasn't going to call back. Realizing she was definitely gone, I sobbed uncontrollably.

Call me crazy, but I never thought Casey and I would end, much less end the way we did. I hoped for more from her. I expected more from her. "That day" in Miami, Casey had done the thing I found most inexcusable— she had been reckless with my emotions. Yes, I had been reckless with Sydney's emotions, but I had never pretended to love her. Although some people probably wouldn't agree, there is a difference. I'm sure everyone can agree that what goes around comes around and it had just come around to me. Casey had just handed me my ass— and not on a silver platter, but on a cheap paper plate. She had shattered my world, destroyed my trust and broke my heart. Worst of all, she had broken my smile— the same smile that had found a permanent place on my face since she had come into my life.

Two days after Casey called, I received a text message from Trish. *Oh, she must be texting me to see how I'm doing and tell me she's sorry and that she knows how hard this must be for me.* I was swamped with anger when I read the message: *I know everything that happened between Casey and you. I only ask that you respect us and keep your distance. Good-bye, Steph.*

Certain that my jaw crashing to the ground had just punctured the hardwood floor, I stopped myself in mid-motion from throwing my phone through the wall, not wanting to add another hole to be patched. I was alone in my condo but screamed out loud. "Is she fucking kidding me?! Keep my distance! I've done nothing *but* keep my distance since I left Miami! That fucking neurotic, jealous bitch swoops in and pretends to be gay and steals my girlfriend so she doesn't lose her best friend and her access to all the tennis tournaments and she has the nerve to tell me to keep my distance! Fuck you! You pathetic piece of shit! Oh, fuck this! I need this shit like I need a hole in my head! They can have each other!" I think I screamed until it occurred to me that my neighbors could hear me talking to myself.

I finally sat back down on the couch and inhaled deeply several times, trying to slow my pulse. My heart was beating wildly and I was gasping for air, as if I'd just sprinted a marathon. It was the most exercise I'd had in weeks.

The hits kept coming. A few days after I had recovered from Trish's surprise text message, the phone call I had been expecting arrived. I considered screening the call but figured that avoidance tactics would only postpone my misery. I nervously picked up the phone when I saw Sydney's number appear on the caller ID. I answered cautiously and got ready to dodge the ball of fury that I was certain was going to be heaved at me. I had visions of Bad Sydney verbally bashing linesmen and chair umpires and figured my lashing would be ten times worse.

On my guard, I sheepishly muttered a simple, "Hello."

"Have you been avoiding me? Shouldn't I be the one mad at you?" Her tone was rather jovial.

I rechecked the caller ID to make sure that it was, in fact, Sydney Foster calling.

"I hope you're at least sorry for what you did," she insisted, half-snickering.

Yep, it was Sydney calling alright! The last thing I needed was for her to make me feel guilty. I already have one Jewish mother who does a really good job of that and I didn't need another one!

She deepened her voice. "I really can't believe you two…"

Shit, here it comes.

I felt the familiar knot forming in my stomach. "Sydney, what we did was wrong and I'm truly sorry for hurting you. I don't know what else to say to you." I had rehearsed my apology in my head a thousand times and had whittled it down to a succinct few sentences. Let's be honest, the bottom line is that things weren't working between Sydney and me and I should have been truthful with myself and with her earlier. I got caught up in something I was not proud of and all I could say to Sydney was "I'm sorry." How many different ways could I admit that I fucked up?

I suddenly heard Melissa beginning to count in my head, "Well, let me see, sugar…one, two, three…" *Don't answer that! It was a rhetorical question! I mean it. Stop counting!* Melissa was at number eight when Sydney's voice overpowered the patronizing one in my head.

"I appreciate your apology. I think you two are shits, but I have a lot of forgiveness in my heart. Once I love, I love forever. I'm sure I'll be okay with this in time and we can be friends."

I thought we had addressed the "friendship thing" when she trapped me in the hallway in Miami. I wasn't interested in pursuing a friendship with Sydney, but I truly was sorry for doing what I did to her. It was never a game to me, but I had been playing by someone's rules the entire time and Sydney became one of the victims. If I were Sydney, I wouldn't cross the street to put either Casey or me out if we were on fire.

Thankfully, the thespian clicked in on Sydney's other line and cut short the phone call that was beginning to make me not only uncomfortable but irritated. Sydney's last words to me were, "We'll talk sometime again in the future. Take care of yourself and go find some happiness. But stay away from Bonnie!" She cackled as she said good-bye.

I clicked off the phone, happy to be in one piece. I was thankful for the thespian at that moment. Sydney was too intoxicated with her new thespian ambrosia to be concerned with me, but my intuitive gut told me she would eventually reach sobriety.

* * *

It didn't take long for the news to spread about the Sydney/Stephanie/Casey love triangle. Once Sydney had uncovered detail after gory detail about my "affair" with Casey, she told anyone who would listen. Not surprisingly, she pounced on the opportunity to be the victim of Casey's betrayal twice in less than two years. Casey's private life was exposed and she and I were the objects of the latest locker-room fodder. Never one to shy from the spotlight, this wasn't quite the type of attention I craved.

I heard from my other friends on the Tour that Casey was walking around the tournaments shrouded with embarrassment, as people talked about our affair. Every time I heard it referred to as an affair, I flinched and saw in my mind the flashing lights of that seedy motel sign that I had imagined the day I got back from Tokyo. The image made me feel so filthy that all I wanted to do was check out.

While Casey dragged her head in shame about the affair and glowed about her straight girlfriend, I spent almost an entire month cloistered in my condo, crying everyday over the loss of her. I took a sabbatical from selling real estate and concentrated my efforts full-time on mending my broken heart. I employed all the usual breakup tactics step-by-step that are surely codified in some breakup manual. Step 1: Take refuge in Ben & Jerry's ice cream (especially Chunky Monkey and Chubby Hubby). Step 2: Talk to the phone and will it to ring (both home and cell). Step 3: Compile lists of "sharp object" music to create a "Sad CD" (overplaying Air Supply's "I'm All Outta Love" and Phil Collins' "Against All Odds"). Step 4: Play Sad CD over and over while repeating Steps 1 and 2.

I was determined never to be hurt by another woman, so I eventually did the only logical thing that a heartbroken lesbian could do— I went on a date with a man and tried to drown my sorrows in testosterone. I figured that Sydney was as close as a woman could get to being like a man, so maybe the transition to the real thing would be rather seamless (although my "boy-toy" would probably have looked more natural in a Hollister Co. skirt than Sydney did). But, alas, my walk on the wild heterosexual side was a flash in the pan, lasting all of one-and-a-half hours.

Nearly four weeks after I had left Miami, I still woke awaiting the day that I would not have to fight tears of sadness at the thought of Casey or the mention of her name. Even though Casey was now a part of my past and daily thoughts of her were becoming less and less, I hate to admit that she still occupied a place in my mind. I was, after all, only human. Unlike her, I did not have the ability to turn my head and instantly shut off my feelings and not look back. I despised that I wondered how she was and where she was. But still, I succumbed to my curiosity and went online occasionally to see which tournaments she was entered in and how she was progressing in them. Somehow, knowing where she was and how she was doing made her seem like less of a stranger. And for some reason, that was still important to me.

Since our breakup, Casey had basically played one tournament per week. Since I left Miami "that morning," Casey's tennis had suffered in much the same way that Sydney's had the year before. Sydney's tennis, on the other hand, flourished and she was inching closer and closer back to Number 1 (the lesbian thespian must have turned out to be a better good-luck charm than I). Sometimes, I can find joy in others' misfortunes, but as much as I would have liked to, I didn't cheer at Casey's numerous defeats. I was heartbroken, not bitter. I knew that the only explanation for her poor performance on the court was that her life off the court was not all she'd imagined it would be. Go figure. Casey's life off the court always spilled onto the court. She was struggling with her game because her personal life was draining all her energy. Her tennis was already in the toilet and I knew that it was only a matter of time before her relationship with Trish followed.

The days I spent welling up over my broken heart were also spent analyzing my experience and trying to put it in perspective. For one month, I had been asking myself how this could have happened to me. I must have sounded like a broken record demanding how and why this was happening and insisting that I didn't understand. It never occurred to me that it happened because, among other things, I had given my faith and my heart to someone with an insatiable appetite for new, shiny trophies whether they were titles or people. Casey and I spoke the same language and were raised in the same country. But with us, there was an intersection of extremely diverse cultures. The more I thought about the role I played, the more disgusted I became. I was amazed at how my capacity for reckless abandon had paralyzed me and prevented me from admitting that love is about compromise, but not comprising yourself, which is exactly what I had done.

On a day when I was wallowing in an especially high dose of self-pity, I somehow managed to peel myself off the couch and clothe my body in something other than pajamas. Wearing jeans and a T-shirt that felt curiously foreign on my body, I dragged myself out my front door.

Ironically, I was sipping a latte at Starbucks, lost in thought about my pathetic life when a man who looked to be in his eighties approached me and said, "Young lady, you're staring at a beautiful day. Why is a pretty girl like you not smiling?"

His question was innocuous and he looked like a sweet old man, but I really was in no mood to humor him with a smile. My response was surly. "Sorry. I just don't feel like I have much to smile about."

His smiled tenderly and said, "Not much is much more than nothing at all."

I said nothing in return, hoping that my silence would dissuade him from proselytizing about how life is short and that there is always something to smile about. I was determined to sit with my frown on my face and dwell on my misery. But, as I watched him walk away, the words that he spoke barely louder than a whisper echoed loudly in my mind. I realized he was right.

I finished my coffee, reflecting on the life that Casey had chosen. An image of Casey and Trish popped into my head. My ride on the roller coaster was over and theirs was just beginning. I thought of the inevitable demise of their fantasy and a chuckle escaped my lips. I heard myself laugh for the first time in weeks. Smiling, I was finally bouncing back.

24

The final "Slam"

For my mom's tenth annual fiftieth birthday (sorry Mom, but one of us had to admit it!), my dad surprised her with a trip for two to Europe— the surprise being that I would accompany her. My dad's not much of a traveler and always jokes, "I have to plan the trips and pay for them, but I don't have to go on them." We were scheduled to be in Paris during the first week of the French Open, the second Grand Slam of the year. I cannot claim that being in Paris during the French Open was a coincidence, but I can promise that I am not a glutton for punishment. My dad had finalized the itinerary the previous fall when I was still enamored with Sydney. The original plan was to enjoy the first week of the French Open in Paris with my mother and the second week with my girlfriend (that was his birthday present to me). But now thoughts of being in the same city as both Casey and Sydney made me uneasy. The mere possibility of running into Casey on the streets of Paris made me nauseous. Carrying an airsickness bag around with me did cross my mind— just in case. Canceling the trip was not an option, but foregoing tennis was. In order to preserve my emotional well-being I decided not to attend the French Open.

A few days after my mother and I had arrived in Paris, I took a break from the musées and galleries and met Ribi for a drink at a bar just off the Champs Elysées. Ribi had won her doubles match earlier in the day and had just come back from Roland Garros. We met to celebrate her first-round victory. We ordered two Heinekens, but before we could make a toast to her success, Ribi received a text message. She rolled her eyes and told me the message was from Sydney, asking if she could stop by and join us for a beer. Certain things— particularly gossip— have a way of very quickly breezing through the locker room, so it didn't surprise me that my arrival was not a closely guarded secret. I knew I had pushed my luck meeting Ribi— especially since both Sydney and Casey were staying at a hotel nearby.

Sydney was like a bad penny— she just kept turning up!

It seemed odd to me that Sydney would waste any time or energy worrying about me or anything having to do with me when she was so in love with the thespian. But this is Sydney Foster we're talking about, so I don't know why I was surprised. A part of me felt sorry for her. Ribi told me that Sydney talked about her new girlfriend incessantly and constantly strutted around the tournaments directing people to the thespian's website and talked about how in love she was. She should have been well on her way to forgetting about me. I was doing my best to erase most of the time I had shared with Sydney and I wished she would pay me the same courtesy. Unfortunately, I knew that hoping for Sydney to pull a disappearing act was wishful thinking.

As we were talking and sipping our beers, I spotted a familiar face that I was not altogether happy to see. I felt an insane nervousness overtake me. I definitely thought I was going to need that airsickness bag— and fast! Casey was walking right toward me. Unprepared to speak with her, I tried to ignore her presence. Unfortunately, I was trapped. A few seconds later, she was in front of my table, just inches from me. At that moment, I wanted nothing more than to be like Samantha from *Bewitched* so I might wiggle my nose and vanish into thin air. I tried to force my nose up and down and side to side, but witchcraft failed me. Try as I might, I was still sitting at the table and Casey was still approaching.

I did my best to maintain my composure but felt as if fireworks were exploding inside me. I couldn't pinpoint my exact emotion. The only thing that was certain was that I had absolutely no idea what to say to Casey. It had been two months since I had seen her and almost as long since we had spoken. The last time I had made eye contact with her, we both had had tears in our eyes as she deserted me in her room in Miami. I trembled as I looked at her and then tried to avert my gaze. When I looked away, her face was burned in my memory. Her blue eyes and her platinum hair seemed to glow in my mind. If I thought I was dreaming, the smell of her perfume floating into my nostrils proved that she wasn't a vision— she was truly right next to me.

Casey looked at me and smiled as she said, "Hi."

My hands gripped the arms of my chair and I could feel my knuckles turning white. My stomach dropped as if I were riding the scariest roller coaster in the park. I nervously opened my mouth to speak and returned her greeting with all that I could possibly muster. "Hello." One word. That's all I could manage.

She was fidgeting and was clearly nervous as well. "Can I talk to you?"

Calmly, I responded, "I'm having a drink with Ribi." That was my way of saying "No" but I couldn't force the word out of my mouth. It was only one word, containing one syllable but even so, I still couldn't say "no" to Casey.

I could tell by her fixed glare that she was not happy with my response. "How long do you think you'll be?"

"I have no idea. We just sat down."

"Do you have plans later?"

Casey prolonged a stare at me and I tried to speak with as little emotion as possible as I answered, "Yes." I wondered what she could possibly think was left for us to talk about. She left me without even the slightest hesitation or consideration. It doesn't get much clearer than that.

Desperate to have an opportunity to speak with me, she looked crestfallen, as if she were about to cry. The tension between us was increasing with every breath we took. "Okay, I'll leave you two alone. Sorry to bother you." She nodded with a closed-lipped smile before saying, "Good-bye."

Glad to see she still gives up so easily and walks away from me without putting up a fight. Jeez! Some soul mate she turned out to be! Soul mates are supposed to fight to the death for their love.

Casey turned to leave. I was confused. The truth was, I did want to talk to her but didn't know what to say. More importantly, I didn't want to expose myself to pain again. It took all of my strength to watch her leave, just as it did in Miami.

Ribi looked at me and said, "You should talk to her. I'm going to text her and tell her to come back."

I didn't want to refuse, and before I could— just for the sake of doing it— Ribi had sent the text. Within seconds, Casey returned. Ribi gave me a hug and got up to leave.

Casey lowered herself into the chair next to me. As she arranged herself in the faux Louis XIV high-back chair, my body stiffened with unease. I reminded myself to breathe in and out, trying to ignore all the secondhand smoke I was inhaling. I gulped the rest of my beer quickly and felt the bubbles traveling swiftly inside me. I was voluntarily sitting next to the woman who was responsible for exhausting my emotions and depleting my reserve of goodwill. Suddenly, I felt a precarious queasiness in my stomach. I couldn't help but feel as if I were someplace I shouldn't be.

When I was a kid, sometimes, for fun, I would sneak into my parents' room when they weren't home, just to snoop around. I have no idea what I was trying to accomplish by nosing around. It's not as if I knew of some secret my parents were keeping from me and I was determined to uncover clues about it. They always kept their door open and never denied me access when they were home, but there was something interesting to me about entering without permission. My missions were always spontaneous and never had a clearly defined goal. Sometimes, I'd just look through the bookcases and sometimes I'd look at the jewelry my mom had left out on her dresser. I wasn't one to try on my mom's clothes, but if I were feeling especially adventurous I'd get on my hands and knees in the closet, remove the false carpet from above the trapdoor to the floor safe and spin the number dial with the combination that my parents had entrusted me with. I wasn't planning some big heist or anything. I'd merely take an inventory of the contents of the safe to confirm that things were as they should be. Within minutes, all items were replaced, the door was closed and locked and the carpet was repositioned so that there was absolutely no trace of intrusion. I figured snooping around my parents' room was a better alternative to cow tipping. No one and nothing got hurt on my missions. This was my idea of living on the edge when I was eight. My unsupervised visits were always short-lived. Once the goose bumps covered my body and I began to feel faint with nervousness from the fear of being somewhere I knew I shouldn't have been, I always sprinted out of the room.

I uncrossed my legs and, for a moment, considered making a beeline toward the door to escape the room I shouldn't have been in. But suddenly, my feet rooted themselves in the floor and my legs felt as if they weighed 1,000 pounds.

Casey broke the awkward silence. "I just wanted to look you in the face and say I'm sorry for how everything happened. I know I hurt you, and I'm very sorry. It was terrible how I handled the situation and I'm really sorry." Her voice was shallow, her tone plaintive.

I listened, guardedly, as she sputtered her three apologies, staring at my reflection in the glass top covering the small wooden table in front of our chairs. My beer bottle was empty, but I fidgeted with the green and white label, peeling it from the top until the flimsy paper separated from the green tinted glass. My throat tightened and I bit the inside of my cheek to stop the tears from falling. As quietly and nonchalantly as I could, I took deep breaths and tried to swallow my emotions. When Casey finished apologizing, it was my turn to break the awkward silence.

I shifted in my chair and crossed my legs before speaking. "Casey, if you came here to apologize to me and ask for my forgiveness…" I paused. My voice was icy. "You're wasting your time. I know you're sorry. You wouldn't be human if you weren't. But what you did to me was inhumane and unconscionable. I won't sit here and tell you that it's okay, just because some time has passed— because it's not. And, I won't forgive you so that you can have a clear conscience. I know you're sorry, but I don't accept your apology. I'm not mad at you, but I *don't* accept your apology." I wasn't about to let her off *that* easily!

For months, I had been trying to get mad at Casey. I hated what she had done, but no matter how hard I tried, I could not loathe her. I couldn't, however, accept her apology, no matter how contrite she was. I refused to be patronized.

She looked as if a wave of despair had just washed over her. "I know I don't deserve even to be sitting here with you, but when I found out that you were just down the road from me, I had to come see you and apologize."

I sat silently, protected by the invisible wall of self-protection I had erected.

Her lips parted and curved into a grin. "I know I don't have the right to tell you this, but Steph, it's really good to see you. I've missed you. You look great."

If thin was "in," I did look great. I had lost my "winter coat" plus an additional few pounds since Casey had left me. It's amazing how fast the "Breakup Diet" melts away the pounds. I was thankful that I hadn't canceled my eyebrow waxing appointment before coming to Paris and that I had chosen to wear a red shirt to meet Ribi. It never hurts to look good in front of an ex.

Silently accepting her compliment, I looked directly into her eyes and said, "I just hope it was worth it. I really hope *she* was worth it— worth hurting me so badly."

She breathed an unmistakable sigh of uncertainty and the smile vanished from her face. "Me too."

"Are you happy?"

She inhaled and paused before she answered. "It's been tough, but I am happy."

Liar!

I knew she was full of shit. I knew her too well. I wasn't sure who she was trying to convince of her happiness— herself or me. Either way, I knew that there was trouble in paradise.

"Is Trish here?" I asked the question, already knowing Casey's straight girlfriend would be arriving the next day.

"No, she gets in tomorrow."

I wanted to volunteer to pick Trish up at the airport and take her directly to the Eiffel Tower and drop-kick her into the Seine and watch her and her stupid Louis Vuitton bag bob down the river with the rest of the flotsam, but somehow I had a feeling that Casey had already made other transportation arrangements for her trashy girlfriend.

"Does she know you're here with me? I can't imagine she'd be happy about that."

Casey lowered her head. "I couldn't tell her. She doesn't trust me when it comes to you. I don't blame her, though. I wouldn't trust me, either." She paused as she kneaded her hands and stared down at the floor. When she looked back up at me, she said, "God, I really fucked things up, didn't I?"

She said it! She finally said the words I had been waiting to hear ever since I left Miami. I didn't want to do the "I told you so" chant because I didn't want to look like the spurned girlfriend, but I did it anyway. I couldn't help but take a small jab at her. "Ahhh, things with the straighty aren't all you'd dreamed they'd be?!" Laughter roared from within me.

"God, I miss that laugh. You always could make me laugh."

I refused to let her sidetrack me. "Casey, I hate to tell you this, but I knew this'd happen. I knew Trish wouldn't be the girlfriend you thought she'd be or who you wanted her to be." Even if Trish were gay, she and Casey never stood a chance at having a successful relationship. They had different ideas of what it means to be in a relationship. Trish would be happy with a superficial relationship as long as she got to be in Casey's limelight, while Casey would be devastated with anything less than an all-consuming bond.

I'm not sure Casey heard a word I said. She continued talking at me. "She's...she's just not you. She's not anything like you. She's not warm or open or loving. She'll never be able to give me what I want."

As if I weren't in the room, Casey rambled on, purging herself of her feelings and frustrations. I sat in silence as she confessed some of the multitude of problems she and Trish were having— Trish's parents weren't taking their daughter's conversion to lesbianism well; none of Trish's friends knew about her relationship with Casey; Trish was controlling and cared more about Casey's tennis than she did about Casey; Trish was obsessed with me (but not in a way that should have been flattering).

When I heard my name, I interrupted her. "What the hell do I have to do with any of this?"

"Trish's totally insecure when it comes to you and she brings you up constantly— on a daily basis. She always asks me if I wish that I would've picked you. She...she just knows how much I love...loved you, and it worries her."

I pretended that I only heard her say "loved" in the past tense.

Casey left *me* high and dry for Trish. I was no longer speaking to either of them and I still live 3,000 miles away! How much more secure could Trish get?

"I deny it to Trish, but I think...I know in my heart that I made a mistake. I had everything with you."

Is this the part where I'm supposed to feel sorry for Casey? Pardon my French, but she's the one who fucked me over. Hell, she fucked Sydney over, too— not once, but twice. And now she had fucked herself over. I'm no Buddhist, but I think this is what they call "karma."

"Do you think there will ever be a chance for us in the future?"

A chance for us in the future?!

I didn't see that question coming, despite all the pining I had done for Casey. Night after night I had wished for Casey to beg for my forgiveness and tell me she wanted me back. Now faced with that possibility, I said the first thing that came to my mind. "How could I ever trust you again?" I looked away from her. Staring past her, I said, "Casey, I thought I was going to spend my life with you and then you just flippantly destroyed me. You have no idea how truly unhappy I was for a really long time after I left Miami, or rather after *you* left *me* in Miami." When these words came out of my mouth, her head dropped and she stared at the ground.

"I just think about the connection that we had…and still have," she said wistfully.

Oh, you mean the one that was so easy for you to toss aside?

Casey was right. We did have a connection. But she had made a choice and she hadn't chosen me. I had moved on with my life and didn't see the point of conjecturing about walking down the yellow brick road in search of some fictitious pot of gold at the end of the rainbow. "I'm sorry things aren't what you thought they'd be with Trish, but I have moved on." I really was sorry that Casey was not happy and that things were not working with her and Trish. No, really. I was. In my mind, I thought at least if they had worked out, it would somehow have made all the pain that I went through a little more justifiable.

Casey was silent as she processed what I had said.

I congratulated myself for being strong. The harshness of my words even stung me.

Finally, Casey spoke, "Never before have words hurt me so badly." She sighed and exploded with tearful frustration. "God, I c-a-n-n-o-t believe how bad I fucked things up! I let the best thing that ever happened to me walk out the door in Miami so I could try to make things work with someone who's not even gay. She's not gay…she's just not! We're not even really girlfriends. We barely ever have sex— if you can even call what we do 'sex'— and when we do it's horrible…she's horrible! The only thing that's different now is that I get to call her my 'girlfriend' and not 'best friend'— but only to her. She won't let me tell anyone we're 'together.' All we do is fight. I mean, I love her, but I'm not *in love* with her. I'm so drained from this relationship that I have nothing left to give on the court. I feel like all I do is cry— because of her and because I miss you. I can't even breathe without thinking of you. It's killing me. I wish I could take back everything that happened in Miami." She stared into my eyes pensively.

Wow, that was a mouthful. But the truth is, Casey couldn't take back what happened that day. She could fantasize all she wanted about what was and what will never be and she probably will forever because she lives a life that is not even loosely based in reality. In her world, they have things like "lets" that are used to replay points when something goes wrong. But I live in the real world and in the real world an "I'm sorry I fucked up so badly" is not enough to negate all the damage that had already been done.

I wondered why she was telling me this. Was she trying to persuade me to take her back? Which part of Casey still being in a relationship with the woman she left me for was supposed be a major selling point to me? One of my mom's biggest pet peeves is when people pay her what she calls "lip service"— when people talk a good game but do nothing to back up their words. I thought back to my days as a practicing attorney and searched my brain to find a precedent that I might have come across forbidding a gay woman from breaking up with a straight woman after the former had persuaded the latter to engage in a mutually consensual romantic relationship. I don't remember ever seeing one.

"If you're so unhappy, why don't you just break up with Trish?" I offered, rather stating the obvious.

"What's the point? I know you will never forgive me. I can't have the person I want to be with, so what's the point of breaking up with her? If I could have you, I would leave her. But I can't. So, what's the point?"

I see. Casey's idea of fighting for me, her "lost love," was not to leave

Trish and do everything in her power to win me back. To the contrary, it was to test the waters first and if I bit, *then and only then* would she cut Trish, her prized fish, loose and let her swim straight (literally) back upstream. Now that's what I call lip service.

Just when I wasn't sure that Casey had anything else to confess, she said, "God, I just really miss you. I miss talking to you. I miss our friendship. I miss everything about you, and that's why I had to come see you."

"Well, you saw me. Once again, you got what you wanted without considering my needs," I added, sarcastically. Nothing had changed with Casey. She was still walking through life guided by her selfishness.

I was desperate to find a diversion from the walk down memory lane that Casey was attempting to force me to take. I found one— Sydney.

Casey told me that she and Sydney had made amends and that they were friends again. I could see right through Sydney's thinly-veiled desire to be friends with Casey. Sydney didn't have many friends on the Tour. Accepting Casey's apology was her twisted way of keeping a hold over Casey. And how was she going to exploit this hold she had over Casey? On the tennis court. Somehow, I knew that Sydney would use Casey's betrayal to her advantage and persuade Casey to play doubles with her again in order to make up for what she had done. A bout of evil laughter escaped me as I thought of the two of them reuniting as a doubles team again.

"What we did was wrong, Steph," Casey said, proud of her revelation.

Is she kidding me? Was she just now figuring that out? I had been telling her that what we were doing was wrong the entire time we were doing it, but she didn't want to hear it.

I refused to dignify her sudden epiphany with a verbal response. My rolling eyes and shaking head articulated exactly what I was feeling— disgust.

I had heard about all I cared to hear from Casey about how wrong we were, how sorry she was and how she was going to be in therapy for the rest of her life for letting me go. I had been glancing at my watch the entire time I was with her. Two hours flew by in what seemed like the blink of an eye. Casey tried to prolong my departure for as long as possible, but when reminiscing turned into grasping for small-talk, we both knew it was time to leave.

Casey nervously spoke, "Steph, thanks for talking to me and for listening to what I had to say. Again, I'm sorry for everything."

Thanks for talking and for listening. Her words reminded me of what she used to say to me after a match: "Thanks for watching and for waiting." I was starting to feel like everything in Casey's life was a game to her. I simply raised my eyebrows and nodded as I abandoned my chair and walked toward the door.

Unlike the last time Casey and I parted ways, this time *she* desperately followed *me* to the door.

A cool breeze blew around us as we stood outside the bar on Rue de Berri. Inhaling deeply, I said, "Despite everything that has happened you know I wish only the best for you." I exhaled hard and opened my arms to give her a hug. She held on tightly as we embraced. As I began to back away, she tightened her grip. When our bodies separated, she could barely make eye contact with me.

No words came out of her mouth and again, she pulled me in close to her and held me tightly for one more embrace. She rested her head on my shoulder and exhaled deeply and slowly. I felt her arms tighten around my back. She lifted her head and focused on my eyes. A tear fell as she whispered, "I made the biggest mistake of my life that day in Miami. I walked away from the love of my life. I wish you could understand how much I love you." As if we were the only two people standing on the street, she grabbed the front of my shirt just under the collar. She clenched her fists and pulled me toward her until our lips were almost touching. "I just want you back. Please tell me how I can get you back." She pounded lightly on my chest as she repeated her plea.

I had a choice to make right then. The direction my life would take was up to me. I could go back down the line with Casey or go cross-court in search of the life I truly envisioned. I thought of the inscription on the necklace Casey had sent me from Atlanta: LIVE THE LIFE YOU HAVE IMAGINED. The love I once had for Casey had been real and profound. It had left a special imprint on my heart. As thoughts of our past ran through my mind, I put my arms around her…and gave her one last hug. Not even my imaginary remote control could erase the mistake of Miami or the pain and betrayal I felt. Some things just can't be taken back and some points just can't be replayed.

As we let go, I said, "Casey, I used to trust in our love, but that trust has been destroyed. We can't go back...we just can't. We have to move forward and leave the past behind." I wanted more than Casey could offer me. The life I imagined was one filled with genuine, pure and honest love and fulfillment.

We were standing in the middle of the most romantic city in the world. The cool air gently brushed against our faces. The Arc de Triomphe was just over our shoulders and the brilliant orange hues of the descending sun signaled the time for what should have been an intimate aperitif. But Casey and I were not going to enjoy a happy ending to our love story and float down the Seine savoring the sky overhead set ablaze with crimson.

She wiped her tears and briefly smelled her shirt, already slightly dampened.

"You nervous that my perfume's on your shirt and she'll smell it before you can wash it?" I laughed.

"No. I was hoping...hoping that I would smell it, so you'd still be here after you leave."

She patted her chest as she used to do when I watched her play tennis. "Please don't forget...don't ever forget about us and what we had...have."

I could never forget what I *had* with Casey and what it taught me.

She stood with me on the street as I waited for a taxi. She looked utterly defeated. "I hope I see you at one of my matches. Don't tell anyone, but I always look for you in the stands. I hope you come this week. I'll be looking for you, Stephie."

Calling me Stephie was Casey's way of subtly flirting with me. She knew that hearing that name from her lips always gave me a special feeling in my stomach. She had left me for someone she had claimed to have loved for years and now she was flirting with me again! It dawned on me that love means nothing to Casey. It was merely a number on a scorecard.

The taxi arrived. We said one last good-bye without hugging and I got into the car. I felt her eyes on me as I told the driver my destination. We drove down the block. I could see Casey from the corner of my eye.

She was standing halfway up the block watching the taxi leave. As the taxi rounded the corner Casey slowly lifted her hand to wave good-bye. Her voice reverberated in my head. "Good-bye, Stephie." Casey was not the person I had given her credit for being. I had finally seen her with clarity for the person she really was— a person who plays games for a living. Casey Matthews no longer made my stomach drop. My head faced forward and my eyes were focused directly in front of me. I never looked back.

* * *

Against my better judgment, I decided to take my mother to Roland Garros before we left Paris. Ribi made arrangements for us to pick up our badges at the credentials office, as I had done at every other tournament for several years. I was reluctant to place myself and my mother in the world I had left months before. But having become accustomed to attending tennis tournaments as a player's guest with a full-access badge, I was glad not to have to wait in line and hand my ticket to an attendant in order to be granted entrance.

As my badge dangled around my neck, it occurred to me that for my entire life I had been on the elite "us" side of "us and them." In the world of tennis, badges are symbols that separate "us" from the rather mundane "them." I was happy that my status had been preserved despite the events of the past few months. Ribi guided us toward the players' lounge— only after assuring me that both Casey and Sydney were out on the courts practicing.

The guards scanned our badges and granted us access to the private area. Instantly, I saw countless familiar faces. As I looked around and saw old friends lounging on the couches— some watching TV, some playing cards, some reading books or magazines and some just talking— I was overcome with a strange feeling. I smiled and waved, realizing that regardless of how much time had passed, most of these people were still in the exact same place as they had been when I last saw them. It felt surreal, as if time stood still on the Tour. Maybe some of them had changed sponsors so they were wearing different clothes, but other than that they were in the same place doing the same things as they had done the year before and the year before that and the year before that. The world that once had seemed so extraordinary to me now suddenly seemed stagnant and unenviable.

After we crossed the threshold leaving the restricted area, my mother and I melted into the sea of tennis patrons. I pointed to the famous Philippe Chatrier and Suzanne Lenglen stadium courts. I caught myself looking over my shoulder incessantly as we walked to a smaller stadium court where Conchi was about to play her second-round match.

We took our seats as the players began their warm-up. A few minutes later, I saw Casey and Trish enter the stadium on the opposite side of where my mother and I were sitting. *Typical. Of course, they're here!* I knew that there was one reason and *one reason only* that Casey and Trish decided to come and watch Conchi play. And it certainly wasn't because they were interested in cheering her on!

Somehow Casey had found out that I was at the tournament and she knew I would be watching Conchi's match. Damn that Ribi! I knew she wouldn't be able to keep her mouth shut! Casey wanted to see me and make sure I saw her. Her eyes were fixed upon me. As surreptitiously as I could, I whispered to my mom, "Don't look now, but Casey and Trish are sitting directly across from us. Trish's the ugly, slutty one in the tight V-necked shirt, Capri pants, and heels and Casey's on her left." As my mom tried to sneak a peek, I whispered, "I'll bet you anything Sydney shows up here within thirty minutes."

Just as my mom spotted the two lovebirds, Casey moved over one seat, leaving an empty seat between her and Trish. Very quickly, it became obvious that the happy couple was arguing. They weren't throwing punches, but they didn't look too happy. They both sat stone-faced staring toward the court.

After a quick glance, my mom looked at me and said, "Steph, neither of those girls has even an ounce of pulchritude or a smidgeon of panache." She shook her head and continued, "Anyway, they certainly don't look happy."

We burst out laughing. *Be careful what you wish because you got it. I knew you wouldn't be happy with that straight bitch!*

The match started and I slid my sunglasses over my eyes so I could focus on the court without squinting but also so I could avert my gaze occasionally to Trish and Casey undetected. As the match progressed, the crowd watched the long rallies between the two baseline players and kept their eyes on the tiny yellow ball. An entire stadium of people did the tennis turn and moved their heads in unison from left to right, right to left as the ball went back and forth from one end of the court to the other. Only two heads in the stadium were still— Casey's and mine. Our eyes were not on the ball, but on each other.

During the changeover at 3-2 in Conchi's favor, my mom nudged me on the knee and said, "Uh-huh. You were right. Twenty-five minutes." She tapped her fingernail on her watch. I had totally forgotten my prediction that Sydney would appear soon after Casey and Trish. My mom quietly pointed to someone coming into the stadium. It was Sydney. She had obviously done some reconnaissance because she knew exactly where my mom and I were sitting. She entered the stadium through a press box that was off limits to the general public, which was just beneath where we were seated. I watched as she strutted by with a John Wayne gait without turning her head toward us.

My mom sighed, watching Sydney walk by and then gestured across the court toward Casey and Trish with a quick flick of her index finger. "Thank God, we no longer have to deal with any of *them* on a daily basis," she said under her breath, shaking her head and giving me a slightly reproving look.

I grinned a tight-lipped smile. *Yes, thank God, we no longer have to deal with any of them.*

I had come clean to my mother after returning to LA and told her the unabridged, sordid story of what had happened between Sydney, Casey and me. Although she wasn't proud of my deceptive role, my mom was thrilled that I was no longer dating either Sydney or Casey.

Sydney had now taken a seat several rows away from us. I whispered, "The second this match is over, we're outta here. I'm not getting stuck talking to that psycho!"

The games dragged on and I found myself looking at my watch between each point wondering how much longer the match would take. As I watched the ball whistle from one end of the court to the other, each shot faster than the last, I reminisced about my life when I traveled with the Tour. It was a whirlwind filled with plenty of ups and downs. I remembered the indescribable happiness, the inconceivable frustration and the unimaginable sadness. As the players changed sides between games, I looked around the stadium and thought of the fun, the excitement, the adrenaline, the happiness, the frustration, the anger, the passion and the heartache that I associated with the game of tennis and with two of the women sitting in the stadium.

Conchi claimed victory in straight sets. I motioned to my mom and nodded my head silently toward the closest exit. As I stood up, I looked across the stadium one last time. Casey and Trish were gone. Within seconds, our seats were empty and we, too, had slipped out of the stadium undetected. We weaved through the crowd that was rushing in our direction. I spotted Casey as we walked past the players' restaurant, which was encased with floor to ceiling windows— as if to showcase the elite. She was sitting at a table with Trish and Sydney. I could not silence the laughter that escaped me at the sight of the comedy of errors on the other side of the glass. In what world would that threesome not be considered a ticking time bomb?

I turned away from my ex-girlfriends and looked at my mom. I realized that I had been wrong earlier when I derived my confidence and my identity from the badge around my neck. Without the badge, I had considered my status to be relegated to the less prestigious side of "us" and "them." As fans crowded around to snap quick photos of the players on the other side of the glass, I considered for a moment who the sports enthusiasts were desperate to get glimpses of— athletes with masterful abilities to place a small ball within the confines of a defined court. Certainly, some of them were ambassadors of the sport and champions of the public's heart. But some of them were simply talented game players with the uncanny inability to function normally and contribute significantly outside the world of tennis clubs, hotel rooms and the players' lounges within which they had encapsulated themselves. The glass separated the real world from a world few people have experienced— a world not based in anything resembling reality. Without a ball and racket in hand, some of the idolized athletes were, pure and simple, nothing more than game players devoid of the most basic abilities needed to function in the real world.

My mom did not raise me to be a game player. She raised me to be a woman capable of compassion and worldly contribution. I continued past the window, catching one last glimpse of Casey, Sydney and Trish. We— my mother and I— are, indeed, separate from "them." But what separates us from them is not a plastic badge around our necks or a double-paned piece of glass, but character, strength and dignity.

I left my law career behind in search of adventure and excitement. Certainly, I got both. The nine months I spent on Tour was one of the greatest adventures of my life. I enjoyed temporarily switching off reality and becoming immersed in an unreal and unimaginable life, but I always knew I wanted more than just volleying back and forth between professional athletes. Just as I had grown tired of ghost deadlines, I had now become disenchanted with the lawlessness and unaccountability I had been showered with. Having circled the globe, my whirlwind travels ended and I found myself craving what I had once despised most— structure and decorum. I walked away from my journey with the girls on the Tour with a few small scars and a handful of enormous lessons learned. I learned that there are both tennis players and game players on the Tour; that a true champion is successful at the game of tennis and at the challenge of life; that truth and integrity are not just virtues but commodities; and that worldliness is not measured by stamps in a passport. Most importantly, I learned that the luster of trophies— won and coveted— fades. The true prizes in life are not displayed in a trophy case or strategically gained by deceit.

I reached for the badge around my neck, but not to present my credentials. Rather, to lift the plastic over my head. I would not be adding this badge to my drawer full of mementos from previous tournaments. I no longer found the badge valuable. I discarded it into the receptacle near the exit. With our newly-found anonymity, my mom and I walked through the turnstiles toward the public exit with all the other General Admission patrons. Once outside, I watched official tournament cars roll slowly by. I could hear the voices of umpires echoing as I walked away from the fantasy world I had lived in. I had finally extricated myself from the bubble that had sheltered me from reality for almost one year. As I pushed through the gates into the real world, I smiled. My adventure was over and the *real* world beckoned. I realized then that all endings are beginnings.